A Reckless
Redemption

Laura Trentham

REVIEWS

AN INDECENT INVITATION...

"Trentham is careful not to settle for easy answers or simple explanations, making for a tale full of unexpected twists and turns and emotional complications." -- RT Book Reviews

"Danger, intrigue, and passionate love--what more could a Regency romance lover want? The first in Trentham's (*Slow and Steady Rush*) "Spies and Lovers" series is a well-written, engaging, and very steamy delight."--J. Harris, Library Journal

"Witty, compelling, and sensuous, Laura Trentham's is a fabulous new voice in historical romance." -- Valerie Bowman, bestselling Regency author

A BRAZEN BARGAIN...

"I loved Rafe from the first book and was eager to read his story. It was wonderful! Both of the Spies and Lovers books are fabulous. I love how Laura Trentham draws me into the story in every way. The characters come alive beautifully."—Lily, Goodreads

"I found this to be an exciting and interesting book. Hot and steamy and pulls just enough heartstrings to make it more than just a quick read."—Kilts and Sword blog

CHAPTER ONE

Cragian, Scotland. Winter 1813

Brynmore McCann entered the stables with her head down and her thoughts on the evening's work. Nerves and dread took up too much room in her body. The biscuits she'd choked down for appearance's sake at tea attempted to claw their way out. Chuffs and the restless shuffling of hooves registered too late. A viselike grip pinched her upper arm, and she was jerked inside a dim, hay-filled stall.

A big, warm body pressed her into the rough wooden planking of the stall. His smell registered. A strange combination of currants and horse, sweet and earthy. Not unpleasant, but lately, every time she was presented with currant bread or wine, her stomach refused what used to be treats.

"You've done your best to ignore me, but I've caught you now, haven't I, you little hellion?" Dugan Armstrong's husky whisper might have been alluring if it had come from someone else entirely.

"You haven't caught me yet." She twisted out of his grip. His fingers would leave their mark on her fair skin by morning. She hated the fear he created in her and tried to hold her ground, but she shuffled backward until the jamb of the stall door halted her escape.

Tall and broad, with blond hair and blue-gray eyes, Dugan was a handsome man with a ready, beguiling smile. The women in Cragian were agog if he treated them to any of his attention. He saved his cruelty for her.

"The papers have been signed. You'll be mine in two days. I'll be the first man to ride between those long, lovely legs of yours, and it's going to hurt. I'll make sure of it." His eyes had no depth, no softness. They were like pieces of sharp shale from the riverbed.

He closed the distance between them and swooped in for a kiss. She turned her face away, and wood slivers bit into her cheek. His lips left a damp trail along her jaw. She should fight back. She *wanted* to fight back, but from experience, she knew her ire only prolonged the agony and gave him a perverse joy.

She ducked under his arm and stumbled out of the stall, wiping her face on her cloak as a shudder of disgust trembled through her. Retreating to the other side of the aisle, she sought comfort in a nuzzle from the nearest horse. She couldn't marry Dugan. Living destitute would be better, wouldn't it?

Spoken like someone who's never been starving, her old friend Eden Drake would have said with an ironic laugh. If her foolhardy plan tonight wasn't enough to stop the wedding, at the very least, Bryn would take away something Dugan craved above all else. He wanted to be her first lover? He wouldn't be.

"Two more days, Brynmore." He stalked out of the stables, slapping a whip against his boots. The noise portended something she couldn't allow herself to contemplate. She stumbled farther into the stables, passed his horse, and had to look away, repulsed by the marks on his coat.

The very first day he'd trotted into their stable yard when she was only ten, she'd known. He had failed her basic tenet of moral fiber. Dugan Armstrong treated his horse poorly.

Old Cadell, the beloved stableman from her youth, judged a man's character by the way he treated his stock, and Bryn had embraced the philosophy. The lashes on the flanks of Dugan's bay gelding only reaffirmed her belief.

She slipped into her horse's stall, huddled in the corner, and rested her chin on tucked knees. Her ancient piebald dropped its head to nudge her shoulder and chuff in her ear while she stripped hay into countless pieces. Would anyone notice if she burrowed into the hay and hid like a mouse?

Bryn was perfectly content to remain a spinster at four and twenty. How then had she ended up in this mess? Her half sister, Mary, along with her husband, Craddock, had devised the match and sprung it on her like a trap.

Wielding her tongue like a rapier, Mary had deftly parried Bryn's arguments and entreaties to stay the marriage. Her sister had been born knowing when to inflict small, torturing cuts and when to eviscerate. Bryn didn't have the skill or stomach to respond in kind. Experience urged her to hide, as she'd done all her life. Only this time her problems surrounded her like a brick wall with nowhere to hide, nowhere to retreat.

The crunch of stone penetrated her reverie. She popped up and laid her arms across the low stall door. Bryn's maid kicked stones along the path. Wearing her best blue dress with a narrow tartan in soft gold and greens cinching a tiny waist, Sarah looked as grim and determined as Bryn felt.

Multiple braids of rich chestnut hair wound from her temples and intersected at her nape. Sarah's hair was her crowning glory, making her plain, even features special. Bryn fingered the ends of the ghastly red mop hanging to her shoulders. No amount of pins could confine the mess.

"Lud, we aren't paying a call to Lady MacShane." Bryn tried to inject a teasing lilt to offset her jumping nerves.

Sarah fluttered hands around her hair, tucking and patting, ruddy color bursting on her cheeks. "I wasn't sure what to wear. You'll be attending to your... well, your *business*, and there are all sorts of extra lads in town for your nuptials."

A horrid stew bubbled in Bryn's stomach. "Don't remind me. The charming groom-to-be just accosted me."

"What did he say? Did he hurt you?" Sarah propped her hands on her hips, looking ready to do battle. The man had almost everyone fooled. But not Sarah.

"The usual threats. My wedding night would be a painful experience with any man, but Dugan wants to make it extra-special."

Sarah covered Bryn's hands over the edge of the stall door and squeezed. "Tonight you'll thwart him."

"He'll hate me even more for it, and my sister's not likely to be understanding about the situation either. I worry it won't be enough."

"Not enough?" Sarah asked in a tart voice. "What else can you sacrifice? Lady Mary—forgive me for saying this about your blood kin—but she only sees what will make her richer and raise her standing in society. As Ma would say, she's a grubber. If she were any sort of sister, she would abide by your wishes."

Bryn didn't argue the point, as she happened to agree wholeheartedly. Instead, she went to work saddling the old piebald. Sarah scooted into the stall to help. She was more a sister to Bryn than Mary would ever be.

After Bryn's mother died birthing a stillborn son, Bryn and Sarah had roamed the hills together and spent hours trailing Sarah's mother, the housekeeper, or idling in the stables with Cadell. Too soon, however, their carefree youths had ended.

Sarah had begun her training for housework, and Mary declared Bryn had turned into too much of a heathen for polite society. Fruitless hours were spent drilling Bryn about silverware, the courses of a formal dinner, the intricacies of embroidery, the pianoforte, and watercolors—the typical education of a young lady of a certain means.

Bryn and Sarah shared her piebald mount, pressed close for warmth. Bryn nudged the horse out of the stables and into the January cold. The ground was frozen but clear. It wouldn't be for long. Clouds gathered far in the west, dark and ominous in the dimming rays of light. Snow was nigh.

"You could have worn something a bit more enticing." Sarah locked her hands tightly around Bryn's waist.

Bryn peeled her cloak open, but the wind barely penetrated the brown, worsted fabric of her dress. Buttoned to the neck, loose around her bosom—like most of her garments—and with long sleeves, the dress was practical, not fashionable. But the woodsy color tempered the red streaks in her hair and matched her eyes.

"It's not like I had much choice. Every dress I own is either brown or gray. Unless you think I should have worn my breeches?" Bryn asked with a small huffing laugh.

"Perhaps you should have. You'd likely get all sorts of ungentlemanly attention in those. That's your aim, isn't it?" Sarah's soft voice in her ear sent a shiver down her spine that had nothing to do with the cold.

"I suppose so." Heat rushed to her face. "I'm nervous. I've never flirted or played coy with a man."

"You're not trying to get one of the lads to court you, for goodness' sake." Sarah paused, then lowered her voice to a whisper. "I managed to ask Agnes a few questions after the nooning meal."

Bryn twisted on the saddle, her heart stuttering into a faster rhythm at the sight of Sarah's grimace. "What did she say?"

"She said men couldn't care less who they lay with. It's an itch they need to scratch. Sometimes they don't even bother with a bed. They lift her skirts, do their business, and leave without so much as a kiss or a thank-you." Sarah tried to mask her shock and distress, but the squeak in her voice betrayed her.

With a shaking hand, Bryn tucked her hair behind her ears,

but the wind negated her efforts. "That's good news, isn't it? It could be finished in a matter of moments. Did she say anything about pain?" She gnawed at the inside of her mouth until the tang of blood hit her tongue.

"She said the first time might hurt a little, but no more than a little prick. Then the half-wit nearly fell over laughing, and that's all I could get out of her."

"Am I doing the right thing?" Bryn's voice quavered. Her hands stiffened, drawing the horse to a halt.

"If you do nothing, Dugan and Mary get everything they want. If you go through with your plan, the marriage can't proceed."

Bryn wasn't as confident of the outcome. Sarah hadn't seen the determination on Mary's face and in her voice. A niggling sense of foreboding fluttered in Bryn's chest. She'd interrupted enough whispered conversations to know some piece of vital information was being withheld.

The entire endeavor was Bryn's idea, and she would need to bear the possible consequences. "I'll be ruined. If Mary throws me out—"

"You have friends hereabouts and in Edinburgh, don't forget. Worry about that only if it comes to pass." Sarah gave her a reassuring squeeze. Bryn nudged them onward, her hands trembling and her shoulders tense, but a steely resolve fortified her bones.

The edge of Cragian materialized through the winter dusk. Bryn guided them to the inn's stables. "If I'm occupied, you're to ride the horse home. I don't want questions raised until morning."

Bryn ignored Sarah's cutting, worry-filled glance. Leading the way into Cragian's only inn, Bryn forced her hands to her sides in a show of calm. Inside, she seethed with anxiety, fear of the unknown, and even a dash of justified vengeance.

A handful of local lads called out greetings, but most of the men packed into the common room were strangers. Strangers were good. Their masters and mistresses were at the house, enjoying Mary and Craddock's hospitality for the evening.

Although the dinner was ostensibly to celebrate her union with Dugan, in truth, Mary and Craddock played political chess. Forming alliances, gaining pawns, plotting coups. When Bryn had pleaded nerves—not a lie—Mary had waved her away, unbothered the bride-to-be would be absent.

Young Gavin, the butcher's handsome son, entertained at a corner table. A prospect? Bryn took a small table by the door, constant drafts swirling under her skirts. A smoky haze gave the entire scene a misty, nightmarish quality.

Sarah pushed through the throng around the bar to order them ales. Perhaps the alcohol would impart courage. False or not, it would be welcome. Bryn ran a finger over the rough planks of the oak table, aware of every indentation and scar.

Male voices buzzed around her, but she gave no heed to the bawdy comments and occasional shouts of laughter. She examined each candidate, assessing and then discarding them before moving on to the next.

Sarah set two tankards on the table and slid into the chair beside Bryn, their knees bumping. "Have you settled on anyone yet?"

Bryn shushed her, but no one seemed to be paying them particular interest. "Is this really the best that Cragian has to offer?"

Sarah looked around the room. "This is better than the usual fare, to be honest. Why do you think I've never succumbed to the fine institution of matrimony? Most of the good ones—bad ones too—have up and gone to Edinburgh."

"Colin Conrad is still about."

"Colin Conrad is not a man to be tupping a woman willy-nilly. Are you mad?" Sarah asked with starch.

Bryn smothered a small smile and waggled her eyebrows. "I

meant he's a fine man who hasn't up and left for the city."

"Are you seriously playing matchmaker for me at a time like this?" Sarah shook her head and gave Bryn her full consideration. "For tonight, think of yourself. Please. Find a man with kind eyes and bed him."

Kind eyes? Would she even recognize such? Cadell had been the only man who cared a whit about her. Once the midwife had ascertained Bryn wasn't a longed-for male heir, her father, Baron McCann, had walked away, not sparing her another thought up to his untimely death almost a decade earlier.

Tonight might change the course of her life. The man she chose might only be scratching an itch, but the damage to her body and reputation would be irreparable. The collar of her dress drew tight, constricting her breath, and in spite of the chilly drafts, an unbearable heat beaded sweat on her forehead. The uncontrollable panic had pressed and constricted her body like a vise more often since the announcement of her betrothal to Dugan. She pushed back from the table and dove for the door. For freedom.

The night braced her upright and held her against the rough planking of the inn in a cold, comforting grip. Her lungs exchanged smoke with crisp, winter air. It felt like a betrayal when her body reacted this way, and she fought hard to regain control. With every breath, the oppressive panic dissipated but left her shaky.

Bryn did what she always did when troubled. She retreated to the stable. Rich, loamy air surrounded her like a warm plaid. The mixture of horse, manure, hay, and leather was so inherently comforting her anxiety lowered in pitch and intensity.

A man's murmur rose through the occasional nicker and whinny. For a long moment she stood still, letting the cadence soothe her like a wild pony. The deep, rich voice mesmerized her, and she found herself under its spell, moving inexorably closer to the open stall. She peered around the door to see a man rubbing down his horse with sweeping, graceful strokes of a blanket.

He exchanged blanket with brush and methodically groomed the horse's flanks, all the while talking nonsense to his besotted mount. The low timbre of his voice lilted with a Scot's brogue. The horse nuzzled the man during his ministrations. A greatcoat and brimmed hat kept his identity a secret.

The edge of his coat and boots were muddy and road worn but of excellent quality. How had such a fine gentleman ended up in such an out-of-the-way village as Cragian? For her wedding? Why then wasn't he at the house with all the other kowtowers?

He circled to the horse's opposite flank, and she caught sight of the lower half of his face. Weakness crawled into her knees, and her stomach took a fearless leap. She knew him.

Dark stubble covered a strong, square jaw. In juxtaposition, his mouth was sensuous, the bottom lip full and curled up in a smile as if caring for his horse was a pleasure and not a chore. Something deep inside of her, something she hadn't even known was lying dormant, stirred to life after almost ten years.

It would be this man or no one. The man who'd once loved her sister. The man she'd loved from afar for too many years. Maxwell Drake. The Fates had made her decision.

Perhaps it was instinct, perhaps it was her sigh, perhaps the streak of lightning awakening her memories crackled the air. Whatever the reason, he swiveled his head faster than a wolf sensing prey, his gaze snaring her.

Shielded by his hat, she couldn't tell whether his eyes were kind, but his smile had vanished, and he looked… unapproachable, unyielding, untouchable.

She shuffled backward, breaking the unseen taut bindings, and ran. With her hood pulled low, she banged back into the common room, drawing nearby stares. She grabbed Sarah's arm and pulled her friend into the narrow servant's hallway.

"What's the matter?" Sarah asked with wide eyes, standing on tiptoe to see over Bryn's shoulder toward the door.

"There was a man in the stable."

"Who?"

Bryn bit her lip. Sarah knew all her secrets. As if the walls leaned in to eavesdrop, she whispered, "Maxwell Drake."

Although her eyes flared even wider, Sarah only pressed her lips together and nodded. "I'll discover which room Jock gives him."

Bryn stayed hidden under her cloak and in the dim hallway, waiting for the door to open and reveal him. When it did, she sagged against the jointed planks of the wall, her relief profound. She hadn't imagined him. He whipped his hat off to duck under the low beam, ran a gloved hand through his thick, dark hair, and rubbed his nape.

Peeling her gaze off him, she examined the crowd of men, but no one showed signs of recognition. An irregular gait carried him to the innkeeper's desk. A limp. A recent injury or an old one? After a short discussion with Jock, he settled at the short bar with his traveling bag at his feet, pulled off his gloves, and signaled for a drink.

A small glass. Not ale then, liquor. He drank it in one go and clapped the glass on the bar top. A barmaid refilled it.

Her color high, Sarah weaved through the crowd to Bryn's hiding spot. "He's got the chamber at the top of the steps. The most expensive one. He ordered a hot bath, but Jock told him it would be at least an hour with the crowd. Told him they were here for a wedding, but he didn't look interested or ask questions."

"I'll wait in his room," Bryn said with sudden decisiveness.

"What if he turns you away? What then?"

Her gaze landed on Maxwell's broad back and bent head. "Then it's over. I marry Dugan, and everyone gets what they want—except for me."

"You're sure?" Sarah sounded anything but.

"I'm sure."

* * * * *

Maxwell Drake kept his face averted, only glancing around the crowded common room once. He didn't look long enough to recognize anyone, and no one recognized him. Even Jock, the old innkeeper, hadn't batted an eye when he'd signed the register as Capt. Drake. His mother had been in the ground six years, but even when she was alive, most of the villagers had acted as if she were invisible or beneath their notice—a whore.

After a fourth glass of substandard Scots whisky, Maxwell let his gaze wander from the scarred wood to the crowd once more. This time he sought a pair of impossibly wide brown eyes set in an elfish face. No luck.

A lass had watched him tend his horse. Her knowing smile had frozen him as if she could see straight into his heart and beyond. The sprite had disappeared before his stiff, sore leg could carry him to the stall door.

No matter. He didn't need a complication. Even so, he scanned the room once again. He turned back and tapped his glass on the bar, ready for another. Coming home had damaged his armor, leaving gaping holes, vulnerable for attack. It was a damned uncomfortable feeling.

He'd spent nearly a decade trying to shake off the dirty village and the starving, grief-stricken boy he'd been. The memories he had quashed after he left Cragian at twenty bubbled up like molten lava burning him with their intensity. The potency should have been diluted by his years serving on the Continent and working in London.

It wasn't. Tomorrow he would find his mother's grave and pay his respects. He would settle his debts so he could move on with a clear conscience and never look back. A hollow, aching pit grew by the minute, and he rubbed a hand over his chest. He supposed it might be his heart—or what was left of it.

His glass was empty again. How many did that make? He normally didn't overindulge. Men fell into enough foolishness without the added encouragement, and truth be told, he didn't hold his liquor well.

He stumbled twice up the stairs, laughing softly. A bath and then bed. The morning would bring with it a hellish headache, but the temporary blunting of his raw emotions in the present was well worth it. He threw the door open with a flourish and crashed into the doorframe.

Steam rose from the tub, and a cheery fire burned in the grate. The warmest welcome he'd receive in Cragian, no doubt. He kicked the door closed with his heel, dropped his bag, and peeled off his jacket, waistcoat, and shirt. Folding them carefully, he stacked them on the narrow dresser. Old army habits were hard to break.

He grasped a low rafter and stretched his aching muscles, taking weight off his bad leg. A gasp from the bed jerked him around. He blinked. Had the local whisky been tainted? The vision gracing the middle of his bed was surely a mirage.

A woman with remarkable red-gold hair loose around her shoulders sat in the shadows of the bed hangings. Her demure, long-sleeve chemise glowed white. Her luminous eyes gave her away—the fairy from the stable.

"Lass, I fear there's been a mistake. Did you wander into the wrong room?"

"No. No mistake, sir." Her voice was husky, and her gaze wandered up and down his chest. Her lips were curled into a bemused smile that sent warmth skittering into his extremities. Arousal followed on its heels.

"You're in my bed a-purpose? To what end?" His brain moved at a crawl, the cogs blunted by alcohol.

"I hope my purpose is obvious. I wish you to bed me. Have

your way with me. Debauch me. Tup me. Whatever it is a gentleman calls it," she said with a fair amount of sass.

"A *gentleman* wouldn't call it anything. Much less consider it with an innocent."

"I'm hardly innocent, sir. I've done it hundreds of times." She brushed the fiery curtain of hair behind an ear. Did it feel as silky as it looked?

"Hundreds?" The corners of his mouth quirked into an unexpected smile, considering the circumstances.

"Certainly. Only a woman of experience would wait for a man in his bed."

Maxwell looked her over again. Although the virginal, practical underclothes were strangely alluring, they didn't match her declaration of experience. Most likely, she had bedded a handful of local lads and was out to make some coin. Perhaps a tumble was exactly what he needed to help him forget what awaited him in the morning.

"How much then?" he asked.

"How much for what?" Confusion reflected in her voice.

"Your services for the night."

After an unintelligible chuff, she said, "I wouldn't charge you, sir. The first bedding is on the house." The woman's shoulders rolled in protectively, filling Maxwell with questions he didn't want answered. Tonight he could only handle simple. Simple, uncomplicated pleasure.

"I'll be gone to Edinburgh on the morrow, never to return. There won't be a second tumble with me."

Serenity wiped imagined troubles off her face. "Tonight will cost you nothing."

"That doesn't seem quite fair." He pulled out a handful of coins and slapped them on the table by the bed. "Take this when we're done."

The woman's gaze held on the money. "You'll bed me then?"

Concealed to the waist by covers, everything but her face and primly folded hands covered by white fabric, she was the antithesis of a seductress. She spoke in a crisp, light brogue and appeared clean. Warning bells pealed somewhere in the back of his drink-addled mind. But decisions were being made by something lower, situated between his legs, and with an infinitely smaller brain.

It had been longer than he wanted to admit since he'd lain with a woman. He didn't relish the emotional entanglements from keeping a mistress. Neither did he normally use whores. The unfair balance of power left him feeling cold, but tonight marked a change in his tightly disciplined habits.

There was no question he was drawn to her. She'd been haunting him since he'd caught sight of her in the stable, and having her carnally available had made him go hard as a stone. Why not indulge himself—just this once?

Without answering, he sat to pull off his boots and thick woolen stockings. Regaining his feet, he released the buttons of his fall, his gaze never leaving the woman on the bed. She clutched the sheet to her chest. Her tense body spoke of fear, but her eyes told a different tale. Her hungry gaze flicked over his body, and her little tongue darted to wet her lips. He pushed his breeches and smallclothes to the floor and stepped out of them, completely nude.

"Oh sweet Jesus," she whispered. Her attention seemed riveted between his legs, her eyes as big as saucers. A woman bedded hundreds of times had surely seen plenty of cocks. Again, warning bells rang dimly though the fog of lust and alcohol but were ignored as easily as a buzzing gnat.

She held motionless as if she were prey and he a predator ready to attack. Actually, the image wasn't far off the mark. Part of him wanted to fall on top of her like a beast. Instead, he bypassed the bed altogether, weaved his way to the tub, and lowered himself into the water with a hiss of satisfaction. His legs dangled over either side of the short tub.

Nothing except the woman's head had moved. Her eyes, beautiful and inquisitive, belied the tension freezing her body. Indeed, the heat of her regard singed. Her words and actions, body and eyes were a contradiction. And much to his dismay, he craved her touch more than he cared about the secrets that lurked.

CHAPTER TWO

"Come wash me, lass." His rich, deep voice hypnotized her, and she scooted to the edge of the bed with no hesitation.

This was not proceeding at all how she'd imagined. While she'd waited, she had stripped to her winter chemise, debating whether a village whore would be waiting entirely nude. Probably. But common sense had won out. The heat from the fire hadn't permeated the room yet.

Based on her woefully limited knowledge, she'd assumed he would settle himself between her legs, stick his *thing* inside her, and be done with it. He probably wouldn't bother to divest her of her underthings anyway.

Instead, he had removed every stitch of his clothing while she watched, torn between maidenly embarrassment and womanly marvel. She was fairly certain that Maxwell Drake in his natural state had ruined her forever.

She couldn't imagine any man matching his physical perfection. His hairy limbs and large feet hanging over the side of the tub did funny things to her stomach, flipping it like a potato cake. The curly black hair over the planes of his chest, leading like an arrow to his groin, made her body heat and pulse in unrecognizable ways.

The play of muscles across his shoulders and back when he'd

stretched had forced her gasp of pure feminine appreciation. And when his breeches dropped to his ankles, his long, hard *thing* had her clutching the sheet to her chest in protective instinct, yet she couldn't look away. Her body thrummed with so many conflicting emotions she couldn't discern whether fear, trepidation, or fascination would emerge victorious.

It was easier not to think but to follow his commands. She'd come this far and refused to allow fear to drive her away. Refused to let Mary and Dugan win.

Closer now, she studied his face in the wavering firelight. He had aged like a fine Scotch whisky. Crinkled lines radiated from his hazel eyes, golden flecks glowing like embers. Did kindness lurk in their depths? She couldn't say.

A straight, prominent blade of a nose hinted at his aristocratic heritage even if it had been on the wrong side of the bed. His full bottom lip offset the sternness of his features, and her fingers twitched, desperate to discover if it was as soft and smooth as it looked. Thick black hair—like many a Scotsman—clumped in waves around his tanned face. He was as handsome as he'd been at twenty but in a more rugged, worldly, masculine way.

Rolling the sleeves of her chemise up to her elbows, she moved behind him, breaking their intense study of one another. "I'll wash your back and hair first." She tried to sound as if she washed men on a daily basis, but she worried her breathy voice screamed virgin.

Maxwell levered himself forward and rested his arms along the sides of the tub, exposing ridges of muscles across his shoulders and back. Timidly at first, she ran the soaped cloth over his back, keeping her touch light. Without his eyes on her, she relaxed and sent her bare hand skimming up his flank. His skin jumped in her fingertips' wake.

She kneaded his shoulders, a visible tension dissipating the longer she worked the hard muscles. His purring exhale grew her confidence. An untutored virgin she might be, but she discovered pleasure in touching him, pleasing him.

An echo of something from her youth—a wild courage—welled in her belly. She dropped the cloth and delved her fingers into his soft black hair, massaging his scalp and tracing his ears. Her attention wrung a rumbling moan from deep in his chest, and his eyelids dropped to catlike slits. Shimmery tendrils of desire bloomed.

* * * * *

The lass tilted his head back and rinsed the soap from his hair. Dazed and dreamy, he laid his head on the warm tin edge of the tub. Having never had a woman, except perhaps his mother, wash him, he hadn't known what to expect. It certainly wasn't this tender, arousing care. She knelt beside the tub and ran a cloth-covered hand and a bare one over his chest lightly. Too lightly. His lungs filled with air, pushing into her touch.

The flickering fire turned her chemise diaphanous. Wet splotches from her work dotted the primly ruffled bodice. It clung to her skin, offering teasing glimpses of the high mounds of her breasts and peaked nipples. She was slim, but the fabric had pulled taut, exposing the womanly curve of waist and hip. Anticipation to see the long length of leg that had flashed him on her walk to the tub smoldered.

She roved her hands over his chest, seemingly in no hurry, and stopped to circle his nipples. He swallowed a groan of pleasure, even though his errant cock lifting out of the water was proof enough he enjoyed her attention.

Her unusual red-gold hair swung around her face like a multicolored, silken curtain. It had been cut to hang at her shoulders, thick and straight. She tucked a swath behind her ear before moving to his other side to wash his arm and hand.

A pair of large brown eyes, thickly fringed, dominated her oval face. Her nose was too thin, her mouth too full, and her chin too sharp, but taken together there was a distinctive attractive symmetry. Perhaps not a beauty by London standards, he thought her lovely and especially liked the impish sprinkle of freckles across her nose. She possessed an otherworldly quality that would be right at home in Queen Mab's court.

His lips curved up in a small smile. His overindulgence of Scots whisky inspired the uncharacteristically whimsical, poetic musings, no doubt.

She traced his bottom lip with a trembling forefinger. The intimate, sweet gesture unsettled him. Confusion wiped his smile away. She snatched her hand away and fisted it between her breasts, wetting her chemise further. He wanted to pull it back to his mouth to kiss and caress each finger in apology.

With her eyes hidden by her lashes, she retreated to the end of the tub and ran the soapy cloth up and down his good leg. The one still strongly muscled. He jerked his foot out of her hands, chuckling softly at the tickling sensation. She tossed her hair back, and her simple smile scythed into his chest. He pressed the heel of his hand hard on his breastbone to stem a startling shot of longing that resonated in the hollowness.

His bad leg was next, and he flinched at the touch of her hands on the red, puckered scar. A musket ball had ripped through his lower thigh, permanently marring his leg. He walked with a limp, but at least he walked. The physician had been inclined to cut it off. Thank God, Maxwell had been conscious enough to stop the man and his saw.

"Does it hurt?" the lass whispered.

"Fiercely in the cold," he whispered back, gauging her reaction.

Not bothered in the least, she massaged the area, and he had never felt anything so blessedly comforting. The constant throbbing ache abated. He ran fingertips across her high cheekbone, wanting to return a measure of the pleasure she bestowed. She pressed into his hand, meeting his eyes.

"Thank you for easing my pain."

She cleared her throat. "Are you all clean, sir?"

A laugh rumbled from his throat. "Not quite, lassie. There's one area that feels terribly neglected. And it's been trying to get your attention the whole while." He shifted his hips, his cock breaching the water.

Her molten brown eyes were wide, and her lips parted slightly as she stared. He couldn't remember ever being so hard and needy. A simple washing from a village whore had left him undone.

He'd lain with more beautiful women, women with more bountiful bosoms, women who knew how to make a man beg. But something about this lass beguiled him. Something about her warmed him from the inside out until he burned for the soothing touch of her hands. Something illogical and unexplainable.

She took up the cloth once more and leaned over the tub, the front of her chemise outlining the curve of her breasts. Unable to wait a moment longer, Maxwell tugged the end of the pink ribbon at her neck, unfurling it. The edges of her chemise fell open, affording him an excellent view of her bobbing breasts.

They weren't large but full and tipped with small, peaked nipples. Quite lovely indeed. The skin of her chest pinkened, the color shading up her neck and into her cheeks. Was it from the exposure of her breasts or the innocent caresses along his inner thighs? She acted afraid of his cock. Whatever the reason, her blushes moved him.

* * * * *

Dismay trembled Bryn's hands. She hadn't expected to have to know what in the devil to do with his thing. What did he want? Delaying the inevitable, she cleaned his inner thighs—very, very thoroughly. The appendage reared out of the water, demanding her notice. What if she hurt him or did something wrong? Finally, holding on to a deep breath, she rubbed the cloth over him, her touch light.

Maxwell threw his head back and arched his hips farther out of the water, startling her hand away. Black hair curled at the base, and a pair of heavy bollocks, rivaling even old man Pearson's wolfhound, hung between his legs. With his eyes squeezed shut, he tugged the cloth from her numbed fingers and dropped it into the water to sink to the bottom. Then he forced her hand to curl around the hard shaft. Covering her hand with his, he taught her exactly what she needed to know.

The rhythm was natural and instinctive. His hand left hers to delve into the top of her chemise. He squeezed one of her breasts and brushed his fingers over her nipple. A moan escaped her throat. Her hand on him stilled, distracted by the tingles spiraling from her breast. Pressing her knees together only marginally eased the growing, restless ache between her legs.

His hips bucked as a reminder to keep stroking. She moved her hand faster to match her quickened breaths and heartbeat, enjoying the unexpected hard-soft feel of him. What were his bollocks like? Natural curiosity overcame the fear of doing something wrong. She dipped her other hand into the water and grazed the heavy sac.

"Christ, lassie," he said with a pained growl.

She snatched her hand away. "I hurt you."

"No," he said with force but continued in a softer voice, "Don't stop, please. You can play there while you stroke... but gently, gently."

She did just that, very gently. His head lolled over the tub's edge, the tendons of his neck stretched taut. Warmth flared in her chest. The power she wielded was new and intoxicating.

Desperate to see another of his fleeting smiles, she stared at his mouth. He snaked his hand inside her bodice once again and raised his head, drawing her gaze to his. His fingertips worked magic on her nipple. As if her gasp was the signal, he thrust his hips up hard, spilling a thick, slick fluid over her hand. She stroked until he collapsed down into the water, motionless.

His sudden surge out of the water rocked her back on her heels, and she braced herself on the wooden floor, her wet hands slippery. Water sluiced down his body, and he shook his head like a hound, droplets flying.

She dropped her focus to the wound on his leg. "Is that all? Are we… finished?"

"Not nearly, lass."

He hauled her upright, gripped either edge of her chemise, and jerked, rending the fabric. It fell down her arms to pile around her feet. Stupefied to be standing suddenly naked, she forgot her role as whore and attempted to cover her breasts and mound with her arms and hands.

He dried with a square of linen, his gaze traveling the length of her body. She would have liked to do the same to him, but his big body set off a maidenly fear. He was several inches taller, and with his broad shoulders and deep chest, she felt dwarfed and vulnerable.

"You ruined my chemise," she said, unable to tolerate his silent inspection.

"I paid enough for the privilege." His tone was dark and ratcheted her nerves higher. "Go lie on the bed."

The bed was a foreign, unknown land, and now the moment was upon her, indecision held her in limbo.

He dropped the drying linen to puddle next to her chemise, two pools of white. She tore her gaze from the safety of the cloth and up his body, stopping where the thing between his legs had sprung back to life, lengthening and hardening.

The sight prompted flight, and she made a dive for the thick coverlet. He ambushed her before she could burrow for safety. Capturing her wrists, he stretched her arms above her head, one heavy leg trapping both of hers. She concentrated on not tugging at her hands while he looked at her body. Her fiery blush intensified, prickling her skin.

He let go of her wrists and moved his hard body fully on top of her. The friction and his weight started a different sort of fire, and it spread quickly, as if her body were dry tinder to a spark.

An indefinable need replaced her embarrassment. In contact with his hair-covered chest, her nipples hardened into sensitive points. Tentatively she caressed the flexing muscles along his flanks.

He flicked her nipple with his tongue before pulling it deep in his mouth. If she'd had a breath to spare, she would have protested the odd behavior. Pleasure and a feeling of rightness overtook her bewilderment. She arched closer and thread her fingers in his damp hair. A throaty, womanly moan reverberated—surely not hers—and she writhed.

Shifting, he pressed his leg between hers, his thigh settling into her mound. The pressure was welcome, and she ground against the hard muscle, seeking relief from the growing ache. He echoed her moan, tossing his head back and pushing his pelvis into her. Then his mouth dropped to hers.

Her first kiss.

She tensed, but his lips were gentle and brushed over hers time and again, coaxing a response. He sucked her bottom lip into his mouth, and she clasped his nape, holding his head close.

She mimicked him, pulling his full bottom lip deep and nipping it. He dabbed at the seam of her mouth with his tongue. Her lips parted on a sigh, and he titled his head to probe deeply. At first contact, she pulled her tongue away, but soon enough she rubbed hers alongside his in gentle, slow strokes. Tender and erotic, the kiss allowed her natural sensuality time to overcome her shyness.

"What's your name, lass?" he asked against her lips.

Bryn's mind wandered, lost in a haze. Name? Not her real one. Her head flopped to the side, looking for inspiration.

"Bootsie," she said and then squeezed her eyes shut. The idiocy. She could have said Mary, Sarah, even Agnes. *Bootsie?* All because his Hessians sat by the door. Lord above.

"Bootsie? That's unusual."

"It's… a nickname. My father was a cobbler," she added inanely. Would her lies send her straight to hell?

No, not her lies. Maxwell's mouth trailed down her neck, and his hand grazed down her bare thigh, returning her to a state of arousal. If she had to confess the night's sins to Vicar Mitchell, repentance for lying naked under this man would be impossible to summon.

"Have you ever climaxed with any of your other customers?"

The crude question crushed the breath from her lungs. When she found her voice, it was reedy. "I'm not sure what you mean."

"If you don't know, then you haven't." The rich, deep timbre of his voice vibrated every part of her. "That's a shame, lass. The men you've been with haven't taught you very much. I'd venture to say they haven't kissed you very well either."

"Was I… was I not good at it? Kissing, I mean?"

"You were good, very good. Once you relaxed." He drifted down and positioned himself between her legs, pushing them apart with his forearms. "I suppose no one's kissed you here either, have they? Did all those lads just push up your skirts and rut you, sweetheart?"

Thankfully, it was a rhetorical question. He swiped his tongue through the very core of her.

"No. You mustn't…" Moisture had gathered between her legs. She tugged his head up and tried to close her legs, but his shoulders were no match for her. "I'm… I'm… wet." She ended in a whisper.

The smile that curved his lips was playful but seemed to understand something she didn't. "Yes, you are. Very. And it's all for me."

Holding her gaze, he wiggled his tongue from her folds to a spot that sent sensation streaking through her. As he licked and sucked, coherent speech became hopeless and embarrassment a distant worry. In fact, her brain quit functioning entirely except for the portion processing the pleasure he wrought between her legs.

"Maxwell." She breathed his name on an exhale, climbing closer to some unseen pinnacle still obscured but so close.

His dark head lifted, but she tugged him back to work, and he obliged. His tongue was warm and firm, expertly appeasing her ache. A thunder of blood filled her ears as pleasure suffused her body. She writhed and bucked, breaking out in a fine sheen of sweat in spite of the chilly room. His mouth stayed with her until the waves receded. Before they completely disappeared, he slid up her body and buried himself in one sure stroke.

She scooched up the bed in retreat, her cry a combination of surprise and pain. He pressed into her, his weight holding her still. Her body stretched to accommodate the invasion.

"You're wet, so wet, but as tight as a virgin." His words slurred together, his face slack with pleasure. The irony would have had her laughing in any other situation.

As it had all night, her body skipped ahead of her conscious thought. Her hips jerked, forcing him a little bit deeper and wringing a groan from her. The fullness of his total possession grew a needy ache that was becoming familiar.

Finally he moved, slowly at first. He slipped a hand under her buttock to tilt her pelvis. The new position catapulted her back up the mountain. As his rhythm increased, so did her pleasure.

"Please, faster… I can almost… harder… I'm almost there… Maxwell, *please*."

He obeyed, driving her hard. The bedframe's squeaks and

their harsh breathing echoed like music. Her keening climax added to the symphony. A few more thrusts had him following with a primal roar, the warmth of his spend bathing her passage.

Too soon he rolled off. She expected him to push her away now that he was finished. Instead, he cuddled her close and nuzzled at her temple and ear. She circled her arms around him, holding tight.

"Was that adequate?" she whispered.

A laugh rumbled, deep in his chest. "Adequate? You're bloody amazing." Although heavy with sleep and drink and satisfaction, a teasing lilt weaved his words together.

She kissed the side of his neck, unable to stop the leap of pride. She'd pleased him.

"Let me rest for a moment, and we'll do it again." His voice trailed off into nothingness. Soft snuffling accompanied his deep, even breathing, and his arms fell slack.

Her body tingled in its newly awakened state. While she would gladly take him inside her again, it was impossible. Her life was no fairy tale unless it was a dark one where a witch waited to gobble her up. Anyway, she'd achieved her goal. Or destroyed her life. She wasn't sure how her story would end.

Burrowing so every part of her body touched his, silent tears leaked and fell on his shoulder. For him, this night would be forgotten before he rode away on the morrow. But for her, this memory would live in a special place that she'd visit when life seemed the darkest.

In the fading firelight, she traced his features, etching them into her heart. She gave thanks to whatever deity brought him to the inn in her time of need, but the inevitable couldn't be delayed.

Not bothering with her torn, damp chemise, she buttoned her dress with numb, shaking fingers. After pulling on her thick woolen stockings and half boots, she sat on the edge of the bed, brushed his thick hair off his forehead, and pressed a kiss on his lips. He sighed and shifted toward her. Once he was still again, she slipped away and braced herself to face the night's consequences.

CHAPTER THREE

Maxwell woke with a pounding head but sated body. Without opening his eyes, he threw out his arm, finding only emptiness. The lass was gone. Had it been a dream? No. Never could he have imagined their encounter in the bath… and afterward.

There was no use lolling in bed after a night's bout with an ill-advised amount of liquor. Shivering in the cold air, he stretched himself out of bed, his bad leg stiff but not aching, thanks to her kneading hands. He plucked the washcloth from the now-frigid water and absently cleaned between his legs. Ready to toss the cloth back in the water, he froze. Red streaked across the pristine white. Blood.

Alcohol no longer impeded his wits. He ripped the coverlet away. Dried red droplets sent him reeling backward. His bare arse landed against the dresser. A string of ungentlemanly curses flooded out of his mouth as he raked a shaking hand through his hair.

Her innocent caresses in the bath should have clued him in. Jesus, he'd made a virgin pleasure him with her hands. Another string of curses erupted, and embarrassment over the utterly ungentlemanly manner in which he'd deported himself made him kick the tub. Cold water sloshed over his feet.

The stack of coins stood untouched on the side table. She had been a dammed virgin, and he'd buried himself inside her with no thought to her comfort. Her cries and squirms had been from pain, not pleasure. Bloody hell, he should be shot.

Closing his eyes, he could almost feel her hands clutching him tightly and her breathy pleas in his ear to take her harder. No, her pleasure had been real and true. He'd barely managed to hold on until she'd climaxed. Her tight, convulsing walls had hurled him into the most amazing spend of his life. A numbing realization surged from the middle of his chest out to fingertips, to toes, nearly buckling his knees.

He'd finished inside of her.

He should have withdrawn and spilled on her stomach. That's what he always did. Instead, drunk on liquor and lust, he'd buried himself as deeply as possible before climaxing. After years being scrupulously careful with his liaisons, he'd risked siring a bastard in the same little village in Scotland where he'd been born a bastard himself. The irony was almost too perfect, and he barked a mirthless laugh.

No child of his would be born out of wedlock, much less raised alone by a woman who may not have the means to care for a babe. He would never subject an innocent to the near starvation and deprivation of his own pitiful childhood. There was nothing for it—he would find the lass.

Who was she? Her name was certainly not Bootsie. How ridiculous. He should have known then. Something else had niggled at him, even in the moment. What?

Maxwell, please… Maxwell, faster… What the devil? No one had called him Maxwell since he'd lived in Cragian. He had been Captain Drake most of his years in the army and plain Drake to all his acquaintances in London. The lass knew his given name.

He jerked his clothes on. With her genteel voice and the floral scent of her hair, she was educated and likely well born. Why would she give her virginity away to a stranger? Why had she picked him? Unless someone *had* recognized him and sent her to his bed.

Resentment simmered.

The *clomp* of his boots down the stairs reflected his anger and frustration. Finding a bleary-eyed Jock in the common room cleaning up from the evening's merrymaking, he spoke harsher than he intended. "Who was the lass you sent to my room?"

Jock stopped midwipe, straightened, and looked Maxwell up and down, working his jaw. "No idea what you're talking 'bout, sir."

"A woman was waiting in my bed last night. Was she sent by you?"

"Lawd, no. I'm running an inn, not a brothel. What was your name again, sir?"

"Maxwell Drake."

Jock's eyes flared and his jaw dropped, revealing a gummy interior. "Never thought we'd see you walk these hills again, boy."

Maxwell's shoulders rose, and a wave of heat rushed through him, in spite of the years gone by. "It's Captain, if you please."

"What did the lass look like?"

How to describe her? Ethereal? Kind? Sensual? "She had red hair."

"As do half the lasses around these parts."

"She was young and beautiful."

"A young, beautiful redhead? Those are rarer. Could be the maid of one of the visitors up at the Craddocks."

It seemed a logical conclusion. Except for the fact she had known his name.

"Ironic, ain't it? Your mother was a redheaded whore too." A familiar, malicious humor curled Jock's lips.

In two ground-devouring steps, Maxwell had the old man

around the throat and backed against the wall. Jock's bony hands scrabbled around Maxwell's fingers, too weak to pull them off. "If I hear another word of disrespect from your mouth about me or my mother, I'll burn this inn to the ground with you in it. Understand?"

The man's eyes bulged, and he fought for air, incapable of an answer. Loose skin sagged over Maxwell's hand, and he shoved the man down in the nearest chair. Shame tempered his righteous fury. Jock was an old man now and should hold no power over him.

Coming back had been a mistake. His plans had gone completely awry. He jammed his hat on, pulled his greatcoat around him against the cold, and swept out the door. On to see Vicar Mitchell. And, if necessary, to the manor to see Mary McCann—Craddock now—to locate his mystery bedmate. Dread mixed with foolish hope turned his stomach at the possibility of seeing the only woman he'd let close enough to break his heart.

* * * * *

Every bit of Brynmore's body shivered. She fumbled with the door leading to the servants' staircase, her movements echoing like hammer strikes in her ears. She'd tarried too long with Maxwell, and the sun had risen on the long walk home. By some miracle, she slipped unseen into her room and whispered thanks to an absent Sarah for having a fire waiting.

She huddled close, absorbing the radiating heat until all the numb, disassociated parts of her body flared to life and reattached themselves with painful prickles.

Sarah bustled in and dropped the cleaning bucket she carried. "Thank Jesus, you're home. I've been so worried." Dark smudges outlined her swollen eyes.

"Did you stay up all night waiting for me?"

"Mary and Craddock dragged me straight into the inquisition upon stepping in the door last night. Dugan had informed them of your absence from the manor. I thought your sister was going to have an apoplectic fit."

"I'm so sorry." Bryn grabbed at Sarah's hand. "No one hurt you?"

"No, but I thought I was sacked for certain. I lied, of course. Pleaded total ignorance as to your whereabouts. I'm to inform the baroness"—Sarah rolled her eyes and stuck her tongue out—"as soon as you get home."

What would she do without Sarah's good humor in the face of her dilemma? "I'd like to clean up first. Do you think you could manage a bath? I'm cold and tired and a little sore."

Sarah's eyes widened, her tone as solemn as an undertaker. "So it's done. Was it like Agnes described?"

"It was…" Bryn closed her eyes. *Amazing, magical, magnificent.* "Not so terrible."

"I'll send up a bath. Start rehearsing what you're going to say to Mary. You'll have to dance on a sword's edge."

The coming interview with her sister might well decide her fate. She tried to muster a convincing argument to retain her independence, but her mind kept casting backward.

Footmen clattered in with the tub and buckets of warm water. After they left, she was thankful for the privacy, even from Sarah.

She stripped bare. Her reflection in the looking glass tugged her to a stop. Cutting her eyes to the side, she stole a peek, as if her mirror image would judge her for it. She shifted and met her defiant gaze straight on.

The sharp angles of her body had rounded over the past few years, and her breasts had finally blossomed from molehills into—well, not mountains—but hillocks, at the very least. She trailed her fingertips from the underside of her breasts, through the valley of her waist, and over her hips. Maxwell had been well satisfied. Perhaps she wasn't as ugly and hopeless as Mary had charged time and again.

With a hiss, she sank into the water. The feel of the washcloth had her reimagining the night with their roles reversed. The memory of pleasure sensitized her skin. She washed away the sticky residue from his spend with sadness. No regret or shame rose.

Had he awoken yet to find her gone? Had he already taken his leave to Edinburgh?

Maxwell had been gone from Cragian for so long she had given up hope of ever seeing him again. He wouldn't remember her. For one thing, he'd only had eyes for Mary. For another, she'd acted like a scared rabbit around him, always running. No, that wasn't quite accurate. She'd acted more like an owl perched in the treetops, waiting and watching.

When Maxwell worked in their gardens, she was there, watching him grow skinnier and skinnier. Watching him never stop to eat a noontime meal. Watching him get winded and weak. Mary had been there too, tormenting him in different ways. Twitching her skirts, tossing her hair, thrusting her bosom in his face.

High up in her tree with the rough bark of the pine scratching her face, Bryn had watched Maxwell declare his love for Mary. He'd asked her to be patient as he made something of himself. She'd tossed him over, informing him of her plans to marry Craddock, twenty years her elder, already rich and due to become a baron on their marriage. Maxwell's devastation had radiated like a cannon blast, and Bryn had wanted to rip Mary apart like a rat with her talons.

A furtive scratching on the door forced her out of the cooling bath. "Mary and Craddock are waiting in the breakfast room." Sarah flipped through the meager selection of dresses in her wardrobe. "When was the last time your sister bought you a new frock?"

Bryn pulled out the length of pink-colored cloth she'd stuffed in the back. A ridiculous fall of ruffles covered the bottom three feet of skirt. "My wedding dress arrived. In all the excitement I forgot to show you."

"*That* color with your hair? Your sister hates you."

"Hates me? Because of the color of a dress?"

"Among other things," Sarah said cryptically. "Your brown wool, I think."

A soft green-and-gold plaid around her waist enlivened the plain brown dress. Bryn pushed at her hair with trembling fingers but left it down. The thick mass rebelled against her attempts at confinement.

No more excuses. The rug-covered stairs seemed to have multiplied overnight. The house was quiet, the guests still abed. What she really wanted was to wrap herself high atop a pine tree and breathe in the sticky sap or climb into the hayloft and bury herself underneath the sweet straw. Those days were gone. She was a child no longer.

Her quaking knees carried her to the door. She took a deep breath and ran her damp hands down her skirts before opening it and slipping in. The snick of the closing door cut off a heated, whispered discussion between Mary and Craddock. They turned and regarded her. In Mary's eyes was something akin to hatred, but it was the cold calculation in Craddock's demeanor that sent shivers through her body.

Bryn stayed close to the door, craving the illusion of escape. Stroking the shiny chestnut ringlets hanging over her shoulder, Mary sashayed in meandering arcs, coming inevitably closer and examining Bryn as if she were an undesirable pest to squash. Mary had always exuded confidence, but as she'd obtained a taste of power, she relied more on intimidation than charm.

Since her marriage, her strikingly beautiful face had hardened into a mask of arrogant insouciance, but her voluptuous figure still drew men's admiring, salacious eyes.

"You were gone all night." Mary's too-placid voice put Bryn on alert. "Tell me, sister, are you ruined?"

"Thoroughly and completely." She forced her chin to stay up.

Like a viper, Mary struck. The quick, stinging blow across Bryn's cheek stunned her.

"Foolish, stupid girl." Mary turned on her heel to throw up her hands at Craddock. "What now, husband? Where does this leave us?"

Craddock rubbed his chin. "We deny any rumors as ridiculous. Insist she is pure. The marriage goes on."

"I'll not start a marriage based on lies. I'll tell Dugan. He won't want me now I'm sullied. My virginity is all he cares about." Desperation colored her words even though the turn of events wasn't unexpected.

Mary wagged a finger an inch away from Bryn's nose. She flinched back, her heels hitting the doorjamb. "He may not want you, but he'll take you as wife and make you pay every day of your life for this mistake. There's too much riding on your marriage to Dugan. It *will* take place, Brynmore, make no mistake." Mary's voice was made implacable with disgust. Turning to Craddock, she said, "She can't be trusted to willingly cooperate."

Bryn's gaze darted to Craddock as she processed the implications.

"Agreed, m'dear." Craddock stepped closer, his expression matching the weather. Cold and ominous. "Now that I realize what lengths you'll go to escape the match, you'll be confined until the vows are exchanged tomorrow."

Bryn felt surrounded on all sides, but she wasn't yet ready to fly the white flag. "You mean to hold me as a prisoner?"

"I can't imagine a few moments laboring under some dirty, rough sheepherder will prove a wise decision in the end. Your roll in the muck was for naught." In contrast to her husband's tightly corralled emotions, Mary's venomous anger swirled around her like a maelstrom.

"Hardly for naught. It seems Craddock could take some lessons from my man, because he obviously isn't doing his job well if you consider lying under him a chore. I pity you." Bryn's words oozed from a wound that had festered for years.

Perhaps the first cut had been Mary's disregard of her mere existence. Every insulting word about her appearance, her deportment, her lack of womanly virtues had added to the damage.

Red usually achieved through rouge slashed Mary's cheekbones. Her upper lip curled, her green eyes as hard and cutting as jewels. "Who was it? One of the butcher's sons?"

"You can physically drag me to the church, but you can't make me repeat wedding vows before God."

"I had hoped not to have to employ underhanded methods, but... I know about your little project." The corners of Mary's mouth ticked up in a travesty of a smile, and Bryn froze, her lungs squeezing. "Your extra donations from my coffers to the vicar will cease."

Flooding relief almost made Bryn smile. Mary had no idea the true extent of her *little project*. She forced a deliberate quiver into her voice. "Extra money? I have no idea what you mean."

"The lazy, disenfranchised poor will have to manage without you." Mary's smug, triumphant overtones acted like bellows to the fire of Bryn's anger.

"Lazy? You sit up here in your manor house, stuffing your face while they go hungry to make sure their children don't cry themselves to sleep."

"Go to your room, and don't bother to join us for meals today. Perhaps it will do you some good to experience hunger yourself. A taste of your life if you do not happily repeat your vows on the morrow. I'll cast you out and instruct everyone from here to Edinburgh that to give you charity will be a personal insult to me. You will be left to scrabble for rotten scraps of food."

"You would do this to me? Your only sister?" Bryn asked more out of awe than real fear. No doubt, the fear and panic would come later.

"Accept your fate with as much grace as you can manage, if you please. You're lucky a gentleman such as Armstrong wants to wed you, considering your infirmity."

"It's not... I'm not sick." Bryn hated the whine that had snuck into her voice. Her episodes had grown so infrequent her panicked overreaction in the common room of the inn last night had caught her off guard. Still, she'd got herself under control before debilitating panic could set in.

"But you are, my dear, and you should be thanking us for seeing you settled so advantageously." Mary opened the door and snapped her fingers. A beefy man she didn't recognize approached. Bryn didn't sense the danger until it was too late. He enclosed her upper arm in an iron grip.

"Escort my sister back to her chambers, if you please."

The footman jailer marched her out of the room. Although she twisted and yanked at her arm, the man did not yield until he shoved her into her room. A rusty outer bolt that had never been used to her knowledge screeched home with resonating finality.

CHAPTER FOUR

Time had stood still in this little corner of Scotland. In a village as old as Cragian, ten years was a pittance. A new blacksmith worked at the corner smithy, but Donahue was still the butcher. Maxwell couldn't believe the old man could still handle the hulking sides of meat, but he appeared as spry as ever.

After wandering down the lane and through his memories, Maxwell climbed to the rectory. Perched atop a rise, the church made a pretty picture standing vigil above the little village, spires reaching for the low, misty clouds. Not much had changed here either. Perhaps the ivy stretched higher upon the stone walls, moss grew thicker around the sides, and more headstones littered the churchyard.

Was old Mitchell still the vicar? Their last communication had been about his mother's death. By the time the crumpled, dirty letter had found him on the Continent, his mother had been dead for months. He'd sent money for a proper headstone but never received word confirming his money had been well spent. If she had been buried in an unmarked pauper's grave, forgotten forever, he would never forgive himself.

Maxwell came across old Cadell's grave, well tended and marked with a large, flat headstone. A bundle of dried heather tied with a purple ribbon lay upon the gray, pitted stone. The stableman had been one of the few who had been kind to him. In fact, he'd always wondered if Cadell had a hand in the life-affirming baskets full of food that had magically appeared on his doorstep, but they'd continued even after his death.

The inevitable waited. He took a bracing breath, the cold air a welcome burn in his lungs. Spying a group of modest stones in one corner, he decided it a likely place to start. Not finding her name on any of the small markers, he gazed over the tall, imposing stones of the gentry to the pauper's graves.

The hollowness was back, threatening to swallow him. His mother was insignificant in the grand scheme of the world. Insignificant to everyone but him. She'd been his world and he hers.

He trudged closer, his gaze flitting over the rich stones like a moth. He almost missed her. The large stone was set among the gentry of Cragian, surrounded by those who'd done their best not to acknowledge her in life. *Eden Drake, 1767–1807. Fare thee well, thou best and dearest.*

A bundle of dried heather tied with a blue ribbon leaned against the expertly carved stone. Squatting on her grave, he braced hands on either side of the stone and laid his forehead against her name. Damnable tears gathered. She hadn't been forgotten.

The crunch of leaves broke his solitude. Vicar Mitchell approached with slow, hesitant steps. The vicar's white hair was a bit sparser, his wrinkles and crinkles more abundant, but a familiar twinkle lit his blue eyes as if there was a bawdy joke he desperately wanted to tell but knew he shouldn't.

Clearing his face of emotion, Maxwell rose and swept his hat off. Would the vicar recognize him after so many years?

"A brisk, good morning to you, sir. Have you interest in a cup of tea?" The vicar sidled closer, squinting at the grave behind Maxwell. The vicar's gaze darted back to his face. "Maxwell Drake?" A welcoming, happy smile accompanied the incredulous words.

"Aye, it's me." Maxwell's voice was rough. He'd come home to bury his past, but instead he found it difficult to keep his emotions from welling up and swamping him.

"My boy. It's a shock to see you after so many years but such a pleasant one. Goodness, you're looking well. You've come to see your mother." The vicar stood next to Maxwell, both of them looking at Eden's grave. Vicar Mitchell communed with the dead with ease. There were no eerie undertones, only a comfortable friendship. "It's hard to believe she's been gone six years. Time flows too quickly."

"Did you receive the money?" It was hard to believe the meager coins he'd managed to spare had wrought this stone. He had only been in the army three years when his mother died. His plans had been mere seeds and hadn't had time to flourish.

"I did, son, but by the time your letter arrived, Miss Bryn had already erected your mother's marker. I used your money to purchase books for the children. I thought you would approve."

"Miss Bryn..." The name lit a faint path through his memory.

"Brynmore McCann. A fine lass. She and your mother became fast friends after you left. Bryn took good care of Eden in her last years, Maxwell. You have nothing to feel guilty about. Your mother often told me how proud she was that you had escaped the legacy of your birth."

Dammit. Maxwell looked to the slate-gray sky and beat the burning sensation back down his throat. "Brynmore McCann was a child when I left."

"Not so young. Ten and five, perhaps?" He clapped Maxwell on the back. "Come inside and visit awhile. I'm freezing my arse off out here. The dead may not mind, but I do."

Maxwell ducked under the low door and entered a room untouched by time or a duster. Motes hung like smoke in the air, tickling his nose. As a child, he hadn't noticed how cramped the rooms were. He'd just remembered them being a safe haven.

"Sit while I fetch some tea." The vicar bustled out, leaving Maxwell to choose between a sagging settee and a lumpy chair. He fingered a leaflet of puritanical essays lying on the table and sank into the settee's cushions.

The vicar backed into the room with a tray laden with two cups, a teapot, and a handful of dry, crumbling biscuits. "You've acquired a limp, I noticed. Were you injured on the Continent?" Anticipation colored the question. No doubt, there weren't many visitors through Cragian to liven up his days.

"Yes, sir. I was wounded while running coded messages in Spain. A musket ball hit me above the knee."

"Were you captured? Did you manage to deliver your dispatches?"

"I wasn't captured. My horse saved my hide actually. I never forgot what old Cadell taught me. I took care of my horse, and when the time came, he returned the favor. Got me back to a regiment of British soldiers, and they sent the dispatches on. The physician traveling with them patched me up, sent me back to England, and I sold my commission."

The vicar spooned copious amounts of sugar into his steaming cup of tea. "Fascinating."

"Vicar. My commission. Is it you I need to repay?"

The vicar rubbed over his jaw and averted his gaze. "Not me. No."

The day the vicar had pressed the papers detailing his commission into his hand, Maxwell had known. The vicar's eyes had begged him not to ask the question. Pride had urged him to throw the papers in Ian MacShane's face. Common sense had told him to take the papers and run. He'd chosen the latter.

His mother would have had him believe fairy folk dropped him in her lap. But as he grew older, the taunts from the village boys and men became more pointed and cruel, and he came to understand what he was—a bastard.

"MacShane?"

"Dead not three months past. Isn't that what brought you home?" The vicar tilted his head and pursed his lips.

Maxwell was sure his eyes reflected back an equal amount of confusion. "I had no idea. Why would his death bring me back?"

"For your inheritance, of course."

"My *what?*" Maxwell asked on a harsh exhale.

"Didn't Lady MacShane or that pompous Edinburgh lawyer contact you?" The vicar shifted and stirred his tea.

"I've been in London the past three years. No one has been in contact with me. Tell me everything, Vicar Mitchell. No more lies or half-truths. I'm a man grown." Maxwell's voice dropped in timbre, the revelations shearing away any soft edge.

The vicar flushed and set his teacup on the tray with a betraying rattle. "It would be a sin, for it was a deathbed confession between MacShane and me. I can't countenance my indiscretion."

"Sir, you've already mentioned it. What harm would it do?" Maxwell forced gentleness back into his voice, as if he were coaxing a horse. "I'd rather not find out from Lady MacShane."

The vicar swallowed hard, but nodded. "He's gone now, and Lord knows, you have a right to know. He told me his one regret in life was not taking care of you and your mother. He bought your commission so you'd have the chance at something else. After you left, he dropped in occasionally to ask if I'd received a letter from you. I believe he was truly remorseful."

"He showed no remorse when he threw Mama out, penniless and round with his babe."

"I think Lady MacShane bears the brunt of the blame. Nevertheless, he didn't contradict her orders when it mattered. He vowed to leave you a bequest. That's really all I know. I assume he followed through with his intentions."

"I came to hate the man. Sitting in his fine house while Mama and I near starved to death." Maxwell took a deep breath to stem an old bitterness that felt fresh. "Vicar, did you discover who left us the baskets? I'd like to thank him, if I can."

The vicar's cup rattled against the saucer. Hot tea sloshed, and he leaped up, brushing at his breeches. "How clumsy of me. Pardon me while I change."

The vicar knew. Whether Maxwell could ferret out all his secrets over one pot of tea was debatable. And did it really matter now?

Restless and armed with new, significant information, Maxwell paced from the sitting room into the chapel through a narrow, connecting hall. He hadn't attended services since he'd left Cragian, but he found comfort in the familiar stone chapel.

Swaths of white silk draped the pews and columns, and orchids drooped their white petals in every window. Against the old stonework and colorful tapestries, the decorations made a pretty picture. It was no tenant farmer getting married. Hothouse orchids, indeed.

Vicar Mitchell joined Maxwell in the chapel in a different pair of worn, patched breeches. "When's the wedding?" Maxwell asked.

"On the morrow," the vicar said as if he were being asked to perform burial rites instead of binding a man and woman in blessed matrimony.

"I take it you disapprove?"

"It's hardly a love match."

"Who's the unfortunate pair?"

"The bride is Brynmore McCann. The groom is Dugan Armstrong. He's from the neighboring valley."

"As I recall, he enjoyed strutting through town and throwing his weight around." Maxwell traced a finger over his bottom lip, a picture coming to mind—a ham-fisted bully joining in with the local lads to hurl epitaphs at him. That sort of thing had stopped bothering him long before that particular incident.

"Sounds about right. It's unchristian, I know, but I don't like the man." The vicar sounded mutinous. "Not nearly good enough for our Bryn."

"She should have told him no when he asked for her hand." Maxwell was unable to muster much sympathy. His own worries burdened him.

"I'm not sure she was given a choice. That sister of hers has kept her close since the announcement. Mary Craddock is a damn menace."

A blade that had been in place for nearly ten years twisted. Something on his face must have reflected his inner disquiet.

"I'm sorry, son. I remember you and Lady Mary—"

"It was years ago, sir. She threw me over quite handily in favor of Craddock. And why wouldn't she? I was destitute with the merest wisp of prospects. Status and money were more important." Drawing from the cold wind whistling past the windows, ice dripped from his words. "Is it truly any different for this sister of hers?"

The vicar huffed a laugh, surprising Maxwell. "You must not recall Brynmore."

Vague recollections of Mary's half sister hovered on the edges of his consciousness like shadows. His only vivid memory had been at Cadell's funeral. The sight of the weeping girl had swelled his heart. He had been reluctant to interrupt her grief to pay his own respects to the man. Instead of embarrassment over her tears, she had welcomed him and offered comfort in return. The skinny girl's tight hug had imparted a measure of solace he hadn't expected. Then, like a wraith, she'd disappeared into the fog.

She had been bundled up with a mannish hat low over her brow, but he recalled being taken aback by her warm, brown eyes. So different from Mary's duplicitous green ones.

Big, luminous, chocolaty eyes that reminded him of…

The world tipped, his hangover coming back to call. His heart pounded his head with a mallet. "What color hair does Brynmore McCann have?" The question clawed its way out of his throat.

"An unusual shade. Not really red but not golden either. Somewhere in between. And such lovely brown eyes. She's a bit freckly, but I've always thought it added to her charm."

Why in bloody hell would highborn Brynmore McCann wait in his bed and pretend to be a whore mere days before she was due to wed? Did she think he wouldn't discover her little charade? Or wouldn't care if she tried to pass his babe off as another's? She had taken him for a fool.

His life was growing more complicated by the minute. His plan upon leaving London had been to pay his respects to his mother, make sure she had a proper headstone, repay the vicar for his kindness, and put the village firmly in his past, never to return.

Now he had a possible inheritance from a father who had never acknowledged him, and he'd ruined the sister of his first love. A woman who even now might be carrying his bastard babe. If he hadn't been in a house of the Lord, he would have unleashed a curse-filled tirade sure to call forth a deadly lightning strike.

There was nothing for it. If Brynmore McCann was to marry on the morrow, Dugan Armstrong wouldn't be the bridegroom.

* * * * *

Bryn sat on her bed, biting her thumbnail. *There's too much riding on your marriage to Dugan.* There were factors at play she didn't understand. Factors that made Mary and Craddock desperate for the marriage to go forward. As desperate as she felt to stop it.

She didn't even know what was in the blasted marriage settlement. Every time she'd asked to read it, Craddock had put her off with excuses. Mary's latest ambitions had to do with getting Craddock elected to Parliament. Her tastes had grown too sophisticated for provincial little Cragian. London called. But how did Bryn's marriage to Dugan help move Mary closer to her goal of shaking Scotland's dirt off her feet?

Would Vicar Mitchell bless the vows if she stood silent at the altar? He might not have a choice, considering Mary's threat of withholding much-needed funds from the church. Bryn refused to force him into a moral dilemma.

She faced two options she'd hoped to avoid. Accept her fate and marry Dugan or escape the match and grapple with an unknown, dangerous future.

Her decision made, she stripped off her woolen dress and pulled her buckskin breeches and boots out of the back of the wardrobe. They were snugger than the last time she'd worn them. The cloth strained across her backside and hugged her thighs.

A simple white shirt and study brown waistcoat came out of hiding as well. The waistcoat was especially tight, and she had to leave the top two buttons undone. No matter, her coat would cover her well enough.

Her only items of any worth had been her mother's—a pair of gem-encrusted combs, a gilded looking glass, and a few pieces of jewelry containing semiprecious stones. Bryn would hate to part with them, but she would if necessary. She wrapped them in a length of plaid and put them into the bottom of her small satchel.

She added her brown woolen gown still warm from her body to the pack along with stockings, underthings, and gloves. Her life packed away in one small satchel. The room barely bore a mark of her existence. Blinking back a fog of tears, she pulled her beaten, brimmed hat down on her head. She needed to be far away by the time Mary came to check on her. Time was her enemy.

She rattled the door, hoping the lock was rusty enough to give way, but it held fast. Her gaze fell on the window. Climbing down would be foolish and dangerous, but it was her only choice. If she broke her neck? Well, she would be out of this mess one way or another.

She tied her sheets together in a makeshift rope. The rock face was rough and would supply footholds. While her immediate destination was in question, Edinburgh was her ultimate goal. It was her best chance of escaping Mary's plans. Plus Bryn wasn't without friends there even if they were the common sort.

Bryn opened the sash and shivered as the brisk wind invaded her now defenseless room. Her window faced the gardens, but the weather was keeping the guests inside. The heavy gray clouds portended a snowfall before the day was over. Sunny blue skies would have been a better omen.

She secured one end of her sheet rope to her heavy, ornate bedpost and threw the rest over the sill, checking the length. The wind whipped it around, making it difficult to gauge how close to the ground it would get her.

She heaved a deep, nervous breath, hitched her satchel over one shoulder, and scanned the gardens. It wouldn't do to have anyone alert Mary before she even made it to solid ground. She threw a leg over the sill, held tightly to the sheet, and glanced down. The ground seemed infinitely farther away than it had at her first check. Heaving in a shuddery breath, she said a little prayer and went over the edge.

CHAPTER FIVE

After promising to visit Vicar Mitchell before he left for Edinburgh, Maxwell jammed his hat on his head and weaved his way through the gravestones. Of course, he would see the vicar again—to bind him in holy matrimony to a woman he knew in only the most carnal sense. The gray snow clouds that loomed overhead matched his mood.

Marriage. He had never been bothered with a compulsion to tie himself to one woman. Certainly there were women he admired, like Lady Minerva Bellingham. Lady Drummond, he supposed, now she'd married the brawny, scarred Lord Drummond. But Maxwell had never desired her, no matter that his brain recognized her physical beauty.

And he had nothing in common with London's young debutantes whose eyes shone with unabashed enthusiasm and innocence. Between his childhood and his time in the army, Maxwell had never been carefree. He felt ancient with his aching, crippled leg and jaded soul.

Maxwell entered the inn's stables and whistled for Primrose. Her answering whinny came from the farthest stall. He'd bought the mare, a hardy crossbreed, in London. She wasn't much to look at, but her rough, warm coat and thick forelegs made her well suited for cold weather and long rides. The sweet-tempered mare had earned her name.

He took his time saddling her, and when he was done, he rested his forehead against her neck. The musky smell of her coarse mane offered a bit of comfort. The weight of an anvil pressed on his chest at the thought of seeing Mary McCann after so many years and in these circumstances.

Despite his attempts to score away his first love and heartbreak, he'd never been able to forget the lass. Foolish. He was foolish. As much as he denied he had a heart, it beat against his ribs, too fast and fearful. He couldn't afford to acknowledge its existence.

Maxwell guided his horse over the familiar terrain. He had trod these paths more times than he could count, finding steady work in the spring and summer with the manor house's gardener.

A heated anticipation of catching a glimpse of Mary had filled those hours. The lass had flitted through the garden nearly every day to flirt and tease. He'd stolen ardently returned kisses beyond the arbor. It had never occurred to him to push his physical suit any further. Mary was a proper young maiden bound for marriage.

The house and grounds had a prosperous feel to them, and expensive carriages were aligned on the path to the stables. Maxwell left Primrose in the hands of a harried-looking groom with instructions to keep her saddled.

He dragged his feet as if his execution were nigh. With his hand on the heavy brass knocker in the shape of an ugly little cherub, a woman's cry carried on the chill wind along with the sound of something large colliding with the pavers. An intuition that had saved his hide more than once on the Peninsula stilled his hand before the knocker made contact.

Crouching low, Maxwell skulked around the side of the house, ignoring the scream of his bad leg. He stopped short at the corner and unfolded his body. Hanging from a sheet with her feet wedged onto the second-floor cornice was the woman he sought. Her hair was loose and blowing wildly around her face. A well-worn, shabby hat lay on the ground.

Making as little noise as possible so as not to distract her, he positioned himself directly beneath her. A call of warning might startle her and cause her to fall. His hands shook as she found purchase on the rough stone, inexorably moving toward the ground. Twice her boots slipped from their hold, and she dangled for a moment before she regained her footing. The woman was either daft or desperate. Maybe both.

As she got closer, the tension scrunching his shoulders to his ears faded, and his singular focus on her feet moved upward. Breeches emphasized the slenderness and length of her legs—legs that had been wrapped around him a few scant hours ago. Her attire was absolutely scandalous and ridiculously enticing.

Ten feet from the ground, she came to the end of the sheet. Mutterings that might have been prayers or curses were carried on the wind.

He shifted in the gravel and braced himself. "Let go. I'll catch you."

His voice startled her. Her boot slid down the rough wall, and her hands slipped off the sheet. Her screaming yelp was abruptly cut off when she made contact with him. The collision knocked the air out of him on a grunt.

One of his hands landed on her buttocks, and he wrapped his arm tightly around her waist. She clutched his neck. To any outside observer it might appear a lover's embrace and not a rescue.

Her body trembled. The memory of her trembling under him in her climax as her hands and legs pulled him closer had him squeezing her taut, rounded buttock. Her breasts were almost bursting out of the waistcoat she wore over a white lawn shirt. Christ in heaven, she couldn't even button the thing properly.

She pushed against his shoulders, and for an instant he tightened his arms around her. What the devil was he doing? He released her but kept a firm hold of her arm to keep her from bolting. Beneath the layers of fabric, her arm was thin yet strong.

"You," she whispered as if he were the devil sprung from hell. "What are you doing here?"

"Catching you." Her discomfiture lent him a sense of dark enjoyment. Why not let her squirm like he had done this morning after her departure?

"You know very well what I meant, Max—Mr. Drake."

"*Mr. Drake*, is it now? That's not what I remember you calling me last night. Brynmore McCann."

She yanked her arm out of his grip. "I had no intention of you ever discovering my identity, Maxwell... Mr. Drake. Blast it, what should I call you?" Her face was flushed, her sprinkling of freckles emphasized. She looked even younger than she had in the shadows of his bed, but by his calculation, she was well over twenty.

"Considering we're intimately acquainted, call me Maxwell." His voice remained harsh.

Silence stretched between them like a prisoner on the rack. She picked up her hat and twirled it in her hands. Even with resentment simmering, he couldn't deny the mannish clothes were becoming to her lithe frame.

He forced a conversational tone. "May I inquire what you're doing climbing out your window and nearly breaking your neck a day before your joyous union? The chapel looked lovely, by the by." A satchel hung on her back. Would she tell him the truth or lie once again?

"Joyous union." She harrumphed. "I'm running away, of course."

"Why?"

Some of the defiance leaked out of her as she looked to the ground. "Because my first plan didn't work."

"And I was plan number one?"

"I'd hoped Dugan would toss me over once I confessed my ruination."

He had been chosen to get a job done—nothing more. The hurt that pricked surprised him. Hadn't he taken his pleasure with her to distract himself from his own worries? He whipped his hat off, ran his fingers through his hair, and jammed it back on.

"Not only are you ruined, but my life is ruined as well. Why in bloody hell did you have to choose me for the honors?"

"I'm asking nothing from you. I made my bed—" She cleared her throat. "I mean, it was my decision. You weren't ever to find out who I was, so don't feel you need to ride up and do something honorable."

"You are a complete ninnyhammer. You surely don't think after I found blood on myself and the sheets this morning, I would do nothing? I may have been born a bastard, madam, but I wasn't raised to act as one. Since you were a maiden, perhaps you don't understand that what occurred between us could lead to a very unwelcome arrival." He ended on a near yell.

Bryn pulled her hat low, shielding her expression. "If there's a babe, I'll take care of it." Her small, tremulous voice made him feel like an arse—which only fired his resentment higher. She was in the wrong here, not him, dammit. He paced and shot her silent glares on every pass.

"Where would you go? How would you earn money to support yourself and a babe?"

Her shrug wasn't reassuring in the least.

"I would not have a child grow up the way I did. If there is a babe, it will bear my name and will *never* be called a bastard. I won't have you suffer like my mother did. No woman deserves that, no matter their sins. You will be married by the morrow but not to Dugan Armstrong. To me."

"I never intended for you to sacrifice your life—your freedom—to marry me." Her brown eyes finally rose to meet his, and the sight did strange things to his insides. "It was only once. We have no idea whether I might be with child."

"It only takes one time."

"I'm not completely ignorant."

"Not anymore," he muttered back.

Color swept her face again, but she didn't drop her gaze. "Mary's trying to force the marriage to Dugan in spite of what occurred between us."

"Did you tell her I was the man who ruined you?" Maxwell tensed.

"I didn't lie to you. No one was ever to know whom I chose. But I don't see why we have to marry. At least not until we know with certainty whether I'm carrying your child. Does it matter if we get married tomorrow or two months from tomorrow?" A hint of desperation threaded her words.

"Even if you aren't carrying my child, I took your maidenhead. You're a lady. Marriage is the only honorable course of action. No doubt half the village knows you shared my bed last night, and the other half will find out today." Another more damning thought occurred to him. "Unless my birth places me below your consideration for marriage." He tried to temper the searing anger in his voice but was unsuccessful even to his own ears.

"That's not…" Her head jerked back as if he'd actually struck her. "You don't *want* to marry me. You'll resent me—"

"I already do. Dealing with this debacle was not part of my plans, I assure you."

"I didn't know what else to do." She worried her bottom lip, plumping it and turning it red. The swirling emotion in her eyes drew him in, and a portion of his resentment faded. She'd been desperate. An emotion he was well acquainted with.

"If Mary is willing to force the marriage even knowing you're ruined, you can't stay here." Maxwell rubbed a hand over his jaw.

"My plan is to make my way to Edinburgh."

"And do what?"

"Hire myself out."

"As a whore?"

Her color rose to new heights. "Of course not. A companion. Or a governess, perhaps."

"I ruined you. No one will hire you for either."

"That is ridiculous. I'm not *ruined*." Defiance flashed in her eyes and reflected in the set of her chin. "You didn't ruin me. In fact, I feel… I feel…" She closed her eyes and took a deep breath, the corners of her lips twitching.

Unable to stop himself, he leaned closer as if she were indeed fey and had cast a spell over him. He wanted to run his fingers down her face and the long column of her neck. "How do you feel?"

Her eyes popped open. "I enjoyed last night. Didn't you?"

Her admission contained no guile or manipulation, only honesty. Memories sparked. He'd thought his alcohol-boggled mind had exaggerated her unusual beauty, but his cloudy memories hadn't done her justice. With innocence and strength and vulnerability in her face and eyes, he couldn't lie.

"Aye, lass, I enjoyed it." Something deep inside him stirred. A yearning. But for what?

He gave in to his urges and stroked her cheek with his gloved forefinger. She swayed into his touch. Even though their marriage would be a sham, the marriage bed held a distinct allure. She would be his to explore every night by rights. The thought fired a possessive, primal response in his body. He dropped his head to take her lips. A sampling of what was to come.

"Brynmore!" The screech snapped him out of his strange reverie.

"Lud, it's Mary," Bryn whispered, turning to stone.

No longer feeling a man of the world, he turned as a callow youth to face his first love. Nerves and excitement and dread turned his stomach. Light-headed, he blinked furiously, trying to reconcile the eighteen-year-old Mary with the teasing smile against this woman's ferocious beauty.

Her hair was the same rich sable, wound and curled intricately around her ears. Her flounced, ruffled gown would have been better suited to a younger lass. Rings twinkled on her fingers, and a strand of pearls played peak-a-boo in her décolletage. Although she was still undeniably beautiful, the hatred in her eyes and the cruel twist of her once tempting mouth took him aback. There was no sign of the girl he'd loved.

How many times had he imagined himself riding into Cragian triumphant and successful to show Mary McCann what she had so blithely tossed aside? The image of Mary he had carried for nearly a decade was irrevocably shattered, and he wasn't sure what new emotion assailed him—grief, relief, shock? He had become preoccupied with the grim sadness he'd toted around since leaving Cragian.

He reached out and found Bryn's hand clenched into a fist. She relaxed at his touch, and he gave her hand a quick squeeze. Whatever the future held, he and Brynmore were linked in a way he and Mary had never been.

"Your mystery lover, I presume? How sweet. It's a good thing I caught you, now isn't it? Dugan is inside waiting for an apology." Her fury was palpable.

She didn't recognize him. Or maybe she didn't remember. An old, familiar pain lashed his heart. His voice was raw with emotion. "Your sister is now *my* betrothed."

"I think not. She is already betrothed with signed and sealed papers. Your attentions are no longer welcome, sir. Be on your way and off my land. Do not return." She waved a bejeweled hand, shooing him away, a threat in her voice.

"And if I won't be off like a beggared dog?" A curious protectiveness had Maxwell stepping partway in front of Bryn. After working for Minerva Bellingham, he wasn't the least bit intimidated by autocratic women.

"I'll give you ten pounds to leave and not speak of this again."

Maxwell rumbled a mirthless laugh. "Ten pounds, Mary? Is your sister not worth more than that?"

He'd finally gained her full attention. "Who are you to address me so familiarly, sirrah?"

Maxwell whipped his hat off and stepped closer. "It's no wonder you don't recognize me. How many years has it been since last we met? Maxwell Drake, at your service."

A flash of something he recognized crossed Mary's face. Maybe, just maybe, she did remember. And held regrets.

"The weather has turned damp and frigid, has it not, ladies? A cup of tea would be very welcome. Why don't we discuss the matter inside?" He forced civility even as his heart tore at his chest.

With a clenched jaw and not another word, Mary turned on her heel and led the way around the corner of the manor house.

Bryn grabbed his arm, her fingers biting. "Don't let them take me. They'll lock me away again. Please."

"I won't, lass." The role of knight-errant didn't settle comfortably on his shoulders, but he could hardly leave her to be devoured by the wolves of Cragian. He was duty bound.

The overabundant use of blue and yellow ruffles in the drawing room jangled. Craddock and Dugan Armstrong shared an early brandy. Whether in celebration or commiseration, he couldn't guess. The men rose as Mary marched over to Craddock and gestured back to Bryn and Maxwell.

Craddock's dark hair was a patchwork over his white scalp, and while his clothes were well made, they couldn't disguise his round belly. The years had not been as kind to Craddock as they had to Mary, and the gulf of years between them seemed even wider. She spoke low to the two men, and Craddock's gaze shot to Maxwell. Instead of the expected anger, his expression was one of scheming determination. Dugan tossed back his drink. Fury pinched his mouth.

Craddock fired the opening salvo. "The prodigal son returns. Sit and let's discuss what can be done to remedy the unfortunate situation we find ourselves in."

The animosity swirling around the room swallowed the weak attempt at social niceness. Disguising his limp as best he could, Maxwell took the unoccupied settee across from Craddock and Mary. He loathed showing any weakness in a situation where the lions circled.

Dugan paced toward Bryn, and she shrank closer to the door and escape. Maxwell had encountered Armstrong's type in the army. The man relished power and enjoyed using it to subjugate others, but the blatant malevolence seeping from the big man as he stared at Bryn was worrisome.

"Sit, sit. Come, Brynmore, Dugan." Craddock waved them both over.

Bryn joined Maxwell on the settee, her thigh pressing into his. She was ashen-faced with her hands fisted on her knees. Craddock, Dugan, and Mary, lined up like an opposing army across the table, emphasized how vulnerable Bryn was to their manipulations. She had no one to champion her. It was a wonder she'd resisted their plans at all, and a sliver of admiration surfaced.

Dugan lowered himself into a chair, his hands on the sides as if he was ready to spring up at any time. "Did you return to spoil my marriage?"

Maxwell quirked an eyebrow. "You give yourself far too much credit, Armstrong. You haven't crossed my mind in nearly a decade. No, my plans did not include Brynmore. Nevertheless, plans change, and Craddock is correct. We must remedy the situation." No one moved or said a word, so he continued. "I would propose that the wedding take place tomorrow with me substituted as the groom. That way, all Mary's hard work won't be for naught."

Mary shot to her feet. "Absolutely not. Dignitaries are attending. We have the MP of the neighboring district upstairs as we speak. To invite them to witness a marriage between my sister and the poor local bastard who ruined her? It's a travesty and would completely defeat the purpose."

Maxwell's eyes narrowed, but before he delved further, Bryn scooted to the edge of the cushion and pointed at Mary. "You will not speak of Maxwell in such a manner. Just because you weren't brave enough to claim him doesn't mean I'm not." Although her hand visibly trembled, her voice was steady.

Surprise but also indefinable warmth heated his face at her defense.

Mary took a step forward. Bryn popped off the settee, and the two sisters stared each other down with such hostility that blows seemed inevitable. He readied himself to intervene, his muscles bunched.

A timid knock heralded the arrival of a young maid. The tension dissipated, and Bryn and Mary retreated to their seats like prizefighters between rounds. The maid pushed a tea tray, her wide eyes darting around the room. Mary acted the hostess and poured.

Maxwell sipped the hot tea and observed the tableau before him. The act of sharing the civilized rite of tea when the undercurrents of barbaric emotions ran rife tickled his dark humor. The maid backed her way out of the room and closed the door with a soft snick.

Dugan drained his cup in a gulp and set it back on the tray with a clatter. "Brynmore will be my wife tomorrow in spite of her foolishness. She will regret her impetuous action." His wintry eyes were directed at Bryn, and more than the hint of a threat colored the words. "Anyway, there's things I've been promised from this marriage. Things that—"

"Enough, Dugan." Craddock cut a hand in the air.

"What sort of things were you promised, Armstrong?" Maxwell kept his voice bland even though his head spun with possibilities.

"That is part of the marriage settlement and none of your concern, Drake," Craddock said.

Maxwell hummed before taking a small sip of tea. "I suppose you're correct. You may as well tear it up. I'll require Bryn to bring nothing to our union. I'm more than able to provide for her. And for a babe, if one has been conceived."

The coordinated intake of breath from all the occupants of the room made Maxwell's lips twitch. The words enraged Dugan, and before Maxwell could react, Dugan yanked Bryn up by the arm and shook her. She turned her face away from Armstrong, cowing slightly from the man's physical dominance.

Anger crackled through Maxwell like fire. He moved behind Bryn and wrapped a hand around Dugan's wrist like a manacle. He tightened his hand on Dugan's wrist incrementally, waiting to see how much the bigger man could tolerate.

Although Dugan topped Maxwell in height, Maxwell was stronger. He kept his body honed by boxing, fencing, and riding. He had been in the army too long not to relish the physical activity, and it kept his leg as strong and limber as possible.

Maxwell increased the pressure until Dugan winced, then he tightened it some more. Dugan's hand opened, and Bryn backed into Maxwell's chest. He twisted Dugan's hand into an impossible angle.

"Stop. Let go of me." Dugan's voice was shrill and breathy. Maxwell twisted another inch before releasing him. Dugan rubbed his wrist and retreated, his eyes wide and filled with a newfound respect—and utter hatred.

Maxwell had made an enemy, and a dangerous one at that.

CHAPTER SIX

Maxwell's arm was an iron vise around her waist. His muscled body made Dugan's seem doughy in comparison, and his warrior's command of the room harkened to a bygone time. He made her feel safe—even if she'd forced him to play the role of her protector.

"Is there anything you need from your room? You're coming with me. Now." Maxwell's breath whispered across her ear.

"Anything of importance is in my satchel."

He loosened his arm, and Bryn retrieved her bag from beside the settee.

"Craddock, Mary, Armstrong. I can't say it's been a pleasure, but it's certainly been enlightening." Maxwell's voice didn't reflect the tension she'd sensed in his body. "I am pleased to see you doing so well, Mary. I wish you continued happiness. Perhaps, after Brynmore and I are wed, you'll come for a visit."

He bowed to the room, clasped Bryn's elbow, and led her out the front door. She looked over her shoulder, expecting to see Dugan charging them, but no one came. The brisk winter air cooled the heat of humiliation and fear tumbling through her body.

"Where are we going?" She easily kept pace with Maxwell's limping quick walk to the stables.

"The vicar's, of course."

She pulled him to a stop. "But we agreed to wait to see if there was a need to marry."

"Bloody hell, woman! You were in that room. Did you not hear them?" He tightened his grip on her elbow until it was almost painful, forcing her to continue walking. As they entered the stable, he gave a low whistle, and an answering whinny came from a corner stall. He led his still saddled shaggy horse out of the stall.

"Something is afoot. You're only a pawn, and as a pawn, you're expendable. They've promised you to Armstrong in addition to something else he wants—badly. And Craddock and Mary are getting something in return from Armstrong. Do you know what it is?" Maxwell pulled her around to face him, but she kept her gaze on the buttons of his greatcoat.

The situation made the weak tea crawl up her throat. Adding to her bitterness was the knowledge she was unimportant and powerless. An expendable pawn. Her selfish attempt to escape Dugan's clutches had only forced Maxwell into an untenable position.

"Craddock wants elected as MP. Or perhaps it's more Mary's ambition. She wants to be part of Society. She's pushing Craddock to get her to London. Dugan's people have votes they need. I haven't a clue what Dugan is getting. I've got nothing anyone could want."

Maxwell slipped a finger under her chin, tilted her face up, and studied her intently for a long, uncomfortable minute. With a grim set to his mouth, he mounted and held a hand out. She put her booted foot atop his, and before she could tense her muscles to help, he hauled her in front of him. She spun to ride astride. He took her hat off and pushed it into her chest.

The horse set off at a brisk walk. With her thighs on top of his and her bottom nestled between his legs, she wiggled to find a more comfortable position. He squeezed her so tightly she grunted.

"What's the matter? Am I hurting your leg?"

He hesitated. "Yes, my leg. That's what's hurting."

"I'd be happy to rub it when we get back to the inn." Silence from Maxwell. "I can rub it like in the bath. Don't you remember?"

It started as a lightning-fast guffaw but thundered into a rumbling laugh that vibrated against her back. Twisting around, her stomach swooped to see his mouth curled up into a genuine smile, his hazel eyes glimmering.

"I remember it well, lass. After we're wed, you can rub it every night," he said in a roughened velvety brogue.

The realization her innocent offer wasn't innocent in the least had a blush sweeping through her, as well as a carnal awareness. His horse came to a stop as the two of them stared at each other.

Her fingers itched to smooth over the crinkles at the corner of his eyes and over his bottom lip. A flash of desire sparked as she remembered running her tongue along its soft contour and pulling it between her teeth. She dabbed her tongue along her suddenly dry lips, and his nostrils flared.

His hauled her around to face front again. She squirmed, and he stopped her with a firm hand on her hip and a low, cursing groan.

"I don't trust your sister or Craddock and especially not Armstrong. I've rented a set of rooms and have business appointments set for next week in Edinburgh. I can't leave you here, and if we travel north together, we must be married."

Bryn studied the passing rolling fields. This land was dearly familiar to her, and she'd never traveled much beyond the next valley. She'd always wanted to go to Edinburgh. How many times had she asked Mary to take her on one of her frequent trips there? Her sister had always put her off with one excuse or another. But her chance to see something of the world had come at a steep price.

"I won't force you into an unwanted marriage. That's what I

was trying to escape to begin with." In a softer voice, she said, "Why can't we wait to see if I'm increasing?"

He ignored her.

Snow drifted from the steel-gray clouds on their approach to the church. Afternoon was waning, and darkness fell early this time of year. The falling snow muffled any noise. No one was in sight, but smoke rose from the chimney of Vicar Mitchell's small set of rooms.

He swung her to the ground, and she stomped her feet against the cold as he settled his horse under a tree near the graveyard. Even in the conditions, he took the time to scratch his horse's forelock and whisper words of praise. The horse nudged him.

"You seem awfully fond of your horse." She cursed the tart edge of her voice. The gentle hands he used to pet and soothe the horse made her crave the same. Did she want to be treated like a horse? The answer was a humiliating yes.

"She's been a reliable, trustworthy friend the past weeks."

"I would have thought you'd prefer a bruising stallion or gelding. What's her name?"

"It's a horse's heart and stamina that are important, not the size nor sex." He cleared his throat before mumbling, "Primrose."

Laughter bubbled out. The tension squatting between them eased. "Primrose?"

"Don't make fun. I thought of changing it, but it suits her. She's a sweet-tempered girl. Now as for you..." His gaze trailed over her hair, which must have looked funny collecting white snow, down to the tips of her old, scuffed boots.

She ruffled a hand through her hair, smoothing it behind an ear. "What about me?"

"You can't go around in gentlemen's clothes." He sounded almost distressed about her attire.

"I've spent more time in breeches than dresses over the years,

Drake. I don't see any reason to stop the practice now. Breeches are much more practical." She ran her hands down the worn fabric covering her thighs.

"You have no idea what affect you have on the male species in those breeches, do you? I hope you packed a dress in your satchel for tomorrow."

As she wondered what affect she had on Maxwell, his words sank in. "You surely don't expect me to ride a horse in the winter in a dress? Anyway, as I recall, I haven't agreed to accompany you."

Maxwell shook his head, turned on his heel, and walked away. She hesitated, but the cold drove her to follow him around the side of the church to the vicar's rooms. Vicar Mitchell, disheveled and sleepy, answered Maxwell's sharp rap. His hair was standing on end, and he clutched a blanket around his shoulders.

"Maxwell, my boy, you caught me napping, I'm afraid. Why, Brynmore, is that you, lass?"

"Aye, sir." Bryn dropped a curtsy, which probably looked ridiculous considering her state of attire.

"We have a matter of some urgency to discuss, sir," Maxwell said.

The vicar's gaze darted between them as he gestured them into his sitting room. "Shall I see to some tea?" He shuffled off without waiting for an answer.

"Did you see the chapel? It's quite lovely." Maxwell's voice had enough dry heat to spark a fire.

"Mary handled the arrangements. If I had to guess, it's ostentatious."

"A little." The corner of his mouth twitched. "We can marry here in the vicar's sitting room then."

"No." She stepped toward him, her hands on her hips. He didn't move. The room was small, and she ended up closer to him than she'd intended. It would be too easy to fall into his plans. Too easy to fall into his hazel eyes and strong arms. Too easy to fall from childhood infatuation into danger. "I won't marry you unless it becomes necessary, and that's that."

The rattle of dishes drew their attention to the vicar standing in the doorway, mouth agape. Bryn sighed and sent a brief prayer heavenward.

"You're due to marry Dugan Armstrong on the morrow." Confusion was writ on the vicar's face.

"Not anymore," Maxwell said ominously.

She cast a quelling look at Maxwell. "I've done something rather impetuous, I'm afraid." She removed the shaking tea tray from the vicar's hands and placed it on the table. The vicar heard deathbed confessions and counseled the villagers in the best and worst of times. It was his job. Yet her fear of experiencing his disappointment was more daughterly.

She glanced at Maxwell, but he appeared unlikely to come to her aid this time. Taking a deep breath, she grasped the vicar's hands. "I was desperate. I hoped if I got myself ruined, Dugan would throw me over. I took complete advantage of poor Maxwell and… and seduced him," she finished in a whisper.

Maxwell turned her so they were face-to-face in front of the vicar. "You took advantage of me, did you? *That* was a seduction? If I hadn't been in my cups, I would have recognized you for a virgin sitting there in that horrid muslin white nightdress up to your neck and tossed you out."

Heated embarrassment whooshed through her, singeing her heart. Familiar feelings of inadequacy sharpened her words even as guilt rose. "You certainly weren't complaining when you ripped my *horrid* nightdress off and pounced on top of me like some beast to—"

The vicar pushed them apart and shuffled to plop in his sagging armchair.

"Is there a possibility of a babe, Maxwell?" Vicar Mitchell looked to the small fire in the grate.

"Yes." Dread dripped from the single word. "I had no plans on acquiring a wife in Cragian, but I'll not leave a bastard to starve like my father left me."

Guilt for putting Maxwell in the situation, shame from her confession to the vicar, and anger at the way they were cutting her out of the decision swirled together.

"Dash it. I don't want a husband either. Men dictate and control because they're bigger. A bully is what you are, Maxwell Drake. You too, Vicar, if you mean to force me to say vows to any man."

"You must, Brynmore." The vicar's eyes were sad but understanding.

"Why must I? Why can't we wait? If my courses come, then there's no reason to marry." Fighting men's machinations was exhausting, and the unfairness cut deep.

"People will talk, and they will be cruel."

She fell to her knees beside the vicar's chair. "But surely after all I've done, they'll—"

"They won't be understanding." The vicar brushed his hand over her hair. "Even the innocent suffer under the stain of sin. Maxwell understands."

Tears blurred her vision as she looked up at Maxwell. A grimness settled on him like the black feathers of a raven. "It's true, lass. Sister to a baroness or not, you'll be a pariah in Cragian."

"Anyway," the vicar said, "you should remove yourself from Mary and Armstrong's reach. I don't trust either of them."

Her foolish ignorance had caused this. She had ruined her life, that much was clear, but damn if she would be responsible for ruining Maxwell's as well.

"I shan't marry unless I'm with babe, but I'll accompany you to Edinburgh, Maxwell. Then, if needs must, we'll marry."

"I won't force you to say vows before God." The vicar

hummed and studied them. "And I trust Maxwell to do the honorable thing."

"I will," Maxwell intoned as if saying a vow. Something passed between the two men. An understanding, but of what, she couldn't discern.

With the decision made, she stumbled to her feet. After having spent twenty-four years caught in an eddy, she was suddenly in the current and hurtling toward an unknown fate.

The vicar rose and caught her wrist before she slipped out the door after Maxwell.

"He's a good man. Trust him," he whispered.

"He hates me." A root of her fear bubbled up.

His smile was knowing and sad and hopeful. "He could never hate you, lass."

She wanted to believe him. Would she see him again? He opened his arms, and she fell into him, burying her nose in his collar. He smelled of Cragian and comfort, things she was leaving behind. "I'll miss you, sir. So much."

"I'll miss you too, Brynmore. All my flock are my children, but you're special."

"The donations—"

"Don't you worry about that."

She nodded and took a step backward from his warm, welcoming sitting room into the biting cold. Maxwell sat on his horse as still and hard as a statue. As she closed the distance, he came to life, offering her a hand.

Words were beyond her, and she was thankful he didn't demand them of her on their ride back to the inn. He and Jock argued about a second room, but there were none to be had with the extra guests at the manor.

Cursing under his breath, he threw his hands up. "I'll be back in a bit." He didn't volunteer any more information before leaving her.

Feeling the eyes of everyone on her, she scampered up the stairs to his room. Memories of the previous night rose like wraiths to haunt her. She stared at the bed. A scratch on the door broke her reverie. A maid delivered a hardy stew and yeast bread, her eyes downcast as if Bryn was tainted. And maybe she was.

The country fare was a welcome change from the nauseating French sauces she had been forced to endure under Mary's London cook, yet nerves stunted her appetite.

If Maxwell was set on them leaving, Bryn had her own plans to settle. She checked out the window but saw no sign of him. The moon was on the rise. She couldn't wait a moment longer. After sending the hostler off with a note to deliver, she pulled her cloak tight and set off for the manor house.

If Mary discovered Bryn in the kitchens, would she be married off before Maxwell even realized she was gone? The confrontation with Mary and Craddock and Dugan had left her more rattled than she wanted to admit.

The snow continued to fall, leaving everything preternaturally quiet. Bryn stopped under the boughs of a straggly pine and took a deep breath. The cold air scratched her lungs and sharpened her senses. The first hours after a snowfall, before the tramping of people and beasts dirtied the pristine covering, were magical.

The weight on her chest had lightened in some respects. The debilitating fear over her marriage to Dugan had faded to a buzz in the background of her other worries. She would be a fool not to consider him a threat, but now her worries were concentrated on Maxwell Drake.

The man was too honorable for his own good. If she was with child, he would insist on wedding her, no matter that he didn't love her. For a moment, before Mary's shrill voice cut them apart, something had sparked between them. Something that might grow into a fire. Then the shock at seeing Mary had revealed something in his face and stance. A longing that had nothing to do with Bryn. Was he still in love with her sister? The possibility worked a deep splinter in her heart.

As she got closer to the manor, she skirted through the trees to the kitchen entrance and peered through the small slit in the window covering. Mrs. Kidd was alone working on the next morning's breakfast while Sarah sat on the long oak servant's table and swung her legs. Bryn knocked five times, three long, two short, and the door swung open.

"My poor dearie. Come in, come in. Sarah and I wondered if you might pay us a visit this evening." Mrs. Kidd enveloped Bryn in a bosomy hug smelling of yeast and flour. Bryn closed her eyes and tried to sear the moment into her memory.

Mrs. Kidd had been the head cook at the manor for a dozen years until the short, bullying London cook Mary had hired usurped her. As she had nowhere else to go, she returned to chopping vegetables and following orders. A combination of a kind and rebellious heart meant Mrs. Kidd was more than happy to set aside food for Bryn's pet project—the baskets she coordinated for the poor.

Mrs. Kidd returned to kneading the dough on the table. The kitchen was homey and comfortable. A huge fire burned in the hearth. Bryn took her customary seat at the end of the scarred table and worried her thumbnail.

"I'm accompanying Maxwell Drake to Edinburgh on the morrow." Both women stopped and looked at Bryn with nearly identical expressions of shock.

"That's a name I haven't heard in an age or more. Maxwell Drake." Mrs. Kidd returned to her work, but her eyes remained unfocused. "I suppose that was the visitor today? But why would you hie off to Edinburgh with a stranger?"

Bryn stared at Sarah. Panic reflected back.

"It sounded to me like Mr. Drake and Mr. Armstrong are

feuding." Sarah shrugged her shoulders.

Bryn grasped the thin excuse. "Yes. Feuding. And Maxwell offered to save me from Dugan."

Mrs. Kidd's eyes were no longer dreamy but as sharp as one of the kitchen knives. "Feuding? How long have I known you, Brynmore McCann?"

"All my life?"

"Indeed. You go splotchy when you're lying, girl." Mrs. Kidd clapped her hands together, and flour puffed like fog around her. "I know you and your sister had quite the row this morning. Tell me the truth."

Bryn pressed her hands against her cheeks. Damn her red hair and freckly skin. No wonder men preferred Mary's classic beauty. "I spent the night with Maxwell Drake."

"Are you telling me you went and got yourself ruined?"

The horror and disappointment in Mrs. Kidd's voice was parental. And in truth, Mrs. Kidd, Cadell, and Vicar Mitchell had played the roles of parents in her life. Sarah moved closer. How many times had they stood side by side as children and been berated for their mischievousness? This wasn't slipping frogs into Mary's bed though.

"I was counting on a different outcome. One that involved my freedom from any man. Only now Maxwell feels duty bound to marry me, but I told him I wouldn't unless there's a babe. He's insisting I accompany him to Edinburgh until we know."

Mrs. Kidd's face took on the color of the flour dotting the table. She plopped in the nearest chair. "What if there's no babe and he tosses you out on the streets in the middle of winter? What then, Brynmore?"

The consequences of her actions set her heart pounding so rapidly she grew light-headed, unable to move past a mental image of beggaring in the streets. "I don't know. Perhaps I'll come back here."

"Yes, I'm sure your dear sister will welcome you with open arms." Mrs. Kidd's dry prediction scraped at her raw nerves.

"It's done. There will either be a babe or not. I'm not here for a lecture or to be talked out of going. I need help with the baskets. I'm meeting with Busby and hoped I could tell him you'd provide a bit of food?"

"Of course I'll help with the baskets. Don't worry. We'll get along fine here without you." Even as Mrs. Kidd's voice reassured, another jab of pain made her stomach ache.

Of course they would be fine. The world would turn, the sun would rise, and everyone would go about their lives as if she'd never existed.

Bryn pushed out of the chair, her gaze on the table. "I guess this is goodbye."

Mrs. Kidd clasped Bryn's wrist, forcing her to look up. She pushed Bryn's hair behind an ear as she would a child. "Can I give you a word of advice?" Bryn didn't relish hearing another depressing prediction of her fate, but Mrs. Kidd didn't wait for an answer. "You've given enough of yourself to this little village. Look to your own happiness."

Tears stung. Would this be the last time she ever saw Mrs. Kidd? "I'll try."

Sarah walked her out the door. The two friends faced each other. "I'm going to miss you something fierce, Bryn. Don't listen to Mrs. Kidd's dearth and gloom. Everything is going to be fine."

Bryn managed a slight smile and threw her arms around Sarah. A tear slipped into her friend's braid. "I'll miss you too. Can you do something for me?"

"Do you want me to short-sheet your sister's bed? Put salamanders in her unmentionables? Anything."

A huffing laugh stole through her tears. She pulled back and put her hands on Sarah's shoulders. "No. Give Colin Conrad a chance."

Sarah moaned. "The man can't even bring himself to talk to me."

"He thinks you're the most beautiful creature on earth. You make him nervous."

"Beautiful?" Sarah fingered her braids and looked over the blanket of snow. "I'll give him a chance if he manages to say hello. Will you write?"

"If I can, I will." It's all she could promise.

A clatter down the hall had her heart racing like a rabbit's. After one more bracing hug, Bryn darted toward the tree line. Only when she was tucked into the fronds of an evergreen did she look back. A figure stood in the doorway. A ripple of fear shuddered through her. The kitchen light sparked Mary's auburn hair and green dress, making her glow like an avenging goddess.

Bryn backed into the trees. Were Craddock and Dugan out searching for her? Every scrabbling animal quickened her pace and made her heart leap. Her footprints in the snow would lead them straight to her, but on the flipside, she hadn't seen any tracks but her own.

The hoot of an owl brought her to a standstill. It came again, and this time she cupped her hands around her mouth and returned the hoot twice. A man stepped out from behind a spruce tree. Bryn ran to him and braced herself against the tree, her knees nearly giving way.

"What's the matter, lassie? Why're you in a tizzy?" Busby asked through a woolen scarf wrapped around his face.

Bryn peered into the trees all around them. All she could hear was her own breathing. "It's nothing. Nothing."

Busby pulled the scarf down to grace her with one of his beatific smiles. It lit his black eyes and caused his entire face to crinkle in such a way it was nigh on impossible not to smile back. His hair was as white as the snow around them but as thick as a lion's mane. "What can I do for you?"

"Thank you for coming. It's a night to be curled up under your quilts at home."

"Aye, aye. What's so urgent?"

"I'm leaving on the morrow, and I need help with the baskets. The Widow Monroe's children must have extra meat. And is there any way you could find some shoes for the oldest lad? He was in town last week and had tried to fill the holes with mud. He'll lose his toes if it goes on much longer."

"Aye, o' course, lassie. No need to fash yourself. I'll *acquire* some shoes for young Dongal." Busby winked. Bryn had learned not to question his methods. "Is Armstrong taking you away from us then?"

"I'm not marrying him. He's horrid."

"I'm not disputing the fact, but then where are you going?"

"I'm leaving for Edinburgh tomorrow." Bryn looked down and twisted a button on her cloak. Apparently, the news hadn't swept through the village—yet. "With Maxwell Drake."

"The bastard of Cragian?"

"Don't call him that, Busby. He's made something of himself." Her hot defense of Maxwell gave away more than she'd intended.

Busby ran a hand over his face. "Goodness me, this is quite a turn of events. Drake was a good boy, always tried to do right by poor Eden. Can he take care of you? Keep you safe?"

"I trust him." And she did, up to a point.

"Dugan Armstrong is not likely to give up until you marry and maybe not even then. I've never seen a more prideful man. You and your Mr. Drake need to take care. Between Armstrong and your sister…" Busby shook his head.

Considering she'd run headlong through the woods sensing the danger Busby hinted at ready to swamp her, she didn't argue the point. The question that had been plaguing her grew more insistent. What had Dugan been promised on their marriage?

"I've come from talking with Mrs. Kidd and Sarah at the manor. They'll fix the baskets, if you can sneak in to pick them up for delivery."

They discussed the particulars for a few more minutes. Then it was time for another goodbye. Bryn's eyes stung with tears as they separated to head in opposite directions.

The quiet woods settled her anxious thoughts. Maybe Sarah was right and everything would be fine.

The breaking of a stick behind her registered a heartbeat before a man grabbed her upper arm and hauled her backward. She kicked her legs to regain her balance. Her scream was cut short by a gloved hand pressed over her mouth.

CHAPTER SEVEN

What in the bloody hell are you doing out?" Maxwell asked roughly.

She fought him until he shushed her. Once she stopped bucking, he dropped his hand from her mouth but not the arm wrapped around her waist. Her cloak and hat had fallen to the snow.

"None of your business." A surprising amount of reflected anger clipped her words. "You scared the life out of me. I thought you were Dugan."

Maxwell was furious for too many reasons to count. The fact the chit had snuck out of his room was bad enough. To make matters worse, the breeches he had forbade her to wear clung to her hips and emphasized her legs.

He preferred his women voluptuous and sensual. Or at least he had. Her lithe body in the provocative breeches drew him like a siren. The feel of her long legs wrapped around his hips skittered constantly on the edge of his consciousness. But it was her bottom, molded by the buckskin breeches, that was driving him slowly insane. Or perhaps it was her lovely, pert breasts straining out the top of the ill-fitting waistcoat making his thoughts go awry.

"What you do is very much my business after our night together. Who was the man you met? If you carry a babe, I must be confident that it's mine."

She grew as stiff as a board in his arms, her breaths puffing white in the cold air.

"I... You are implying that I would... I would..."

"Would what? Wait in dishabille in a man's bed bent on seduction? Oh, not to mention, any cock would do, wouldn't it? Anything to break that pesky maidenhead of yours and leave you ruined for your betrothed." He hated his petulant, scorned, jealous-sounding tone.

Bryn pushed at his arm, and he released her. She whirled to face him, her hair fanning out. Maxwell wouldn't have been surprised to see the snow steaming at her feet from the strength of her fury.

"You followed me." Bryn swept up her cloak and hat and put them back on.

He'd been startled to see her emerge from the inn after he'd concluded the business of procuring her a mount and sending correspondence to Minerva Drummond, his former employer and friend. He'd waited and wondered whether Bryn was seeking him, but it was clear soon enough that she wasn't. After he handed the little mare to the hostler, he'd tracked her footprints.

"Aye. I did."

"You don't trust me." Hurt was ripe in her voice.

Damnable guilt rose even though it was underserved. Wasn't it? What did he really know of her except that she'd pretended to be a whore and turned his life into a complicated mess? "Who was that man?"

"A friend. I wished him farewell." The brim of her hat cast her face in deep shadow.

Truth or lie? He didn't know. Did it matter? If there was a babe, he would be bound to her no matter her moral proclivity. Or lack thereof.

To be fair, she seemed loathe to force his hand unless there was a babe. The escape of a lifetime commitment should have filled him with relief, but instead, it had sent him into a snit. Perhaps it was his unruly cock proclaiming its opinion.

"You'll not be running unbridled through Edinburgh. Is that understood?"

"I'm not a blasted horse, Drake." She turned on her heel, her back ramrod straight, her pace bruising.

Maxwell refused to call quarter because of his leg, and by the time he clattered into the common room, his thigh radiated waves of agony. His vision narrowed. The hot water of a bath would ease him. Pain buried the anger over Bryn's escapade. He ordered a bath and focused on the mountainous climb up the stairs.

If he'd been alone, if the eyes of every patron—especially Bryn's—weren't boring holes into his back, he would have dropped to his knees and crawled up the last few steps. Pride be damned.

He stumbled into the room and collapsed on the bed, leaving the door open for the servants to bring the bath. Scurrying feet and the splash of water invaded his pain-muffled consciousness. The door shut and time passed. The bath awaited, but Maxwell lay wrapped in a blanket of agony, unable to walk the few feet to the bath.

A splash of water brought Maxwell out of his fitful doze. He cracked his eyes open to see Brynmore McCann's luscious arse slipping into the tub from the corner of his eye. His instinctive shift for a better viewing angle sent shards of pain through his leg and threatened to wring a groan from him.

After a few deep breaths, an ache in an entirely different place took some of the focus off his leg. By the glances she cast in his direction and her hurried washing, she obviously assumed he slept. Her arms moved in soft white arcs, soaping and rinsing her hair, running the cloth over her body.

With another furtive glance over her shoulder, she rose. Water sluiced down the beautiful arch of her back and over her buttocks. She toweled off with a piece of linen and slipped a thick winter night rail over her head but not before a glimpse of the underside of a pert breast tormented him further. Sitting in front of the fire, she combed her hair, a domestic scene only a husband or lover would be privy to. A surprising underpinning of contentment tempered his pain-fueled lust.

He remained as still as the dead, and when she approached, he closed his eyes. What would she do? Prod him awake with the fireplace poker to make him sleep in the chair? No less than what he deserved.

A long moment passed. A tug on the boot on his good leg had him tensing. As it pulled loose, she staggered back into the door. No use in pretending he'd slept through the clatter. He opened his eyes and raised his head. "If you want me naked, all you have to do is ask, lass."

"I hardly— I wasn't trying to get you naked, you blasted man. Your boots are dirtying the quilt."

He dropped his head back to the pillow and wiggled his other foot. Even the small movement sent pain blazing through his thigh. She worked the boot off his bad leg. A grunt escaped him.

The boot thudded to the floor, and the bed dipped at his hip. He started when her hands landed on his thigh. She massaged around the old wound, casting the same magic she had the previous night. The tight scar tissue relaxed under her touch, and a sigh of relief hissed from between his clenched teeth.

The minutes stretched to infinity as the pain holding him captive surrendered to her touch. Her fiery golden hair swung back and forth across her shoulders and brushed her neck. She worried her bottom lip and paused to tuck her hair behind her ears, giving her the look of a pensive elf.

He flexed his leg, and only a slight echo of the brutal, stabbing pain remained. "Thank you, lass. It's better now. You must be cold. Go on and get under the quilts."

The question in her eyes didn't need to be spoken aloud.

"I'll not touch you again until we're married," Maxwell said so emphatically he wasn't sure which one of them he was trying to convince.

Bryn buried herself under the covers. He rolled off the bed and walked across the floor with minimal discomfort. After stripping naked, he washed. He didn't bother looking over his shoulder. His skin heated from her gaze, and not even the lukewarm water diminished his erection.

Pulling his breeches back on, he extinguished the candles and slid under the thick quilt, staying well on his side of the bed. The glowing embers in the hearth cast a hazy light over the room. Tension thickened between them. He wanted to thank her for her care or apologize or roll on top of her and...

"Not any man would have done— When I saw you in the stable..." Her voice treaded between them like a skittish cat. "If it hadn't been you, I would have married Dugan and gone to him a virgin. I had nearly given up, but then... I found you."

The one time he'd confided in a mistress about his birth and the privations of his youth, she'd been unable to hide her aversion. He'd walked out of her rooms, never to return. Bryn had seen the ugliness firsthand and had still chosen him. Through his resentment, satisfaction hummed.

"What were you doing out tonight? Tell me the truth." He gentled his voice and banished the vitriol.

"I needed to say goodbye to people who have helped me. That's all."

He wanted to believe her, but something about her furtive race through the woods filled him with doubt. "I suppose you'll be sad to leave Cragian."

"I suppose." Her voice was thoughtful and not teary in the

least. He wanted to question her further, but she sighed. "It's been a long day, hasn't it?"

A portion of the tension between them ebbed. "Aye, and we have a stop to make before we head north to Edinburgh."

Bryn turned on her side and tucked her hands between her cheek and the pillow. "Are you thinking what I'm thinking?"

As he was thinking how innocent and pretty she looked, how sweet she smelled, and how maybe one kiss wouldn't break his promises, he said darkly amused, "I very much doubt it. What are you thinking?"

"We should make an attempt to get my marriage settlement."

"And you think Craddock would hand it over if we ask nicely?"

"Well, no. But I could distract him while you search."

"Do you know where he keeps it?"

"Not for certain, but he keeps a drawer locked in his desk."

"Too dangerous. Let's pray distance will discourage Armstrong." He turned on his side, putting them face-to-face.

"Where are we stopping then?"

"MacShane's holding. I need to see old Lady MacShane. Has her son married?"

"Not yet. Lord Albert's mother doesn't approve of the gentry around Cragian. Or in all Dumfries for that matter. She'd much rather him take a season in London and bring back a proper English lady."

A strange hollowness settled in his chest at his half brother's name. Maxwell had never met him, but Albert MacShane was the last link to his father, and although he didn't want to be, he was curious.

"Do you know him? What's he like?"

"He's written a book about Scottish flora. And he hunts. Plays cards and drinks. Mary and Craddock invited him to the manor house often. He's not without influence." In a hesitant voice, she continued. "If you're after revenge or something of the sort, be warned that you and Albert are not evenly matched."

His thigh flexed as her jab landed. "I assure you, even with my leg, I can be a formidable opponent. If you're worried that I can't protect you—"

Bryn laughed, husky and sensuous. "You dolt. I meant you would make mincemeat out of poor old Albert. I saw how you handled Dugan, and he's not the wilting violet Albert is. You make me feel quite safe."

He harrumphed, but a now familiar damnable warmth squeezed at his chest. "I'm not after revenge. My years at war excised the aggression and hatred bred into me by my treatment here. And then some."

"Was your time in the army horrible?"

"Horrible? There were horrible, terrifying moments. Men who had slept next to me one night would die the next day. The battles were brutal and bloody." He closed his eyes, and images that had imprinted on his soul flashed. "But it wasn't always horrible. I remember a sunrise over the Pyrenees, the colors chasing away the blanket of stars. Fields of dazzling yellow sunflowers and the buzz of a million bees, so bright and loud you had to shield your eyes and plug your ears. I remember the blue of the bluest sea stretching to forever."

When he opened his eyes, she had scooted closer and propped herself up on an elbow, her mouth parted in a bemused smile. "I can almost see it myself."

"If I hadn't received my commission, I'm not sure what would have become of me."

"If you hadn't been wounded, would you still be serving?"

Maxwell considered his answer a long moment. "I suppose I might be. The work felt worthwhile."

"Where did you go after you left the army?"

"I was good with numbers, and long hours waiting in the ranks honed my skill with cards. I went to London and made a small fortune, dissecting lords from their money, but gambling was only a means to an end. I made connections, and some of those connections owed me favors. I was put in contact with a solicitor looking to retire from handling the Duke of Bellingham's affairs. It was an unusual situation, and the man was having a difficult time filling the position."

Her eyes sparkled. "You worked for a duke? How exciting. What was he like?"

"A spoiled, pompous little prick." Maxwell's lips twitched at her shocked gasp. "For all intents and purposes, I worked for his sister, but she married recently, and the duke came into his majority. I left before he could sack me."

Maxwell considered himself a quiet man—some might say dour—who kept his own counsel. He had never lain in bed with a woman… talking. If there was a woman in bed, he made sure she was well pleased but never lingered. This was a different sort of intimacy.

"Once I gave up cards, I began to dabble in a different sort of gambling. Investments." Maxwell's wealth was modest by some's standards, but compared to his childhood, he was rich as a sultan.

"That's amazing."

He shrugged. Was it? It had consisted of hard work and long hours. Feeling like he had revealed too much of himself, he deflected to her. "It's obvious you and Mary are not bosom sisters. What transpired to incite such hostility?"

* * * * *

Bosom sisters? Sharing secrets and giggling with Mary was beyond her imagination's capabilities. "After Mama died, I ceased to exist for the baron, so I attached myself to Cadell."

"Did you not have a governess?"

Bryn tsked. "Papa was obsessed with having a son, remember? Mary and I were encumbrances. No, that's not fair. We weren't useful, therefore we were beneath his notice." Maxwell squeezed her forearm. The simple gesture and the understanding in his hazel eyes made her keep sharing things she normally kept locked away.

"I missed Mama, but little by little, I forgot her touch, the way she smelled, and Cadell was more a father to me than the baron. Cadell made me read book after book to him as he worked on the horses. He couldn't read. It was a way of educating us both, I think." Tears gathered, and she rolled to her back to keep them contained.

"Cadell was a good, fair man. Where was Mary during all this? She should have been seeing to you like a big sister."

"I much preferred her inattention compared to being a pawn in her schemes." Bryn cut her watery, blurry gaze to him. "After father died, Craddock was offered up as the new baron, and she had her sights set on being lady of the manor."

"I never had a chance, did I? How could I not see?" He rubbed at his forehead.

"She craves power. When she was younger, it came from manipulating the boys and men in Cragian." Fears rose up. "She craves a different sort of power now, I think."

"Why have you not married before now? Did you never ask her for a season in Edinburgh? With your connections and beauty, you would have been pursued by countless suitors."

Distrust ran roughshod over her heart. In her inexperience, she couldn't read truth from platitude. Mary had only ever called her ugly and ill formed, with her red hair and skinny boy's body, and sick because of her anxious malady. Yet Maxwell hadn't touched her as if she were ugly. What did she believe?

"It was never convenient for Mary," she said simply.

"You'll have your chance to experience Edinburgh now."

"Yes," she whispered. A chance. A chance at a different

future. As the fire faded, the silence filled with portent.

"Did I hurt you last night?" His voice was so soft and deep and mesmerizing, and seconds passed before the meaning of his question registered. "I wasn't as gentle as I would have been had I known—"

"A bit sore is all. More from your... size than from the loss of my— I'm fine." She waited for the quilt to combust from the amount of embarrassed heat she was emitting.

"It's going to be a long, cold day tomorrow." The squeaking bed frame broke the heavy silence as Maxwell turned, his back blocking the weak light from the fire.

She was intensely aware of his big, warm body even though they didn't touch. After his breathing became deep and regular, her body relaxed and her grip on the sheet loosened, sleep claiming her body.

CHAPTER EIGHT

Blessed warmth surrounded her. Usually by morning when the fire had gone out and the dawn chill stole into her room, she was ready to get up and move instead of shivering beneath her covers. Something was different. She wiggled back into the source of heat, only to be startled awake by a deep groan.

Her eyes popped open, and the winter dawn displayed an unfamiliar collection of furniture. It took a handful of blinks to conclude she was not at the manor house in her drafty, corner room but at the inn in Cragian. And that was no furnace keeping her warm. Maxwell's body curled around hers. Their legs notched together like a wooden puzzle toy, their fingers laced.

Embarrassed by the seemingly tender embrace, she attempted to extricate herself. She wiggled but didn't make any headway from under his heavy arm. In fact, it clamped tighter around her waist.

"Don't move." His sleep-roughened voice was like a caress. The puff of breath and scratch of whiskers against her neck sent a pleasant shiver through her body.

Something hard nestled against her bottom, and realization streaked through her. His hips rocked against her. She arched her back, pressing into him. Any logical argument to keep her distance was forgotten in the need he inspired.

He muttered something about promises and breeches before

he pushed her away and flopped onto his stomach, burying his head in the pillow.

Without his warmth, a chill crept to her bones, and goose bumps rose on every inch of skin. Bryn darted from under the covers to grab her satchel. "Don't peek."

"Wear a dress. Wear a bloody dress or I won't be responsible for my actions." His muffled command came from the pillows.

What did that mean? Would he beat her? Was he no better than Dugan? Anger, resentment, and a dash of fear formed a lump in her belly. She was sick of being told what to do, whom to marry, how to bloody well dress.

She grabbed up her buckskins and stared at Maxwell's muscled shoulders where the quilt had fallen. Like a blind woman, she remembered the contours, the strength in his body. Yet he'd only ever been gentle and protective of her, even though her actions had vastly complicated his life. Of course, Maxwell was no Dugan.

Guilt dissolved the anger, and practicality stepped in. If they were going to call on Lady MacShane, a dress it must be. Washing and dressing with speed, she slipped out of the room with one last look at Maxwell.

* * * * *

The door creaked and the latch clicked. Maxwell rolled onto his back, his cock straining painfully against his breeches. He looked down with a mirthless laugh. Her innocent wiggling nearly made him spend in his breeches like an adolescent.

He'd awoken before dawn slightly embarrassed but mostly aroused to be holding her. When he'd tried to pull away, she held him firm. Her throaty seductive protests had hardened him further.

He hoped to God the chit had put on a dress. If the soft, faded buckskins curved over her bottom like a lover's hand, he would have to haul her back up to the bed and shatter the promise he'd made to keep his hands off her. The possibility made his cock throb in anticipation.

Maxwell levered himself up and rubbed his face. After washing himself in the old bathwater, he scraped at his night beard in the small looking glass and packed his satchel, casting one more longing look at the bed. A rather large, aching part of him prayed she'd defied him and worn those breeches after all.

He was halfway down the stairs when her lowered voice changed the direction of his thoughts. "Let go of me. Maxwell will be down any moment."

Protectiveness roared, but he wasn't foolish enough to charge into battle without identifying the enemy. He stopped at the foot of the stairs and lurked.

"Did he take you again last night? Are you enjoying my castoffs? He'll never love you as he loved me. He was my *slave*."

Mary's words rubbed salt in a raw wound that had never fully healed. He stepped around the corner. She had a tight hold on Bryn's upper arm, twisting it.

"Let her go." His voice cracked them apart.

Mary whirled. Her dark red velvet dress hugged voluptuous curves. A vee at the bodice exposed the cleft of her breasts. Curls were gathered below one ear, and rouge pinkened her cheeks and deepened the red of her lips. Mary possessed a beauty like Helen of Troy. Manipulative and destructive.

Bryn's face had lost all color, her freckles dancing over her nose and cheeks. The sisters couldn't be more different in looks and attitude. Mary approached on a whisper of velvet and cloud of flowery scent. She assessed him head to toe with a brazenness he'd only encountered among London's demimonde.

"Let's not make a scene. Perhaps we should discuss this in private." Mary's tongue darted out to skim over her upper lip.

He flicked his gaze to the patrons who were observing the unfolding drama wide-eyed and slack-jawed. Between Bryn's two nights in his room and Mary's appearance, he thought it rather too late for discretion. However, he gestured to a small, private dining room to their right, his voice dry. "We certainly wouldn't want to generate any more gossip for the local mill."

Maxwell stepped inside, but Mary stopped Bryn from following. "You wait here while we discuss the situation, Brynmore."

Bryn's gaze remained downcast. Mary closed the door in her face, and Maxwell had a terrible feeling he'd taken a misstep in their game of chess.

Mary's heavy-lidded eyes, pouty lips, and flushed cheeks were the mask of a seductress. The once lovely, enticing girl had turned into a beautiful, irresistible woman. She advanced, stopping a scant few inches from pressing herself into him. He held still while she trailed a hand down his chest, fingering the lapel of his coat.

"You were always handsome, but my goodness, you've grown into a gentleman. You've done well for yourself then? Your jacket is very fine."

"Yes, I've done well. You should have had faith in me." He tried to keep his tone mocking, but his dry mouth roughened his voice.

"Maxwell, darling, let's be frank, shall we? My boyish, virginal sister could hardly have satisfied your, no doubt, considerable needs." She trailed a hand down to cup him between the legs. Shock held him still. "You deserve a real woman, one with certain assets I know you're very fond of." She fingered the neck of her dress and peeled it back.

His gaze followed without conscious thought. Her manipulations were brash and vulgar. Nevertheless, his cock, already primed from the morning's torture, hardened under her hand. Mary smiled as she stroked the length of him. Taking his silence as acquiescence, she pressed herself close, her large, soft breasts against his chest.

How many times had he dreamed of this? Countless.

"Can we make a bargain? Take me to your room and do with me what you will as many times as you wish. When we're finished, I'll take Bryn with me. Dugan will still marry her and promises, if there is a babe, to claim and protect it with his name. There will be no bastard, I assure you." The fringe of her lashes veiled eyes that were more calculating than lustful. "You must have wondered over the years what it would be like to lie with me."

Christ, it was true. The women he had taken as lovers bore a strong resemblance to the woman caressing him so blatantly— always voluptuous, dark-haired beauties. Was he tempted?

Hell yes, he was, and he hated himself for it.

He closed his eyes. An image of the red-haired woman waiting outside the door cooled his lust. He'd never betray Bryn and hand her over to Armstrong.

Maxwell wrapped his hands around Mary's upper arms, and a triumphant spark lit her face. He pushed her away. "It's been a long time since I was susceptible to your schemes. Aye, I loved you truly, but you never felt the same."

"I did, but…" She grabbed at his sleeve, a desperate thread in her voice "Maxwell, you couldn't take care of me the way Craddock could. I don't love him. I've never loved him. I loved *you*."

In her vibrant green eyes, Maxwell sensed a kernel of truth underneath the emotional manipulation. He brushed by her but stopped with his hand on the latch, looking over his shoulder. "Is Craddock aware you're bargaining with your body?"

Mary's face hardened, stripping her soft beauty away. "The marriage will take place. If I were you, I would step aside and allow it to happen."

"Are you threatening me?"

"There are dangerous men about, Maxwell. Scotland is still an untamed place in many ways," she said with a cryptic, mirthless smile.

"Bryn and I are leaving Cragian. I wish you and Craddock well, but leave us the hell alone." He opened the door.

Bryn stopped midpace. Her fresh-faced beauty compared to Mary's calculated sensuality was a welcome shock.

"Come," he said gruffly.

"With you?"

Mary tugged on her gloves and sashayed toward them. The casualness of her approach wasn't reflected in her emerald-hard eyes and the tension curling her shoulders forward. "Farewell for now, sister. I can see why you so vehemently defended your mystery lover's skills yesterday morning. He's quite well endowed." Mary's gaze dropped to between his legs, and Bryn's quick intake of breath echoed in his ear.

The corner of Mary's mouth quirked, and she ran a finger down the lapel of his jacket before she added, "If only we had more time, Maxwell, but alas, I'm due for breakfast and must offer a suitable excuse for your absence, Brynmore."

Mary pulled the veil of her hat over her face and swept out of the room into a waiting carriage. Maxwell turned to Bryn. She had blanched, but instead of hurt or embarrassment, her brown eyes eviscerated him. "Did you touch her? Kiss her?"

"I did neither." Shame at his weakness clipped the words short. And he wasn't lying. He hadn't touched Mary, except to push her away. But he hadn't looked away or batted her hand off him either. Echoes of the power she'd held over him as a young man swirled.

He strode out the door toward the stables, assuming Bryn's compliance. She kept pace, and he intercepted several pointed, probing glances, but she stayed silent.

After a tussle over a sidesaddle, which Maxwell won since he was paying, they rode away from Cragian in stony silence. She had insisted on wearing the mannish brimmed hat, which she pulled low on her brow. He couldn't imagine her in the millinery confections the ladies wore in London anyway.

They maintained a brisk pace in spite of the fresh snow on the path. The sky looked as gray and ominous as it had the previous day, but the snow was held at bay. For now. The temperature was nothing compared to the chill coming from Bryn. He owed her something, if not the total damning truth.

Nudging Primrose with his heels, he came alongside her mount. "Your sister offered a proposition. Her body for my use if I turned you over to Dugan, who promised to claim a babe as his own. I said no."

She turned as far as her sidesaddle would allow in order to face him, her demeanor thawing. "She's ruthless."

"Or desperate." The gray clouds pressed all the way to the horizon.

His worries turned from Mary's machinations to Lady MacShane. Odds were excellent she would refuse to see her late husband's unacknowledged by-blow. He was on a fool's errand.

Bryn pointed. "I see the chimneys. Lady MacShane renamed it Riverwalk. A bit pretentious if you ask me. More like Scrubwalk with all the brambles on the road. The river's a good two miles over the dale."

He met her attempt at normality halfway. "The gentry here have nothing on the peers in London. Even the esteemed Baron and Baroness Craddock would be considered country bumpkins. I would almost be tempted to venture back to see them make a bow in London."

"What's London like?" The biting air had returned color to her cheeks, and her brown eyes had the warm comfort of a cup of chocolate. How quickly she went from being intimidated by Mary, angry with him, and now curious about the world.

"Dirty, foggy, smelly, and crowded. But exciting, beautiful, and interesting as well. I'm glad to have lived there for a time but not sad to leave it behind either. As much as I sometimes hated Cragian, I missed Scotland."

"I've hardly ventured out of Dumfries. Will I like Edinburgh?" Her nervous shift on the saddle underscored how different she was from Mary. Indeed, unlike any woman of his acquaintance.

"Edinburgh is nothing like London, of course, but it's where the best of Scotland gather when not tending to their estates." It's why he'd chosen to settle there, after all. His plans included offering his services to those same men. But there was another aspect he hadn't considered. He might be expected to socialize, and Bryn, as his wife, would be by his side.

Her cloak was good quality but plain, as was the brown wool dress under it. Everything she wore was designed to blend into her surroundings like a tree in the forest. Did Bryn choose to hide, or had Mary forced her to? A mossy green would suit her well. And a dark blue would cool her fiery hair and add sophistication.

"You'll need to be kitted with a proper wardrobe once we've arrived."

* * * * *

For once, Bryn agreed. She would need sturdy woolen gowns, but financing a new wardrobe posed a problem. Her pin money from Mary had gone toward buying shoes, clothes, and other sundries for struggling families. Her future hadn't seemed precarious until recent events.

As soon as they reached Edinburgh, she would pawn her mother's baubles and buy one or two serviceable gowns, perhaps at a secondhand shop. She was fair with a needle and could alter them to fit.

As they approached the manor house, a footman, his white wig askew on his head and wearing only one glove, careened down the stairs to help Bryn dismount.

"Saw ye coming up the drive and said to me mistress, 'Who's that a'coming? 'Specting company?' But she said, 'Nay.' So I thought I'd better get gussied up not knowing who ye might be. And it's Miss McCann. Where's yer sister?" The footman looked toward Maxwell as if he were Mary in disguise.

"Lady Craddock didn't accompany me today." Bryn smiled but couldn't bring herself to flutter her lashes like she'd seen Mary do. "Since your mistress is at home, I assume she's receiving."

"Erm… let me check on that, miss." The footman tripped up the steps.

"Show us directly to the drawing room before we catch a chill, won't you?" She handed her reins to a young groom who'd run up.

Maxwell started to interject, but she shushed him. He raised his eyebrows but said no more. Maxwell may be used to dealing with London's finest, but she was used to dealing with Cragian's finest.

If Lady MacShane was aware her husband's by-blow was on the front steps, she'd order the door slammed shut and barred. If Maxwell needed to see the woman, the least she could do was help him gain an audience.

The footman never stood a chance. She maneuvered around him to the drawing room, ignoring the proprieties. Despite the outward show of bravado, her hand shook when she raised it to rap sharply on the door. It swung open with a creak.

Lady MacShane didn't bother to look up from her needlework. Her singsong voice was laced with disdain. "You know I hate a rude, loud knock, Hamish. I prefer a more demure scratch. That's how the servants in London announce themselves. Now, who was that coming up the drive?"

She and Maxwell exchanged a glance. Before he could open his mouth, she stepped forward with faked enthusiasm and a perfunctory curtsy. "Lady MacShane, it's been too long, hasn't it? Terribly sorry to arrive unannounced, but it couldn't be helped, I'm afraid."

A cap in a virulent shade of puce covered Lady MacShane's iron-gray hair and glowed against the black fustian she had worn since her husband's death. Her jowls hung low, and her thin lips curved into a frowning sickle.

Laying down her sampler, she assumed the position of an imperious eagle on the edge of the settee and surveyed Bryn as if she were a rodent let loose. And she hadn't even spotted Maxwell yet.

"Miss McCann. What in blazes are you doing here? Are you not to be married this very afternoon? Shouldn't you be preparing yourself for your groom?"

Bryn's mind drifted a moment as to how you prepared yourself for a groom—was there a special baste or a bitter medicine? "Dugan Armstrong and I have decided we don't suit. I don't love him."

"Love? What's love got to do with marriage? Foolish gel, ride back and throw yourself on his mercy. You won't find anyone as handsome or rich as Armstrong to marry you. Look at you. Hardly a great beauty like your sister. Are you addled?" Lady MacShane stood and rapped her cane on the floor for emphasis.

"Most likely I am." Lady MacShane's assessment pricked her feelings, but it's nothing she hadn't heard from Mary a hundred times. "I'm here for another reason, actually. I'd like to introduce you to Captain Maxwell Drake, decorated war hero. He is recently arrived from London."

Maxwell stepped out of the shadows. Lady MacShane drew in a great breath and swung her ire to him. "*You*. You would dare show your face in my home? Are you here for money? Is it your aim to bludgeon me and steal the precious memories of my dear husband?" Her bejeweled hand was at her neck as if Maxwell planned to leap across the room and strangle her. "Hamish, help me."

One dark look from Maxwell froze the footman halfway into the room. "Lady MacShane, let me assure you that I'm not after your money or your jewels or your precious memories." Sarcasm dripped from every word. "I'm here to read my father's last will and testament."

"Absolutely not. If you aren't after revenge, then why do you want to see MacShane's will, you lowborn cur?"

The insult made Bryn gasp, but Maxwell didn't seem bothered. "If there's no mention of me or my mother, then why won't you allow me to read it?"

Lady MacShane gave an unladylike snort. "It matters not because I don't have it. It's in Edinburgh with my solicitor."

Maxwell stared her down, but she didn't falter. Finally he said, "As luck would have it, we're headed to Edinburgh. What is the firm's name? I'll be sure to pay your solicitor a visit."

Her jowls quivered, but she rattled off the name. It was all the information they were likely to get without resorting to torture, and while it looked as if Maxwell might enjoy locking Lady MacShane in a dungeon, retreat was the wisest course of action.

Bryn backed toward the door. "We must be on our way, Lady MacShane. There's a long road in front of us, and—"

"Does Mary know you're whoring yourself with such an animal?" Lady MacShane's malice hit her like an artic wind, yet something else stirred in the old lady's eyes. Fear?

The way Mary and Lady MacShane could tear people apart over a civilized cup of tea had always been intimidating. Bryn would sit to the side and wish for escape. But she'd stayed silent, always silent. To have the insults directed at her was shocking.

"You will not speak of my betrothed in such a fashion, Lady MacShane." In Maxwell's voice was a threat to tear the old lady limb from limb.

"Betrothed?" The lady tutted. "Dragging the McCann name through the muck. Your sister must be devastated."

Was this a taste of how Maxwell had been treated as a child in Cragian? Even with all the insults Mary had aimed her direction, she'd never felt less than a person—an ungainly, unaccomplished, unwanted person, but a person nonetheless. Words formed. She would stay silent no more.

Bryn sidestepped in front of Maxwell. "He's not an ani—" She bit her lip, unwilling to attach the word to him. "Maxwell is a hundred times the man Dugan is, no matter his birth. Good day to you, Lady MacShane. May we never meet again."

Bryn took a step back and bumped into Maxwell's chest. He turned her and nudged her into the entryway. The warmth of his hand on her shoulder steadied her in the midst of the old woman's bitterness.

Hamish galloped ahead of them and opened the front door. His eyes were wide, and he bounced on the balls of his feet. He would be in the kitchens relaying the confrontation before they were out of sight. They waited outside for their horses to be brought around.

Maxwell didn't seem agitated in the least, his stance casual and his hands loosely clasped behind his back. Her stomach tumbled, and she broke into a light sweat in the aftermath, yet her anger kept the hated panic at bay.

"How can you be so calm about that... that despicable, horrible, detestable, ugly old woman?"

Maxwell's eyebrow and mouth quirked up in unison. His hazel eyes danced. "Although a useless endeavor, you did a fair job defending my honor."

"She called you an *animal*," she said, the last horrible word on a whisper.

He chuffed, still holding on to his half smile. "What Lady MacShane hurled was nothing compared to what I endured growing up. I was insulted, with much saltier language I might add, on a daily basis. The lads beat me up and pushed me around for years—until I got big enough to defend myself. I know what and who I am."

Did an old pain linger? Bryn understood the scars hateful words could leave. "You're better than all of them. If I could go back, I would do more." She cursed her tongue.

"More?" His dark brows rose, and his voice turned mocking. "What more would you have done? Called the boys out on my behalf? I would have liked to have seen that, a ten-year-old sprite with dueling pistols."

If he discovered her hand in the baskets, his pride would never recover. And for a man like Maxwell, who had grown up with nothing, his pride was his most valued asset.

She forced a tease and winked. "I'm a fair shot, I'll have you know." Her smile faded and she whispered, "Why did you tell her we're betrothed?"

"Aren't we?"

"As long as the marriage contract exists, I'm still legally betrothed to Dugan."

"A piddling detail. If you're carrying my child, we will find the nearest blacksmith, marry over the anvil, and consummate the marriage without delay."

A spark passed between them, threatening to light banked embers. In place of the dread she harbored at the thought of a wedding night with Dugan, anticipation danced.

The hostler arrived and broke the spell. After giving her a leg up himself, Maxwell led them down the drive in a fast trot. A galloping horse approached from the open grouse field to their right.

Lord Albert MacShane pulled up short, blocking the drive. His horse was lathered and puffing clouds into the air. Bryn cut her eyes to Maxwell, unsure how to proceed. "Lord MacShane. This is Captain Drake. We've been to see your mother."

MacShane stared at Maxwell as if studying new plant life. "I can't imagine the visit went well."

"It didn't," Maxwell said.

Maxwell's calmness and Albert's lack of animosity quelled the tension stiffening her shoulders.

"Mother is rather high-strung." Albert rubbed his nape, a too-bright smile coming to his face. He stood in his stirrups and held out a hand. Bryn's breath hitched. Maxwell hesitated a moment before reaching out to clasp Albert's in a brief handshake, broken by their skittish mounts.

Although the two men bore a resemblance, Maxwell's features were blatantly masculine, while on Albert, the full lower lip and sharp cheekbones took on an effeminate cast.

Albert spared her the briefest of glances. "I was returning to ready myself for your impending nuptials. Am I to assume those won't be taking place as planned?"

"You assume correctly." Bryn wished she didn't blush so readily.

"Lord MacShane, perhaps you could help me." Maxwell's face stayed impassive. "I wanted to lay hands on our father's will."

Suspicion shuttered Albert's curiosity and good humor. "Why would you be interested in such?"

"I was told there might be mention of me or perhaps my mother."

Albert's gaze dropped to the scrub lining the lane. "I'm not sure who insinuated such, but I assure you, there was no mention of either of you. I must return to see how Mother is coping with her shock." Albert tipped his hat and tapped his heels against his horse's flanks, sending them trotting toward the stable.

In contrast, Maxwell gave Primrose a gentle pat and nudge, their pace sedate. She could tell nothing about the direction of his thoughts from his expression. Unable to tolerate the silence, she said, "Can we safely assume you're mentioned in the will?"

"Indeed." His voice was as blank as his face.

"Do you think old MacShane tried to legitimize you or left you a great deal of money?"

"I'm not sure, but I'll discover the truth." He nudged Primrose into a trot and left Bryn staring at his back.

Hours later, Bryn's view had changed little. Late afternoon sunlight filtered through the clouds and cast a premature dusk. The clouds had grown thicker and darker all day. Maxwell's mood had spiraled in concert.

Although Bryn tried time and again to engage him in conversation, his monosyllabic answers had finally discouraged her. The day passed in an exhausting silence, yet as the minutes ticked off, her mood soared.

She trotted up next to him and smiled. If she'd been on the ground, she would have danced a jig. As it was, she bounced in the saddle. He gave her a side-eye glance and then turned fully for a thorough inspection. "Why are you so cheerful? It's freezing, and we're still miles from the nearest inn."

"Despite the weather and your gloomy disposition, I would rather freeze to death on the road to Edinburgh with you than be standing in Cragian's chapel, choking out vows to a man I detest."

A combination of victory and relief made her want to pump her arms or jump up and down or give him a hug. She hadn't caved to everyone else's demands of her. Maybe for the first time in her life. Even with the uncertainty of the future, freedom made her giddy.

"Congratulations. Thrilled this debacle has worked to your advantage." The bite in his voice deflated her bubble of euphoria.

He was right. She had escaped Dugan only to become a burden to Maxwell, and he would never forgive her. Her smile wilted. She twisted the reins, and her horse skittered ahead.

"Wait, Bryn, I'm—"

A distinctive crack in the woods silenced him. She turned

around and held still. He scanned the tree line, his mouth pulled into a grim line. The stretch of road was flanked by a dense forest. The dimming winter sun cast long shadows, making it difficult to see more than twenty feet in any given direction.

"What—"

He held up a hand to shush her. Both the horses shuffled, perhaps reacting to the sudden tension crackling the air or perhaps to an unseen threat. Her mount tossed its head and trotted forward, its nerves affecting her. The air rushed close to her face before the report the musket echoed through the woods.

"Bloody hell, ride, woman!"

CHAPTER NINE

She froze like a wild animal caught in a trap. Maxwell dug his heels into Primrose's flanks and slapped her horse on the rump as he passed. Her mount bucked forward. She listed off-balance in the sidesaddle.

A tree on her left splintered a split second before the report sounded. Maxwell moved beside her.

"The woods. Head into the woods," he yelled.

She pointed her horse into the thick copse to their right. The pounding of her heart and the clatter of horses' hooves echoed in her ear. She hunched over, making herself as small as possible. Her breaths were quick and sharp.

Commotion behind her had her glancing over her shoulder. A riderless Primrose bolted to the left.

Maxwell. His name roared through her.

Bryn pulled hard at the reins, but crazed with fear, her horse continued to crash through the trees. Maxwell. She had to get to him. He needed her. She kicked free of the stirrups and leaped off. Her hip and shoulder hit the frozen ground, but she rolled to absorb the fall like Cadell had taught her.

She patted her body. Her shoulder and hip throbbed, but she'd live. It was Maxwell who needed help. She scrambled up and through the patchy snow, searching for him. Her frantic fear made her heart gallop and her breathing fracture.

Spotting the shiny black tip of his boot, she stumbled to his body and fell to her knees. He lay unmoving and spread-eagle, half-hidden in evergreen fronds. The left half of his face was covered in blood. She pressed her ear against his chest and sagged to hear his strong, steady heartbeat.

Blood oozed out of a cut to his forehead. She used her teeth to start a rip in her thick muslin petticoat. Using the swath, she staunched the cut on his forehead and wiped the blood away. It might leave a scar, but it would heal without needing to be stitched. Another cut bled along his neck, but it too was shallow and mostly bluster.

An examination of his body didn't reveal any breaks or blood. She felt his skull and found a lump. He'd knocked his head. A long-ago warning from Cadell amplified her worries. People didn't always awaken from such falls even if they had no other injuries.

She turned her concern to their surroundings. Someone had shot at them. Could it have been a hunting accident? Unlikely, considering more than one shot had rung out. They were easy prey stranded in the woods with no horses. The man, or men, could come back at any moment and finish them off, and Maxwell was too heavy for her to move far. None of it boded well.

She forced her breathing to slow and heard nothing besides her own heart beating in her ears. Another danger loomed. It was growing darker and colder by the second.

An evergreen tree with drooping branches close by would offer them some concealment. She grabbed Maxwell by the boot heels and dragged him fully underneath, muttering apologies even though he couldn't hear her.

Once under the meager protection of the tree, she smoothed his hair back. He was pale beneath the red streaks of blood. "Please wake up," she chanted through cold, numb lips.

What now? Cadell had always told her to think like an animal. They needed shelter and warmth. She used evergreen boughs to create a makeshift bed. Once not a speck of snow was visible through the fronds, she rolled Maxwell onto the boughs.

Dare she start a fire? While death by bullet was a possibility, death by cold was a certainty. Except the smoke and light would surely draw attention. Anyway, his flint and all her things were packed in Primrose's saddlebags. She rubbed her temples and tried not to surrender to the threatening tears.

She smoothed the marks they made in the snow and settled herself on top of Maxwell, spreading out her skirts like a blanket. She pulled more loose boughs over them. The cold snuck past her puny efforts at warmth. As darkness fell, she settled in to monitor the rise and fall of Maxwell's chest.

* * * * *

Warm puffs of moist air and large wet lips caressed Maxwell's face. He tried to angle away from the large woman with rancid breath, but she was tenacious. Hair tickled his chin, and he tried to push the lady off, but his hands were tied. Was he being held prisoner?

His time in the army had taught him patience under duress, and he forced himself to consciousness without movement or panic. Memories flooded him. He and Bryn on the road… shots fired… a desperate ride into the woods… then nothing.

Physical sensations bombarded him—a throbbing pain in his head, the bitter cold seeping into his back, the lump shivering on his chest, and finally the caress of a large, hairy muzzle at his cheek.

Primrose. Dear, sweet Primrose was nudging him awake. He almost kissed her back. Saved again by a horse. The huddled, trembling figure on his chest had his arms trapped. *Brynmore*. How long had he been unconscious?

Full dark was upon them, made deeper by the trees. Maxwell

pulled his numb arms from under her body. Pinpricks followed the path of blood. He grit his teeth until they faded and shook Bryn. "Wake up, lass."

"Leave me alone. I'm so tired." She pushed at his hands.

"You can't sleep. Get up." He rolled her off him and got to his hands and knees. Nausea churned his stomach and drove bile up his throat. Black edged his vision.

She rubbed his back and over his arm, her voice penetrating the roar in his ears. "…never wear breeches again if you'll be all right."

"Is that a promise?" His voice came out rough, with none of the tease he'd intended. He wanted to lie back down, which would be suicidal in these conditions.

She helped him stand. He beat back the surge of pain in his head and leg. Primrose offered support on one side and Bryn the other. There was some black humor to be mined, but Maxwell didn't have the strength to dig.

"We'll be dead by morning unless we find shelter. Up you go." He cupped his hands for her foot. Getting Bryn in the saddle was the easy task. It took him three tries to haul himself up, his movements jerky. He huddled over Bryn for support as much as warmth.

"Does your head hurt terribly?" she asked.

"Everything hurts terribly," he said. "What about you? Did you fall as well? Are you injured?"

"I jumped off to find you, and the disloyal piece of flesh and hair ran off and left me." Her disgust turned his lips up until the implication settled in his pain-ravaged head.

"For the love of— Someone shot at us, you daft woman. You should have ridden for safety. He could have taken or killed you."

"Believe me, after I couldn't get you to wake up and realized the horses were gone, the grim possibilities circled like vultures. But"—she twisted in his arms so she could see his face—"I couldn't leave you. For a moment I was afraid you were dead." She snaked her arms around his torso and squeezed his already tight lungs.

He swallowed past the lump jammed in his throat that didn't seem to be associated with the knot on his head. Bryn might have died. For what? To save him? Jesus, no one would have come looking for him. No one would have missed him.

Just because a slip of a lass had risked her life to save his was no reason to turn mawkish. He cleared his throat. "While I appreciate the sacrifice, there would have been no use for both us to die."

"I wasn't planning on either one of us dying. Who shot at us, do you think?" Her voice was muffled against his greatcoat. He liked her arms around him even if she only sought his warmth.

"Most likely Dugan or someone he hired, wouldn't you think?"

"It might have been Albert. He could have followed us from Riverwalk and waited until we entered the forest to attack."

"Damn, we're a fine pair, aren't we?" Both of them had stirred the pot enough to have someone out to kill them. Or him, actually. Both Dugan and MacShane would want him dead.

"You don't have to sound so amused that two factions have cause to murder us."

"You're safe enough. Everyone wants me out of the way. Of course, if Dugan gets his grubby hands on you, you'll be dragged to the nearest blacksmith." He sniffed the air. "Is it the knock to my head or is that smoke?"

Primrose picked up her pace, perhaps sensing oats and a rubdown in her near future. A small, well-tended farmstead appeared through the trees. He pointed, his arm worryingly heavy and numb. "We'll slip into the barn."

"Blast that. I'm going to finagle our way into the house. I would battle Beelzebub himself to sit in front of a fire."

"It's the middle of the night."

"You see to Primrose. I'll see to gaining us a place by the hearth." She jumped down and clutched at Maxwell's good thigh until she gained her footing.

"Wait for me, Brynmore."

* * * * *

Bryn tipped her head back and met Maxwell's shadowed gaze. The command in his voice was natural. No doubt, he had been used to having his orders followed in the army. But while she would never be comfortable calling on the Lady MacShanes of the world, she moved among farmers and herders with ease.

"I'll be fine. I'm much less intimidating on my own."

He broke their gazes first with a heavy sigh. Perhaps the bash on his head had addled him. "Do what you can then, lass."

She waited until he was out of sight before approaching the cottage. Dormant roses were planted around the door. Good, there was most likely a woman of the house. Lantern light flickered through the shuttered windows. Odd that, but perhaps the family kept late hours. Whipping off her hat and fluffing her hair, she pasted on what she hoped was an I'm-not-a-murdering-thief smile and rapped on the door.

The door cracked open. A man peeked out, his eyes wide, his mouth agape, and his hair disheveled. "What in the world? Where did you come from? Are you a witch?"

Trepidation stole her bravado, but Maxwell needed a fire. He was cold and wounded, and she needed to tend to him. "A mere woman lost in the woods and desperate for a warm fire. My... husband is sheltering our horse in your barn. If it's not too much trouble, could we bed down at your hearth? We're nearly frozen through."

A low, keening cry echoed out the door. Of all the farmsteads in Scotland, they had to wander into a madman's. Bryn took a step backward. "On the other hand, perhaps we'll move along."

"No! Come in. You must help me." The man grabbed her forearm, his fingers digging sharply into flesh. She planted her feet, but she was no match for his brawn. He dragged her through the door and slammed it shut.

A blast of fear heightened her senses. A blazing fire lit the room. Devilish shadows danced along the walls. A black pot hung over the flames, billowing steam. Sheets and blankets and strips of linen littered a wooden table. The tortured moaning renewed with fervor.

Bryn backed against the door and scrabbled for the latch. "Sir, my husband is a large, strong man. He'll kill you if you hurt me."

The man barked a laugh and dropped her arm to run a hand through his hair, standing more strands on end. "I'm not going to hurt you, lass. It's my wife. A babe is coming, but something's not right. It's been going on forever. And I can't ride off and leave her here alone to fetch the doctor. He's a good ten miles away and stays half-drunk anyway. She's in such pain, and I don't know what to do. Please." Desperation threaded his hoarse voice and shined in his eyes.

How could she turn her back and do nothing even if it was only to offer a bit of comfort? Words came tripping out of her mouth. "I've not had any experience birthing babes, but I've heard women talk." My God, she sounded ridiculous. The only births she'd witnessed were lambings.

Instead of laughing, the man nodded. "Yes, just please help me."

"When did the pains start?"

Words poured from the man, some relevant, others not. Bryn picked through the torrent. After an untroubled term, the woman had been laboring for almost twenty-four hours. Another long cry emerged from a side room. The man covered his mouth and turned away.

Taking a deep breath and blowing her hair off her forehead, she tiptoed toward the room. She poked her head around the jamb. The woman's head was thrown back in a keening wail, the tendons in her neck standing out. Her dark hair was plastered against her forehead with sweat.

Bryn's stomach tried to run for the door. Was this torture in her future? The fuzzy worry of a babe solidified into terror and slithered through her body, dizzying her. The woman's pain passed after an interminable age. When she opened her eyes, she jerked into the pillows at the sight of Bryn in the doorway.

A hand at Bryn's back propelled her into the small room, her numb legs moving on instinct. The man led her to the side of the bed, wrung out a cloth, and ran it over the woman's forehead with gentle care.

"I'm Reese, and this is Meredith. Sweet, this is…" The man looked at Bryn, his face blank.

"Brynmore McCann, madam. At your service."

"I'm very happy to meet you, Brynmore McCann. Are you a midwife, perchance?" Another pain took hold of Meredith, saving Bryn from answering.

Chaos reigned in her head. What had Cadell told her about labor in ewes? The pain was necessary and welcome. The pain grew the birth canal and expelled the lamb. The woman's cry faded into a tired sob. This pain did not seem welcome, and the baby wasn't coming.

Bryn stepped to the woman's side and took her limp hand, chaffing it between both of hers. "I need to discover how close you are to delivering. May I?"

Meredith's beautiful blue eyes looked into Bryn's like she was a savior. Fear crawled out of her stomach and closed her throat to a river reed. At Meredith's nod, Bryn lifted the sheet to the woman's waist followed by her night rail.

Without urging, Meredith bent and spread her legs. As if in a dream, Bryn positioned herself to examine the birth canal. She squeezed her eyes shut and imagined Cadell at her shoulder. She popped her eyes open. The birth canal had grown round enough to accommodate a baby's head, but none was visible, not even a hint of hair or scalp.

Examine the ewe. Ease the lamb out. But first always wash, Cadell whispered in her head. Soap and water. Cadell had always scrubbed his hands until they were raw. He'd rarely lost a ewe and was much sought after by the local herders.

"I need…" The words came out as a croak, and she cleared her throat. "I need soap and hot water to wash." Reese shot out of the room.

"Is everything going to be all right?" The fear in the woman's voice cut through Bryn's own fears. This might very well be Bryn in a few months. Did she want a hysterical midwife at her side admitting she didn't know what in blazes she was doing?

Bryn slipped off her cloak and rolled her sleeves to her elbows. "Everything is going to be fine. I need to determine where the baby is positioned so we'll have an idea of how much longer it will be before you meet your son or daughter. Do you have a name picked out?"

Bryn forced her lips to curl upward. It was enough to calm a pain-addled Meredith, who managed a weak smile in return and relaxed against the pillows. Before she could answer, another pain racked her body. Bryn's imagination jumped from one horrid possibility to another.

Reese balanced a basin of steaming water in one hand and strips of linen and soap in the other. A pounding sounded on the front door. He started and spilled water over his hand. "That'd be your husband, I suppose."

Reese set the water down and bolted back out of the room. Male murmurs undercut Bryn's rising panic. Maxwell was here. The thought of him in the other room steadied her nerves, and her thoughts straightened into logical lines.

While she washed, she talked about the weather and the beauty of the snow. When her hands were red from the hot water and soap, she dried them and positioned herself between Meredith's legs once more.

Bryn closed her eyes and explored with one hand. Expecting to feel the dome of a little head, she grabbed something smaller and squirmy. A foot.

Meredith's baby was breech. *Remember the two choices?* Cadell whispered. She could turn the baby in the womb or try to pull it out by its feet. She had seen both done—to ewes. How did Cadell decide which course to take? She moved back to Meredith's side and pressed on her belly. Meredith moaned, but the baby moved, still high.

Bryn bit her lip and washed a small amount of blood off her hands.

Meredith's eyes brimmed with tears. "What is it? Tell me."

"The good news *and* the bad news is that I felt a very wriggly foot."

Meredith's head fell back against the pillows. "He's alive. Can he come out like that?"

"He can, but I only felt one foot. It might be one leg is up and one is down. I can try to turn the babe in your stomach, but it might be painful."

"Painful? It can't be worse than what I've already endured. Do it." Determination hardened the woman's eyes and voice.

"I'll need the men to press on your belly while I push his little foot back up."

Meredith nodded her assent, another contraction stealing her attention. Bryn slipped out the door. Maxwell stood inside the door, his gloves off but his coat still on. His eyes were protective and questioning. Without saying a word, he infused her with confidence.

"The babe is breech. I'll try to coax the fellow around but require some muscle." Bryn didn't take her eyes off Maxwell.

Reese cursed and strode to his wife.

She shuffled toward Maxwell. "I need you."

The admission crashed around them, encompassing more than just help with the birth. Finally he nodded, shrugged out of hat and cloak, and limped toward her. His forehead was crusted with dried blood, dark red against his unusually pale cheeks. His pain radiated to her and made her ache in concert. But he was in no danger of dying. The same couldn't be said for Meredith and her babe.

"I can't do this." Her voice was at a whisper. Panic centered in her chest radiated to her extremities, causing them to tremble. Not now. She couldn't deal with one of her episodes now.

Maxwell took her shoulders and squeezed, drawing her focus to his face. "You can. You saved one life already today. Mine. I have faith in you."

It was as much the confidence in his eyes as his words that beat the panic back to manageable levels. "You'll be at my side?"

"Always."

The word made her breath catch, but she had no time to tease out the meaning. Another wail drew her back into the birthing room.

She directed the men to stand on either side of Meredith's belly and demonstrated. "Maxwell, push from the top and around. Reese, you push from the bottom. I'll tuck his little foot back up. You must keep pushing until I tell you to stop, no matter your wife's cries."

Both men looked like she was forcing them off a cliff at sword point. She waited until Maxwell and Reese were in place, their hands on Meredith's belly.

"Are you ready, Meredith? Try not to tense," she said. The woman nodded. "Gentlemen? Here we go. Push!"

While the men pressed, Bryn poked the little leg upward. Meredith writhed, her screams ringing in the small room. Bryn lost her grasp on the babe's foot, and a sob cracked her composure. She tried again, pushing the foot even higher. Everything shifted.

Maxwell eased off. "I felt the babe move. Is he in the right place now?"

Black hair appeared from the birth canal. Bryn jerked backward. For a moment she couldn't move. Meredith bore down with a long, animalistic yell. The babe emerged, and as if watching someone else, Bryn caught the warm and slippery body with both hands.

The black-haired babe squalled. Shock held her still as she stared at the cherubic-faced, screaming, bloody devil. Maxwell wrapped the babe in a swath of linen and took him from her. Reese tied the cord and cut it with a knife. She stood with her bloodied hands out as if she still held the baby.

Maxwell swayed with the babe, and the screams reduced to a whimper. A genuine awe-filled smile curled his lips before Reese scurried around the bed to take the baby out of his arms.

Meredith laughed. "Let me see. Is the babe a boy or girl?"

Bryn hadn't had the wits to check between its legs.

"A fine baby girl," Maxwell said.

"A girl," Bryn whispered. By the way Meredith and Reese cooed and stroked her face in wonder, a baby girl who would be well-loved. Tears stung the back of Bryn's eyes as a long-held pain reared in her heart.

Meredith's soft murmuring was interrupted by a groan as she curled over her belly. The afterbirth. Bryn resumed her position between Meredith's legs. "One more push will see it done."

Bryn guided the afterbirth out, her stomach roiling at the blood. But not too much, she didn't think. Cadell had always said birthing was a beautiful, bloody experience. Not convinced of the beautiful aspect, she wrapped up the afterbirth and set it aside for burying later.

She washed in the basin she'd used earlier, mesmerized by the swirling pink water. Drying her hands, she glanced at Meredith. Although shadows ringed her eyes and her hair was a sweaty mess, she smiled as she nursed her little girl and leaned against her husband.

"I'll return in a bit with fresh water to clean you and the babe." Bryn backed away.

The heat she craved earlier threatened to overtake her. Nothing could hold her panic at bay now. Her forehead prickled with sweat, and her stomach heaved. Stumbling out of the room, her vision narrowing, she thought to make for the door, but all she could see was Maxwell, and she veered toward him.

CHAPTER TEN

B ryn was ashen-faced, her freckles standing out against her pale, smooth skin. And she looked at him like a shelter from the storm. Part of him wanted to run from her, from the responsibility, but another part of him wanted to snatch her against him and bury his face in her hair. He felt like a hunted hare, not sure which way to turn until the decision was taken out of his hands. She fell into his chest, and he wrapped his arms around her to keep her upright.

Her trembles cascaded through him, and he pulled back. Was she crying? Her face had splotched, and prickles of sweat dotted her forehead, but no tears. She pulled at the neck of her gown, her eyes unfocused.

He swept her into a cradle hold and sat in an oversize, leather armchair with her on his lap. He pushed her hands away and unbuttoned the neck of her gown. Her shudders diminished with each heaving breath. Not knowing what else to do, he took his handkerchief and wiped her face.

Her color evened. She fingered the floppy edges of her gown and shimmied to rise. Her voice was creaky, not quite back under her control yet. "I'm so sorry. Let me—"

"No, don't move."

Her squirms ceased, and she leaned back into his arms with a sigh. "I'm not sick. My attacks have come less frequently over the years. I can usually tame them on my own."

"Attacks?"

Her breathing was still too rapid, as if she'd run across the moors. "Mary calls them nervous attacks. It's one reason she's never taken me to circulate in Edinburgh. She's afraid I'll cause a scene because I'm so weak. Plus my looks."

Nothing in her explanation made any sense. His gaze coasted over her hair and face. Her silky hair begged for his fingers. Her beautifully full lips called to his own without a word being spoken. And her lithe body... well, it didn't bear discussion what part of him answered that call. He could hardly admit any of it to her, but he could dispel Mary's other argument.

Weak? Hardly.

"Let's review the day, shall we? You blustered your way into Lady MacShane's drawing room, leaped off your horse to save me from a man—or men—with evil designs, and single-handedly delivered a breech babe. Sweetheart, you are the furthest thing from weak."

"But I panicked—"

"A completely normal reaction. I've never seen anyone as cool under pressure as you were with Meredith. She drew on your strength." It was the truth. Even in the midst of war, he'd rarely come across a man as collected as Bryn had been directing them in the birthing room.

Her head lolled on his shoulder, and she grabbed his biceps, pulling his arm around her. He didn't hesitate and gave in to his desire, burrowing his face in the hair at her neck. Her body turned lax, and she heaved a sigh, her breathing slowing.

Too soon she rolled off his lap and stood. He let her go with an embarrassing amount of reluctance. When he'd held the babe, a sense of marvel crashed into his terror, resulting in confusion. In a scant few months, he might be holding his own babe. His and Bryn's babe.

A roil of emotion he'd assumed long dead left him rattled. He clenched his hands around his thighs to keep from reaching for her. Now he was the one close to panic. The throb in his leg and head reared higher, and his stomach knotted. He closed his eyes and leaned his head back.

Wispy touches across his forehead registered through the pain. He opened his eyes. She was close, her eyes warm and soothing like a thick plaid.

"Let me see to your wounds," she whispered.

"I don't need your help." He harshened his voice, making an effort to distance himself from her, already feeling too vulnerable. It had no effect on her.

"I know you don't need my help, but you're getting it anyway. Slip off your jacket and shirt."

Beyond arguing, he obeyed, unbuttoning his waistcoat and pulling his torn, bloody shirt over his head. He sat back, and she moved between his spread legs, putting him eye level with her bosom. The brown wool gaped and afforded him a shadowed view of her breasts. A white chemise concealed her curves. But he remembered too well how her nipples had hardened with just the brush of his gaze. He shifted in the chair.

Her hands moved like butterflies over his skin, cleaning the cuts on his neck and forehead and washing off the dried blood. She leaned over to examine the bullet crease on his neck. Her hair swept forward to tickle his shoulder. He wanted to nuzzle into the cleft of her breasts and run his hands along her hips. He clenched the arms of the chair to control the compulsion.

His desire ran deeper and wider than the physical, and therein lay the problem. In two short days, Brynmore McCann had somehow managed to worm her way past his defenses and into his rusty, unused heart. Her problems and pain and worries were his.

How had he allowed it to happen? After Mary rejected him, he'd guarded himself well. More than one lover had accused him of heartlessness. His intention was not callousness, but he'd never allowed himself to care about a woman beyond simple pleasure.

She straightened and set her hands on her hips. His gaze wandered up to her face. A wrinkle appeared between her eyes. "Your pain must be considerable."

"My leg and head ache, but I'll live."

"You look as if you might rip the arms straight off the poor chair."

His fingers were white against the dark leather. He forced pliability into his hands, although tension stiffened his shoulders. "It's been a rather trying day."

"Forever the master of understatement." She fiddled with the open neck of her gown, her eyes veiled but examining him. His stomach muscles jumped as if she'd grazed him with her fingertips. "Do you have another shirt? I'm afraid this one is ruined."

"In my satchel by the door."

Once she was out of sight, he heaved in two great breaths and filled the cracks in his armor. She was back too soon, shaking out a clean, white shirt. When she tried to help him put it on like a child, he snatched it out of her hands and finished the task himself.

Water splashed. "I'm going to wash Meredith and the babe."

Wearing a happy, dazed expression, Reese shuffled out of the little room, straight to a shelf on the wall and pulled out a dusty bottle. "A present from my father-in-law. I don't imbibe often. Would you like a glass?"

"God, yes," Maxwell said with more feeling than he'd intended. The numbing effect of alcohol would be welcome.

Maxwell made to rise, but Reese waved him back into the armchair and pulled up a sturdy, straight-back kitchen chair. "Your wife is bloody amazing, if you don't mind me saying. She saved Meredith and the baby. If I'd lost them—"

Reese and Maxwell looked in opposite directions. Bryn wasn't even officially his betrothed, yet the thought of losing her made him toss down half his glass in one swallow. The burn cauterized the ache in his chest.

"You're welcome to stay here as long as you need," Reese said in a roughened voice. "Meredith is grateful for the company. She grew up in a vicarage in Edinburgh, you see, around scads of other ladies. The farm is so isolated she's had a hard time, especially since her confinement."

"I appreciate that, but I'm afraid Bryn and I are in a bit of trouble. We were accosted on the road, which is how we ended up seeking shelter with you, and I got this." Maxwell gestured to his head before emptying his glass.

"Robbers?"

"Of a sort. Whoever it is may come looking for us. We don't want to put your family in danger."

Reese leaned forward and poured another finger of liquor in Maxwell's glass. "I'm a handy man to have around in a fight."

"I'd not ask it of you. You have Meredith and a new babe. The best thing we can do is leave in the morning. I don't want to travel on the main road to Edinburgh though. Is there another route?"

"Aye. Longer but less traveled."

Maxwell tipped up his glass and glanced toward the door shielding Bryn. "Tell me how to find it. We need safe."

* * * * *

Bryn wrapped the sweet-smelling, pink-skinned baby in a soft blanket and handed her off to Meredith. Dirty sheets were piled on the floor, and both mother and babe were clean.

"Have you settled on a name?" Bryn asked.

"What think you of Elizabeth Brynmore Douglas?"

Bryn stared at the little girl sleeping in her mother's arms. A girl who would bear her name. "I would be honored, but it's not a usual sort of name, so don't feel you have to—"

"I have the feeling after coming into the world the way she did, she's not going to be the usual sort of girl." Meredith's smile was tired. "I'd like you to be her godmother."

Tears burned behind Bryn's eyes, and she dropped her gaze to the basin to finish washing her hands. "I'm not sure we could attend the christening. You see, Maxwell and I are in a spot of trouble."

"I wondered. Your husband appeared rather beat up."

"We were attacked on the road."

"Reese and I will help you. Do you need money?"

"Kind of you to offer, but we don't need money." But as the words left her mouth, a ping of awareness shot through her. Wasn't the root of all evil money?

After Meredith and the babe were settled, Bryn gathered the soiled sheets and retreated. Reese joined his wife, closing the door behind him. Meredith wasn't the only one exhausted. Bryn dumped the sheets in a corner. Maxwell was sprawled in the leather armchair, sipping on a glass of amber liquid and staring at the fire.

"The baby's name is Elizabeth Brynmore," she said.

Maxwell's eyebrows quirked. "A fine and righteous name. You saved both their lives tonight."

With Maxwell occupying the armchair, that left her a stiff-backed wooded chair or the floor to sleep on. In her state of exhaustion, the woven rug in front of the hearth looked heavenly. She stutter-stepped to the hearth and dropped to her knees.

"What the devil are you doing?" Maxwell asked.

She had no strength of will to deal with grumpy, gruff men. "Going to sleep."

"Not on the floor." He grabbed her wrist, tugged her toward him, and maneuvered her into his lap. He pressed his glass into her hands. "Drink the rest."

She swirled the liquid. Firelight striated the whisky into golds and browns. Tipping it up, she drank it in two gulping swallows. The burn stung her nose, but as the warmth spread, the tension in her body dissipated. Whatever had been holding her together dissolved.

Panicked tears, sad tears, worried tears, and mad tears came in a silent storm, and she turned her face into Maxwell's shoulder, hoping he wouldn't notice.

He brushed his hand along her cheek and pushed her hair back. A hiccup escaped. Two errant thoughts ran through her head. The first was regret that he was going to see her face turn splotchy, and the second was that she'd never seen a man look as terrified in her life as he did in that moment.

"Why are you crying so? We're safe. Everyone will live."

"It's been a harrowing day, and crying makes me feel b-better." Her tears slowed, and she took a deep, shuddering breath. Sometimes life called for a good cry, a way to clean away all the ugliness, Cadell used to say.

"Feel *better*?" He sounded horrified at the notion. "You must stop immediately."

In contrast to his harsh command, he gathered her close and nuzzled his bristly cheek against hers. He smelled of winter's pine and leather and whisky. She closed her eyes.

"Stop," he whispered hoarsely in her ear. He kissed her temple and skimmed his lips along her jaw. "Please stop."

His mouth found hers, his lips soft. She nipped his bottom lip and sucked it into her mouth. He tightened his arm around her and cupped her nape, bringing her even closer. Her lips parted, and he took the invitation to sweep his tongue against hers.

The kiss went on and on, their tongues playing and teasing, their lips grazing and pressing. Her body thrummed with an energy she'd thought lost after the day's trials. Her breathing grew shallower and faster until she had to pull away to catch a lungful of air.

He dropped his forehead to her collarbone, his hair tickling her chin. With his weight holding her still and the warmth from the fire and from his body, contentment tempered her arousal.

CHAPTER ELEVEN

Maxwell did not deal with emotional women well. He'd seen women cry before, but they had been calculated tears in order to sway him to provide money or jewelry or a more permanent commitment. Women's pretty tears never moved him.

These were not pretty tears. As her face had gone splotchy and her eyes swelled, helplessness tore at him. He would give anything—*do* anything—to stop her crying. Even break his promise.

In fact, between her tears and the whisky, his promise not to touch her seemed selfish. He'd kiss her sadness away. Except his kiss of comfort flamed into a kiss of passion.

His cock throbbed against her hip. What the devil was wrong with him? He never allowed base emotions or needs dictate his actions. Yet around her, he couldn't seem to stop himself. He set the tumbler on the side table. It was the alcohol's fault once again. Liquor and Brynmore McCann were a bad combination, one he'd be sure not to repeat—again.

But for now he rested on her chest and laid a kiss on soft, fair skin where the curve of her breast began. Her body was lax, and he raised his head. She was asleep, her lips parted, her breathing even.

He should leave her to sleep alone in the chair, but instead of rising, he gathered her close and rubbed his chin against her soft hair. Firelight flickered behind his closed eyes.

Something jostled Maxwell awake. He blinked, his eyes sandy and blurred. Morning light reflected off the snow and poured through the windows. The fire in the hearth sputtered as cold air sped down the chimney. Reese came into focus, bent over him with a hand on his shoulder.

"Riders are approaching. Two of them," the man said shortly.

A pulse of nervous energy shot from Maxwell's stomach and startled him into action. He stood and dumped Bryn on the chair. She grunted but curled up in the warm spot he'd left like a sleepy cat.

"Wake up, lass. We have to leave." Maxwell grabbed her wrists and pulled her upright. Her eyes were open but unfocused. He looked to Reese. "Can you stall them at the door? We'll go out the window and circle around to the barn."

"I'll do my best. Here's your things."

Pounding sounded on the door. Bryn took her cloak from Reese and followed Maxwell to the window. Dark circles under her eyes highlighted her pale, tired face.

Maxwell opened the sash and climbed out. His bad leg seized. He stumbled before catching himself against the rough planks of the cottage. He held a hand out to help Bryn. After throwing one leg over the sill, she stopped and put a hand on Reese's arm. "Perhaps someday soon we might meet again in less harried circumstances."

"You would be most welcome in any circumstances, Mrs. McCann," Reese said with a bravado Maxwell hoped didn't get him in trouble. The door rattled again with the force of the men's knocks. With a grim smile, Reese pushed her into Maxwell's arms and shut the window.

Maxwell pulled Bryn down on her haunches. The pounding came again, this time accompanied by a rough, uneducated voice. "Open up before I break it down!"

"Bloody hell, man, my wife's given birth this night hence. You'll wake the babe with your caterwauling."

On cue, little Elizabeth Brynmore, perhaps sensing the importance of the moment for her namesake, let out a lusty cry that echoed throughout the cottage and drifted outside.

Under the noise of the spate of crying, Maxwell crept to the edge of the house and peered around. No sentinel in sight. The barn stood across an empty space with no cover. Had they run across Primrose yet? If they were any sort of competent blackguards, they would have checked the barn first.

The throbbing pain in his leg would have to wait. He jerked his head at Bryn and took off in a hobbled run. She was like the wisp of a breeze at his side, her feet hardly making a sound. He stopped at the corner of the barn. The gaping crack in the double doors confirmed his suspicions.

Without taking his eyes off the man, he whispered, "Stay here. If I'm overwhelmed, make for the woods and hide."

He slipped through the doors and scooted to the side to wait for his eyes to adjust from blinding brightness to dim shadows. The man leaned against the stall door and offered Primrose a handful of oats.

"Come 'ere, you nag. Let me in to see that saddle."

Primrose, bless her, apparently took the insult to heart and nipped at the man's outstretched hand. Oats flew in the air, and Primrose snuffled at the floor to gather what she could. "Ungrateful wretch. Mayhap I have a taste for horsemeat."

Maxwell approached from behind. Primrose's head rose with a whinny. The man's balding pate glowed like a bull's-eye. Maxwell muffled a startled curse as a long, thick stick appeared at his elbow.

Bryn had followed him like a bloody wraith. Against his orders. She pointed the stick at the man who was trying once again to lure Primrose close to the stall door and wagged it toward Maxwell. He grabbed the stick from her hand, poked the blunt end into her shoulder, and pushed her out of the way.

A few more quiet steps put him within striking distance. The man was still unaware of the danger. With a lunge, Maxwell brought the stick around and hit the man on the temple. He stumbled, swayed, and crumbled into a jumble of arms and legs.

"I told you to wait outside the barn," he whispered.

"You needed a weapon."

He took in a great gust of air but let it go with a shake of his head. "I'm trying to keep you safe."

Color flushed her face, and the rising sun sent a beam to land on her hair, catching it on fire. "You're daft if you think I'm going to diddle outside while you face danger alone."

She looked ready to annihilate him herself. When she took a step forward, he pulled his head back, but she bypassed him on the way to Primrose and his saddle. He joined her, and they had Primrose saddled in minutes.

He gestured her to follow him out the back of the barn. "We'll cut through the forest to the east road. You ride her out, and I'll cover our tracks."

"But your leg. Why don't I cover—"

"I'm fine." He bit the words out. Fine was an exaggeration, but he'd been through worse. Much worse. And he wasn't about to leave Bryn without an escape. If the men found them, she could ride to safety.

He gave her a leg up, and she walked Primrose through the drifts and the scrubby line of trees. He smudged their prints from the snow with the branch from the nearest evergreen tree.

Once the barn was out of sight, he dropped the evergreen branch and whistled for Primrose. Both horse and woman looked back at him. The brim of Bryn's hat had wilted low over her face, the edge dripping melted snow.

With both of them still silent, he mounted behind her. She

collapsed back into his chest.

They rode in silence. Each plodding step without attack released a portion of his tension. The trees grew sparser until only brush and rocks littered the countryside. The animal path intersected with a soggy, muddy mess of a road, narrower by half than the main road they'd been chased off the day before. They met no travelers in either direction.

The afternoon passed, the terrain growing rockier. Dark gray clouds overtook the sun. A foggy, misty rain obscured their view and blanketed them in an unnatural silence.

Bryn fell asleep, and he tightened his arm around her lax body to keep her comfortable. She snuggled her face into his neck and burrowed in his chest. He fought his own exhaustion. It made him inattentive and careless, yet he could feel it winning the battle.

His breath puffed white and hung in the sodden air. Although it didn't snow, the air felt colder and heavier. "I see a farmhouse ahead." His words rumbled hoarsely.

He prodded Primrose into a faster walk, circling back and approaching the barn out of sight from the farmhouse.

She hopped down at the barn door. "I'm going to ask for—"

He shushed her with a hand over her mouth. "Quiet. They'll know we're here."

She cocked her head. "They're going to find out we're here when I go beg for some food."

"No begging for anything," he whispered. "And, for Christ's sake, keep your voice down. We may have been followed."

"There was no sign we've been followed. I understand caution, but we must eat."

His stomach rumbled on cue. His body didn't remember the days without food as a child and demanded something besides air. "I'm coming, just in case."

He took a step forward, but she lay a hand on his chest. "In case of what? I can handle myself. You see to Primrose."

He grabbed her wrist and pressed a coin in her hand. It wasn't much, but to offer more invited their hosts to slit their throats. "Give them this, but emphasize it's all we have."

She nodded, pulled her cloak around her, and ducked back out of the barn.

He stared at the empty space she left. She was a mystery. Around Mary, she acted unsure and frightened—smaller somehow than the woman who'd faced challenge after challenge on the road with him.

Maxwell finished seeing to Primrose and piled hay into a corner of the roomy stall, checking out the door every few seconds for a sign of Bryn.

She appeared with her arms full, and he met her halfway to help carry a skein and a half loaf of still-warm bread, leaving her with two trenchers of stew.

They huddled in the hay, shoulder to shoulder, eating. The stew was rabbit with carrots and potatoes, hearty and delicious. He tore off a hunk of bread and sopped up every bit. The skein contained a weak, sweet wine. Between the two of them, they finished every drop.

"I don't think anything has ever tasted so good." She leaned her head against his shoulder and sighed.

He set the empty trenchers to the side. "It was kind of them. What did you tell them?"

"We are newly married and on the way to Edinburgh to start our life with nothing in our pockets." She yawned noisily like a child, and he hid a smile in the collar of his cloak. "They wished us health and happiness and blessings."

"Let's lie down. It's going to be a cold night."

"Aye. I'm so tired."

He was too, yet once they were settled with their cloaks and a plaid for blankets and hay all around them for warmth, sleep proved elusive. She scooted fully into his body and sighed. It was dark in the barn and under the hay. A comfortable, safe nest. Perhaps that's where the question was born.

"Why do you let Mary bully you?"

* * * * *

B ryn didn't protest or pretend she didn't take his meaning. "Once Mary wed Craddock, she decided to turn me into a model young lady and make an advantageous marriage for me. And them, I suppose. To that end, she took up my neglected education. My lessons proved difficult."

For years, Bryn had woken with a roiling stomach. Elocution and dancing instruction were her morning misery. By the time her afternoon pianoforte lessons commenced, her mind had been a jumble and unable to process the sheet music. The attacks that heated her body and made her want to run away had started a few months after her lessons began.

His arm tightened around her waist as if she didn't need to explain further, but she found herself saying, "Mary would stand over my shoulder as I played the pianoforte or practiced my needlework and point out every flaw. Said I'd never make a proper wife."

"Men don't give a damn whether their wives can embroider a silly pillow or play a boring drudge."

She chuffed a small laugh. "Don't they? What matters then?"

His breath tickled the hair at her temple. His hesitation made her guess he had only been humoring her, but finally he spoke. "Kindness. Humor. And the kind of strength that might not be obvious but shores up a life like the limestone in the cliffs."

As no-nonsense and practical as Maxwell seemed, sometimes his words cast magic. She tried to dispel it before she was ensnared.

"Fine words, but men want beauty."

"Beauty, aye. But there's many kinds in the world."

Did he think she was beautiful? More beautiful than Mary? Reality smacked her. Bryn wasn't a great beauty like Mary. Her looking glass didn't lie. "Mary got one of the village women up to the house to dye my hair."

"That's ridiculous. You have lovely hair." He fingered the ends, and a shock tore through her as if her hair were alive. She brushed her hand over her neck and pulled the offending strands out of his hand.

"No. It's atrocious and too brassy. Men want a shiny chestnut, like Mary's, or pretty blond curls." When she'd spotted herself in the looking glass for the first time after the dyeing, she'd cried. It was black as night and made her look like a sickly witch.

"I suppose your sister instilled such nonsense in your head."

She wished she could see his face.

"I cut it all off," she whispered, her lips barely moving.

"You cut your hair?"

"It used to be to my waist, but I couldn't stand it so black and ugly. I thought Mary might commit murder when she found me." The moment was etched in her memories. Black hair clumped around her like dead ravens. Her sister's scream. Bryn couldn't even claim hysterics, for she'd grimly and methodically cut it off within an inch of her scalp.

A kernel of rebellion had been planted that day. She'd provided baskets for Maxwell because she couldn't bear the thought of him starving. But those same baskets had provided a way to defy her sister. Satisfaction at seeing the money her sister valued funneled back into Cragian had kept Bryn's spirit from withering.

"Mary is beautiful," she choked out.

"Indeed, she is." His words clawed at the festering wound on her heart. "As are you. Only you have yet to discover your power."

Power. A funny choice of words since she'd been powerless against the Fates most of her life. She made decisions when forced into a corner like a feral dog. And like a dog, she would rip at her own limb to escape the traps set for her.

She sat up and turned toward him. Cold air knifed between them. "I have no power. You said yourself that I'm merely a pawn."

He pulled her back down into his warmth and pressed her face into his chest, but she squirmed, not sure what she was trying to escape.

"Don't fash yourself. Let me get you warm. Settle... settle...," he whispered to her in the same soft, comforting brogue he used with Primrose. "You have a special sort of power, Brynmore. Trust me on this."

His velvety voice soothed her. A small part of her brain protested. She was woman, not horse, and this man would use her as everyone in her life used her.

She didn't care. In his arms, she felt protected and strong at the same time. Two states of being that were foreign to her.

She wiggled closer. One of his hands stole over her back to the top curve of her bottom. She lay on his other arm like a pillow, his breath puffing on her forehead. Her free arm stole around him and pressed into the hard planes of his back. If the farmer's wife discovered them, she would certainly believe they were wed.

She slid toward sleep, warm for the first time all day. "Why aren't you bothered by the cold?"

She had almost drifted off when his chest rumbled words. "I learned to bear it. The shack Mother and I shared was full of holes. Barely a notch above sleeping outside. The floor turned to mud in rain or snow, and we had only one cot."

She breathed his name. He hugged her tighter, and she pressed her lips against his jaw. He heaved a sigh. "Go to sleep now, lass."

For once, she did as she was told without an argument.

CHAPTER TWELVE

Maxwell closed his eyes, his body rocking naturally with the motion of the horse. A tortuous mimicry of sex. Her bottom shifted back into him again. Even separated by his breeches, her dress, and both their cloaks, he had no trouble picturing her naked rounded backside pressed against his cock.

He imagined bending her over in front of a looking glass so they could both see and pushing inside her. He'd not been drunk enough to forget the feel of her, tight and hot and wet.

"—an inn. Our attackers have given up."

"What are you blathering on about?" After the night they'd spent in an embrace in the farmer's barn, he convinced himself his predicament was her fault. If she hadn't up and seduced him, he would have been in Edinburgh, safe in his rented rooms with his new life begun. Alone. There would be no half brother or jilted fiancé out for his bollocks, no uncomfortable nights on piles of hay, no constant thrum of need and want.

"We've seen no one who wishes us harm on the road. Can we take a room in an inn tonight?" She favored him with a sunny smile in spite of gray clouds overhead.

His insides twisted like a wrung-out rag. A bed and a fire and Bryn waiting in a chemise. Or less. "No, we bloody well can't."

She turned away, taking her smile with her. He wished she'd

whine and complain like a normal woman. Instead, her smiles and laughter warmed him in unexpected places. Places he'd thought locked, the key misplaced.

"They'll be no need of an inn tonight. We'll be in Edinburgh by afternoon." He tempered his voice in weak apology.

Once in Edinburgh, he needn't spend time with her. Or even see her. It would be a waiting game. If she carried his child, they would marry by special license or over the anvil, if necessary. If not... He didn't want to consider the alternative.

He tugged her into his chest and breathed into her hair. She smelled like fresh hay and a crisp winter's wind.

"When are your courses due?"

Bryn started. "Ah, I'm not exactly sure but not yet."

A shot of satisfaction, relief, and resentment coursed through him. The emotional stew had too many ingredients and left a bitter taste in his mouth.

After hours of silence, Edinburgh materialized through the fog. Ornate spires clawed into the clouds as if trying to sneak into heaven. The castle loomed on the hill, nearly swallowed in white. Ancient cobblestones echoed underfoot. The fog muffled and distorted sound. Hawkers called out their wares, but they were indistinct, crowding into an opposite street.

Maxwell had come to Edinburgh before joining his regiment as a newly minted lieutenant, and he'd known in his bones he'd be back someday as man or ghost to roam the streets with long-dead clansmen and lairds.

With the castle still in sight, he guided Primrose onto a quiet street lined with town houses. Primrose's clops echoed off the stone. A handful of people were out, scurrying with cloaks pulled tightly around faces.

A fission of energy had him sitting straighter. Success and autonomy were in his grasp. His plan was to offer the same sort of services he had to the Bellinghams but on a nonexclusive basis. He would act as steward or advisor for several property owners instead of one and take a cut of their profits instead of a salary. And he would turn a profit or that he had no doubt.

"Here we are. Eighteen Barrow Road." Maxwell dismounted in front of a town house with green shutters. Knobby, brown stone fit with the rest of the ancient city, but Maxwell knew it to be a façade. The house was only a decade old, if that. It was a newly prosperous area of Edinburgh, perfect for reaching out to landed aristocrats and wealthy gentry. While the ghosts of the city beckoned, he desired to live like a modern man.

He helped Bryn down. She clutched his forearms, digging her fingers into his muscle. A tiny moan escaped. The memory of her moans and pleas their night together in Cragian ignited an ember in his belly, no matter how road worn and weary he was. Would he ever be able to forget?

Damn his hands. They circled her waist to support her more fully.

The front door opened and cut them apart. A middle-aged lady with salt-strewn black hair stood in the doorway. Candlelight wavered behind her, but the diffused light of the afternoon lit her expression. Shock? Disapproval? Or merely surprise?

Maxwell tackled the steps as best he could with his stiff, sore leg, his limp more pronounced than usual. "I'm Mr. Drake. May I assume you are my housekeeper, Mrs. Soames?"

The lines creasing her forehead smoothed, and in a heavily accented brogue, she said, "Indeed, I am, and pleased to finally make your acquaintance, sir. We were growing concerned. We expected you nigh on two days ago." Mrs. Soames glanced at Bryn with shiny, dark eyes, but her discretion did her proud.

"I was delayed by the weather. And I acquired a guest. My betrothed, Miss McCann, will require lodging. Could you ready a chamber for her?"

"Indeed, Mr. Drake. And I'll send young Seamus around to

see to your horse." She gestured them into the town house, tutting about the cold and damp.

The dim, characterless entry made it difficult to get a lay of the land. A young man in a natty blue uniform barreled out of a side corridor, smoothing his coat with one hand and his hair with the other.

"This is Henry. Your footman and man of all work. Henry, send young Seamus to tend to the horse, and tell Isla to ready another chamber for the young lady. Will there be anyone else arriving, Mr. Drake? A chaperone, perhaps?"

Bloody hell, the thought hadn't crossed his mind. He hummed. "Yes, we're expecting her any moment."

Bryn's swift breath was audible, but he didn't dare look over at her.

"Is this the drawing room, mayhap?" He cupped Bryn's elbow and opened the door on their right. Warm greens and browns lent a welcoming, charming feel. Although it wasn't lit, fuel was stacked next to the hearth. This was more to his liking. "We'll both require baths at your earliest convenience, Mrs. Soames, but first some tea and whatever the kitchen has available, if you please."

"Yes, sir." She backed away and disappeared into the shadows. The jangle of keys grew faint until they disappeared.

Bryn stood in the middle of the room, still in her cloak and chafing her arms. If he was tired, she must be close to collapse. Although his last years in London had been comfortable, years spent surviving first Cragian and then the war had hardened him.

He squat in front of the hearth and got a fire crackling. The glow and warmth spread. He stared into the hypnotizing flames.

"We made it." She had come up next to him without his notice. Color flooded her cheeks, and her hair sparked in the firelight.

"Aye." His throat was dry. Where was the blasted tea?

"Are we safe?"

If only troubles were so easily left behind. His father's will and her betrothal agreement loomed like harbingers. "Perhaps, but most likely not."

"Always the optimist." She side-eyed him with a half smile.

Mrs. Soames reentered and deposited a laden tray on a low table in front of a settee. "The lady's bath is filling now, sir."

Bryn took a piece of dark bread, slathered it with butter, and took a bite, expelling a sigh.

"Thank you, Mrs. Soames." Maxwell followed the housekeeper into the entry.

"Should we expect the lady's chaperone this evening, sir?"

Darkness had fallen. Mrs. Soames's candle cast long shadows along the walls. "Miss Bryn's chaperone might be detained a day or two. There is to be no gossip, is that understood?"

Mrs. Soames seemed to grow taller. "Certainly not, sir. I realize we have only corresponded through letters, but I've run houses twice this size with efficiency. I do not tolerate gossip."

As he had little choice, he would have to trust the woman. "Did you get my trunks?"

"The books are unpacked and on the shelves in your office, and your clothes are in your room." She gestured across the entry to the closed door. "You've received correspondence over the past week, sir. I've stacked the missives on your desk."

"Very good, Mrs. Soames."

"Should I be expecting a trunk with the lady's things, sir?"

Damnation. "We met with some misfortune on the road. Thieves. She'll require a new wardrobe. Is there a dressmaker you could commission?"

A look of sympathy softened the stern lines of her face. "Indeed there is."

"Could you ask her to come around with samples at her earliest convenience? It will consist of a large order."

"I'll send a note in the morning, sir."

Henry, the butler/footman, clomped down the steps, slowing as he caught sight of Mrs. Soames. "The lady's bath is ready. The kitchen is heating water for the master's now."

"Thank you, Henry," Mrs. Soames said. "Shall I escort the lady to her chamber?"

Maxwell nodded. Bryn stumbled out of the room like a sleepwalker and swept up the stairs in Mrs. Soames's wake. He finished every scrap of food left on the tray and drank tea until he was called for his own bath.

Henry led the way to his room. It was at the far end of the upstairs corridor. Candlelight flickered at the bottom of door halfway down the hall. Bryn was likely naked in a steaming, fragrant bath, her skin pink and flushed, much as it had been after—

He quashed his thoughts. A single candle and small fire lit his chamber. The door closed with a snick. Finally he was alone.

He stripped out of his road-worn clothes and slipped into the bath, the heat loosening his muscles and easing the pain in his leg. The state of being alone wasn't unusual. In fact, silence had been a boon companion for as long as he could recall.

The past days with Bryn should have been grating. It hadn't been. She understood the beauty of silence and didn't fill it with inanities.

Only when the water cooled did he heave himself out, his leg's protests muffled. The air nipped at his damp body, and he pulled on small clothes and wrapped himself in a plaid folded on the end of the bed.

He hesitated between bed and door. Muttering a curse, he padded barefoot into the hall. Light shone through the cracks in Bryn's door. He rapped. Nothing. Had she fallen asleep in the bath?

He pushed the handle, and the door swung open with a long creak. The bath was empty. The bed was not.

She was curled in a tight ball on the coverlet, a pillow clutched to her chest, the gold in her damp hair muted. The night rail she wore was reminiscent of the one she'd seduced him in—thick and covering her from neck to feet. She'd even tucked her toes under the hemline. The lass was likely to freeze to death.

His already chaotic emotions tumbled. He rolled her and peeled back the covers. A few throaty noises later, she was covered. Between the blankets and the fire, she would be warm enough without him. It was only concern for his possible babe.

Yet he didn't move. He tucked a lock of hair that had fallen over her cheekbone behind her ear. The skin of her jaw was soft under his fingertips. In his memories, the rest of her body was just as tempting. He forced himself to take a step back, his hand drawing into a fist.

He was an addict, and she was his drug. He'd hoped the brief touch would satisfy his craving, lest it overwhelm him and he find himself at her bedroom door every night begging entrance. One touch had only fed his craving.

He would distance himself from her until time revealed his path forward. But if she was carrying his child, they would marry, and he would keep their marriage bed warm indeed.

* * * * *

Bryn had been ambushed.

Maxwell had set the trap, and Mrs. Soames had sprung it.

And now she found herself a dressmaker's doll in the drawing room, arms out while Mrs. Wilson pinned a set of sleeves onto a forest-green dress.

Maxwell performed a perfunctory knock and cracked the drawing room door open. "May I enter?"

"Yes, sir. She's decent enough," Mrs. Wilson said through a mouthful of pin.

Maxwell closed the door behind him and paced around her as if surveying a battlefield, his hands behind his back, a solemn expression on his face. "Is your client behaving?"

"Aye, sir. Although she's been trying to convince me she needs less, just as you predicted. Also, she's fighting me on the colors. Insists on brown or gray." Mrs. Wilson removed the pins and blew a piece of hair off her forehead.

"I'm standing right here, and my ears are in perfect working order." Bryn couldn't keep the tartness from her voice, even as she realized Maxwell was doing something nice and necessary, considering breeches were her only other option.

Nevertheless, she didn't like the idea of being indebted to him. A riding habit, a ball gown, five warm winter woolen dresses, and five summer frocks were being commissioned. She would end up with more clothes than she had left behind at the manor house. Just how much money did the man have? What would happen if her courses came? What would she do out on the streets in a ball gown?

Maxwell wandered over to the fabric samples laid across the back of the settee.

"Two serviceable gowns are sufficient, Drake." The thought of how much the dresses would cost made heat rush through her. She took slow, deep breaths.

"I'll not have you dressing like a servant." The delicate fabric was incongruous against the blunt roughness of his hands.

They were big hands, the backs tanned. She couldn't see the calluses on his fingers, but the memory of them brushing against her skin heated her in other more intimate ways. The night had been lonely and cold. Had he felt her absence as keenly as she'd felt his?

A silky midnight-blue fabric pooled to the floor like a waterfall. He draped it over her shoulder, covering the green wool. The fabric caressed her neck, cool and silky. It was sensuous and not at all practical. "This one, Mrs. Wilson."

Mrs. Wilson cocked her head. "You have a good eye, Mr. Drake. A blue cools the heat of her unusual coloring. Quite a stunning choice for the ball gown."

He pushed her hair over her shoulder, his fingertips glancing over her collarbone. Was the touch accidental or intentional? "Stunning, indeed."

Shivers erupted. Stunning? Maxwell stood close enough for his scent to envelop her. It was the same soap she'd used in the bath, but on him it was earthier and drew her like a cinder girl to the hearth.

He whirled away with such suddenness she flinched. Moving with an economy that spoke of impatience, he pulled a dark blue broadcloth and instructed Mrs. Wilson to make a riding habit and a silvery gray that was a far sight from the drab color she was used to for another day dress.

"And this green? The color is lovely on her. Don't you agree, Mr. Drake?" Mrs. Wilson tucked and rustled the green dress around her. Maxwell's slow perusal down her body brought to mind a sheep auction.

"The neckline is too high. Can you notch a vee in the front?"

Mrs. Wilson nodded. "Would you be wanting her to wear stays?"

Bryn only managed a huffing protest.

"With her lithesome figure, she hardly needs them in her everyday gowns, but I want the ball gown cut low. Not scandalous, but Miss McCann's assets"—Maxwell waved his hand in the air— "should be highlighted, don't you agree?"

"Aye, her bosom is very fine. She'll be a pleasure to dress, sir."

Bryn covered her bosom with a hand, her tongue thick in her mouth. She'd never been so flustered in her life. They were discussing her as if she were livestock.

With the ghost of a bow, Maxwell quit the room, leaving behind a thick fog of silence. A ticking clock on the mantle was like the hammer to an anvil. Bryn closed her eyes. Did Mrs. Wilson think Bryn was Maxwell's mistress? And wasn't she, of a sort? Explaining their complicated situation would only make matters worse.

"Goodness, lass, he's quite taken with you." No condemnation, only curiosity threaded her voice.

Bryn looked over her shoulder at Mrs. Wilson, who was pinning the back of the dress, a smile on her face. "What? No. What makes you say so?"

"What man takes such an interest in his lady's clothes if he isn't? And the way he looked at you. I needed a fan. He'll want to marry with haste."

"Marry?"

"You're betrothed, are you not?" Mrs. Wilson raised an eyebrow.

"He's— We're—" Bryn blew out an exasperated sigh. What could she do but agree? "We are betrothed."

Pins in her mouth, Mrs. Wilson hummed as if the secrets of the universe had been revealed. As the dressmaker continued to poke and prod and measure, Bryn wished she could acquire some of that knowledge to help with her confusion.

CHAPTER THIRTEEN

The hum of voices and a clatter outside the front door pulled Maxwell from his ledgers and out of his study. Had Armstrong or Craddock or MacShane found them? Not bothering with his jacket, he waited in the shadows for Henry to open the door, the muscles along his shoulders bunching.

Fabric rustled. Holding a book to her chest and pale-faced, Bryn rocked on her feet at the entrance to the drawing room, looking ready to bolt. She was wearing the green gown the seamstress had modified.

The color highlighted her creamy complexion and complemented her hair. The soft wool molded to her body. Lush curves had been hiding under the baggy, brown monstrosity she'd worn for days on end while they traveled. As if he needed reminding. The memory tormented him nightly in his dreams.

Their gazes met across the entry. He wanted to tell her how lovely she looked. Wanted to assure her of her safety. Whether she carried his babe or not, he'd protect her. With his life, if necessary.

Henry opened the door. The bubble of tension popped. It was neither Dugan nor Craddock nor his brother, Albert. Three strangers, two older gentlemen and a matronly lady, stood on the stoop, arguing.

"For all that's holy, Edie, we're not in London, I'm sure he—"

The opening of the door cut off whatever else the gentleman was going to say. "Ah, there you see? It wasn't too early to call."

The man who led the way into the modest entryway was used to power and deference. Although his hair was thinning and gray and he appeared to be well into his fifth decade, he exuded a vitality that was somehow familiar. A peer, certainly, but something else tickled Maxwell's memory.

"You must be Maxwell Drake. My daughter-in-law raved about you in her letter. Best man of affairs in all of Britain. Smart, dependable, and imminently honorable. Let me apologize for the early hour and the lack of calling cards. I find the older I grow, the less time I have to waste on trivialities." He handed off his hat and cane to Henry.

At the mention of a daughter-in-law, Maxwell's memory notched into place. The man had the energetic air of his daughter, Lady Lily Masterson. "Lord Windor. I had the pleasure of meeting both your daughter and son last year."

"Sharp on the uptake. Good. I don't have time to waste on idiots either." The earl rubbed his hands together with a smile.

"David, really." The other gentleman moved forward with a shake of his head. By the lines of his face, he was close to Lord Windor's age, although his hair was still thick, the dark shot through with white. "I'm Lionel Masterson, Mr. Drake. The earl's daughter, Lily, is married to my son, Gray. And this is Mrs. Edith Winslow, a family friend. As Lady Minerva regards you as a brother, we're all family of sorts."

A brother? Maxwell supposed he'd been as close to Lady Minerva as anyone in his life, besides his mother.

Mr. Masterson the elder had kind gray eyes and an overall aura of unruffled competence. Maxwell nodded, his shoulders relaxing as he turned to Mrs. Winslow. The effect of the bright tangerine gown Mrs. Winslow wore was like the summer sun finding its way inside. Even more than her appearance, her good humor and energy gave the impression of a handsome woman. She offered her hand, and he performed the social niceties by rote.

"A cup of tea or, better yet, coffee wouldn't be remiss, Drake." The earl moved farther into the house, apparently intending to make himself at home.

Henry lay everything on a side table in the entry. "I'll let Mrs. Soames know there are visitors, sir."

Maxwell nodded and gestured their guests into the drawing room. He half expected to find Bryn had scampered away to a hiding spot, but she had been caught by the earl and backed into the side of an armchair.

"And who might you be, young lady?"

"Brynmore McCann, my lord, of Cragian, Dumfries." Bryn managed a credible curtsy.

"Quite a pleasure to make your acquaintance, my lovely Miss McCann." The earl took her bare hand, bowed, and pressed a kiss on the back.

Something primal reared inside Maxwell. No matter the earl's age, he wanted to rip him away from Bryn. Instead, he laid a hand on her shoulder. "She is lovely." *And she's mine.* The unspoken addendum hung in the air as if it had been said—loudly.

The earl's vivid blue eyes narrowed, but Maxwell sensed amusement, not anger. "Ho. Minerva thought that's the way the wind blew."

Mrs. Winslow, laughing loudly, slapped the earl on the arm with her reticule. "David. You're incorrigible. You must forgive us, Miss McCann, we've been in each other's pockets since summer, traveling the whole of Great Britain. Lionel's the only one who's managed to maintain a sense of decorum."

"My dear Edith, you had no sense of decorum even before we began this adventure," the earl said as they settled side by side on the settee. Mr. Masterson took one armchair and Maxwell the other. Bryn was left to perch next to the earl.

After the arrival of the tea tray, Bryn hesitated only a moment before pouring for them all. Maxwell cleared his throat, drawing everyone's attention. "Not that you aren't welcome, but how did you find us?"

The earl laughed and slapped his knee. "I love the Scots. Your forthrightness has its charms after navigating London's treacherous waters, where innuendo and deceit is the order of the day." The earl took a sip from his cup, his pause designed to heighten expectation. "We were apprised of your whereabouts by Minerva, of course. We're here to help."

Maxwell stiffened. His natural inclination was to refuse. He had learned not to rely on anyone for help or happiness. That path led to disappointment.

Before he could get a word out, Bryn turned and touched the man's arm. "Lord Windor, we would be most grateful for assistance."

"The pleasure is ours. I've been going out of my mind, to be perfectly frank. If I see one more ancient, crumbling church, I'll have to be committed. Rafe and Minerva's letter detailing your concerns arrived in the nick of time."

The letter he'd sent to Minerva from Cragian had arrived faster than he'd expected. Maxwell had written hoping for level-headed advice from his former employer about his situation, not reinforcements. As if things weren't complicated enough already. "I'm not sure—"

"I was informed of your arrival, but Mrs. Winslow convinced me to give you time to settle in. You look quite ravishing in your new dress, by the way, Miss McCann. Green really does suit you."

As he recalled, the earl had been a high-ranking diplomat with the British government and had spent much of his time traveling. "Informed by whom? Diplomatic contacts?"

The earl pursed his lips, humor dancing across his face. "Of a sort."

"Now that you're retired from service, can you not be honest?" Mrs. Winslow asked before turning to Maxwell. "Lord Windor was more than a diplomat, Mr. Drake. I'm afraid his thirst for intrigue will never die."

The earl sat back, crossed his legs, and laid an arm across the back of Bryn's end of the settee. "Let's discuss strategy. We have several weapons at our disposal. Lionel can interpret the legal mumbo-jumbo of any legal documents. Mrs. Winslow has made friends with a substantial portion of Society in Edinburgh, and my name can gain us entry to any residence. Brief us on the situation."

Maxwell took a deep breath, looking around the room at the four people gazing back. Did he have a choice but to accept their help? Days stewing over their not insubstantial problems hadn't produced a viable solution. "I may or may not have been bequeathed something in my father's will. His widow claims the will is with the family's solicitor here in Edinburgh. A Mr. Pickett."

"Should be simple enough to obtain as you're a son," Mr. Masterson said softly.

Maxwell grit his teeth against the ingrained rise of shame. "An illegitimate one, I'm afraid. And unacknowledged at that. I haven't been able to secure an appointment."

An uncomfortable wave passed through the room as if he'd detonated a cannon. No one but Bryn met his gaze. He stayed focused on the unblinking understanding he saw there.

"I've seen enough of the world to not judge a man for a father's sins, and this twist only makes things more interesting." No embarrassment or disgust laced the earl's voice. In fact, excitement thrummed in his face and body, his leg bouncing. "I've also lived long enough to understand that information is always attainable. For a price."

"Yes, well, I'm afraid that's only one of our problems." He sketched out Bryn's escape from Cragian and Armstrong, leaving out the scandalous details of why Maxwell was now acting as her protector.

"Do you recall a visit from a solicitor, Miss McCann?"

"I do not. And I would have remembered. Mary and Craddock returned from Edinburgh with the contract in hand. I was made to sign without an opportunity to read it."

Bryn's hand had crept to her neck in a protective manner, and Maxwell was flooded with the urge to drive his fist through a wall. Or Craddock's face. He was only beginning to understand the strength of will Bryn had exhibited to escape.

"If the contract was drawn up in town, perhaps they used Mr. Pickett as well," Mr. Masterson said. "And if not, he'll know who handled the affair. It's a small city, after all, and people talk."

"Mr. Masterson, I've been wondering... could Dugan Armstrong force me into marriage or sue for breach of contract?" A hesitancy hitched Bryn's voice.

Maxwell scooted to the edge of the cushion. If Dugan attempted to take Bryn from him, Maxwell might just turn into the animal Lady MacShane had accused him of being.

Mr. Masterson rubbed his bottom lip. "Not force, I don't think. But he could sue. Are you inheriting a large sum of money, Miss McCann, on your majority or marriage?"

"No." The denial was accompanied by a rattle of her teacup. "At least I don't think so. No one has ever intimated that I have any inheritance whatsoever."

"Yet their insistence the wedding continue after..." Heat bloomed in Maxwell. "Bryn's sister was expecting something valuable out of the union. As was Armstrong. We just don't know what."

"Could it be that Armstrong loves you, Miss McCann?" Mr. Masterson said softly, exchanging a telling look with the earl. "I've seen men driven insane with love. Even driven to kill."

A wistfulness twisted her smile. "What he feels for me is closer to disdain than love. I have no accomplishments to tempt a husband. Certainly nothing worth killing over."

A protest hovered on Maxwell's tongue, but it would reveal too much, and he stayed silent.

"Killing? Has something happened to make you believe our interested parties might turn violent?" The earl cast his gaze between Maxwell and Bryn.

Maxwell detailed their flight into the woods. Instead of concern or astonishment over their possible deaths, the earl broke into a sunny smile and rubbed his hands together. "Jolly good! This gets more and more tangled."

"David, really, they could have been injured or worse." Mr. Masterson's worry was in his frown.

"But they weren't. They look alive enough to me. The stakes are higher, and immediate action is required. We need to discover what's in Lord MacShane's will and Miss McCann's betrothal contract. Discover who has the most to lose."

"Mr. Pickett isn't likely to hand any of it over, is he?" Bryn asked.

"No, but I'm wondering if perhaps Drake, Lionel, and I shouldn't go to try to wheedle it out of him anyway. A bit of charm, a show of muscle, and perhaps we can obtain a reading in his office. Lionel can find the interesting bits, can't you, old boy?"

"Certainly." A flash of humor lightened Mr. Masterson's face before it tightened once more as he looked to the ceiling. "Mr. Drake, if I'm inferring your situation correctly, a chaperone would not be remiss. Even Edinburgh society will cut you if it becomes common knowledge the two of you are under the same roof without oversight."

"You're absolutely correct. In fact, I was planning to advertise for someone suitable today." Maxwell tugged at his suddenly constricting neckcloth.

"We can offer a solution." The earl turned to Mrs. Winslow. His sigh was deep and long-suffering. The woman was sitting straight up and still balancing her teacup on her lap, but on closer inspection, her eyes were closed. The earl lifted the cup from her lax fingers and said loudly, "Edith. Wake up, woman."

Mrs. Winslow's eyes popped open. She shook herself slightly before taking the teacup from the earl and asked, as if she had not quite heard the question, "What was that now?"

"Drake and Miss McCann need a chaperone and are wondering whom to employ."

Mrs. Winslow pursed her lips and stared Maxwell down. "Employ? My good sir, I chaperoned Lady Lily through her first season in London, and I'll be more than up to the task in Edinburgh. There is no finer chaperone in all of Britain than yours truly."

Feeling caught in a maelstrom out of his control, Maxwell turned to Bryn. "Is that acceptable to you?"

"As no one else has landed on our doorstep, I'd say Mrs. Winslow would be more than welcome as my chaperone." Her voice was dry with a humor he appreciated.

Between the earl, Mrs. Winslow, and Mr. Masterson, the way forward was set. After deciding the first order of business would be an appointment with Mr. Pickett, their three visitors left in a whirlwind, with promises Mrs. Winslow would be back with her things by evening tea.

Once the door was closed and Henry had cleared the tea tray, Maxwell found his voice. "That was unexpected."

Laughter bubbled out of Bryn, but it was the nervous variety. "You could say that. Do you trust them?"

Trust. Mary had decimated his trust and his heart. Acting as an exploring agent for Wellington had only reinforced the necessity of handling his own business and keeping his own counsel. Yet Minerva hadn't sent a simple reply, she'd sent her lordly father, a matron, and their man of business. They offered help with nothing to gain as far as Maxwell could determine.

"We have no choice but to accept their help. I can't get the documents we need." The edge of his bitterness sharpened. The truth of his birth could very well affect his fledgling business venture. As it stood, Edinburgh society wasn't aware of his shameful association with Lord Ian MacShane. Yet he couldn't leave the matter alone. He must know the truth.

She touched his arm. He hadn't noticed her move, but now that she stood close, a light vanilla scent enveloped him. The soft brown of her eyes showed no pity, only understanding and an echo of fear. He had an urge to wrap her close, bury his face in her neck, and let her body soothe him.

Foolishness. He straightened his neckcloth and took a step back. Her hand fell to her side. "Could you discuss arrangements for Mrs. Winslow's arrival with Mrs. Soames?"

"Of course," she said softly. This time the unmistakable glint of pity was in her eyes before she turned away. He retreated to his study, but the solitude he craved felt more like loneliness.

CHAPTER FOURTEEN

The next morning, with Mrs. Winslow settled in the town house, Earl Windor and Mr. Masterson gathered in Maxwell's study. A simple note from the earl had secured them an appointment that morning at ten. Maxwell had personally visited their offices his first day in Edinburgh, only to be turned away with platitudes to return when the gentlemen solicitors weren't so busy. It was loathsome to have to use the earl's name to gain entry to the place when Maxwell had the money but not the name to garner true respect.

"It's frustrating to be shuffled off," Maxwell said.

"It's the way of the world, Drake. At least the world we live in." The earl puffed on a thin cigar and lounged in one of the leather padded chairs. "If you hold such egalitarian beliefs, perhaps you'd feel more at home in the Americas."

"Have you been, my lord?"

"Briefly after the revolution. Quite an interesting mix of people all thrown together. A hierarchy exists, but money is king, and there's little differential between old and new. You'd do well."

"I considered it, but with war broken out there once more, I want no part of it." Maxwell steepled his hands at his chin. "I spent too many years on the Continent. I hardly want to throw myself back into the fray in a different country. Moreover, I have unfinished business here, and now that I'm back, old roots are growing deeper."

"Could a pretty red-haired woman have something to do with those deepening roots?"

Maxwell cast an irritated look at the earl and didn't answer. As if it was any of the old lecher's business. He'd intercepted the appreciative looks the earl had bestowed on Bryn, and each time, he was nearly overwhelmed with the need to throttle a man twice his age. Jealousy was not an emotion he was familiar with, and now he'd been nearly unmanned by it twice where the chit was concerned. It was damned inconvenient. Not to mention embarrassing.

The earl pulled out his pocket watch, checked the time, and clicked it shut. "While I would love to let the fool stew, wondering what the coming interview is about, I believe we should garner as much good grace as possible. Let's not be late, gentleman."

As they arrived, it was clear the staff had been forewarned. Two young clerks offered tea, coffee, and even whisky to the earl, bowing and scraping and turning Maxwell's stomach. Lionel Masterson witnessed the display with more amusement than resentment.

"Doesn't it bother you how people kowtow to him because of his title?" Maxwell whispered.

"Not a bit. I would never want to be in his shoes."

Interest in the man who had stood at the earl's side for years replaced Maxwell's annoyance. Lionel was calm and unruffable and took the earl's diatribes in stride.

"The prestige and money hold no allure?"

"Pah! Those things don't truly matter, Mr. Drake. I had something that the earl never attained even with all his money and prestige, something much more elusive and precious—love, a happy marriage, a happy home." Lionel peered closely at Maxwell. "I would never have been free to marry my Betsy were I in the earl's position. She was from country gentry but not the bloodlines necessary for breeding in the peerage."

"That sounds cold-blooded."

"Quite so. Honestly, if my son hadn't thoroughly compromised Lily Drummond, who knows whether the earl would have approved of the match."

Maxwell coughed at Lionel's casual mention of Lily's premarital antics. "Would she have walked away and married another more suitable man if the earl had disapproved?"

At that, Lionel laughed. "I imagine she would have kidnapped Gray to Scotland had that been the case. I had the distinct pleasure of raising Lily and Rafe alongside Gray, for all practical purposes. The earl was off doing what he does best." Lionel gestured at the scene unfolding. "I'm afraid my more enlightened viewpoints may have rubbed off on *all* the children."

Their conversation was cut short as the earl gestured them forward to follow a young clerk into Mr. Pickett's office. Introductions were made, and as soon as Maxwell's name was spoken, Mr. Pickett tensed, his Adam's apple bobbing. The impeccably dressed Pickett made his way around the desk and perched on the edge of his chair as if ready to take flight.

As there were only two chairs facing a large impressive desk, Maxwell hovered in the background, letting the earl take the lead. Not that he had much choice in the matter.

"It's quite an honor to have your business at our fine establishment, my lord. What might I help you with today?" Pickett smoothed a hand over his balding pate. Did Maxwell detect a hint of sweat? He propped his shoulder against a large bookcase and crossed his arms. Pickett's gaze darted in his direction but didn't stick.

"I wasn't entirely forthcoming with my needs earlier, Mr. Pickett." A lazy insouciance overlay steel in the earl's voice. "We have two pieces of business today, both are delicate and involve information. Firstly, I would like to know if you handled the marriage settlement of Dugan Armstrong and Brynmore McCann."

Pickett sniffed, his expression souring. "No. I handled all of Baron McCann's business, God rest his soul, and Craddock's as well, but he brought a solicitor from Glasgow down to negotiate the settlement."

"Do you remember the man's name?"

"Aye. Buscomb. Sad business that. He was robbed and killed by highwaymen on the way back to Glasgow. Notorious, dangerous road from here to there."

The earl straightened like a hunting dog catching a scent. "Quite sad. Convenient too, wouldn't you say?"

"Convenient?" Pickett's surprise didn't appear feigned. "You mean to say he was killed with intent?"

"Was the business done here or in Dumfries?"

"Here. It was Mr. Sutherland who hosted Buscomb, Craddock, and Armstrong."

"Interesting indeed."

The name Sutherland meant nothing to Maxwell, but the earl's knowing tone had him taking mental notes.

Pickett half rose, gesturing toward the door. "Well, if that's all—"

"No." The single cutting word had Pickett plopping down hard in his seat. "My second piece of business has to do with my good friend, Mr. Drake. I've taken a keen interest in his situation, you understand."

"And what business would that be? Our firm has never dealt with Mr. Drake." Another glace ricocheted off Maxwell.

"Mr. Pickett. I find such pretenses tiresome." The earl readjusted the hint of white peeking out from the sleeve of his Weston jacket and picked a piece of lint from the lapel. "You handled the last will and testament of one Ian MacShane of

Dumfries. Is that correct, sir?"

"Y-yes. I did witness and file his will. But I'm still not sure how this concerns... Mr. Drake, was it?"

The earl's casual manner flipped on its head, and he rose, placing fisted hands on the desk. "I'm a busy man. You wouldn't be roiling in nervous sweat casting alarmed looks Drake's way if you weren't entirely aware of the reason for our visit."

Pickett pressed back against the chair, garbled out a noise, and pulled out his handkerchief to pat his forehead.

Lionel didn't stand but sat forward. "Mr. Pickett, you know as well as I that if Mr. Drake is mentioned in the will, it is your responsibility to read him the pertinent parts and make the proper bequeaths. The question is simple. Is Maxwell Drake mentioned in Lord MacShane's will?"

"P-perhaps?"

Maxwell pushed off the bookcase, but instead of trying to intimidate the man, he spoke as if soothing a horse. "Mr. Pickett, has someone threatened you in order to keep the will a secret?"

Pickett nodded, staring at Drake, lips compressed into a thin, quivering line. Holy hell, was the man going to start crying?

"Did you know the man who threatened you?"

"N-no. A letter." His voice gained strength and rose an octave. "I have a family, good sirs, a wife and three children whom I dearly love. The letter was quite clear and detailed terrible things that would befall them if I were to disclose the information you seek."

In the ensuing silence, the earl and Drake exchanged a loaded look. Here was a man who most likely wanted to do the right thing but was being strong-armed.

"I understand your position now, Mr. Pickett." The earl relaxed into his chair and stroked his jaw. "Let's speculate a moment. What if you leave the document in question on your desk this evening? And what if the document is exactly where you left it tomorrow morning when you arrive for work?"

"We lock our offices, my lord."

"Very good practice, Mr. Pickett. You never know what kind of miscreants might be lurking in the dark of night. You... just... never... know."

Everything stilled. Then the earl stood and rubbed his hands together. "I believe our business is satisfactorily concluded, gentlemen. We've taken up enough of Mr. Pickett's time. Good day, sir."

The earl led the way out, Mr. Masterson on his heels. Maxwell lingered a moment, but Pickett was staring down at his splayed hands on the desk. Pity rose for the man. He was but a pawn in the game afoot.

When they were safely ensconced in the carriage, the earl asked, "How are you at picking locks, Drake?"

"Rubbish, I'm afraid. I was an exploring officer during the war, not a thief."

"Send Penny along with him," Lionel said.

"No. I will accompany him." The earl's chin jutted, and his tone veered autocratic.

"That would be unwise, David."

"But blast it, I want to go." The earl's voice took on an unattractive petulance.

"You haven't fully recovered from your ordeal last year. The nights are too cold, and if you're caught, you couldn't run to safety. It's a game for younger men now." Mr. Masterson raised his eyebrows as if daring the earl to argue. He didn't. Only rapped his cane once in obvious frustration and looked out the window.

"Who's Penny?" Maxwell couldn't imagine a woman taking part in their clandestine activities. A picture of Bryn in breeches escaping out her window or sneaking through the woods came to mind. Perhaps he knew one woman up to the task.

"Pendleton is ostensibly our coachman, but he's a man of many talents," Mr. Masterson said.

Back at the town house, Maxwell directed Seamus out to watch the horses so the coachman with many talents could join them. Maxwell stopped in the study doorway. Bryn paced in front of the grate.

Another dress had been delivered, this one a cornflower blue. It was high-necked and long-sleeved but molded the supple curves of her body. Mrs. Wilson was as talented as any London modiste.

It appeared as if Mrs. Winslow's lady's maid had taken hold of Bryn, because instead of swinging around her shoulders, the silken mass of her hair was pulled back into a loose chignon, highlighting her delicate bone structure. In the sophisticated gown and with her hair back, she appeared polished and more mature, ripe and womanly.

If the chit began circulating socially in Edinburgh, a multitude of men would soon be panting after her. Better men than Armstrong certainly. Better than Maxwell as well—titled, landed men. Only if she wasn't carrying his child though. If that were the case, he wouldn't delay to make her his, whether she wanted him or not.

Suddenly grim, he imagined Bryn laughing at some other man with her big, chocolaty eyes. The urge to rip at something nearly overwhelmed him. No one noticed his inner anguish. He'd become adept over the years at hiding all emotions.

"Well, what news?" Bryn touched his arm. The light brush seemed to burn through the layers of wool and cotton to his bare skin, branding him.

Words deserted him.

The earl swept to a chair and pulled off his gloves, taking command of the room. "We have much to discuss, gentlemen."

Bryn lowered herself onto the edge of an ornate chair Maxwell had been afraid to test with his weight. "I'm not leaving."

The earl cocked his eyebrows, a half smile quirking his lips. Mr. Masterson settled into an adjunct armchair. Penny the coachman sidled inside, still cloaked and holding his hat. Dark hair hung to broad shoulders that gave the impression of a hulking frame under the greatcoat. His face was pockmarked and bland, but his eyes were bright and darted around the room. A twinkling stud in one ear reminded Maxwell of the adventure stories he'd discovered one afternoon in the vicar's room when he was ten.

"What do you know of this Mr. Sutherland?" Maxwell asked the earl in a gruff voice.

"Having circulated in Edinburgh for the past few weeks, Lionel and I have crossed paths with Sutherland several times now. He has money and respect, but something about the fellow strikes me as disingenuous. Lionel?"

"Agreed. I disliked him on sight. Are you acquainted with him, Miss McCann? For your brother-in-law and your intended seem to know him quite well."

Bryn shook her head. "Mary and Craddock never brought me with them to Edinburgh. What's his involvement?"

Mr. Masterson sketched out what they'd learned before adding, "After drawing up and witnessing your marriage contract, Mr. Buscomb of Glasgow was tragically and conveniently murdered by highwaymen."

"He died because of me, didn't he?" Bryn took a shuddery breath, her eyes on Maxwell.

"If he did die because of this business, the blame is not yours," Maxwell said.

"Does Sutherland have a copy of the marriage contract? Can we obtain it?" She scooted forward on her chair, her foot tapping.

"He's our most likely lead at the moment." The earl crossed his legs and shifted. "Lionel, didn't we receive an invitation to a dinner party at his house?"

"Indeed we did. I intended to send our regrets, but it seems we'll need to attend after all. I'll make our acceptance dependent on invitations issued to Drake and Miss McCann, as they're old family friends."

"Thank you so much for your help," she whispered.

The earl waved off her gratitude. "Really, m'dear, as I said earlier, you're doing us a favor. I haven't been so content in ages. I do love a good mystery."

"Speak for yourself," Mr. Masterson said dryly. "I enjoy touring crumbling old churches and castles myself."

"Bah. You always were a stuffed shirt, Lionel, moldering away at Wintermarsh."

"I love Wintermarsh, and more importantly, I loved helping Gray, Lily, and Rafe grow into admirable adults." Lionel Masterson's voice was edged with heat.

"You're entirely correct. I do apologize." The earl inclined his head, his voice strained.

Mr. Masterson rapped his hands on the arms of the chair. The tension dissipated. "Onto Drake's little problem. Penny, we have arranged for Mr. Pickett to leave a file on his desk containing Lord Ian MacShane's will."

"Should be easy enough to slip in, grab the papers, and get out, none the wiser." Penny's voice sounded as if it had been battered over rocks. "I was making notes of the windows and entrances while you gents were inside doing your business."

The earl tapped steepled hands on his chin. "Here's the rub: the file must be returned on the desk before morning. Mr. Pickett's family is in danger if certain parties are aware he handed the file over."

"That makes it twice as dangerous." Penny turned slightly to examine Maxwell. "You should come with me then and read it there. I don't fancy two rooftop scalings. Haven't had as much practice lately as I used to get. How're you in a tight spot, Mr. Drake? Will your leg hold up?"

"I'll pay dearly for the abuse tomorrow, but it'll hold up. I've been in more than my fair share of tight spots. I won't panic."

The discussion continued. Routes, times, meeting places. As an exploring officer, he'd learned to manage the long periods of boredom shot through with intense danger. The feeling of setting off on a mission wasn't foreign. Nevertheless, it had been years, and nerves had him bouncing his good leg. He hoped the instincts he'd relied upon to keep him alive hadn't been lost.

* * * * *

No one paid any attention whatsoever to Bryn, which wasn't, in fact, an unusual state of affairs. She welcomed her invisibility, staying as motionless as possible in her little chair. She'd been ready to put up a fuss if they'd attempted to banish her, but Maxwell had only stared at her with his mysterious eyes.

The need to find out what was in her betrothal papers was superseded by worry over the plan that emerged. Scaling rooftops, climbing walls, picking locks—Maxwell would get himself killed or hanged. What if his leg gave out at the wrong moment and he plummeted to his death? Her stomach crawled up her throat.

The men departed, and she laid in wait for him to return from seeing them off. The moment he stepped into the study, she pounced. "What the devil are you thinking, Drake? You can't climb a brick wall. Your leg will give out and you'll fall."

"Then I fall." His tone dispassionate, he moved to the desk to sort through a stack of papers.

"And leave me—" *Alone.* She didn't say it. Neither could she articulate why the thought was unbearable. "What if there's a babe?"

His head whipped up. The smoldering fire in his hazel eyes banished the cold dispassion. "I'll be as careful as possible, but I have to bury this part of my past."

"What does it matter what he bequeathed to you? You don't

need the money. Let it be." A begging note crept into her voice, and she laid a hand on his arm, needing to feel the warm life in his body.

"Do you have any idea what it was like growing up and seeing MacShane driving through Cragian in his fancy carriage doing nothing but splashing more muck onto me. Onto Mother. He never acknowledged me, never offered a ha'penny to help feed or clothe me. It got so bad after Mother got sick we nearly starved to death. I could have rotted in that hovel for all he cared."

The bitter vehemence in his voice made her tighten her hold on him.

"I want to know he had regrets. I want to know if he had to do it over, he would have—not acknowledged me perhaps—but showed a human level of decency and kept us from suffering. I was his *son*. The only thing that kept us alive were the baskets."

Bryn's hand drew into a fist around the wool of his jacket. He knew. He knew she was the one. His penetrating gaze laid her heart bare.

"Maxwell, I—"

"Wait. Have I been blind? Did *MacShane* send the baskets?"

Bryn choked out something between a sob and laugh. She shook his arm. "Please don't get yourself killed for a man who's already dead."

Agitation drained from his body, and he half sat on the edge of the desk, covering her hand with his. "Is it only for the babe that you care what happens to me, lass?" His voice had taken on the velvety texture he used when talking to his stock.

She was no better than a horse, because she swayed toward him and clutched at his lapel. "Of course not, you stubborn, demented man."

"Then why? What have I done except ruin you and nearly get you killed?"

"I bear the responsibility for my decisions." But she would

also claim the pleasure. Too much wanted to pour out of her. The past. The present. And even though the future was obscured by a dark curtain of uncertainty, she held hope close. Instead of revealing the maelstrom, she popped to her toes and kissed him.

He stilled, his lips soft against hers but unmoving. What had she done? Mortification stripped away the pent-up need and worry that had prompted the impetuous action.

She pulled away, but with his breath still warm on her cheek, he sprang to life, banding his arms around her and holding her close. Yet he didn't kiss her. Instead, he nuzzled her neck.

Unable to examine the affection in his actions while she was in his arms, she loosened her clutch on his jacket and skimmed her hands up his chest to wrap tightly around his neck. He trailed his lips across her cheek.

The wait for his lips to touch hers was excruciating, and her breathing shallowed. After an eternity, he kissed her. Not with the rough carnality of their one night together but with a gentleness even more devastating.

Her body awakened, memories of their joining searing away her questions and doubts until all that was left was the moment. Her knees wobbled, but the solid strength of his arms anchored her to his body.

He was her sun, keeping her in orbit and restoring gravity. And her sun was scorching, burning her fears to embers until all that was left was need and desire. Wrong or right, she wanted more.

He rotated them, scooped his hands under her buttocks, and lifted to sit her on the edge of the desk. Their tongues sparred. Papers fluttered to the floor around his feet. She parted her legs and cradled his hips. The pleasure he wreaked on her body was profound, but ecstasy lay further down the path they tread together. She was no longer an innocent.

He didn't rip her clothes off this time. His kiss calmed, and their stormy passion ebbed until she was left trembling on the shore. Yet he didn't release her or push her away. He ran his hands up and down her back and tangled his fingers in tendrils of hair that had escaped, the tug sending prickles of sensation through her body.

"I like your new dress and your hair." His rumbling, velvety brogue was like a physical touch as pleasurable as the kisses he trailed over her jaw.

"Do you? Better than my breeches?"

"While your arse is undeniably tempting in breeches, I don't like to think about other men appreciating you as I do."

"Do you appreciate me as much in a dress up to my neck?"

"It's a different sort of appreciation, imagining what's hidden under this lovely gown."

"You don't have to imagine." The inviting, pleading tone of her voice should have summoned embarrassment, but it didn't. All she could focus on was her desperation.

"I'm the only man who knows that what's underneath is more beautiful than the fine new trappings." He slid a hand from her ribcage to her breast. His thumb glanced over her nipple, and he captured her lips once more.

She ignited into a mass of nerve endings.

"Gracious me!" Edith Winslow stood framed in the study door.

As if a bucket of icy water had been poured over her head, she weakly pushed at his chest. Maxwell took a stuttering step backward and left her to lean against the edge of the desk and shake her skirts. Mary would have taken great pleasure in humiliating her and locking her away. What would Mrs. Winslow's punishment be for acting a wanton?

Bryn didn't wait to find out. She bolted past the woman and up the stairs to her room to hide.

CHAPTER FIFTEEN

Maxwell stared at the papers on his desk. He had work to finish and appointments to prepare for. The reckless enterprise to obtain his sire's last will and testament loomed. Yet his thoughts circled Bryn like carrion. If he didn't die from an unfortunate fall that evening, the sexual tension pushing and pulling at the two of them would kill him forthwith.

Did she recall their one night together every single time she closed her eyes? Did she have to fight the urge to sneak into his room? Would he have lifted her skirts and taken her on the desk if they hadn't been interrupted?

He pulled at his hair. Where was his honor? Was he no better than his father? The temptation she presented was torture. Bryn was under his care. No matter what had transpired to bring them to this point, she *was* an innocent. Too naïve and trusting.

Nothing would get accomplished until he burned off the frustration and aggression tightening his muscles. A hard ride wasn't possible in the city. But there was another place he could go. A pugilist salon on Waring Street. Maxwell grabbed his hat and cloak and set off on foot in the crisp, winter air.

Each stinging lungful of air regulated his heartbeat. He exhaled and concentrated on the white whirls. Cutting down a long narrow alley, he slowed as his ardor cooled and his leg twinged.

Boots clacked behind him, echoing off the stone walls eerily. The hairs on the back of his neck vibrated. Two steps later, a rough-hewn man wearing a tweed cap and coat entered the alley in front of him. Coincidence? Perhaps, but Maxwell's gut told him he wasn't going need the pugilist salon after all.

The approaching man was a stranger—short, lean, and with the look of an old tomcat who'd survived on the streets. The footsteps behind him made steady progress. Taking a peek would erode Maxwell's one advantage—surprise. He forced a smile as the capped man drew closer.

Maxwell was no stranger to hand-to-hand fighting. His time as an exploring officer for Wellington had been fraught with danger. Although he was sorely out of practice, the instincts that had kept him alive heightened as if he were back in the war. The intent in the man's eyes gleamed a heartbeat before his lunge. Maxwell met him with a jab across the bridge of his nose. A burst of red splattered down the man's chin. He staggered backward, hands cupped over his face.

Maxwell swung around. The second man was cut from similar cloth. Both were past the bloom of youth, grimy, and lit with desperation. The man's gaze darted between Maxwell and the other man. He stopped less than six feet away and crouched, pulling a knife from his boot and brandishing it as he inched forward.

With a grimacing smile, Maxwell slid a dagger from his boot as well and gestured him forward. The man slashed the knife toward Maxwell's midsection. Maxwell jumped to the side, and the man's momentum sent him stumbling forward, his shoulder bumping the brick wall.

Maxwell circled and took stock. His heart pumped hard and filled his ears with noise. Blood trickled out of the first man's nose, and he was doubled over, occupied by his own pain.

Maxwell concentrated on the man with the knife. He lowered his shoulder and slammed into the man's chest. The man's lungs emptied, and he went to his knees. Maxwell pressed his advantage, kicking him in the stomach and driving him to his back.

Maxwell trapped the man's wrist under a boot and pressed until his hand opened and the knife fell to the cobblestones. Maxwell kicked it away.

The first man staggered toward them, a penknife flashing in his hand. Before Maxwell could evade him or go on the attack, he careened into Maxwell and knocked him backward into the wall. The blade caught him on his left flank. The sharp edge cut through his clothes to flesh.

Maxwell jabbed an elbow into the man's throat and then again on his already battered face. The man fell to his knees. The second man scrambled up and ran, his foot strikes echoing. Did he sense defeat, or would he return with reinforcements? Time was short.

Maxwell crouched over the man on his knees, his side stinging. "Who hired you?"

"Bugger off."

Maxwell shoved him to the cobblestones, put his boot at the man's throat, and pressed. The man arched and his legs kicked. Maxwell pressed harder. "Let's try again. Who hired you?"

"The apprentice gang." The man's voice veered high from lack of air and fear.

The gang roamed the city, usually at night, robbing and beating lone, typically well-to-do gentlemen. They were generally discontented youth with no prospects. How in the world had Maxwell garnered their attention after a scant three days in town?

"Why me?"

"Dunno. Orders were to kill or maim you. Told us you were a cripple, for Christ's sake."

At the word "cripple," Maxwell ground his boot, inciting an airless groan and continued writhing. "I'm hardly a cripple. Now, I want a name."

"He'll kill me."

"*I'll* kill you if you don't talk." Maxwell forced a casualness he didn't feel into his voice and ran a finger down the blade of his dagger for show. He'd seen enough death to last a lifetime and didn't relish taking a life.

"If I answer, you'll let me go?"

Maxwell eased the pressure on the man's throat. "If it's a truthful one, yes."

"Danny McAfee."

"Tell me about him."

"He's naught but twenty and leads the whole gang." More than a hint of acrimony colored the man's voice.

Had the youthful uprising of out-of-work apprentices unbalanced the natural order of things in the underbelly of Edinburgh? "Who does McAfee answer to?"

"No one."

Maxwell narrowed his eyes. It was unlikely that McAfee rose to the top of the heap on his own. Still, the information should be easily obtained. Maxwell removed his foot. The man rubbed at his throat with both hands and took heaving breaths.

"I would recommend that you take a moment to gather yourself and exit at the opposite end of the alley. I'll not be so forgiving if you follow me. Do I make myself clear?"

"Aye, sir. I'll not follow you, sir." The man's nod was comically emphatic. Maxwell believed him. For now. Given another chance and more money, he would return.

Maxwell backed away, keeping his eyes on his adversary. The man sat up but otherwise didn't move. After putting a fair distance between them, Maxwell turned and forced an even gait. Out of danger and with the excitement ebbing, his side throbbed in time with his heartbeat. He pulled off a glove and pressed a shaky hand against the wound. His fingers came away bloody.

* * * * *

Expecting a shaming, Bryn joined Mrs. Winslow for tea. After all, Mrs. Winslow was her chaperone, and Bryn deserved a dressing down considering what she'd done with Maxwell and even more so considering what she'd *wanted* to do with him. Not that she planned to admit as much to Mrs. Winslow.

Bryn's nerves had her squirming on the settee, waiting for the tray of tea and preparing for the other woman's condemnation.

What Bryn endured was almost worse.

"—a footman, he was. Of course, I noticed the lad as he hauled my trunk up the stairs. All those bulging muscles. In fact, before he left the room, I noticed something else bulging and gave him—"

Maxwell threw the door open into the drawing room and leaned on the jamb. Bryn shot up, her tea sloshing, hopeful never to learn what Mrs. Winslow had given her brawny footman. The heat prickling her neck eased, and a smile born of relief came naturally.

Something was amiss. Maxwell's mouth and eyes were tight, and a gray pall marred his tanned complexion. Her smile wiped away, she took his arm. "What's happened?"

His eyes flared as they stared at one another. His gaze fell away, and he swallowed hard. "I was accosted. A wound on my side needs attention, but at the moment, I would very much appreciate a drink." His tone was so calm and polite he could have been discussing the weather.

Too much had passed between them, and too much simmered under the surface for her to be fooled. Not caring their chaperone perched on the settee with wide eyes, Bryn took his hand. Blood stained his trembling fingers. She guided him to sit.

"I'll gather supplies. Mrs. Winslow, could you fetch a tot of brandy?" Bloody linen peeked from a rip in his jacket under his left arm, but she was unable to tell how long or deep it was.

"Have you experience stitching cuts, lass?" His question set her own fingers trembling.

"None, and according to Mary, I've a useless hand at embroidery. I'll send for a physician."

"No. You do it."

"Maxwell, no, I—"

"Yes." He wrapped his hand around her nape and pulled her closer. "We're likely being watched. I don't want anyone to witness a physician visiting. You must do it. You birthed a breech babe. Stitching me will be simple. I have faith."

She feared his faith was misplaced. His hand fell to lie on the cushion, the blood in stark contrast to the cream upholstery. Mrs. Winslow held out a glass with brandy lipping the rim.

"A bit more of a tot, isn't it, Mrs. Winslow?" The amusement in Maxwell's voice steadied Bryn's knees. A mortal injury would surely stymy his bleak humor.

"Being accosted deserves more than a mere tot, Mr. Drake," Mrs. Winslow said.

"Mayhap you're correct."

He took a swallow and heaved a sigh. By the time Bryn had torn a clean sheet into strips and the hot water arrived, the glass was empty. The tightness around his mouth had eased, and his eyes were glassy.

Now that the moment was upon her, Bryn clutched the strips. "Show me the wound."

Maxwell's face creased as he struggled with his jacket. Bryn slipped her hands under the jacket, sliding it over his shoulders and off.

"Let me." She slid the disks free on his waistcoat and performed the same maneuver.

He picked at the torn fabric of his shirt and tried to see the wound. "How could you tell I was hurt?"

"Your eyes, your mouth, the way you moved," she whispered

as her hands gently tugged his shirt from the waistband of his breeches.

"Oh my. I can't... the blood." A handkerchief muffled Mrs. Winslow's voice. Pale, she sidled out of the room but left the door cracked open a foot.

Bryn pushed his shirt upward and eased it off. For a moment the sight of his bare chest held her arrested, his soiled, torn shirt clutched in her hands. But then her attention fixed on his wound, and she felt as sick as Mrs. Winslow had looked but for a different reason. Maxwell might have died.

The gash along his side was long. A little deeper or longer or closer to a vital organ, and they might be calling the undertaker. Blood oozed and trickled down his side in narrow rivulets of bright red. Pressing a folded piece of cloth against the gash, she touched her fingers against his heart. It beat solid and strong. Tears flooded her eyes.

He covered her hand with his and pressed it flat. "You're going to fix me, aren't you, lass?"

His skin was warm, the muscles underneath her hand hard and strong. He was counting on her. A shuddery, deep breath gained her a semblance of control, and she nodded.

Cleaning his wound was an arduous process. A multitude of fabric threads were stuck in the dried blood around and inside the wound, and as gentle as she tried to be, he flinched. Carefully extracting everything she could see, she poured a small amount of brandy over the top for good measure. He hissed. The worst was yet to come. She filled his glass again and waited until he'd drank a good portion down.

"Do it. I've been through worse with my leg."

The needle wavered in her fingers. She held her next breath, pinched the skin, and took her first stitch. He groaned through his teeth.

Seeing him in distress only increased the tremble in her hands.

Maxwell emptied the glass and laid his head back with a dark chuckle. "I've gone soft. I had to stitch myself up a time or two."

"I wouldn't say you've gone soft." Bryn touched a thin white scar along his ribs. He shifted, the muscles flexing.

Maxwell's head lolled back on the settee, and Bryn snuck glances at him as she continued her work, but the brandy seemed to have done its job.

As she took the last stitch, he asked, "Do you think about that night in Cragian?"

Bryn froze before coming to her senses and tying off the thread. "Sometimes."

A lie. She thought of their night together so often she worried she'd embellished the memory.

Maxwell gave a mirthless laugh. "'Sometimes,' she says, 'Sometimes.' That night haunts me."

Her heart spurred, and her face flushed. "The brandy has gone to your head."

"Perhaps." His voice was dreamy and faraway, his eyes barely open. "You told everyone that you're no great beauty. Balderdash. Why wouldn't that cretin Armstrong kill to have you in his bed? I might consider it if our positions were reversed." He listed farther over onto the settee, his head pillowed on a throw.

The daft man couldn't hold his liquor worth a quid. She touched her hair, the bane of youth. A ball of warm feelings in her chest muted the varied and numerous insults her sister had unleashed so many times they'd scored her heart.

His chest rose and fell with deep breaths. The shot of fear at how close he'd come to death was tempered by relief. He would have to bow out of the night's foolish errand with his injury. Perhaps the attack was a blessing in disguise. She pressed a clean linen bandage on the wound and worked long strips around his waist to keep it in place.

"Why can't you see your beauty, Bryn?"

His voice startled her. A fixed intensity banished the faraway look in his hazel eyes.

"No one noticed me in Mary's shadow. All the lads thought the sun rose and set with her—even you."

"I was a fool." No small amount of regret lurked in his voice. "Mary's beauty fades as yours blooms."

Could he be right? Was that why Mary had never given her a proper introduction into Society? This time when Maxwell's eyes closed, they stayed closed. A snuffling snore soon followed.

Bryn covered him with a blanket but stayed on her knees at his side. She allowed her fingers to play in his hair and trace his bottom lip. She had used him poorly in Cragian, too innocent to predict the events she would spin into motion. Yet it was difficult to summon the proper regret when he kissed her or talked of her as if he considered her worth fighting for.

She laid a hand over her belly. What would happen if she wasn't carrying his babe? Her heart wept. Leaving him would break it. Somewhere along the road to Edinburgh, she had fallen from childhood infatuation into love with him.

CHAPTER SIXTEEN

Maxwell bolted upright. The sudden movement sent a burst of fire across his side. He pushed the blanket off and checked Bryn's work. A neat row of stitches, the skin reddened but not inflamed.

He checked the time, pulled his ruined shirt over his head so as to not scandalize the servants, and dragged himself to his room to rinse his mouth and change into something less ripped and bloody. A light repast of bread and cheese settled his stomach. He wasn't sure whether it was the liquor, nerves over the night's endeavor, or his admissions to Bryn that was the cause.

By the time he emerged, feeling close to human again, the earl and Lionel were sitting side by side on the settee, sharing a pot of tea as Bryn paced by the window.

The earl set his teacup down and scooted to the edge of his seat. "Miss McCann informs me there has been another attempt on your life, but you're looking hardy and hale."

He didn't feel either. "I'm well enough. This time it was two hired thugs. Claimed that Danny McAfee, leader of the apprentice gang, hired them to kill or maim me."

The earl and Lionel exchanged a glance. Both looked worried, which in turn worried Maxwell. He'd expected the earl to scoff at the attempt as yet another adventure.

"They're opportunists. I've never heard of them targeting someone specific and in broad daylight." The earl rubbed a finger along his lip.

"They must have been watching the house. I went out unexpectedly and to nowhere they could have anticipated. They cornered me in an alley."

"Perhaps the gang is branching out into hired work."

"Perhaps, but I suspect someone else is giving McAfee orders. Any ideas who that might be?" Maxwell shot a look at the earl.

"I'm not in possession of such information. Yet." The earl's mouth twitched behind his finger. "Besides avoiding them, I haven't given those upstart apprentices much thought."

"Do they have a purpose?" Bryn had tucked herself next to the thick velvet drapes—her eyes bright and her chin sharp—like a bird at hunt.

For the first time, Lionel spoke. "They organized with grand ideals of better pay and shorter hours. Blame the system, not the men."

The earl made a phishing sound. "They're little better than common thieves."

"They're likely watching the house right now. Tonight's plan is foolish beyond the extreme." Bryn peeked out the front window before twitching the drapes closed.

"She's right," the earl said. "You'll need to sneak out the back."

Bryn stalked forward, the air crackling with her anger. "No. He should stay here. Safe. You're all fools. Well, perhaps not you, Mr. Masterson, as I haven't heard your opinion on the matter, but definitely you two." She wagged her finger back and forth at the earl and Maxwell.

The protectiveness in her voice gave him pause. It felt like more than a night bound them. "I'll be fine, I promise."

"You can't promise me that." She stomped a foot. "Let me help. I could stand guard outside the building. Or even scale the wall in your place. You're injured."

"Absolutely not." Maxwell rose, his throbbing side a reminder Bryn's point was valid. "You'd be a distraction, making it even more dangerous. Edinburgh is not safe at night. Or the day, for that matter. You are going to stay here with the earl and Mr. Masterson. Is that understood?"

She narrowed her eyes. "I understand." *But might not obey*, her defiant look said as if she'd spoken aloud.

He turned toward the two gentlemen. "Make sure she doesn't follow me. Tie her up if you have to."

"We'll do whatever's necessary," the earl said over Lionel's stumbling protests.

He stalked out the drawing room door, refusing to look back even though he wanted one more glimpse of her.

"Stop right there, Drake." Bryn grabbed his arm and pulled him around, his wish granted.

Anger radiated off her, but her eyes were soft, wide, worried. For him. How long had it been since someone had worried over his well-being? With her hair escaping its pins and her face flushed, she was lovely. He tucked a piece of hair behind her ear.

"Have you noticed you call me Drake when you're annoyed?" he asked softly.

"Keep yourself alive, *Drake*, or I'll never forgive you." She grabbed the lapels of his jacket and laid a hard kiss on his mouth. With an eviscerating look that seared, she turned on her heel and disappeared into the drawing room.

He felt like he'd taken a physical hit, shaken and off-balance. For the first time in forever, he had something to live for. Someone to survive for. Which was exactly the sort of thinking that would get him killed. He blew out a long breath and made his way through the narrow mews at the back of the town house, making friends with the shadows.

He moved behind the row of houses and tipped his hat at the random hostler that roused at his passing. No one raised an alarm.

Nearing the main thoroughfare and the tavern, Maxwell pulled his hat low and scanned the milling crowd of working men looking to take the winter's chill off with some ale and entertainment. The scene appeared wholly ordinary. He slipped inside and found Penny slouched at a corner table that afforded him a view of the front doors.

Penny gave him an almost imperceptible shake of his head, which Maxwell interpreted to mean they shouldn't be spotted together much less observed leaving together. He made his way to the bar and ordered an ale, not bothering to remove his hat, gloves, or greatcoat. He took a sip, his stomach protesting the addition of alcohol.

Penny weaved to the back of the tavern and disappeared down a narrow hallway. Maxwell left his ale for the front door and strolled down the street, waiting for Penny's signal.

"Are you ready then, sir?"

Maxwell reached for the knife in his boot before the voice registered as friend, not foe. Penny stepped out of the alley as if birthed from the darkness.

"As ready as I'll ever be. Did you learn anything of interest this afternoon?"

"Nothing of note. Typical sort of building. We'll head round to the back. Lucky for us, the ledges are wide. It should be an easy climb."

They reached the back of Dewey, Pickett, and Franklin, and without further ado, Penny fit himself to the bricks and climbed as if he were an eight-legged spider. If this was Penny out of practice, how good had the man been in his prime? Penny reached the second-floor ledge without a single misplaced foot. Maxwell, on the other hand, had scrambled for purchase half a dozen times, the wound on his side throbbing.

Penny checked the first window, found it latched, and moved on to the next. It opened soundlessly, and he swung himself inside. Maxwell's entrance was less graceful and louder. Penny shushed him, and Maxwell mimicked his stillness. The silence felt vast.

"Someone else is here," Penny whispered.

They had landed in a library of sorts. Leather-bound books lined one wall from floor to ceiling. Pickett's office was located at the front of the building. Penny guided them out and down the hall, unerringly toward their target.

They stopped outside, the boards under their feet creaking. A candle flickered from under the door, and the sound of drawers rattling came from inside.

Penny held up three fingers and counted down one finger at a time. Maxwell nodded, understanding the intent. At the signal, Penny threw the door open to reveal an open window and a snuffed, smoking candle on the floor. A stiff, cold wind blew papers around the office.

Maxwell ran to the window. A man dressed in black jumped the last dozen feet to the ground, rolled to his feet, and ran off with a limping gait. Penny pulled the window and draperies closed with a swift glance up and down the street to see if anyone bore witness to their predecessor's escape.

"Blast and damn." Penny was the picture of calm. "Let's see if the bounder got what we came for."

Maxwell wanted to wail and tear at his hair. So close. They'd been so close. They riffled through the papers, not finding MacShane's will. The man might have run off with it or it might well be buried under the mess.

Penny checked out the window through a crack in the drapes. "Sir, we shouldn't tarry."

Maxwell kicked and sent papers flying off the floor but led the way back to the library.

"Careful now. Coming down's a sight more difficult than going up." With that piece of comforting advice, Penny tossed a leg over the sill and made the descent look like child's play.

Maxwell took a deep breath and followed but left the window open. If Penny expected him to close it whilst balanced on the ledge, he could go piss in the wind.

Although it took Maxwell twice as long, he landed on the ground unscathed except for aching muscles and a sore side. Relief and eagerness to see Bryn offset the disappointment of the night, and he quickened their pace home.

* * * * *

Bryn meandered the drawing room and chewed on her nails. Mrs. Winslow had joined them for the vigil. While the earl and Mrs. Winslow engaged in half-hearted flirting, Lionel Masterson's attention wandered from her to his book, and though he seemed on the verge several times, he didn't speak.

Heavy footsteps echoed. She launched herself into the entry and scooted around Penny to Maxwell. Not caring who saw them, she ran her hands from his shoulders to his wrists and then from the top of his chest to his waist, cataloging that all his parts were in working order and there were no extra holes or gashes.

"You're alive. And unhurt?" None of the tightness from the afternoon was present around his mouth and eyes.

"I'm well enough. Although your confidence is underwhelming, lass." The amusement in his voice didn't dent her worry.

"Please don't make light. The evening has been torture. Imagining…"

Penny's voice rumbled indistinctly from the drawing room. She pressed her cheek against his chest, feeling the sharp edges of his buttons but needing to hear the strong cadence of his heartbeat. "Was it worth the risk?" she asked.

"We were beaten to the punch." Frustration stamped out any lingering humor. "The blighter escaped out the window before we could catch him. Left the office ransacked."

"I'm sorry."

He took her hand and squeezed before putting a proper distance between them and gesturing her into the drawing room to join the others. She stayed on the edges and observed.

The earl paced and tapped his temples as if trying to fit this new puzzle piece into the mystery. "Either the devil caught wind of our visit to Pickett and took it upon himself to get the will out of his hands, or Pickett himself betrayed us."

Penny swirled a glass of brandy, his hip propped against the window sash while taking the occasional peek outside. "He was damnably unprofessional. Pardon the language, ladies. I'm used to Miss Lily."

"What makes you say that?" The earl stopped and tilted his head.

"He'd no talent for tossing an office. Papers pulled out in droves from the drawers and scattered. The will could have very well been there, but there's no way any of us could have found it in that mess."

"Perhaps that was his intent," the earl said.

"Perhaps." Penny sniffed as if offended by the man's standards when it came to the proper techniques of breaking and entering. "His exit was none too skillful either. Climbed the front face where anyone could have seen him, panicked, fell the last dozen feet or so, and then limped off."

Lionel rubbed his chin. "Whereas the men who attacked Drake in the alley were paid professionals. Could we be dealing with two different factions, gentlemen?"

"It's possible. Considering Bryn and I are both seeking information no one wants found." Maxwell ran a hand over his face and sat, unable to mask a wince.

It took all her willpower to not hover over him. Instead, she took the seat across from him and fisted her hands in her skirts.

The earl's voice danced on the edge of urgency and excitement. "Unless we want to wait until someone actually manages to kill Drake off, it's imperative we attend Sutherland's dinner party."

"Should I reconnoiter Sutherland's house?" Penny asked.

The earl rubbed his hands together. "The man will likely hire on more servants for the house party. Offer yourself up as a footman, Penny."

"I can't abide fancy duds, sir. They make me feel strangled." But Penny's voice was resigned, his protest weak.

"A few days is all we need. It'll allow you to get inside and see what this Sutherland gent is really like. See if the rumors are true. Think of our advantage if we know the layout beforehand. It will save us considerable time."

"I'm *supposed* to be retired." Penny emptied his glass with a swallow and clunked it down on the table. "I spent three lovely years with Miss Lily, tending flowers and driving her around London. Very relaxing—minus the incident with Penhaven."

"Men like us never retire, Penny." The earl's half smile was met by a snort.

"Only because men like you won't let me."

"I'll forge you a reference, and we'll hire a temporary driver tomorrow."

"Aren't you all forgetting something?" Bryn popped up. Everyone's gaze on her sent a flush up her neck, but she concentrated on Maxwell. "The dinner is days away. How will you stay alive until then?"

"I can take care of myself."

She huffed.

"They've tipped their hand. I'll stay close to home and away from dark alleys. I can certainly take appointments here instead of traveling," he said.

"How's your venture progressing, Drake?" the earl asked.

"Almost too well. Between the letters of introduction from Lady Minerva and yourself, I have more work than I can reasonably handle. Enough to hire a clerk or two once things settle."

"That's wonderful news." Lionel rose. "It's late, and this old body isn't used to keeping London hours. David, why don't you rouse poor Edith?"

Mrs. Winslow listed toward the armrest like a ship whose ballast was uneven. The earl touched her shoulder, and she came to as if she had only blinked her eyes shut. The earl escorted her to the bottom of the stairs and kissed her hand before following Lionel and Penny out the door with farewells.

Maxwell pressed a hand against his side for an instant before casting her an inscrutable look and disappearing into his study.

Mrs. Winslow trudged up the stairs, stopping halfway. "Are you coming, Miss Bryn?"

Bryn stood at the bottom of the stairs, her hand on the banister. She glanced back at the closed door of the study. "I should check Maxwell's stitches."

"I'll trust that's all you'll be checking?"

Considering the state in which Mrs. Winslow had found her and Maxwell earlier that day, she could hardly blame the woman for asking. "Of course that's all."

Mrs. Winslow descended far enough to lay a hand over Bryn's. "Darling girl, I understand something of love. But if you want your Mr. Drake to come up to scratch, you must play a more elusive game."

Bryn swallowed. If this was a game, the rules were a mystery.

Mrs. Winslow squeezed her hand, her expression unusually

serious, before turning and climbing the stairs. Bryn waited until she heard Mrs. Winslow's door close before she tentatively knocked on the study door.

"Enter." His voice rumbled.

There was time to escape. She could hie to the stairs and lock herself in her room. Her hand trembled on the latch. Crossing over the threshold seemed tantamount to crossing another line.

Discarding all common sense, she slipped inside. Slumped in an armchair, Maxwell looked worn and haggard, his face pale, his eyes drawn. All her doubts took flight. He needed her.

"Do you feel feverish?" She placed a hand on his forehead. Not to run her fingers along the hair at his temples or to trail down his cheek, although that's what her errant hand did anyway. "Let me check your stitches. With the carrying on, you might have ripped them."

"Not feverish, just bone-tired." He acquiesced to her demands, pulling his shirt from his breeches and twisting to the side.

She unwound the bandage. He'd bled through the cloth, but her stitches had held with no sign of angry red skin or pus. She rewrapped the wound. Maxwell dropped his shirt and settled into the chair with his knees spread wide and his hands dangling off the armrests, his eyes closed.

He was a stern, sometimes dour man. Others might call him cold. But she knew better. Their night together had proven him to be flesh and blood, passion and heat. And countless times afterward, she'd glimpsed the boy she'd been infatuated with behind his gruffness.

She drank him in. From his dark hair to his sensuous mouth, across his broad shoulders and chest to the bulge she could see faintly outlined by the black woolen breeches.

"I'm not sure what's going on in that head of yours, but if you keep staring like that, my breeches are likely to combust."

Bryn's gaze popped up to find his half-lidded eyes on her. She backed to the door. "I should go. Mrs. Winslow…"

Emotion seethed in the depths of his eyes. Not cold at all, but an inferno. Yet he didn't speak.

She fled to her room, cursing her cowardice, and dreamed about a wholly different outcome to the evening.

CHAPTER SEVENTEEN

The next days passed in fits and starts. The invitation to Sutherland's soiree arrived, and Mrs. Wilson appeared twice for fittings. The midnight-blue fabric Maxwell had chosen had been fashioned into a gown so beautiful it took Bryn's breath away.

She was a far cry from the skinny girl who'd spent most of her youth in breeches. The dress showcased the curves of a woman, the fabric light and airy and fairylike. What would Maxwell think?

She had barely seen him. He spent his days meeting with genteel, well-dressed gentlemen and widows and locked himself behind his study door in the evenings. Whatever intimacies had passed between them seemed forgotten. By him, at any rate.

Whenever the earl and Lionel Masterson came by, the gentlemen retreated to the study. The exclusion grated. Was she not as much a part of this as Maxwell?

Observing a disaster unfold, especially as her actions had set the disaster into motion in the first place, didn't sit well. Her natural inclination to help along with a hefty dose of guilt left her feeling at sixes and sevens.

On the third such evening, the bell pull brought everyone to the entry. Henry opened the door, and Penny stepped inside. A young woman followed close behind, her eyes furtive and darting. She refused to give up her cloak, clutching it around her body. She took a step into Penny, and he put his hands on her shoulders, forcing her in front of him.

"It's all right now, Gertie. You're safe here."

Bryn forced a smile in the face of the girl's fear and held out a hand as if taming a wild animal. The girl was naught more than ten and six. "My name's Miss Brynmore, Gertie. And this is Mrs. Winslow. It's a cold night. Would you care for some tea in front of a warm fire?"

"There's nothing to fear here, girl. They're good sorts." Penny's voice rumbled, sounding more intimidating than comforting, but the girl nodded, her shoulders unfurling from their defensive scrunch.

Bryn never took her gaze off the girl nor let her smile lapse. "Come and warm yourself."

Gertie took a handful of steps forward, glancing over her shoulder at Penny. Only when Penny put a hand on her back to guide her forward did she enter the drawing room as if expecting a trap to spring.

The earl, Lionel, and Maxwell entered with raised voices and loud footfalls. Gertie scurried toward a corner, her panic palpable. Bryn shushed them with a hard, warning look. The girl was terrified, and being questioned by any one of them might make her retreat into silence.

"Gertie has information, if she's willing to share it with you all," Penny said.

Gertie's fear centered on the wall of masculinity that filled the room. Bryn touched the girl's arm and whispered sotto voce, "They look intimidating, but they're pussycats. I promise."

"Meow," Maxwell intoned with a quirk of his lips.

"Don't worry about them at all. Will you tell me what you can about Sutherland?"

The young girl stared down at her hands. They were red and chapped, the nails broken in places. "I'm a maid of all work for Mr.

Sutherland. Jobs are hard to come by, and it's been good money, but I'm a good girl, I am."

"You seem like a very good girl, Gertie," Bryn said gently.

"Go on. It's all right," Penny said.

"Whispers about Mr. Sutherland had made it to me ear before I applied for the position, but I have younger sisters to help take care of. Ma is all alone since Da passed." She paused a moment to look around. "He's never... not with me, but I've heard the others talk."

"About what?" Bryn asked gently.

Gertie's voice dropped. "Sometimes he brings a girl into his room. There's talk of boys too. And him wearing fancy gowns."

A pall blanketed the room. Bryn wasn't sure what she'd expected, but not the outrageousness of Gertie's claims.

The earl chuffed. "Sutherland would make a right handsome woman. What do you think, Lionel?"

A shocked sounding laugh spurted out of Lionel. "I must say that was a bit of a suprise."

The information spun in Bryn's head as she tried to make sense of it. Her gaze sought Maxwell's, full of questions he most likely wouldn't answer for her.

Sure enough, his gaze skittered away, a flush coloring his face. "It's scandalous to be sure, but how does it relate to our problem?"

"Perhaps it doesn't," the earl said, "but information is valuable and can be bought and sold like goods. If true—or even if it's only rumors—the information could provide leverage for Miss McCann's marriage settlement."

"I'd best get back." Penny turned his hat in his hands and shot a look toward Gertie. "I don't think she should return to Sutherland's. Is there something here for her?"

Gertie sidestepped toward Penny. "I'll not be burden or charity case. I'll—"

Maxwell cleared his throat. "Miss Bryn requires a lady's maid. I hadn't had the chance to advertise for one, but I'm a believer in fate, and it seems to me, we can help each other. You don't ever have to go back to Sutherland's again, if you don't want."

Color burst in Gertie's cheeks, marking her as almost pretty. "I'm good with hair, I am."

"Will Gertie suit, Bryn?" Maxwell asked without taking his eyes off the young girl.

"She will indeed." Although she was unlikely to find in Gertie the kinship she'd felt with Sarah, it would be nice to have someone nearer her age in the house. For as long as she would be here, at any rate. Bryn led her out into the entry where Penny swept his cloak on. "I'll introduce you to Mrs. Soames, the housekeeper. She'll get you settled into a room."

"Do be careful, won't you, Mr. Pendleton?" Gertie said.

"Don't worry about me, miss. I'll sleep with one eye open." He gave her an exaggerated wink. Gertie's giggle was high-pitched and relieved. He slipped out the front door as if he were oiled, a cold winter draft the only evidence left behind.

Bryn introduced Gertie to Mrs. Soames and worked out the details of her employment. By the time she returned, the drawing room was empty. She rapped on the study door. Nothing. She raised her hand to knock again, when the door opened.

"Did you get the girl settled?" Maxwell asked.

"I did." She took a step forward, but he didn't step back or invite her into the room. He was alone. "She's as skittish as a mouse. I wonder at what she's seen and heard."

"I hope hiring her as your maid was acceptable."

"It was very quick thinking and kind of you."

He rubbed his nape. "Yes, well, good night then."

He shut the door in her face, and she stomped a foot. She veered between sadness and anger at the walls Maxwell had erected so easily.

Bryn woke at dawn after troubled dreams. In them, she'd been tossed on stormy seas, powerless against the forces of wind and water. Her ability to steer her own ship was gone. That had to change. If there were decisions to be made about *her* future and *her* life, she planned to be a part of them.

She lurked outside Maxwell's study. A well-heeled gentleman with a bushy white mustache exited and shook Maxwell's hand.

"Can't tell you how delighted I am with our arrangement, Mr. Drake. The earl spoke so highly of you, and your portfolio is impressive. Always had my money in sheep, but your tactic of spreading the risk is sound. Can't tell you how much sleep I've lost during some of our harsh winters, wondering if the flocks would survive."

"It's my pleasure, Mr. Lowry. I look forward to our association. You should expect to receive quarterly reports."

"It was certainly worth the trip down from Kinross."

Bryn started and spoke without thinking. "Kinross?"

Both men turned. She took a step back into the shadows but then clenched her jaw and forced herself forward. If she wanted power, she had to claim it.

"Terribly sorry to interrupt, but my mother was from Kinross," she added.

The old man blanched as if he'd seen a ghost and swayed backward, the doorjamb halting his retreat. "It's impossible."

Bryn exchanged a glance with Maxwell. His eyebrows rose as if to say, *Go on now that you've started.*

"I'm Brynmore McCann, sir. My mother was Katherine Kinnon before she wed. Did you know her?"

The man's mouth moved, but nothing came out.

"Perhaps a chair, Maxwell?" Bryn stepped forward, worried the man might swoon.

Maxwell caught one arm and Bryn the other, and they guided him back into Maxwell's study and into a chair situated across from his desk. She came around and squatted at his knees, putting them closer to eye level.

"Are you well, sir?" She covered his trembling hand.

His mustache quivered on the start of a smile. "Katherine's daughter."

"You knew my mother?"

"Aye. Your grandmother was heartbroken when Katherine left Kinross for the south and even more so when news of her death reached us. But we were told she and her babe died?"

"They did, but that was to be my brother. I lived. My grandmother?" The word bounced around her head until the reverberations could be felt in her heart. She'd been told she had no family left.

"You look so much like her it's uncanny." He covered one of Bryn's hands in both of his. "No one was told of a daughter. Your grandmother will be thrilled."

Now instead of giving comfort, she clutched the man's hands for balance. The revelation left her light-headed. "Are you saying that I have a grandmother who is alive?"

"She was hale when I left her at the house yesterday morn," the man said with a twinkling smile. "We married two summers past, both having lost our spouses years ago. I suppose that makes me your grandfather of a sort."

"Why was I never told?" She didn't expect an answer. Anyone who might know was either in Cragian or dead.

Maxwell cupped her elbows and helped her rise. She leaned into his strength as he guided her to the seat next to Mr. Lowry.

"No one mentioned a grandmother?" Maxwell asked.

Bryn rifled through her early memories. "Not that I can recall, but I was naught but five when Mama passed. Papa paid me no mind. He was obsessed with siring a male heir. I wouldn't put it past Mary to keep the information from me out of spite. Or to use it when it would be most advantageous to her."

Mr. Lowry gnawed on his upper lip, his mustache dancing. "Miss Katherine and Winnie, your grandmother, left things in a poor state. She didn't approve of your papa being a widower and so much older than Miss Katherine. Winnie has lamented their falling out more times than I can count. Not setting things right before your mother died has haunted her. Stubbornness runs in the family, it does."

"I would have never guessed." Maxwell directed a wry smile toward Bryn.

"Do you think she would want to see me?" Bryn asked in a small voice.

"Want to see you? She'd insist upon it. In fact—" Mr. Lowry looked back and forth at the two of them. "I'm not privy to your current situation, but you can rest assured you'll always have a home with us."

"Bryn is being attended by a chaperone while staying in Edinburgh." Dark truths hiding under the surface roughed his voice. Their gazes locked, and like applying a flint, a fire sparked to life no matter the distance he was trying to put between them.

"You're a fine gentleman, Mr. Drake. And I'm sure Winnie will want to thank you for taking care of her granddaughter. I'll send word this very day, but I know she would want me to extend an invitation for you to stay with us in Kinross at your earliest convenience, Miss McCann. And yourself as well, Mr. Drake."

Welcome was evident in the man's expression. Her throat tightened. "I would be most happy to visit once my business in Edinburgh is concluded."

"Winnie will mean you to stay, Miss McCann, I can assure you of that. You could even open up your house if you want. It's been vacant for several years but in good repair."

"My *house?* Whatever do you mean?"

"Why, the house that was left to you on your grandpapa's death. Oh goodness me, of course, you don't even realize... Well, you're an heiress, my dear. The house is nothing grand like you'd find in London perhaps, but it has several bedrooms and a grand dining area and even a small ballroom."

"A ballroom?" Her imagination couldn't keep pace with the revelations. Even Maxwell looked stunned.

"Part of the money you're investing, Mr. Drake, is rightfully Miss McCann's, of course." He sounded genuinely thrilled.

After years spent observing Mary's ambition for more money and power, Bryn couldn't fathom his jolly acceptance of her existence. She searched his face for ulterior motives. "You don't mind?"

"My dear girl, Winnie and I are rattling around up there alone. My boys are dead and Miss Katherine too." His eyes gleamed with tears although his lips were still turned up into a smile. "This news is a godsend. A miracle."

"I don't know what to say," Bryn said.

"Say you'll come to Kinross as soon as you're able. Mr. Drake has our direction. I'll start to Kinross as soon as my business is concluded to prepare for your arrival. I can't wait to see her reaction to the good news." Mr. Lowry rose, and Bryn followed suit. His energy was infectious. The three of them made their way to the door. "Perhaps you could write to her, Miss McCann."

"Of course. I'll write her this very hour."

Mr. Lowry enveloped her hand in both his gnarled hands and nodded as if affirming she was flesh and blood before taking his leave.

"Well then." Maxwell's voice rumbled. He gestured toward the study, and she followed him like an automaton.

"I had family who wanted me, Maxwell. All those years..." The lump formed from the loneliness and torment of growing up with a father who barely acknowledged her and a sister who hated her.

"All those years made you who you are today. Anyway, if you had left Cragian, what would have happened to me?"

"Wh-what?" She tensed.

"There would have been no one to save my hide in the forest after I bashed my head."

He still hadn't guessed about the baskets. The pinpricks of relief were bittersweet. "If I had left, there'd be no one out to kill you in the first place."

He propped his hands on his desk, his gaze on the tips of his boots. One of his fingers tapped the desk like a timekeeper. Then all his fingers took up the beat. He was like a spring ready to pop or a snake to strike. He pushed off the desk and paced, the sound muffled by rugs. Yet she could feel each boot heel strike in her chest.

"I suspect Mary was aware of not only your grandmother but your inheritance as well. I would wager that's what Dugan would have received upon your marriage," he said.

The dark place in her heart recognized his suspicion as truth. Mary had used her with little thought for her happiness. "What was Mary receiving in return?"

"What does she want above all else?"

"Respect. Adulation. Power."

"Perhaps Dugan had promised them a cut of your inheritance once you were married?"

"No, not money. Craddock and Mary have plenty." Now more than ever, she needed to play a part in finishing the drama with Mary. "I can discover her plan at Sutherland's party. Her tongue gets the better of her when she's provoked. And no one can provoke her like I can."

"The earl and Penny are trained operatives, Lionel is a

solicitor who understands legalities, and I have war experience. How would your provoking Mary further our goal?"

The fact she had no good answer for his question did nothing to quash the fury that alit within her. "This is as much my problem as yours. Why won't you allow me to help?"

"Because those people have tried to kill us already. Why won't you allow me to protect you, woman?" After days of presenting a blank slate of indifference, the raw emotion in his face and voice was startling to see. "It would kill me to see you hurt." The admission cost him dearly.

"How do you think I feel when you're injured because of me?" She put them toe-to-toe and tipped her head back. "I want this over and done with before they actually succeed in killing you, you blasted man."

He caressed her cheek with his fingertips. His touch held memories of their one night together and promises of more. He might not love her, but he wanted her. Something he'd awakened in her rose and stretched in anticipation.

"You'll do as I say, Bryn." His face had softened, but his voice retained its autocratic bent.

If she let go of her anger, what was left was even more dangerous. She'd cared for Maxwell as a child, but as a women, her feelings ran deeper and stronger. It was the difference between a shallow, bubbling brook and a loch with waters so deep you could drown in them. Bryn was drowning, and like a drowning woman, she clung to her anger like a buoy.

She turned on her heel and stomped a retreat to her room. Gertie jumped away from the closet at her entrance and tried to dart out with a mumbled apology. It wasn't until she had almost made her escape that Bryn noticed her tear-streaked face.

"What's amiss, Gertie? Is it your room?"

"No, miss. My room is very nice, and I don't even have to share it." For some reason more tears gathered and her chin quivered.

"Then what is it? Tell me you don't miss working for Sutherland."

"Certainly not. Last night was the best night's sleep I've had in ages, but my friend, Elspeth—" She covered her mouth.

"You're worried for her, aren't you?"

"Aye. She's naught but five and ten and pretty. Prettier than I. If she catches his eye…"

Bryn straightened her shoulders. If it had been Sarah in such a fix, Bryn would have gone to hell and back for her. "I'll get word to Penny. He can smuggle her out and bring her here."

"But this is a small house. Mr. Drake won't want another mouth."

"Let me handle Mr. Drake. You run along to Mrs. Soames, and I'll let you know how I get along this evening."

Bryn waited until Gertie was gone before returning to the study. She knocked and entered before Maxwell answered. A gray-haired man turned in his seat, and Maxwell half rose, his impatience with her interruption writ large across his face.

"Excuse me, gentlemen. Mr. Drake, may I have a word?" Her dress had turned into an oven hot enough to boil water. She retreated to the entry.

Maxwell joined her, closing the study door softly behind him and whispering, "What's the matter?"

"Gertie is quite upset because she has a friend at Sutherland's that may be in danger."

"In danger how?"

"From his roving eye toward young, pretty girls."

"Has he acted inappropriately with the girl?"

"I don't believe so."

Maxwell's gaze darted to his study door.

"Not yet anyway," she added. "But she's an innocent."

"This information is from a young girl we barely know. One who may be prone to dramatics." Maxwell shuffled a hand through his hair. "What would you have me do? Knock on his front door and tell him I'm there to save all the young, pretty girls in his employ? That would be foolish in the extreme."

"We can't do nothing."

"You can't save everyone, Bryn. It's not practical. What I can do is send word to Penny to look out for the young girl and—"

"Elspeth."

His mouth softened with his sigh. "Elspeth. I'll do what I can. Now, I have to finish with Mr. Marlowe." He disappeared behind the study door.

You can't save everyone. The words echoed through her. She'd learned the truth of them many years ago, but she could save one. Like she'd saved Maxwell.

CHAPTER EIGHTEEN

That evening, Maxwell sipped on whisky and half listened to the earl and Lionel argue over the plans for Sutherland's dinner party. He couldn't tear his thoughts away from Bryn. She'd been so earnest in her desire to help, not just with the investigation but also with the young maid caught in a terrible situation. He'd done as he'd promised and sent word through the earl to Penny about Elspeth. He could do nothing more.

A knock on the front door was a welcome interruption. Wearing finer clothes than Maxwell had ever seen him in and with his hair pulled back into a queue and his earring gone, Penny was transformed. While he would never rank as the most handsome of footmen, he was a far cry from the piratical, shadowy man who scaled walls and spied.

The earl stood as Maxwell led him into the study. "What's the matter? Why aren't you at Sutherland's? Were you followed?"

Penny looked affronted. "O'course I wasn't followed. What do you take me for? A green recruit?"

"Out of practice." The earl sank back down, his lips twitching.

"I'm here to pass on the sketch I made of the house. However, there's a more pressing matter. Unless I'm mistaken, I just saw Drake's young lady scale out of a back second-floor window on a rope made of sheets. Wearing breeches." Penny dipped his head toward Maxwell.

Heat whooshed through Maxwell. He was torn between screaming and laughing. Brynmore was taking her fate into her own hands.

"Is she running away?" Lionel asked, half rising.

"Impatient with our all male schemes and taking matters in hand, more likely. Did you pass along my message to Penny, my lord?"

"Not yet." The earl waved his hand. "It seemed insignificant compared to the greater plan."

Of course the fate of a little maid wouldn't matter to a man like the earl. Bryn was different. Her kindness made her vulnerable. And brave and wonderful.

He tucked a knife into his boot and, after a moment's hesitation, took the cane from where it leaned unused in the corner. The blasted thing represented weakness yet could also be used as a weapon.

"You're going after her." Lionel had a knowing smile on his face.

"Of course." His barked answer crackled with emotion. He cleared his throat and forced a flat, dispassionate tone. "It's dangerous, especially this time of night. Too many men out of work with idle hands and hungry bellies. Those gangs would see her as an easy mark, and heaven forbid they discover she's a woman." He jammed his hat on his head. "I trust you gentlemen can let yourselves out."

"Take Penny," Lionel said.

Penny gestured down his body to his heeled shoes. "I'd be more of a liability than help dressed like this. Anyway, I must get back before questions are raised."

Penny pointed Maxwell in the right direction, and he moved down the street as fast as his leg would allow. First he would spank her. No. First he would kiss her, and then he would spank her.

Panic threatened to overwhelm him as various scenarios, each more dire than the last, took hold of his imagination.

Lanterns cast dim circles of light that only succeeded in making everything beyond appear even darker and more sinister. Small groupings of men, a few women, and three skinny, grubby boys populated an intersection in front of a tavern. No sign of Bryn and decision to be made. Which direction?

Feeling time slip like sand through his fingers, Maxwell made his way over to the boys, one of whom quickly hid something in his pocket.

Maxwell swept off his hat and leaned on his cane to appear less forbidding. "Hallo, lads. I'm looking for someone and was hoping you could help me. A redheaded… lad." He fumbled over the word, not sure if she had passed as a man.

The boys burst out laughing. "You mean a redheaded lady in breeches?"

Maxwell gritted his teeth. "Yes. Which way did she go?"

"It'll cost you, guv." The lad, who couldn't be more than ten and two, spoke with the bravado of a man.

Maxwell pulled out a ha'penny.

Another lad, older but perhaps not wiser, piped up. "But, Billy, the pretty lady gave us more."

Billy raised an eyebrow at Maxwell.

"Well now, I can best her, I believe." Maxwell pulled a sovereign out of his pocket, and their eyes grew as round as saucers. He acted like he was ready to flip it to them but pulled his hand back at the last minute, teasing them with the small fortune.

"First, information. When was the lady here, and where did she go?"

Billy stared at the sovereign Maxwell rubbed with his fingers. "She was here naught five minutes ago, sir. She wanted directions to Hightower Road. Looking for a certain house, and she asked if we knew anything about a man named Sutherland."

"And do you?" Maxwell asked.

In the lad's eyes was knowledge no boy should have. "We've all heard the rumors."

"Which direction did you point her?"

Billy rubbed the back of his neck. "Well, guv, there's the rub. I'd not be a good Christian lad if I sent that lovely lady to Sutherland's house this late at night. There's no telling what sort of mischief she might fall prey to."

How did Bryn do it? How did she befriend every man, woman, and child in her path? "She won't be safe until I see her home."

"You promise you don't mean to hurt her?" Billy asked.

"I only want to protect her." The sincerity and desperation in his voice was all too real.

He and Billy locked eyes for a long moment. Finally the boy nodded. "Right then. I sent her that way." He pointed toward a street that fell quickly into shadows. Blessing the bit of good luck, Maxwell flipped him the coin.

* * * * *

Bryn stopped, put her hands on her hips, and turned in a slow circle. This didn't seem right at all, but it was the direction the young boy had pointed her in. His confidence and sweet face had inspired her trust.

The street grew narrower and the stoops on either side looked more and more dilapidated, the smell of poverty growing more apparent. Sutherland lived in a more affluent part of Edinburgh, and she still hadn't crossed Hightower Road. She could ask someone or turn tail and go home.

The street was deserted. In the sudden stillness, the clack of boot heels reverberated off stone. Tendrils of fear coursed through her, and she froze. Run or hide?

Running with no idea where she was going might get her into even more trouble. The alleys were dark. She would wait until the man passed and then make her way back toward the crowded square and home. Her righteous anger had faded, leaving a sick recognition that tonight's mission had been foolhardy at best, dunderheaded at worst, and prompted by hurt feelings and pride.

She darted into a dim alley on her left and huddled in the gray shadows, unable to move deeper into the darkness. The mystery of what lay beyond her vision turned her feet leaden. Whatever it was smelled horrible.

The *clack* grew louder and closer. She tried to sink into the craggy stone. *Go by, go by, you don't want me.* Her prayers went unanswered. The man stopped before he passed the opening. A black, hulking menace.

Bryn's heart beat in her ears. Could men smell fear? She was rife with it, her palms clammy against the cold stone. The man pivoted toward her and took two steps with a noticeable limp.

"Maxwell." She breathed his name. Relief made her dizzy.

"What in blazes possessed you to venture out alone at night? Firstly, you could have broken your pretty little neck scaling out your window, which I am nailing shut tomorrow, by the by. Secondly, anyone could have accosted you on the streets. Thirdly, if that young boy hadn't steered you in the wrong direction, you could be fighting off, from all accounts, a sexually depraved lunatic. Good God, woman—"

She launched herself at his chest, rocking him back on his heels. While normally she would defend herself, she was so happy he was here her eyes filled with tears. Wrapping her arms tightly around him, she burrowed against his warm, muscular chest and was relieved when his arms came around her.

"You're right," she said.

"I am?" The consternation in his voice made her want to

smile, but fear had only loosened its grip, not retreated.

"I was angry you brushed me off this afternoon. That girl needs help, Maxwell."

"Penny is aware. Even if you'd managed to get Elspeth out, she would be replaced by another girl and another. Sutherland must be exposed to be stopped. He's the head of the snake."

"You're absolutely correct, of course. I've been reckless and foolish." Her voice was thick from the tears caught in her throat.

"You scared the bloody hell out of me." He ran his hands down the length of her body as if to assure himself she was in one piece.

"I'm dotty, dippy, and soft-headed. Yell at me some more. I deserve it."

"You're safe. We're safe. After our long walk home, I might still take you across my knee though." The slight tease in his voice settled any worries he might be serious. He rubbed his chin alongside her temple, dislodging her hat. "I found you. Thank God, I found you."

She tightened her arms around him, grateful to be found.

Men's voices, raucous with drink, echoed. "The toff headed down this way. Can't have got far with that limp."

A lantern sent long shadows down the street and clawing into the alley, leaving nowhere to hide. Maxwell muttered a curse and gestured for her to move farther into the depths. Bryn pulled her hat low and shuffled backward, keeping her footsteps soft and her eyes on the alley opening.

Her heart, which had barely recovered from her ordeal with Maxwell, sprinted away and left her body trembling.

A man made large by a lantern's light filled the alley entrance. "Here we are then. Another gentleman as well? Two fer one." Three men gathered behind the outspoken leader, enough to block any escape. Short bludgeons swung or tapped against legs.

The alley ended in a wall of brick, too high to jump or climb. They were trapped. It was only a matter of when and how the men won.

This was her fault. Her foolishness. Maxwell clutched his cane like a short quarterstaff. He would put up a good fight, but too many men pressed into the alley. Would they kill Maxwell? What would happen when they realized she was a woman?

If only she could spirit them back in time before anger got the better of her. She would never forgive herself if Maxwell was hurt.

* * * * *

Maxwell studied the men clogging the alley. No, more boys than men. Untested and untried in true battle. They viewed him as a weak target. While his limp hampered his ability to run, he had faced worse odds in close-quarter fights.

A deadly, cold calm washed through him. Not wholly unfamiliar, but it had been years since he'd faced death. No matter the cost, he would protect Bryn.

"What are you gents after? My purse?" Maxwell slid his cane so a hand rested on each end and deftly unlatched the hidden clasps.

"For a start. Why don't you both toss over your purses, and we'll consider going easy on you?"

"I decline your kind offer."

The man chuckled and shook his head. "Fine then. Mar him, lads!"

Three men moved forward, but the alley was narrow enough to allow only two to advance shoulder to shoulder. The other man trailed ineffectually. Maxwell whipped his arms to the side, releasing a short saber and a dagger from his cane. The men stopped. One looked over his shoulder at the leader.

"Go on then, don't be bashful." The cocky leader shoved the

closest man forward.

Maxwell's instincts took over. He cut the man across the chest and shoved him away. Behind him, Bryn let out a squeal as the man howled. The leader pushed another man closer. This man brought his bludgeon up with a holler, leaving himself exposed. Maxwell jabbed the hilt of his dagger into the man's nose. He dropped his bludgeon and crumpled to the ground, the sound coming from him animallike.

The leader roared, grabbed a boy with spots on his face, and shoved him forward. Enough was enough. Maxwell threw his dagger toward the leader's torso, hoping to hit a shoulder or arm. Instead, it lodged deep in the man's throat. Everyone froze.

The lantern slipped from the man's hand and cast eerie shadows over the bloody tableau as it sputtered. He touched the hilt protruding from his throat and stared at Maxwell. It was not the first time he'd killed, but war had a different set of rules. Watching the life leak out of the man was difficult.

The man went to his knees and then tilted until he fell over like a cut tree. Blood stained the stones. The boy with spots didn't move, and the man whose nose he'd broken took a shuffling half step to the side. They were rudderless without a captain.

Maxwell pulled a dagger out of his boot and gestured. "Any other takers? Or are you lads going to let us go?"

The boy with spots backed out of the alley and called in a high-pitched, frightened voice, "Black Crag! Help!"

That sounded ominous. Better to retreat now. He grabbed Bryn's wrist and stalked toward the mouth of the alley.

"Back away, lads, and let us walk out. No one needs to be the wiser," Maxwell said.

As the lads hypnotically obeyed his command, a commotion at the street stopped him.

A bear of a man blocked their escape, extra men on his heels. A lad picked up the fallen lantern and illuminated Black Crag. He was the meanest, scariest, nastiest-looking man Maxwell had ever laid eyes on.

Tangled black hair hung to his shoulders, and his similarly colored beard was thick and unkempt. A prominent forehead graced by two bushy brows concealed his eyes, but Maxwell guessed they were of the beady and cruel variety. Beyond the intimidating visage, his brawny strength was undeniable. The seams of his pants protested the bulge of muscles they were expected to gird.

Maxwell braced his feet apart, ready for a battle he wasn't sure he could win. Bryn had moved to his side, unprotected and vulnerable.

"For pity's sake, get behind me and take cover. If you see an opportunity, run as fast as you can," he muttered in her direction, not willing to take his eyes off his formidable opponent. "Don't wait for me. Don't look back."

Black Crag toed the man on the ground over. "What's this then? You bunch can't handle a couple o' sorry gents? Pathetic. This is my last job, and if I get bloody, there'll be hell to pay at home." While he continued to grumble, Black Crag cracked his knuckles and neck.

"If you want to avoid bloodshed, I would recommend letting us walk away unscathed," Maxwell said.

"You seem a decent fighter, guv. Why don't you give over your purse and let's all be friends."

"Not likely." Maxwell clenched his teeth and prepared for the fight of his life. But more importantly, for Bryn's life.

If Maxwell could get the man on his back, he might have a chance. The lad holding the lantern raised it higher, throwing Black Crag's face in full relief. It was fearsome.

Before Maxwell could go on the offensive, Bryn launched herself at the giant. Her hat fell to the stones, and her hair cascaded to her shoulders, sparking in the light of the lantern. Maxwell reached out, his fingertips brushing her jacket but unable to grab hold.

"Thomas Kennedy! I thought that was you."

The mountain of a man caught Bryn in his arms and twirled her about, laughing. At least Maxwell assumed the grinding, chesty noise was laughter.

"Brynmore McCann. Why in the devil are you skulking about in an alley in Edinburgh dressed like a gent?" Thomas set her down and put his hands on her shoulders.

"I almost didn't recognize you with a beard."

"It's good to see you, lass. How's Ma and the kids?"

Did the terrifying man just ask about his... mother? The shift from threatening to dismember Maxwell to jovial unbalanced him.

"All's well. Your brother will be as tall as you soon."

Thomas glanced at the knot of men at the mouth of the alley. "Off with you then. You'll not be robbing my friends tonight. And take Dirk here." The men picked up the dead man and scattered like roaches.

"Who's this?" Thomas turned to face Maxwell. A pair of blue, twinkling eyes lined with laughter peered from under his dark brows.

Bryn moved next to Maxwell. "Maxwell Drake, Thomas Kennedy. Maxwell grew up in Cragian, too, if you recall."

Thomas stroked a hand down his beard. "I remember. Seems as you've done well for yourself, and if our little Brynmore vouches for you, you're good in my book."

Maxwell's near clobbering seemed to be water under the bridge. The big man rubbed his hands together, a look of pure mischief lighting his eyes. "Are you up for a little adventure?"

"The evening has proved adventurous enough. We should head home, Bryn." Maxwell could only imagine what Thomas "Black Crag" Armstrong considered an adventure. Although the

Armstrong family was well known in Cragian, Maxwell could only recall a pack of black-haired siblings, all big and rawboned, even the girls.

"You two will be safe enough with me. It's not far." Thomas's voice turned singsong. "I'll see you both home safely after the dancing."

"Dancing? I love a good reel." Bryn grabbed Maxwell's hand and said, "We'll be safer on the streets with Thomas."

Maxwell allowed her to tug him out of the alley and into the unknown with more than a little trepidation.

CHAPTER NINETEEN

Bryn followed Thomas through a maze of alleys and streets. Maxwell's profile was stern, and she was surprised he'd ceded control without an argument. The night stretched and took on a magical quality as if they'd been spirited away by the fey.

Pipes, tin whistles, and strings lilted through the dark night and quickened her feet. A two-story wooden house stood at the next crossroads. It leaned to the right and appeared to be shaking from the inside out. A group of four men gathered outside, holding steaming cups of drink to ward off the cold.

Maxwell stopped them at the steps. "This is Molly's."

"Have you been here before?" Bryn asked.

Maxwell sputtered, "Of course not," over Thomas's chesty laughter.

"Molly's is a house of business on occasion. Tonight, though, it's playing host for the neighborhood. Quite reputable gentlemen and ladies attend, and if the men happen to take notice of the wares and come back later in the week to sample them? Well, Molly's a bright one, she is."

"It's improper. Bryn, we should—"

"Ach. You worry too much." Thomas aimed a sly smile at Maxwell. "Methinks it's not the wolves beyond the door that are the danger to Miss Bryn."

"What the devil are you implying?" Maxwell squared off with Thomas with an echo of the aggression from the alley. Bryn glanced back and forth at the two men, wondering at the undercurrents.

"You can't fool Black Crag, Mr. Drake." Thomas pushed through the front door. A cry of greeting went up for Thomas.

A house of ill repute. If the ladies had the evening off, Bryn couldn't tell it. They sashayed around the room, serving ale, in dresses that exposed their ankles and were so low-cut she was sure there would be an accident if there hadn't been already. She was torn between being scandalized and curious.

Self-conscious in her mannish clothes, she tugged her hat off and tried to tame her hair. A lost cause. She could never compete with the whores in experience or womanly attributes.

Mostly men populated the room. Not as well-heeled or well-behaved as the gentlemen and ladies Mary and Craddock invited to their social functions but patrons with money nonetheless.

A three-piece band—pipes, fiddle, and tin whistle—was positioned on the second-floor balcony. The music floated around the room, visceral and tickling her senses as if she could see and touch the music as well as hear it. Bryn soaked the notes up.

Thomas was at the bar, giving a pretty blond-haired woman a buss on the cheek and a squeeze of her bottom. Her blue dress was modest and pretty, but she had a way about her that was compelling and a little dangerous. Thomas whispered in her ear, and the woman's sharp gaze clashed with Bryn's.

The woman closed the distance, and Bryn stood transfixed. She was a bit older than she looked from afar, perhaps thirty, but her beauty would last well into old age.

"Tommy tells me you're friends from home." The lady's country accent didn't match the picture of elegance she projected.

"We are all from Cragian, yes. This is Maxwell Drake, and I'm

Brynmore McCann. It's a pleasure to make your acquaintance." Standing in the middle of a whorehouse, Mary's lessons in deportment chose to bubble up, and Bryn bobbed a curtsy.

A blush rose, and feeling foolish, Bryn looked away. At the closest table, a woman was sitting on a man's lap, twirling her fingers in his hair while his hands roved.

"Jane." The woman clapped twice and shook her head. "Not tonight, dear."

With maximum contact, Jane peeled herself off the man and whirled away, her skirts exposing a good amount of leg. It seemed both natural and orchestrated.

"I'm Molly Duncan. The owner and operator of Molly's." The woman's voice contained both pride and hesitation as if she was used to being cut.

Bryn had watched too many women suffer through poverty or suffer a husband who beat them. Molly had taken her life into her own hands and ran a successful business. Who was Bryn to judge, considering what she herself had done to escape a marriage?

"You've built an impressive trade here," Bryn said simply.

Molly's smile widened and exposed laugh lines at her eyes. "I'm proud of it, I won't deny. I take care of my girls. Make sure they're kept clean and healthy, and if a man uses them ill, then he's no longer welcome."

"That's admirable, I'm sure." The conversation had taken on a surreal bent. "Are you and Thomas… friends then?"

Molly laughed. "We're getting married."

"That's wonderful. I've known Thomas for many years."

"He's mentioned your kindness with the—"

"Will you stay here then?" Bryn snuck a glance at Maxwell, but he seemed more concerned about a nonexistent attack from within.

The Kennedy family was poorer than most around Cragian,

although they'd scrabbled together an existence until Thomas's father had died. That's when Bryn began dropping off baskets for the family. One slip of the tongue would give her away to Maxwell.

"Aye. I'm well established, but tonight was the last night Tommy will do Sutherland's dirty work."

* * * * *

The mention of Sutherland swung Maxwell's full attention to Molly. "Sutherland is behind the apprentice gangs? Why? Unless he's hiding his debts, he's richer than anyone in Edinburgh."

"Not so loud, Mr. Drake. Sutherland has eyes and ears everywhere." Molly's gaze darted around the room even though she didn't move her head. "Everyone has something to hide, and I'd say Sutherland's secrets are deep and plentiful."

"But to organize gangs?"

"Sutherland has convinced the men tasked with keeping the peace to look elsewhere while the lads terrorize the city. It's appalling."

"He must be getting something in return."

"You can be sure he is, but I don't know what." Darkness crossed Molly's face before it cleared, although her bright tone seemed forced. "You must dance with your lady, Mr. Drake. Her toes have been tapping since she walked in."

Molly tinkled a laugh at odds with her no-nonsense, tough-as-nails demeanor and left them to play hostess. Molly Duncan was not a woman to cross.

"Will you dance with me?" Bryn's face was lit with a childlike expectancy.

"I'm not spry enough to dance." The excuse rolled out with practiced ease. He'd used his injury to avoid dancing for years, but this was the first time he regretted it. Dancing with Bryn meant he could touch her without justifications.

Before Maxwell had a chance to change his mind, Thomas grabbed Bryn's hand and pulled her onto the floor. Her throaty laughter cut him as Thomas whirled her about him.

Not hampered by skirts, Bryn's footwork was on display. As were her long legs and hips and the curves of her breasts. The night's danger had stripped away his carefully constructed ruse of indifference. The distance he'd put between them was a sham.

He wanted to sift his fingers through the silken mass of her hair while she lay under him or feel it tickle his cheeks as she rode him to oblivion or perhaps bury his face in it while he took her from behind like a rutting beast. As if she cast a spell over him, he moved closer to the dance floor, the torment heightened.

Her dance was all primitive beauty, as old as the pipes themselves, and he was transported to a time when their ancestors must have done the same around druid stones. She commanded the room with a confidence that Mary had tried to pulverize.

She stripped off her jacket and flung it to the side to the cheers of both men and women, leaving her in a white shirt and waistcoat. Her back was to him, and his attention was on her beautifully rounded arse. He'd dreamed about that arse—and other assorted body parts—since the night at the inn. The dreams were a reality within his grasp. The space between them crackled with lust and need. And he needed—badly.

He crossed his arms and braced his legs apart, holding himself back even though his gaze never left her. The look she arrowed over her shoulder struck him in the heart. Once their eyes caught, they held, neither able to look away from the other. She turned, her body still in the throes of the music.

She was woman incarnate. Her gaze brushed down his chest to linger at the juncture of his legs. Maxwell could well imagine what she saw, his cock in heavy, full arousal. Lightning sizzled in the air, and he expected to hear thunder rumbling in the distance at any moment. One song ended and another began, the frenzy building like climbing a mountain of longing.

Did she understand her danger? Most likely she was still too innocent. One night and a few kisses and caresses in his study did not add up to experience. If she moved within reach, it would be over for them both. His strength of will had been demolished.

* * * * *

Everyone in Bryn's periphery blurred. Only Maxwell mattered. Energy thrummed and drew her to him. She danced close enough to touch him yet didn't. She spun away, confident his gaze remained on her. The music and the want in his eyes granted her a bravery she'd longed for all her life.

Like they were tethered, she returned. This time she laid her hands on his shoulders, soft like the brush of a bird's wing. He didn't push her away, and her confidence blossomed with knowledge he'd imparted to her.

She ran her hands from his shoulders to his biceps. The muscles tensed under her clutching fingers. Standing immobile on the edge of the floor, he had looked so strong, almost as if he had been cast from marble, but he was indeed flesh and blood and man.

As if her hands worked ancient alchemy, releasing him from his stone imprisonment, he darted an arm around her waist and pulled her close. Flesh and blood, indeed. His erection pressed along her hip bone. A blush raced through her body, the heat stoking her desire higher.

No liquor clouded his eyes or his judgment tonight. Yet he still wanted her. He smoothed his hands over her buttocks. She nearly incinerated. But he wasn't done. Pressing her higher, he fit himself against her lower belly and rocked against her. A different sort of dance.

"Maxwell, what—"

His mouth descended on hers like an invading army, no quarter given. Hard and unyielding. His teeth nipped her lips. Dominated in every way, Bryn surrendered. Or maybe Maxwell was the one who'd given in. Whatever had changed, he took what she was only too willing to give.

The roaring in her ears drowned out the crowd and music, her heart moving her blood faster and faster. She looped her arms around his neck, the same time he scooped his hands under her.

"Wrap those long, sweet legs around me, lass." His velvety brogue was undeniable—as if she would deny him anything in this moment.

He carried her, his leg not seeming to bother him in the least. The catcalls and whoops of the occupants of the crowded room penetrated her daze, and she buried her face in his neck. Her embarrassment wasn't enough to tell Maxwell to stop. Up the stairs they went.

At the top, in the shadows of the hallway, Maxwell nudged her face up to his and captured her lips in another carnal assault. He cracked open the first door. A barrage of curses and a high-pitched shriek had him backing away with a rumbly laugh and moving to the next.

The room was blessedly empty. He kicked the door shut. The hinges rattled. The rickety wood planks got no rest. He turned and pressed her against the door. Like an uncaged beast held too long away from food, he devoured her.

Instead of fright, his elemental response drove her own primitive urges. She bit his neck, running her tongue along the skin she'd caught between her teeth. He tilted his head on a groan. Frenzied music filled the air and made words unnecessary. Her senses were overwhelmed, leaving no room for doubts or horror.

The rough wood at her back contrasted with the silky skin she stroked through the collar of his shirt. As he kept her a welcome prisoner, he roamed his hands over her body and rocked against her. The same fluttering pleasure she'd experienced in his bed in Cragian took flight, and she chased it, knowing where it led. The throb between her legs grew more intense.

Peeling his torso away, he cupped her breasts and squeezed. The layers of fabric did a poor job hiding her response. Her nipples were hard and aching, and as if he understood, he pinched them. Sparks erupted and arced from her breasts to between her legs.

He unhooked her ankles and took a step back. Her knees had forgotten how to perform their duties, and she leaned against the door, her breaths coming in pants. His gaze skimmed down her body.

He fingered the lapels of her waistcoat. Slowly he drew his hands into fists around the fabric, the tug against her sensitive breasts unbearably arousing. Instinctively her back arched, begging for his touch without words. His sudden jerk left her gasping. In a blink, he'd torn her waistcoat and shirt to her waist. Two buttons hung by loosened thread, but the rest were gone. Her shirt's jagged edges would be impossible to mend. Tendrils of chill air caressed her skin.

Shock held her still as he peeled the sides apart, exposing her. His mouth had gone slack, his eyes glassy as if he'd imbibed, yet she knew different. She risked a glance down. Her breasts were plump, her nipples pebbled.

"You're lovely, Bryn. So lovely." His mouth closed over one breast, pulling her nipple into his hot mouth. His hair tickled her skin, and she thread her fingers through it, the thick waves curling over her skin in a caress of its own.

He scraped his teeth over her nipple. A gasping moan escaped. Wetness had gathered in preparation for taking him. This time there was no fear or embarrassment. She wasn't an inexperienced maiden, and she knew what she wanted.

Leaving her shirt to frame her bare breasts, he fumbled with the buttons of her fall. "I would never have imagined myself so anxious to get into a pair of breeches."

The shot of levity lessened the intensity of the moment and brought with it tenderness. As his hands continued to fumble with her breeches, he took her lips, this time slowly, devastatingly, and she clutched at his jacket.

The buttons of her fall slipped free, and Bryn could feel cool air against her hip. He urged her toward the bed. She planned to undress him and kiss every inch of his chest and lower. All the way to his…

Her plans were for naught. He spun her, pressed her face into the quilt, and jerked her breeches down to pool at the tops of her boots, her buttocks exposed.

"Beautiful. Perfect." His words were like a brand on her skin.

Could he see how wet and ready she was for him? Could he tell how much she wanted him? The imagining made her even more desperate for him to claim her. She shuffled her feet farther apart and popped up on her toes.

"You're tempting me beyond all reason, lass." Finally he touched her, kneading and squeezing her buttocks.

Bryn fisted the quilt on the bed, muffled her groan, and writhed under his hands. "Maxwell, please."

"I told you I'd punish you if you wore breeches again, didn't I?"

She would do anything if he kept talking to her in that velvety brogue. "You did."

"What should your punishment be?" he inquired almost idly. The spank he gave was soft but unexpected. She jolted away from his hand. "More of that, like a disobedient child, or perhaps something more befitting a woman?"

Even more unexpected, he trailed a finger through her core. He hummed and rubbed the spot where every nerve ending in her body was focused. She rotated her hips against his fingers. If he stopped, she might die.

He stopped.

She twisted around and grabbed his wrist, flicking her hair out of her eyes. "Don't you dare tease me now, Drake."

His gaze was combustible and darted down to her breasts. The corners of his mouth curved up as he leaned in and surprised her again. Instead of kissing her, he rotated his wrist in her hand and sucked the fingers that had been stroking her.

He closed his eyes like he'd tasted something truly delicious. Her grip loosened, her senses adrift. The only thing that mattered was riding this wave to completion. She was an animal, her craving primal.

She leaned on her elbows and pushed her bottom into him. Cloth impeded her single-minded focus. He curled his body over her, his breath hot in her ear. "Are you ready to be ridden hard?"

She was ready for everything and anything he could give her. "Yes. Do it."

His knuckles brushed her bare bottom. At the realization he was freeing himself, her anticipation ratcheted up tenfold. She spread her feet apart as far as her breeches would allow and canted her hips up. The head of his heavy erection glided through her folds and pushed inside her.

With one strong thrust, he buried himself fully, wrenching a cry of pleasure from her. For a moment he held himself inside her, his fingers biting into her hips. She wiggled. A cross between a groan and husky laughter accompanied his first thrust.

She didn't care. All she cared about was the pleasure he promised with each drive forward. The tension that had festered between them culminated like a storm ready to break. He held her down with one hand as he fulfilled his promise and rode her hard. Yet what coursed through her was power.

His thrusts slowed, and the pressure on her back eased. His heat curled around her, and he snaked a hand to where they were joined. "I don't want to fall alone, Brynmore."

She undulated against his fingers and splintered into pure light. As she pulsed around him, the wet rush of his spend released deep inside her.

He collapsed on top of her, his weight pressing her into the sagging mattress, the quilt soft on her cheek. She wanted to crawl on top of the bed and entwine herself with him.

"Tell me I didn't hurt you." Although it was a command, his voice was pure anguish.

"If that was your idea of a punishment, I'm returning all those dresses you bought me for breeches." Her voice was muffled in the quilt.

Maxwell erupted in a deep, resonant laugh. Her stomach fluttered. The man needed to laugh and smile more. Or maybe he didn't. These moments were rare like shooting stars, and selfishly she wanted to reserve them all for her.

Still inside her, he nuzzled the side of her face. "Are you sure you aren't a fairy, for you surely have bewitched me."

Unexpectedly tender and whimsical, his words wound around her heart. "I'm merely a woman."

"There's no 'merely' to it. You enchant everyone who crosses your path."

"Do I?" Her tongue felt clumsy. What was he saying? Did *he* find her enchanting?

"Here now, we'd best not linger as we're not paying customers." He levered himself up, leaving chilly air to snake between her legs. She snapped her knees together, stood, and yanked her breeches up.

Her surroundings registered like a devil's finger tracing her spine. A whore's room. What did that make her?

Her shirt hung open, and she turned her back to him while she fastened her breeches. Her shirt and waistcoat were ruined. The two buttons left did a poor job disguising exactly what had happened. She prayed her jacket hadn't walked off with someone downstairs. Of course, after their indecorous exit, anyone with half an eye and sliver of a brain would know exactly what they'd been up to. The abject embarrassment her desire had dampened roared to life, and she covered her face.

Maxwell slipped his jacket over her shoulders. "For what it's worth, I'm sorry."

She slipped her arms in the sleeves, her pathetic gratefulness warring with a lick of anger. He couldn't accuse her of deception this go around. "What are you sorry about exactly?"

"Dragging you upstairs. My rough treatment. I've never lost control like that. No matter what's passed between us before now, I shouldn't have taken advantage."

She dipped her head and deftly buttoned his jacket over her ruined shirt. As if Maxwell returning had fundamentally changed her, instead of cowering or retreating, fury sent strength coursing through her body. Yet there was something familiar in the fury. It had flared at Mary, at Dugan, at her own perceived weakness many times. But now it caught hold like a tenacious weed.

"I'll not feel shamed for this night. I wanted it. As did you." She raised her gaze to his and set her chin.

"Marry me, Bryn, and we can set this right."

"I'll not trap you into marriage. You'll resent me, and I won't be responsible for making us both miserable."

"You'd be miserable?" His voice took on an icy edge.

A selfish part of her wanted to marry him. Yet it would hurt her too much to be the cause of his unhappiness. Any answer she gave would reveal too much. She remained silent.

"If you're with child, you'll have no choice but to marry me."

"I know." The words emerged on the merest whisper. Her strength ebbed. All she wanted now was to curl up in her bed and have a good cry. She pushed past him to the door.

The music had stopped, and the common room was sparsely

occupied by men interested in continuing the evening with one of Molly's girls. She stepped to the left to allow a buxom redhead and a grinning middle-aged man to pass them on their way up the stairs.

Bryn glanced over her shoulder. The couple entered the room she and Maxwell had vacated. The woman's giggle was cut off by the door closing.

"I'll see to acquiring transportation," Maxwell muttered.

Thomas sat at the bar in the common room, talking to Molly who was polishing glasses behind it. Bryn gathered her jacket and approached the couple at the bar, unable to quash a burgeoning shame faced with Thomas's knowing half grin.

Thomas quirked an eyebrow. "That was quite a dramatic exit. Is Drake the marrying kind?"

"It's complicated. Are there any hacks about this time of night?"

"I've got the wagon out back waiting if you don't mind a little hay." Thomas exchanged a secretive, serious look with Molly. "If you need help of any kind, you only have to ask for Black Crag or Molly. You could stay with us a spell if you wanted."

She swallowed, his kind offer pushing her closer to an outburst of emotion she could hardly afford. "I appreciate the offer, but Maxwell and I have business to finish."

Molly burst out laughing. "I'd say you finished right proper upstairs."

"Ach, Molly, quit teasing the lass. She's naught like you and me. The offer stands for as long as you need. It's little enough to repay your kindness over the years."

"Thank you, Thomas. Molly." She nodded at them each in turn. "I'll remember."

Drake returned, shaking his head. "Nothing out."

"I promised to see you both home safely. I'll pull the wagon around." Thomas disappeared out the back.

The three of them sat across the seat. Bryn was sandwiched between the two men, grateful for the warmth they provided. She had offered Maxwell his jacket back, but he refused, probably not wanting Thomas to bear witness to the devastation he'd wrought on her clothes.

Thomas gave a low whistle of appreciation, eyeing Maxwell speculatively as they pulled onto Barrow Street. "Mayhap I should have taken a little donation from your purse after all, Drake. Seems as though you have some to spare."

"At your own risk, Thomas." Under the tease in Maxwell's voice was the hint of a real threat. Maxwell offered a hand, and Bryn clambered out of the wagon, cold and exhaustion seeping into her limbs.

She called out her thanks and waved as Thomas drove away. Once he was out of sight, she turned and trudged up the stairs. Maxwell waited on the stoop. A loud *crack* echoed through the streets. She froze. The hairs on her neck rose as her body sensed what her mind was slow to comprehend.

Danger.

"Bloody hell, not again." Maxwell grabbed her wrist and yanked her the rest of the way up the steps, protecting her with his body as he struggled to unlatch the door. Another report sounded. Maxwell grunted and stumbled against her, but his arm was strong around her waist as he shoved her in the house.

Panic infused her bones and turned them as weak as a stalk of grass. She leaned against the wall for support. Maxwell strode into his study and emerged with a pistol. She clung to his arm, but he shrugged her off.

"No! What are you doing? Someone is shooting at us." Hysteria crept into her voice.

"I came to the same conclusion," Maxwell said drily. "This has got to stop. I'm going to find the bastard."

He ducked out the door and was lost to the shadows.

CHAPTER TWENTY

Maxwell was furious. This was the second time they'd been shot at, not to mention the incident in the alley. Him dying was one thing, but he wouldn't allow Bryn to be hurt. His move to the stone wall was swift and silent. The clash of boots in retreat reverberated out of the nearest alley. He edged along the wall in darkness untouched by moonlight.

Based on the report and where both bullets hit, one next to the door buried in the stone and one grazing his arm, his would-be assassin had lain in wait across the street and retreated down the alley.

He slowed and took a quick look around. Deserted. A glow on the ground to his right drew his eye. He dropped to his haunches. A half-smoked cigar. The stubs of two others had been discarded close by. He sniffed. He had never enjoyed cigars, but several of the officers and his comrades partook to pass the idle hours or to calm their nerves before battle.

Sniffing again, he closed his eyes. This brand was favored by the officers, mild and expensive. Interesting. After stubbing out the cigar and slipping it into his pocket, he followed the alley and stopped at the mouth, a wider street stretching to either side.

He cocked his head, listening. The man was close. Now to flush him out. Maxwell picked up a rock and pelted it across the street. It hit a shutter, the clang echoing. His prey got spooked. Movement blurred on his left. Maxwell pursued as quickly as his damnable leg would allow. The man moved fast, and the distance between them grew, a greatcoat concealing his build. They moved inexorably toward the richest part of the city. Finally the man outpaced him, and Maxwell stopped giving chase, winded but satisfied.

He'd gathered valuable information. The man was well-off. He wore quality garments and smoked fine cigars. Subterfuge did not come naturally to him. When scared, the man had headed toward home, which was not Thomas's neck of the woods. Also, although not as prominent or inhibiting as Maxwell's, the man had a limp, suggesting he was the man who'd ransacked Pickett's office.

Maxwell meandered back to the alley and recreated the shots. A shaft of moonlight illuminated the door to the town house, as good as drawing a bull's-eye. Either the man missed on purpose, he didn't have the stomach for killing, or he was an abysmal shot. That alley was no more than twenty feet from their front door.

As he limped across the street, the door swung open, framing Bryn. She would have made a terrible spy. Emotions flit across her face and reflected in her body language. Artifice was her sister's strength; Bryn's was honesty.

And right now she was mad as hell.

As he gained the entrance, she launched herself at him, punching him on his grazed arm and again in the belly.

"What the devil, woman?"

"Don't you ever. Do. That. Again!" She punctuated each word with a slap or jab.

They scuffled a moment in the entry until Maxwell corralled her wrists in one of his hands. Rousing the household would lead to awkward questions.

Frog marching her into the study, he closed the door with his foot and pinned her against it. It seemed incongruous that not even an hour ago, they had been in a similar position under entirely different circumstances.

"You are a total and complete dolt. Why did you run after an armed man? You could have been killed." At least she had the good sense to keep her voice down.

"For the love… Stop kicking me. You're hurting my leg."

She stopped kicking but twisted and bucked against him. Her lithe body aroused a physical response. One he was sure would earn him a knee in a very sensitive area. He let her go and stepped away.

"I wasn't in any real danger." While ultimately true, that fact had been less clear when he'd set off after the man. "The man had fired twice, and odds were he didn't have any shots left. Anyway, he made his escape before I gave chase."

The man's noisy retreat added to the mounting evidence pointing to a layman. An experienced criminal would have been quieter and more careful not to leave anything behind.

"What if he'd had friends waiting and led you into a trap? What if he'd skewered you as you came out of the alley?" The tremulous quality of her voice told him more of her worries than her words.

"You have a bloodthirsty imagination." He rubbed a piece of her hair between his fingers and was gratified she didn't pull away. "I'm fine."

"I can see you're not fine, Drake." She touched his elbow.

Between the cold and the energy that had pumped through him at the first gunshot, he'd forgotten about his arm. Now that she'd reminded him, it throbbed in punishment. Not only his arm but his leg as well. He'd pushed himself beyond his limits this evening. Before his injury, he would have caught his would-be assassin. It was frustrating.

"I would appreciate some help cleaning my wound." When she crossed her arms in response, he added, "Please? I'll make a muck of it."

Her eyes softened even though her stance remained rigid. "I suppose I can't let you die of fever. Go pour yourself a tot of liquor."

She left, and he did as he was told. After downing his more-than-a-tot of brandy in two swallows, he pulled off his shirt, wincing at the sting on his arm. Another shirt ruined. A few more attempts on his life and a shirt order from the tailor would be required. He laughed softly to himself, a sure sign the brandy was taking effect.

Time passed. Bryn returned with a basin of water and clean linens and knelt at his feet.

"Are you still mad at me, lass?" All he needed was an angry, impassioned woman with her hands on his wound.

"Yes," she said shortly.

But he needn't have worried. She was gentle, her ministrations almost soothing.

"It's shallow and clean. No need for stitches." She sat back on her heels and looked up at him.

The brandy had warmed him from the inside. His hand, disconnected from any conscious thought, caressed her cheek, and her lashes dropped as she leaned into his touch. The same hand made a trek to her hair, sifting through the silk.

He stretched his bad leg out straight, muffling a groan.

She tilted her head. "Your leg pains you."

It was a statement and not a question, so he didn't feel obliged to answer. He closed his eyes, wanting to ask—beg was more like—her to ease the pain, but he was unable to get the words out. Asking for help exposed his weakness.

But it seemed she was a mind reader. She kneaded his leg around the old wound. He watched through barely open eyes. Her bottom lip was caught between her teeth as she concentrated on healing him. Her hands were magic. She was magic.

No, if tonight proved anything, she was flesh and blood. He'd taken her like a man possessed in the whorehouse. She should have been furious with him. And she had been. But not about the act itself. It had been his bumbling, pompousness afterward. His insistence on marriage.

Now that pain wasn't his companion, a wave of exhaustion swamped him. Why didn't she want to bear his name and children? Was he not good enough? The question circled his head, finding no answer, until he drifted to sleep.

* * * * *

The next day dawned gray and ominous. After the long, harrowing night, Bryn didn't awake until early afternoon. The gloom kept her abed. The old Bryn would have never lolled in bed so late. Of course, the old Bryn would have never done many of the things she'd done over the past weeks.

Preparations for Sutherland's dinner party would begin in earnest in a few hours. Part of her wanted to seek out Maxwell, wondering how deep his regrets had grown after their passionate encounter. But there was no use trying to ferret out his feelings. He buried them so deeply she wasn't even sure *he* understood them.

So she avoided him and concentrated on writing a letter to her grandmother, worrying over every word. How much should she reveal to a woman she didn't know? Bryn wanted to believe the best of her grandmother, but recent events had taught her to question everyone's motivations.

Moreover, she didn't want to increase any guilt her grandmother carried. What could Bryn say about her mother and father? Her father had been detached but not cruel. Her mother had seemed content with her lot, although what did a five-year-old understand about marital contentment?

As she sealed the envelope with wax, Mrs. Winslow gave a

perfunctory knock and strolled through her door, Gertie on her heels.

"It's time to get dressed and coiffed, my dear."

"Already?" Their departure for Sutherland's was a good two hours away.

"There's much work to be done." Mrs. Winslow eyed her critically.

Her eyes wide with questions, Gertie whispered, "Elspeth?"

Bryn shook her head. "No news yet, but Mr. Pendleton is aware."

Gertie seemed satisfied, even though Bryn questioned whether she should or could do more.

There was no time to plan. Gertie laced Bryn's stays tight and plucked her eyebrows. An attempt was even made to curl her hair. It went poorly. Finally Mrs. Winslow declared it a lost cause, and Bryn heaved a huge sigh of relief as Gertie laid the hot tongs aside.

"Curls may be in fashion, but your beauty is timeless." Mrs. Winslow paced around her, looking this way and that, then finally snapping her fingers in triumph. "Braids. Here and here, and then wind them together and pin here."

Bryn endured the painful tugging, hoping the result would be something more sophisticated than usual. She wanted to do Maxwell proud.

Gertie held out the midnight-blue dress, and Bryn stepped in. It only took a few adjustments before she was taped and tied. Mrs. Winslow twirled her finger in the air, and Bryn dutifully spun for a final examination.

"My dear, Mr. Drake will be stunned by your beauty."

Bryn stepped closer to the looking glass. The transformation wasn't magic. She still looked like herself but a different version. A prettier version.

The braids highlighted the varied hues of her hair, and pinning them up exposed her neck. The blue color complemented her skin tone and hair. Bryn skimmed her hand over the swells of her breasts. Never had she worn a dress that exposed so much.

The sleeves hugged the curve of her shoulders, leaving the rest of her chest bare. The back scooped to the bottom of her shoulder blades, and for some reason when she turned around to examine herself, it was almost as shocking as the front.

New silk stockings with pretty garters and matching kid slippers completed her ensemble. The tactile sensations of her silken legs rubbing and the rustle of the flowing gossamer dress reminded her of intimacies with Maxwell. For the first time she understood the power Mary wielded. Some of that power surged through Bryn. The dress was a talisman.

She pulled on elbow-length gloves and made her way to the drawing room. The murmur of male voices drifted out. Nerves bundled like kindling in her stomach.

She glided to the doorway, hoping to slip in without any fuss, but the conversation stopped and the gentlemen rose in unison, greeting her in silence. Maxwell cut a strikingly masculine figure. His dark hair was combed back and tamed with a touch of pomade, his aristocratic features on display. He was dressed in all black and white with a simple cravat. The coat emphasized his broad shoulders, and his breeches were cut close, his muscular thighs apparent.

The continued silence made her doubt what she'd seen in the looking glass. Had she grown spotty?

"Come now, I don't look *that* different, do I?"

* * * * *

The uncertainty in her voice prompted Maxwell to offer a compliment, but he was frozen, only able to swallow weakly.

Did she look different? Yes, but not better, because nothing was as tempting as Bryn in her breeches, but… different. She was a woman in the gown, and as he'd surmised, the color was exquisite on her. The gauzy overlay sparkled in the candlelight. Her hair was up in braids, and his gaze traveled the long distance of her neck to explore the curves and shadows of her bosom.

His conclusion was unarguable. Her breasts were perfect, beautifully pale and quivering slightly on each indrawn breath. Torture was knowing that her concealed dusky nipples were just as perfect.

Lionel bestowed compliments, and the earl stepped forward to press a kiss on her gloved hand. Instead of gallantry, Maxwell wanted to throw her over his shoulder and repeat the madness that had infected him at Molly's.

But he'd promised himself he would not allow another transgression of the sort—unless they were wed. He clenched the back of the chair to keep himself from pouncing.

Like a clodpoll, he only managed to choke out, "You look nice," in a rusty, harsh voice.

Disappointment and hurt flashed over her face, and he had the urge to drop to his knees and apologize, but he stood, lips compressed, doing his best to dam his emotions.

Mrs. Winslow entered the room in a flourish of red velvet, dissipating the awkwardness. Her dress was cut scandalously low, and the earl looked as stunned as Maxwell felt, but in contrast, he almost tripped over his feet to press a kiss on the merry widow's hand.

"You look ravishing this evening, Edie."

"Why, thank you, David. You look rather ravishing yourself." The earl blinked a few times and then burst out laughing, his eyes twinkling.

He offered Edie his arm, which she took graciously, and said, "Shall we? We have much to accomplish this evening."

Bryn's chin was up and her shoulders back. The only chink in her confidence was the way her gloved fingers twisted together.

Lionel cleared his throat. Maxwell stared at Bryn.

Lionel muttered, "Good Lord, Drake," before stepping forward and offering Bryn his arm. She took it with a smile and a slicing glance in his direction.

He was an idiot, and he'd better figure out where his brains were hiding before they arrived at Sutherland's, or his life—and maybe Bryn's—would be forfeit. The thought was sobering enough to move his feet toward the carriages.

* * * * *

Disappointment wilted Bryn like a flower. Whatever power she had felt reflected back at her in the looking glass had been false. It was all so confusing. How could Maxwell be frosty and distant one moment, then explode with a heated passion the next?

Mr. Masterson patted her hand and whispered, "You've got poor Mr. Drake in knots, my dear."

Startled, she glanced over to see his gray eyes twinkling merrily. "I believe you're very much mistaken, Mr. Masterson."

"He was stunned. Some men are not good at expressing themselves, but never doubt that such a man feels as keenly as the most verbose poet."

Mr. Masterson handed her into the second carriage to join Mrs. Winslow. The men entered the other.

"I was sorry to miss your entrance, dear. What did our Mr. Drake have to say?" Mrs. Winslow smoothed her gloves and fiddled with her curls.

"He said—and let me make sure I quote him exactly—'you look nice.'"

Mrs. Winslow's eyes widened. "Oh my. He *is* smitten."

"He seemed completely unaffected, I assure you."

"*Seemed* being the key word. Look at you. For goodness' sake, you are beyond *nice*. He was too in awe to think of a more appropriate compliment. He's stingy with his words in the easiest of contexts. Imagine if he's flummoxed."

First Mr. Masterson and now Mrs. Winslow. Were they right? She had little time to mull over the issue. The carriage rumbled to a halt in front of a majestic house. Lanterns lit the walkway and up to the door. Sutherland's residence mimicked a neoclassical Greek style. Columns flanked the entry topped by intricate scrollwork.

She picked apart the plan. So many things could go wrong. Mrs. Winslow's job was to distract Sutherland after dinner. Maxwell and Penny were to obtain the marriage contract. Lionel would then meet them in the gardens to decipher the fine legal points of the document. Then they would all make an escape, and Penny would return the contract.

Apparently, Bryn was expected to hold up a wall while everyone else exposed themselves to danger on her behalf. After the foolishness of her nighttime foray, she hadn't protested her exclusion, yet the unfairness settled like an ugly stain she couldn't quite rub out.

A footman handed Bryn out of the carriage. The modernity of the sprawling town house made the manor house in Cragian seem medieval. She squinted to make out the details of an elaborately etched fanlight. A strong hand took hers and guided it to a hard arm.

Maxwell glared stoically ahead, fairly stomping into the entry where a staid, dignified butler waited. Maxwell slipped her cloak off, his hands lingering a heartbeat longer than was proper on her collarbones. Her breath caught, and she held still, but he only handed off her cloak and divested himself of his outerwear.

Waiting for the butler to announce them, he leaned to whisper, "You look bloody gorgeous, and I want to peel that dress off you inch by inch."

It was a wickedly delicious thing to say. And unexpected. Her ears buzzed, and heat bloomed through her body, accompanied by a surge of satisfaction and desire.

The large drawing room was understated in its elegance. Soft greens and blues made the space feel both masculine and feminine. Clean lines dominated—no flounces or ruffles in sight.

At the announcement of their names, everyone turned to examine them. Bryn's gaze flit from one face to another. Strangers. Had the scandal that had brought her and Maxwell together filtered from Cragian to Edinburgh?

A lean, dark-haired gentleman of average height swung a glass of champagne with a grace that matched his saunter. Yet a crackling energy emanated like a racehorse at rest.

The man's lazy, drawling speech was at odds with his calculating black eyes. "I'm Charles Sutherland. I've been most anxious to meet you, Mr. Drake." He raised his brows, took a sip, and pitched his voice too low for anyone else to hear. "It's an odd world we live in that a poor, sniveling bastard can rise to such heights, isn't it? I'm sure you never imagined yourself in such a place."

The calm, confident manner in which Sutherland delivered his insults demolished any semblance of politeness. Bryn tensed, ready to go on the defensive. Maxwell squeezed her elbow and answered drily, "It hardly compares with the Duke of Bellingham's, but for Edinburgh, it will do."

Sutherland's eyes widened and his mouth tensed. The champagne glass was no longer swinging idly but straining under Sutherland's clenched hand.

Maxwell continued with a confidence that matched Sutherland. "Nevertheless, I am most grateful for the invitation. With winter upon us, Miss McCann has been bored in town with only her chaperone for company."

Sutherland turned his gaze on her. She wished he hadn't. His blatant perusal of her bosom made her want to hunch her shoulders.

"Miss McCann." He performed a perfunctory bow but didn't reach for her hand. Good thing too, as her free hand had a death hold on her skirts. She didn't want to touch him. "Mary led me to believe you were a homely chit. Perhaps Craddock needs to get his wife fitted with spectacles. You're quite a vision."

Sutherland turned his head but never broke his gaze from hers. "Lady Mary, Craddock. Come see who has joined my little soiree."

Rocks tumbled in Bryn's stomach. The crowd parted for her sister and brother-in-law. Although Mary wore a smile, her color was high and her movements were stiff.

"A pleasure to see you again, Lord and Lady Craddock. I very much enjoyed our visit in Cragian," Maxwell said with a smoothness that was belied by how tense his arm had turned under her hand.

Mary perused Maxwell like he was a buffet she planned to sample. "Maxwell, my, you're looking quite fetching this evening. We need to find an alcove and reminisce about old times." Mary traced the low neckline of her gown with the tip of her fan.

Red burnished Maxwell's cheekbones. The arrowed glance Mary aimed at Bryn was contemptuous and triumphant. A few weeks ago, Bryn might have yielded the battlefield and planted herself in a corner for the rest of the evening.

A wellspring of anger bubbled up. She raised her chin and forced a half smile. "I find I've quite enjoyed Edinburgh, Mary. A shame you never thought to present me. We are accompanied by Earl Windor, lately arrived from London. Have you been introduced?"

"I haven't had the pleasure." Mary's smile qualified more as a grimace.

"Perhaps I can perform introductions. Or not. He's a busy man, and you and Craddock are barely country nobility." Although Mary was the master at wielding words as weapons, Bryn had studied Mary's weaknesses for years and her aim was true. Her longing to climb to the highest reaches of Society was a huge chink in her armor.

"I can't believe you would deign to show your face in public, my dear, considering your current status." Venom injected Mary's voice. She brushed Bryn's skirt with her fan. "And blue? I would have thought a nice brown would have suited you better. You look like wilted heather."

Mary's insults missed their mark. Before she could respond in kind, Maxwell said, "Bryn is the loveliest woman in the room. Every man's eye is upon her. Including your husband's."

Craddock was indeed watching them from a dozen feet away where he'd been waylaid in conversation by a thin, white-haired gentleman. Whether he was actually looking at Bryn wasn't clear, but the seed Maxwell planted sprouted, and Mary stalked off.

"That was quite untrue. But appreciated." Bryn gave his arm a squeeze.

Maxwell huffed. "It was the absolute truth."

The two of them moved farther into the room. Maxwell was acquainted with several gentlemen through his investment venture, and the gentlemen and their wives greeted her warmly as he performed introductions.

During the mindless chitchat, she mulled over the possibility of Mary and Craddock complicating their plans.

"Mr. Dugan Armstrong." The butler's announcement wrapped a cold fist around her heart. The sip of champagne in her mouth soured.

The lady beside her leaned in as if imparting a secret. "Ah, Mr. Armstrong. Are you acquainted with him? The poor man was thrown over the day before his wedding. He was to marry some poor country chit out of the goodness of his heart, and she ran off. Lady Craddock's *half* sister. Can you imagine? The girl must be mad."

"Perhaps not *mad*," Bryn said, "just angry."

"I can't imagine it. Mr. Armstrong is so handsome and genial."

Making her excuses to the woman who thought her mad, she sidled over to Maxwell, seeking his strength and protection instinctively. He had become her stable in times of need. A glance at her face had him scanning the room for the cause.

Armstrong weaved through the drawing room, his destination clear. Bryn tucked herself close to Maxwell and braced for the confrontation.

CHAPTER TWENTY-ONE

*B*loody, *bloody hell*. Maxwell barely kept himself from cursing aloud. Mr. Bowman was a potential client, and a drawing room brawl would destroy Maxwell's credibility in Edinburgh. Successfully navigating the evening was proving to be more difficult than he'd anticipated. Although, having the players all in the same room would ratchet up the tension every minute. At some point, the façade would fray and the truth would emerge.

Maxwell retreated a few feet to an unoccupied corner, Bryn at his side. Armstrong stopped two feet short of them. Too close for politeness's sake or Maxwell's peace of mind. Armstrong's gaze lingered along Bryn's décolletage, and Maxwell fisted his hands to keep from shoving him away. That's what Armstrong wanted. To stoke a physical confrontation where he could respond and claim to be victim. Maxwell played a different sort of game. One that would win.

"Our marriage contract is valid whether you're soiled or not, Bryn. I'll marry you and bed you before the winter's end. He can't stop me." Armstrong raised a hand to touch her, but she batted it away. Armstrong was a kettle ready to boil. "There's plenty your cripple can't teach you. I'll be more than happy to oblige."

"That's quite enough, Armstrong." Maxwell kept a smile on his face but forged iron in his voice.

"You're not man enough to face me."

"On the contrary, didn't your hired lackeys report back to you?"

Ruddy color painted Armstrong's cheeks, making him appear younger and less sure of himself. "Don't know what you're talking about, Drake."

Maxwell hoped Dugan wasn't a card player, because he was a poor bluff. "Perhaps. But since it's been nothing more than a nuisance—"

"Nuisance? You haven't stepped foot outside your town house all week." Armstrong's satisfied expression fell as he realized what he'd given away.

"I've been busy with meetings. Apparently, *you've* been busy watching me."

"Next time I'll be the one to—" Armstrong snapped his mouth closed. When he spoke again, it was a guttural whisper. "Watch your back, Drake. You might find a hole in it."

He spun away and was lost to view on the other side of the room.

"He means to kill you and won't give up no matter what happens. You've tweaked his ego." Bryn's voice was thin with worry.

"I believe you're correct." Maxwell shrugged. "Quite unfortunate."

"*Unfortunate?* I'd call it disastrous. How can you act so blithe about the possibility?"

"Armstrong I can handle. He's impetuous but not terribly bright. I can work the situation to our advantage as soon as we determine what he's gaining by marrying you. If it's your inheritance, then I'll buy him off. The problem arises if it's something less tangible."

The call for dinner arrived. Guests milled about, organizing for the procession. The woman Bryn had been conversing with earlier sidled over. "Miss McCann, how exactly are you related to Lady Craddock again?"

Bryn leaned in and whispered sotto voce, "I'm her *mad* half sister." The woman's eyes went wide before she turned and scurried away.

"What was that about?" Maxwell asked.

"The gossip is that I'm queer in the attic for abandoning such a handsome, upstanding man such as Dugan."

"Regretting your decision?" Dark humor dried his voice.

"I bless the day I found you again, Maxwell." Sudden raw honesty pulsed between them. Her eyes were warm pools he could drown in. His heart thumped an answering call against his ribs.

Maxwell opened his mouth and then promptly shut it. He'd cursed the morning he'd awakened to find her virgin blood on him. His life had splintered since she'd crashed into it like a cannonball.

But what he'd rebuilt was bigger and fuller than anything he'd imagined. He'd assumed the years that stretched before him would be lonely ones. He'd planned on it. Even gloried in the melancholy. Everything had changed. She'd changed everything.

Sutherland strolled by. "Drake, your place is in the back of the line, if you please. Miss McCann, up at the front with me, my dear."

It was touch and go whether Maxwell was going to allow her to leave him. Finally out of reach, the massive, gaping hole she'd left was clear.

* * * * *

A local vicar of some standing escorted Bryn into dinner. He was middle-aged, gone to paunch and a distractible sort, but pleasant and jolly.

Once in the dining hall, Sutherland took her elbow in a

proprietary grasp. "My dear Miss McCann, I have placed you at my table with your sister and Mr. Armstrong. We're all agog to hear how you're amusing yourself in Edinburgh."

The insinuation wormed through her. Had Sutherland heard about her foray at Molly's? She recalled Molly's warning that Sutherland had eyes and ears all over Edinburgh. She was seated next to Craddock and across from Mary and Dugan. The seat to her left was as yet unoccupied.

The earl took his place at Sutherland's right and next to Mary. He winked and gave her a bracing smile. She had one ally at the table, and Dugan could hardly drag her away in the middle of a dinner party. She could concentrate on avoiding the sinkholes of their questions.

Maxwell, Mr. Masterson, and Mrs. Winslow were seated at the farthest table away. Footmen moved forward to fill wineglasses.

"Miss?" A familiar voice whipped her around. Holding a carafe, Penny stood at her elbow with a raised eyebrow and a barely discernable smile.

She gasped but covered with a clearing of her throat and a mask of indifference. "Yes, please."

Her stomach rejected even the thought of food. Bryn did her best to not look at Dugan, but his gaze never left her. He hated her. Why hadn't she been strong enough when Mary had blindsided her with the betrothal announcement and say she did not wish to marry.

Instead, a chain of events she could not have predicted had been put into motion through her cowardice. A measure of remorse was hers to bear. Not for breaking the engagement but for allowing the farce to continue until she'd been so desperate to involve Maxwell against his will.

As the seat to her left was as yet empty, she turned to Craddock. "How did you leave Cragian?"

"Same as always."

"Has the lambing begun?"

"How the devil should I know?"

"You are responsible for your tenants. You should know everything that happens on your land and to your people," Bryn said.

As he gestured for the footmen to start serving soup, Sutherland asked mildly, "You care a great deal about the less fortunate among us, do you, Miss McCann?"

"Shouldn't we all care, Mr. Sutherland?"

"Certainly. But instead of worrying about a tenant or two, the greatest change can be instigated by working within the system."

Bryn fiddled with her spoon, her appetite nonexistent. "The government, you mean?"

"The House of Commons, Parliament. There are monies available for roads, bridges, and charitable purposes. With the right influence, those monies can be directed where it's truly needed."

A sound that might have been a warning came from Mary.

With an undisguised irony, the earl said, "And you're the man who can justly appropriate the monies and distribute among the needy?"

Sutherland lounged in his chair like a lion lying in wait for its prey. "Scotland has been too long ignored by those in power. We need strong leadership to demand what's rightfully ours."

"And one man could accomplish such a feat? That didn't work out well for your bonny prince, now did it?"

The jab wiped Sutherland's enigmatic smile away. "Not one man, but many."

Before the confrontation had a chance to conclude, Lord Albert MacShane made his way to the seat next to her. "So terribly sorry, Sutherland. Mother felt a bit peaked earlier, and I was late getting off."

"I hope she's recovered."

"She is. I rather think those spells are only to keep me close." His laugh was too high-pitched and grating.

"Well, no matter, you're here now and haven't missed the main course. I believe you're acquainted with most of the table."

While Sutherland introduced Albert to the earl, Bryn quashed her astonishment so it wouldn't reflect on her face. All the players were in attendance tonight, but what part would they play? Hero or villain?

"How long have you been in town, my lord?" she asked.

Albert dropped his fork, the clatter drawing eyes. "Only a few days now."

"I'm sorry to hear of your mother's sickness." Bryn channeled her resentment of Lady MacShane into the dissection of the quail on her plate.

"Mother is well enough. She's an old dragon, but she can still spit fire." A cynical amusement tinged his voice. Dark circles ringed low under his eyes, and he had lost weight, his face gaunt and his jacket loose.

"Are you quite all right, Lord MacShane?"

Staring dispassionately at the quail lying on his plate, Albert asked, "Are you staying with Mr. Drake?"

"Aye, with Mrs. Winslow as my chaperone."

"What's he like? Is he a good man?" It seemed Albert's appetite matched her own. He skewered the quail, methodically pulled off the meat, and set it neatly in a pile to the side, not taking a single bite.

Was this simple curiosity about his half brother or something more sinister? What would the truth hurt? "He's remarkable. He overcame a childhood of deprivation and amassed a fortune."

"I didn't know who he was when I was a child, you know."

"If you had, would you have crossed your mother and father to help him?"

He hesitated, moving the food around on his plate. "I don't know. But I asked for a brother more times than I could count. Mother never told me I already had one. Is he like our father, or is he a kind man?"

A wash of sympathy came over Bryn. Albert had not been deprived of food or shelter as a child, but he'd lacked something Maxwell had been rich with. Love. "Very kind. Funny too in an ironic kind of way. He doesn't laugh often, but when he does—"

Bryn took a gulp of wine. She'd said too much. If Albert was out to hurt Maxwell, her nattering could put him in danger. The way his smile and laugh could turn her inside out and put her heart on offer was of no consequence to Albert.

Tracing the tip of her knife around the edge of the plate, she continued. "He's tough from his time in the war. Good with a pistol, knife, or his fists. Ruthless with those who cross him."

Albert pulled at his collar as if it were strangling him. "Excuse me, Miss McCann."

Bryn turned to watch him leave, crossing glances with Maxwell. Returning her attention to the pit of vipers that doubled as a dinner table, she found Dugan whispering to Mary, but Mary aiming daggers with her eyes at Bryn.

"What were you and Lord MacShane discussing so intimately, Bryn? Are you already bored with my castoffs?"

"Mind your tongue, Mary," Craddock said harshly.

The undercurrents of anger and danger and secrets were as complicated as a Jacob's ladder, tying them all together in a myriad of ways.

Stilted small talk about the weather, politics, and horses accompanied dessert. Albert never returned. Dinner ended, and the after-dinner rituals commenced. She had no time to discuss matters with Maxwell before the men closeted themselves to drink brandy and smoke.

Bryn followed Mary into the drawing room, where the ladies

would gossip and drink port. She felt a bit like an insect flying straight into a spider's web.

CHAPTER TWENTY-TWO

Maxwell stepped into the billiard room, a tingle setting his nerves on edge. Albert MacShane leaned against the window sash in the far corner, looking out into the dark. His late entrance and early exit had raised alarms. But the final piece to the puzzle had been his slight limp.

As soon as the brandy had been passed around, Maxwell wasted no time in approaching Albert. The man snipped the end of a cigar.

"Lord MacShane, I was hoping to join you, but I'm afraid I'm fresh out." Maxwell projected what he hoped was an open, honest air while MacShane rifled his jacket for another cigar.

"Certainly. My pleasure." MacShane fumbled the handoff and apologized profusely.

Maxwell ran it under his nose and sniffed. Mild, expensive, familiar. "An excellent cigar."

"Mother detests the habit, but smoking helps settle my nerves."

"Are you nervous now, my lord?" Maxwell said blandly.

"No, of course not. Why would I be?" The tremble in his hands as he lit a match belied his words.

"The officers in my unit would smoke this same type of cigar before battles." Maxwell made no move to light the cigar. "The smell brings back memories."

"Good or bad ones?"

"Like most of life, some of both. Tell me, Lord MacShane, how did you hurt your leg? Did you fall off the side of a building perchance?"

The man swayed and grabbed the back of the nearest chair. "What are you going to do? Have me arrested? K-kill me? It was foolish, but mother insisted. Oh Christ—"

"Calm yourself, MacShane. I'm not plotting revenge against you." Maxwell interrupted when heads swiveled in their direction.

"For what it's worth, the night I sh-shot at you, I didn't even mean to hit you. I closed my eyes and squeezed the trigger. I was a nervous wreck."

Was that news supposed to console him? "Is what's in our father's will worth killing me over?"

"I don't know," Albert said heavily.

"What?" Stupefaction sailed Maxwell's voice higher. "Are you telling me you haven't read it either?"

"Mother's kept it under lock and key. Told me not to worry, that I was heir to the house and fortune. I didn't think anything of it, to be honest, until you came calling. She went around the bend after you and Miss McCann left."

"Did you follow us that day and ambush us in the forest?"

"No, of course not." Horror-tinged surprise was written large on his face, even though he himself had shot at Maxwell the night before.

Although it would have tied things up neatly, Albert's amateurish attempt on his life didn't align with the ferocious attack in the forest.

It seemed Albert was after the same thing he was. Information. "Did you locate the will in Pickett's office?"

"I pulled all the files out of the cabinets, checked his desk drawers. Nothing."

"Did you check on top of his desk?" Maxwell asked drily.

"Mother had warned him you might come calling. Why would he leave it out for anyone to see?"

Maxwell barked a humorless laugh. "A quick tip: don't leave your estate to start a career as a thief or assassin."

"Bloody hell, I won't, Mr. Drake. You have my word. The past few weeks have taken a decade off my life. All I want is to go home and study my plants. I have some interesting experiments going on in my greenhouse that need attention."

"That's for the best, I'd say."

"I plan to get my hands on Father's will one way or another." Albert chewed on the inside of his mouth and cast him a look from under his lashes. "If you would like, I'll make notes of the pertinent parts and send them on to you."

"Why would you do that for me?" Although Maxwell didn't consider Albert a threat to his life, neither was he ready to bestow his trust.

"You're my brother." The simple statement skewered Maxwell.

For years he'd secretly wished for MacShane the elder to acknowledge him. He'd wanted a family. He'd wanted a brother. But he'd given up on such foolish dreams during sleepless, hungry nights in their cottage. He opened his mouth, but words failed him.

Albert had no such misgivings. "Miss McCann sung your praises at dinner tonight, minus a rather ominous threat as to your abilities to maim a man. I fear I've judged you based on Mother's opinion, and I'm coming to understand she's unable to be objective where you're concerned."

"What exactly did Miss McCann say about me?" The words were out before Maxwell could stop them. Albert's eyebrows rose in a mirror image of his own, and Maxwell's breath caught painfully.

Albert only smiled. "I appreciate your forgiveness and understanding, Mr. Drake."

"Call me Maxwell."

"And I'm Albert." They shook hands. "I'll take my leave now. I have a feeling I might get my first decent night's sleep in an age."

Could they perhaps become friends? The odd turn of events tipped Maxwell off-balance and made him fear their plans wouldn't withstand the unexpected.

Maxwell maneuvered to the earl and Mr. Masterson, who were at the mantle in discussion.

"Drake. Did you make a new friend?" The earl swirled the brandy in his glass, his eyes twinkling.

"Mayhap I did. Although the blighter did try to kill me."

"Lord MacShane was the mysterious pistol-wielding man in the alley?"

"None other. And he was the intrepid burglar that mucked up Pickett's office. He claims the shenanigans were all his mother's doing, and I tend to believe him. All poor old Albert wants to do is go home to his greenhouse."

Mr. Masterson asked, "What about the will? Did he clue you in to its contents?"

"He hasn't read it either, if you can believe it."

"I'm not sure that I do," the earl said.

"His dear mama has kept it under lock and key. He's promised to obtain a copy and send me the pertinent parts, but I'm not sure he's strong enough to wrest it from her hands."

"Dear Lord, I worry for the future with the number of milksops running around." The earl's mouth tightened with real annoyance.

"Let's look at the bright side. One faction out to kill me has been eliminated."

Raucous laughter and a fist pounding on a nearby table drew their attention. Sutherland sat in an armchair flanked by Craddock and a local magistrate. Armstrong and a handful of others formed a semicircle around them.

"But what about the vote? Men will decide at the polls."

Sutherland flicked a hand. "I'll help the men decide. Most of them don't care as long as their families stay fed and warm through the winter. Craddock has Dumfries well in hand, and I *own* Edinburgh," he said with such relish that Maxwell imagined him with a conquering army. "And if we can clear up a little matter soon, we'll control even more."

The slight glance between Sutherland and Dugan Armstrong hit Maxwell like a gunshot.

Sutherland rose gracefully and announced, "I believe it's time to rejoin the lovely ladies in the drawing room, gentlemen."

* * * * *

Bryn stood in the corner of the drawing room and wished she could call for the carriage and go home. But tonight wasn't about her comfort. She had to keep her eyes and ears open. The trouble was Mary had given her the cut direct, which had emboldened the ladies of Edinburgh to do the same. Not that Bryn blamed the ladies for following Mary's lead. Any woman who treated her with a modicum of kindness would be subjected to Mary's sharp tongue.

Mrs. Winslow, who had circulated in Edinburgh for several weeks now, was still included in conversations, but it was stilted. The women gathered on settees or at card tables, laughing and talking, and were doing such a good job ignoring her that Bryn felt invisible. She was a child again, on the outside looking in.

But was being invisible so bad? She could slip out with everyone none the wiser and perhaps discover what Mary and Craddock had promised Dugan. If she could unravel the betrothal, she'd be free.

She meandered to the door and out. The plans Penny had drawn up had been thorough and clear. She bypassed the staircase and tiptoed down a dim hallway to the last door on the left. Pressing her ear against the cool wood, she heard nothing and cracked it open. Sutherland's study was empty.

First, learning from Albert's mistake, she riffled through the papers out on the desk. Nothing pertaining to her and Dugan's marriage, but she did find a list of names she recognized with a number associated with each man. All the men listed were either peers or political appointees. A few were crossed through with a thin black line. Bryn hesitated and then folded the paper and tucked it down her bodice, well into her stays.

All but one of the drawers of his desk were locked, and the one that wasn't contained nothing of interest. The walls were lined with bookshelves and a handful of pictures. There had to be a hiding place somewhere. She spun, examining the space. Her eye caught on a vibrant oil painting of a woman in dishabille. It was lovely and tasteful but stood out because it was so different from the rather mundane watercolors.

On instinct, she ran her fingers along the edge of the frame. A small lever clicked, and the picture swung open on well-oiled hinges. A wooden box was built into the wall with an elaborate locking mechanism. Her heart accelerated. She hadn't expected to get this far. Now what?

Footsteps in the hall rippled panic through her like thrown pebbles in a puddle. She secured the picture and darted to a full-length corner wardrobe. Taking a deep breath, she pushed inside and closed it as the study door opened.

Whoever had entered was being very quiet. Was it Maxwell? Or Penny? She pressed her eye to the narrow crack where the hinges attached, but it was well jointed. So much so, very little light seeped into the darkness.

What if the door jammed? Would she suffocate and die? Was this to be her coffin? Closing her eyes, she took deep breaths and imagined herself in the Cragian stable under the hay.

Noises penetrated her spiraling terror. Men's voices, muffled but growing louder. The doors to the wardrobe opened, and a big body pressed in. She lashed out, catching the man on the shoulder. A whispered epitaph stilled her.

She breathed his name, "Maxwell."

He shushed her.

Several men poured into the room. Only a few planks of wood separated them from a fate she didn't want to contemplate.

Maxwell slipped an arm around her waist and aligned himself behind her. It was a tight fit. Clothing hung behind and around them, and the corner of a shelf poked into her leg. If this were to be her coffin, at least she shared it with the man she loved.

"…and Brynmore McCann."

At her name, her attention turned outward. Had that been Dugan's voice? Or Craddock's?

"How difficult is it to kill one man?" Sutherland's voice was no longer charming and hospitable, but sharp and intimidating.

"He decimated the two men you hired. One thought he'd managed to slip a knife in his ribs, but the blackguard looked healthy enough tonight." Definitely Dugan, and he'd moved closer. A bang shook the side of the wardrobe, and she stifled a gasp with her hand.

"Let's approach the situation from a different angle. If we can't dispose of Drake, we take the girl instead." Sutherland again.

"You've got a vicar in attendance, don't you?" A zealot's excitement colored Dugan's voice. "If I can get her upstairs, would he perform the ceremony?"

"Of a certainty. I've his bollocks on my desk." That elicited a laugh among the men. How many? At least four, including

Sutherland and Dugan. "But you're impatient, Armstrong. That's your weakness. She has protectors tonight. Would she come quietly?"

"Not likely," Dugan said.

Sutherland spoke again. "Let her go home tonight and settle back into her routine. Surely she goes shopping or visiting with that dotty chaperone. What do you say, McAfee? Can your boys handle a snatching?"

Maxwell tensed behind her as a rough voice answered, "Aye, they can, sir. What're the rules? Can they have a taste before handing her over?"

"No fucking her. But she deserves some punishment for letting Drake take her, don't you think?" Dugan's words made her head swim, and she clutched at the arm circling her waist. Of course she'd known he was cruel, but she hadn't guessed the extent of his depravity.

"It might even make her grateful to be handed over to you. You can ride in and save her from McAfee's boys. You'll have her on her knees in thanks." Sutherland's voice contained a salaciousness that made her feel dirty.

"Drake doesn't seem the type to sit idle waiting for a ransom note. You'll need to get her wedded and bedded with haste." Sutherland was on the move, his voice not as close. "Gentleman, please stay to finish your drinks. McAfee, I expect you two can find your way out discreetly after you've finished. Come with me, Dugan."

With Sutherland and Dugan gone, the discussion lost its seriousness and veered into horse racing and the possibility of a game of whist later. The tension ebbed out of her body. They only needed to wait until the men moved on. With Maxwell with her, her fears stayed manageable.

The feel of Maxwell pressed against her from shoulders to knees edged out the blur of conversation. The darkness was no longer menacing but enveloped her like a protective cloak.

Tactile awareness mounted—Maxwell's breath stirring the hair at her temple, warm and tickling, the slight stubble of his jaw rasping erotically against her cheek, and the strength of his forearm around her waist.

His thighs flexed against her as he slid a foot between her own. Awareness of the hardness pressing into her buttocks came with a sudden clarity. He wanted her despite the peril. Or perhaps because of it?

Danger rubbed her senses raw, every stimulus dancing the edge of pleasure and pain. She arched her back and wiggled her bottom. His arm turned to stone around her waist. He tilted her forward and traced his fingertips along the delicate line of her collarbone.

Desire blossomed like a moonflower, showing its beauty in the darkness. His lips fell to her cheekbone, and a sizzle streaked along the path he trekked to the delicacy of her ear. A moan welled up. He circled his hand around her throat to silence her.

Madness. Utter and complete madness. Men who would be happy to rip Maxwell limb from limb and were planning on abducting and defiling her sat mere feet away. Yet passion flared. He roved his hands from her throat to her collarbone to the swells of her breasts. With each pass, he delved farther inside her bodice, until his finger grazed over a budded nipple, and she quivered.

She slipped a hand between their bodies to glance over his erection. His sharp intake of breath and the buck of his hips grew her confidence. One of his hands stayed to tease her nipple, squeezing gently, while the other gathered the fabric of her skirts.

The sensation of the fabric brushing her skin made her squirm. His hand branded her thigh. She turned her head and nuzzled his jaw. He took her mouth in a kiss that stripped away reality. The wardrobe fell away. They could have been standing on a heather-covered hillock with a star-filled night sky that stretched to forever.

His hand didn't stay idle. Wantonly, she slipped her legs farther apart and prayed he'd find the slit of her drawers. He did. His touch was light. She needed more and compressed her lips to keep from begging. Still grasping his erection, she squeezed him. Like prodding a horse, he jerked, and his finger slipped through wet heat. He bucked his hips into her hand and buried his face in her neck.

But he gave her want she demanded. He rubbed her sensitive bundle of nerves with his thumb as a finger pressed inside of her. The rhythm he set was slow and decadent. A tiny part of her brain was attuned to the men outside the wardrobe, but they had grown quiet. No, not just quiet but silent. She and Maxwell were alone. She surrendered.

She covered his hand with her own and pressed him deeper as her body clenched and pleasure spiked. She clutched at his erection, wanting it to replace his fingers more than she'd ever wanted anything. Too much cloth stood in her way.

Even though the men had left, the two of them stayed pressed together in the wardrobe. He played along her slick, aroused folds before removing his hand. Her skirts fell to the floor as her body clenched around nothing, unsatisfied.

The unwelcome voice of reality intruded from outside the wardrobe. "Drake?"

CHAPTER TWENTY-THREE

Maxwell pushed the wardrobe door open and ducked out. Bryn, not sure her legs would support her, wobbled out and plopped in the nearest chair. Penny's eyebrows shot up, but he said nothing.

"We had to hide when Sutherland and his cronies came in," Maxwell said with such briskness that Bryn almost believed nothing had happened.

"Did you manage to find the contract before you were interrupted?"

"Not in any of the desk drawers."

"There's a locked box behind the oil painting of the lady. There's a hidden latch you must release at the bottom." She pointed toward the oil painting. Neither man hid their surprise. "I'm not completely useless, you know."

While the men worked on picking the lock, Bryn returned to the wardrobe to examine the contents. There were a few odd-looking dresses cut so low Bryn wasn't even sure they would cover a woman's bosom. A cylindrical object made of solid glass drew her eye, and she picked it up studying it intently. One end was tapered, and one end was capped by a bulbous projection. What was it? It almost looked like a...

"Oh. Oh my." She shoved it back on the shelf. She glanced

over the rest of the objects with newly awakened eyes and saw harnesses and whips and cuffs. Her face burned. She closed the door and leaned against it.

Penny opened the box and stepped back to let Maxwell rifle the contents. "I've got it," Maxwell exclaimed softly.

Bryn plucked it out of his fingertips and skimmed the first page. Maxwell snatched it back, holding her at bay when she reached for it.

"No time for games. You'd best get back, Mr. Drake." Penny turned to Bryn. "Mrs. Winslow has informed everyone you're not feeling well and left early. I'm afraid you'll have to wait for everyone in the carriage."

"I'd feel more comfortable somewhere I can keep my eyes on you." Maxwell took her hand.

"I can hardly waltz back into the drawing room after excuses have been made. I'll be fine."

Penny rocked on his feet by the door. "Every minute raises the chance of our discovery. You've been gone too long as it is, Drake. I'll take care of Miss McCann."

They slipped into the hallway, and Maxwell squeezed her hand. "For God's sake, stay in the carriage. Do you promise me?"

"I promise." After everything he had risked for her, it was a small enough concession. Anyway, they had the wedding contract in hand.

Penny led her through a narrow hall to a little room that smelled of flour. "Out the window with you, miss."

The window wasn't much wider than her hips. "Are you serious?"

"Come now, I know you're familiar with the technique." His voice was rife with tease.

"Not before I met Maxwell. And not in a dress," she muttered. The window slid open noiselessly. A frigid breeze burst into the room.

"Always have an escape plan ready. Out you go then." Penny offered a hand as if she were climbing in a carriage and not out a window.

Bryn hiked up her dress, and Penny helped her maneuver her legs and hips out. She dropped and caught herself on her hands and knees in the grass.

The quiet thud of Penny landing came a moment later. She stood and dusted her hands together. He took her elbow and guided her through a small garden. Her dress was no match against the bitter cold. Her bones shook.

A brick wall rose in front of them. Mentally preparing herself to climb it, she was thankful when Penny led them to a small wrought iron gate. It appeared rusty and disused, yet it opened with nary a squeak. Carriages lined the lane on the other side of the wall.

He handed her into Maxwell's carriage, and she wrapped herself gratefully in her cloak as her toes found a hot brick. "I must return before I'm missed. I'm afraid Sutherland has his suspicions already."

She grabbed his arm. "You're not putting yourself in unnecessary danger on my account, are you, Penny? Why must you return at all? We have the contract."

His smile spoke of intimacy with danger she hoped to never cultivate. "I'll be fine, but the earl and your gentleman, Mr. Drake, might require my talents. Now, you settle in for a spell. Close the curtains, miss, and don't leave."

"I won't." She had no intention of stepping outside again.

Penny nodded and slipped away. The interior of the carriage was dark and close, and Bryn settled onto the squab, remembering another dark, close place. She closed her eyes and let her mind drift. What was Maxwell doing? Had Mr. Masterson had a chance to read the contract yet? Was there an easy way out of this mess?

Voices outside the carriage brought her to an instant alert.

Most likely a groom. Yet fear zinged through her body. She slid off the squab and crouched on the floor of the carriage. The men grew closer, the whispers forming discernable words.

"Keep clear. Right there is the axle. Not that one, you dolt, but next to it." Muffled responses followed. "We're to follow it home. If they don't crash then, we'll loosen it more."

More whispering followed, and Bryn only caught a few words. "Kill him… snatch her… accident, who cares…" Her blood congealed, making her heart pound with effort. The carriage shook and bounced with whatever maliciousness they performed.

The clack of boots faded, and she peeked out of the curtains. The two men were mere shadows. Did their identity matter? If not those two, then it would be another set of hired lackeys.

The far carriage door swung open. Shock held her in its grasp. Craddock's bulk blocked the opening. She had one chance for escape. Move. She needed to move. Like being shot from a pistol, she scrambled to the far door and fumbled with the latch. A chance. All she needed was a chance to run.

She pushed the door open, but Dugan stepped into the space, sealing off her escape.

Bryn put herself between the two men and looked around the carriage for a weapon. Her foot glanced over the still-warm brick.

Ignoring her, Dugan looked over at Craddock. "I told you she wouldn't have let some old biddies scare her off. She's got too much pride for that. What have you been up to, Bryn?"

"I wasn't feeling well, and instead of making everyone leave, I decided to wait for them in the carriage. That's all there is to it."

Dugan harrumphed. "I doubt that's the extent of it. Do you think she discovered anything?"

"Sutherland keeps anything of importance locked up tight, so I very much doubt it," Craddock said.

"Sutherland said we should wait, but when opportunity knocks and all that. What do you say?" The smile that crested

Dugan's face was colder than the night.

Craddock nodded. "Take her upstairs, and I'll corral that dotty old vicar and Mary. Then you can consummate the loving, heartfelt vows, although I think it best if we witness the bedding to make sure it's legal and binding."

"Yes. And it will be all the sweeter with Drake downstairs with nary a clue." Dugan reached for her, and she reached for the brick. She brought it around as hard as she could but misjudged the weight, her aim off. Instead of hitting his temple, it glanced against his shoulder.

"You bitch!" Dugan grabbed her wrists and pulled her out, her arm scraping along the door.

She shrieked, but Dugan covered her mouth and nose with a meaty hand and pulled her back against him. She bucked and clawed like an animal, but his hand over her face only tightened. Air became scarce. Her lungs burned. She pulled at his wrist but couldn't break his hold.

"Damnation, she's a hellcat. Knock her senseless with that brick, Craddock," Dugan said.

"Wouldn't be wise. Even a vicar in Sutherland's pocket might balk at legally binding you with an unconscious woman." Craddock stepped closer, and she lashed out with a kick, catching him on the shin. "She'll soon learn her place."

"That's right. Under me." Dugan's laugh made tears spring to her eyes.

His hand shifted enough to allow a breath, but before she could use it on a scream, the sharp point of a knife pressed to her side.

"Believe me, I would be more than happy to gut you for all the trouble you've caused us, but you still have something we need. I could cut you, shallow but painful. In fact, if you died in a few weeks from a fever, all the better. I'd be happy to play the grieving widower." The relish in his voice resonated with an evil truth.

Whether from fear or the cold, her body went numb, and she stumbled along. The poke of the knife in her side wiped all rational thought from her head except survival.

He propelled her forward, toward the darkened back entrance of the house. Craddock veered down the hall toward the party while Dugan hauled her up a narrow set of servant's stairs. They emerged in a dimly lit guest corridor. The sound of the gathering below drifted to them. So close yet too far for help. Dugan stopped at a door halfway down and toed the door open, shoving her inside.

Away from Dugan and the knife, her brain whirred to life. The room was sweet-smelling and blue and white. She leaned into the massive post of the bed, averting her eyes at her likely wedding bed unless she could gather her wits and escape.

Dugan stood in the doorway and twirled the knife in his hands. His half smile had nothing to do with humor or happiness and everything to do with satisfaction and triumph. Voices and footsteps came from outside the door.

Sutherland was the first through the door, followed by Mary, Craddock, and the hapless vicar that had escorted her into dinner.

"Wasn't expecting to perform any civic duties this evening. I would have passed on that glass of port otherwise." The vicar's voice betrayed his nerves.

"True love can be impetuous, can it not?" Sutherland was all blithe charm. How many masks did the man have at his disposal? "Armstrong and Miss McCann have been betrothed for some time—the agreement is downstairs in my study. They both wish for a small ceremony and a speedy consummation, isn't that right, Armstrong?" The stare Dugan and Sutherland shared contained an energy and vigor that Bryn didn't understand but set her on edge.

"Aye, that's right, Vicar," Dugan said never breaking eye contact with Sutherland.

Although panic stalked close, she didn't lose control of her senses as she had all too often. But could she feign an attack or swoon? Mary's eyes were narrowed on Bryn as if she could read her mind. No, any weakness shown on her part would be exploited. She would have to wait and hope for an opportunity to escape.

The vicar's face had flushed, and he looked from one person to the next, his gaze landing on the door. "This is most irregular."

"Yes. Which is why you'll receive a donation worthy of your time." Sutherland pulled out a purse and jangled it. "And your silence."

The vicar licked his lips. Was he reacting to the money or the threat in Sutherland's voice? "What are the groom and bride's full names?"

"Dugan Michael Armstrong."

"And the lass?"

Bryn measured the distance to the door—too far—and kept her mouth shut. No matter what happened, she wouldn't make this easy on anyone.

Mary pinched Bryn's arm in a move reminiscent of childhood. "She's nervous, is all. Her name is Brynmore Katherine McCann."

"Brynmore... Brynmore..." The vicar intoned her name several times. "An unusual name. I've only heard of one other soul with that name."

For the first time, the vicar met her eyes. A connection flared between them, sparked by her name. She took a step toward him. "Yes, sir. My name is quite rare."

"And how long have you resided in Edinburgh, lass?"

"Only a few weeks. I traveled from Dumfries during the snow."

He reached for her hand and patted it. "I'll need to see the betrothal contract, Mr. Sutherland."

"Why?" Sutherland narrowed his eyes. "Surely my word is enough."

The vicar's hand trembled. He was afraid of Sutherland. Well, that made two of them. She grasped his hand and squeezed. Only this man's courage and honor stood between her and a fate that would lead to her death.

"If the contract is in order and the bride has no objections, then we'll see about a ceremony this evening. Otherwise, the blessed event can wait until morning, surely."

"I'll get the contract. It's binding." Sutherland slammed the door on the way out.

Any delay was welcome. Maxwell would turn the house upside down for her, but when would he discover her absence?

Sutherland crashed back through the door a moment later. "It's bloody well gone!"

Dugan, Mary, Craddock spoke on top of one another.

"It was in the lockbox."

"Who took it?"

"Where is it?"

"Aye, it was locked up tight." Sutherland turned baleful eyes upon her. "Have we underestimated you, Miss McCann? What were you up to earlier this evening? Search her, Lady Craddock."

Mary wouldn't find the betrothal documents, but she might discover the curious paper Bryn had stuffed down her bodice. She held her arms out and spun in a slow circle. "Go right ahead. You'll find nothing, because I don't have them."

"It's only a matter of time, Bryn." Mary checked her cloak but not her dress.

The vicar backed toward the door and held his hand out to Bryn. "Without the documents, I can't in good conscience perform a ceremony blessed by God. I'll escort Miss Brynmore back downstairs to her chaperone, shall I?"

Sutherland propped his fists on his hips but didn't protest.

"You're going to let her leave?" Incredulousness sailed

Dugan's voice high.

"This is only a delay. Let them leave." Sutherland turned away and stared out the window.

Bryn didn't hesitate. She left at the vicar's side. Maxwell and the earl stood at the bottom of the steps, the intensity of their discussion coloring the air. She pulled out of the vicar's grasp and skipped down the stairs.

Maxwell. She must have spoken, because as his name reverberated in her head, Maxwell and the earl turned. He took the steps two at a time, meeting her on the first landing. They grabbed hold of one another, his lips murmuring her name over and over.

Puffing slightly, the vicar joined them. "I'd advise you to move the lass somewhere safer."

They continued down the stairs and huddled in an alcove. Guests were beginning to leave, and they kept their voices low.

"I thought I'd lost you." He took her hand, his thumb rubbing the back.

"Craddock and Dugan ambushed me in the carriage and dragged me upstairs at knifepoint. The vicar was on hand to perform a ceremony."

Maxwell's hand tightened on hers. "Are you… unhurt?"

"I'm fine. The vicar's quick thinking foiled their plans."

The vicar bowed his head. "I'm much ashamed to admit that before I heard the name Brynmore, I would have proceeded, damned as I would be in God's eyes. Sutherland is a powerful, dangerous man to cross."

"Have we met before, sir?"

"You've met my daughter, Meredith. If I'm not mistaken, you're godmother to my newborn granddaughter, Elizabeth *Brynmore* Douglas."

Bryn shook her head. Fate was a mystery of twists and turns, and she could only thank the stars this twist had been in her favor.

The vicar cleared his throat. "Sutherland will try again. A different vicar, another time."

"Yes." Maxwell's voice was heavy with portent. "My lord, would you and Penny escort Bryn to the carriage and remain with her until I arrive?"

Although he posed it as a question, it was obvious he would brook no dissension.

She laid a hand on Maxwell's arm. "Wait. They've tampered with the axle. Two men are planning to follow the carriage and attack when we break down."

"I'll drop a word in Penny's ear," the earl said. "He should be able to take care of it."

Maxwell gave a brisk nod and turned his attention to the vicar. She felt dismissed. Pigeonholed. As if Maxwell only cared for her when it was convenient for him.

The earl flipped the hood of her cloak over her head. "Let's not draw any more attention than necessary to your reappearance, shall we?"

Instead of sneaking out the back, the earl guided her out the front door, but they didn't speak to anyone except for Penny who was out front loading guests into their carriages. Their whispered conversation didn't interest her as much as what Maxwell and the vicar were discussing inside.

CHAPTER TWENTY-FOUR

Having Bryn out of his sight and his protection settled like an itch he couldn't scratch. This evening had revealed how precarious their situation was. His desperation after discovering her absence had been terrifying in more ways than one. He'd felt like he'd lost an arm or a leg or a... heart.

Maxwell turned to the vicar. "For obvious reasons, Bryn and I told your daughter we were married as we traveled together. Quite out of necessity, I might add. We were accosted on the road by Sutherland's lackeys, which is how we ended up begging shelter that fateful night."

"Goodness, he wants the lass badly." A flash of fear showed in the vicar's eyes before he stood up straighter. "What can I do?"

Maxwell stumbled over his next words. "I... Well, I'm hoping you'll indeed perform a marriage ceremony. Tomorrow. I need it legal and binding, sir."

"What about this betrothal contract? Does it exist?"

"Aye, unfortunately, it does, but with the mounting evidence that Armstrong means Bryn harm, surely we can circumvent it—in court if necessary."

"An English court perhaps but not one in Edinburgh. I'm not sure you realize how far Sutherland's arms reach into this city. I'll most likely pay dearly for this display of mutiny," the vicar said.

"You as well, Mr. Drake."

"Perhaps a visit to your daughter is in order until it blows over."

The vicar smiled. "Yes, a fine idea. I'll leave tomorrow after I make your union official."

"Thank you, sir." The two men shook hands.

A moment of doubt assailed Maxwell. Would Bryn agree or stare at him as if he'd grown devil horns? She might not like it, but she *would* marry him on the morrow. For her safety and his sanity.

"Lord Craddock and Mr. Armstrong look ready to do battle, Mr. Drake." The vicar took sidestepped toward the door.

Maxwell glanced over his shoulder to see Craddock and Armstrong descending the stairs like two bulls. "Go on, Vicar. Until the morning."

The vicar moved faster than his spindly legs and belly would suggest.

"Where is it?" Armstrong bit out with no prelude.

"Where's what?" Maxwell blanked his expression. Lessons from bluffing his way through checkpoints during his days as an exploring officer were at his fingertips.

"You bloody well know what we want—the betrothal papers. I'll sue for breach of contract." Armstrong raised his clenched hands, and Maxwell readied himself in case a punch came.

"You're welcome to try, but any magistrate will find your little machinations to have me murdered quite interesting. At the very least, I'll ensure your name is dragged through muck, and your schemes will be for naught." Even though his voice was calm, serene even, Maxwell had the urge to pull the knife from his inside pocket, slit Armstrong's throat, and watch him bleed out in the middle of Sutherland's marbled entry hall.

"You'll not have another peaceful night, Drake." Armstrong jabbed a finger an inch from Maxwell's face. Maxwell didn't so much as flinch. What bullies like Armstrong wanted above all else was people to fear him.

People to fear him. The words went on repeat in his head. But who? He would certainly gain Bryn's inheritance on marriage, which would widen his reach over a handful of tenants and their sheep. There must be more.

He sketched a bow and retreated. Let them think he was scared and running. The night air cooled the bloodlust singing through his veins. Bryn, the earl, and Mr. Masterson huddled in the cold next to the carriage as Penny's muttering snaked from underneath.

She looked small and slight next to the two gentlemen. Weak even, if he didn't know any better. Nothing—not abductions or attacks—had dented the essence of her spirit. Yet if Armstrong and Sutherland and Mary had succeeded in their machinations, would Bryn's spirit have survived?

A well of emotion rose. He turned away so she wouldn't glimpse his face and guess at the depth of his feelings. It was bad enough he'd let his guard down in the study trapped in that blasted cabinet. Suppressing this consuming need for her was exhausting.

Penny scooched out from under the carriage, wiping his hands on a rag. "Should get you home safely, but I'd have your stable master examine it on the morrow."

"Edie is staying warm in my carriage, Drake. Do I need to get her?" The earl's brows rose.

"No. Propriety is not as important as Bryn's safety. Let's leave this place."

The earl and Mr. Masterson climbed into their carriage. Bryn took her place, and Maxwell sat on the edge of the seat across from her. Flicking open the drapes, he scanned the road and kept his hand on a loaded pistol. No one bothered them, but he could feel the shadowy menaces stalking them. He would defend Bryn. With his life, if necessary.

They gathered in Maxwell's study on their arrival to peruse the contract. Lionel read out the pertinent parts. Bryn was indeed an heiress. A manor house, twenty thousand pounds, and a good bit of land were hers. Dugan would assume control on their marriage. Perhaps he would petition for a knighthood or barony to solidify his standing.

Yet a piece of the puzzle was missing.

Maxwell dropped into his chair and propped his elbows on his knees, his hands dangling. "Murder, kidnapping... Is this all about Bryn's inheritance?"

"Money and greed can turn a man's soul to evil. I've seen it. I've used the fact to my advantage," the earl said.

"Maybe so."

"Wait. I took something from Sutherland's study." She presented her back and wiggled and shimmied as she dug around in her bodice. "Here it is."

She handed over a piece of parchment. Maxwell spread it open on the desk, and all of them bent over to examine it.

"Those are elected officials all through Scotland," Maxwell said.

"What are the numbers?" Bryn asked. "Bribes?"

Lionel pushed away from the desk and paced, slow and deliberate. "Not bribes. Votes. Each number represents votes. My guess is the ones struck through are politicians they've bought. Armstrong wants Bryn's inheritance not only for the money but the land and votes. He wants standing and respect."

Maxwell banged his fist on the desk. "Yes. And Sutherland wants to control Scotland from his seat in Edinburgh. He wants the power of a king, the ability to steer the country. He's just amoral, intelligent, and brash enough to do it. He's already succeeded in Edinburgh."

"What's next?" the earl asked contemplatively rubbing his lip.

Maxwell flicked a glance toward Bryn. "Things will be clearer in the morning, I think."

Lionel cleared his throat. "Perhaps so. It's late and cold, and my bones are crying for bed."

Bryn retreated up the stairs with a backward glance full of secrets. He stared until she faded into the shadows.

The earl trotted down the front steps, but Lionel hesitated. "What are your plans regarding Miss McCann?"

"Bryn and I have an appointment with the vicar tomorrow morning."

"She's amenable?"

"I don't care. She's marrying me, and that's the end of it." His voice was harsh and more than a little desperate.

Lionel's eyes were kind, and the pat he gave Maxwell on the arm was fatherly. What would life have been like with a man like Lionel in his life? Old regrets and longings pressed and made it difficult to take a breath.

"A word of advice, Drake? Use a bit more tact with Miss Bryn. I was married for many years, quite happily because Betsy's feelings and opinions were important to me. I didn't trample them." Lionel tilted his head. "She loves you, you know."

Maxwell swallowed. Did he know? Neither of them had spoken of love. She had used him, altered the path of his life. But his new path was sweeter and fuller than the barren road he'd traveled alone.

"And whether you've admitted it to yourself or not, you love her."

"I… I…"

Lionel's smile was as kind and understanding as his eyes. "You're a good man, Drake. Be the man that Miss McCann deserves."

Lionel ducked into the carriage after giving him one long, last look. Maxwell wished he had the experience to interpret everything Lionel seemed to want to impart, but he didn't.

Stalking back to his study, Maxwell tore his cravat and collar off and braced his hands on his desk, the silence crypt-like. The craving to mark her as his was overwhelming. If not with his babe or a wedding ring, then in some more intangible way. It wasn't a want but a need. He needed her. He loved her, dammit.

He wasn't happy about it though. Since leaving Cragian, he'd entombed his heart. Brynmore had snuck into his room at the inn, slipped past his defenses, and breathed life into him.

One careless word or action from her would destroy him. If she understood the power she held over him, she could manipulate and torment him the rest of his days. He wanted to capture her heart and hold it under a knife in retaliation for stealing his away.

He moved up the stairs and stopped in front of the door he had stood in front of so many nights. This time he would enter. He reached for the handle as if his hand belonged to someone else.

Welcome enveloped him on his first step over the threshold. Candles cast a warm glow, and a fire crackled. Bryn rose from a chair by the hearth, wearing a virginal white nightgown made almost translucent by the light behind her. Tied loosely, the gown hung off one shoulder, her red-gold hair licking the delicate white curve of skin like flames. She had never looked more ethereal and otherworldly, her face in shadow, her body lit from within.

Charming, blithe words couldn't force themselves past the lump in his throat. He didn't feel charming and blithe. He was vulnerable and fearful and fought the urge to fall to his knees at her feet in surrender.

* * * * *

The fire and the candles aglow around the room highlighted Maxwell's face. It was almost as if he were scared of her, ready to bolt if she took so much as a step toward him. She held out a hand.

He approached as if he were a wounded animal seeking a balm, stopping within reach yet not touching her. Tentatively, she stroked down his arm, took his hand, and linked their fingers. A squeeze was the reward for her patience. She trailed her other hand up his chest. He'd removed his collar and cravat already, and she curled her hand around his neck, pulling him down to her.

As soon as their lips touched, he came to life, wrapping his arms around her, his grip almost painful. He needed something from her, although she wasn't sure what. He clutched at her hips, her buttocks, her back, as if trying to pull her inside him. In contrast, she ran her fingers through his hair and down his face, softly, soothingly, calming his fervor.

She shushed him as his mouth careened down her bare shoulder, nipping her and then licking in atonement. Her nightgown rose, the edge tickling past her thighs reminiscent of their interlude in the cabinet, but he didn't stop. Cloth obscured her sight for a moment, then drifted to the floor in a white heap. His hands were once again frantic on her bare skin.

Her naked body pressed against his fully clothed one in a crazily erotic buffet of sensations. The rasp of the fabric rubbed against her sensitive skin, and buttons bit against her breasts and belly.

Her world tilted and spun as he picked her up and laid her on the bed. He stood looking down on her. His silence, in combination with the intensity of his demeanor, unnerved her. Even after all that had passed between them, she felt naïve and unable to speak her heart.

He attacked the buttons of his waistcoat, peeling it off and letting it fall. His shirt followed. She propped herself up on her elbows. The flickering fire highlighted the play of muscles along his shoulders and arms as he wrestled with boots and breeches. He was beautiful and perfect, and she loved him.

Naked, he stood before her aroused but defiant, looking grim.

Bryn's eyes pricked with tears. She blinked. Maxwell had stood alone, apart, untrusting for most his life. Painful lessons imparted by Mary had only reinforced his attitude. Would he ever accept he didn't have to keep himself apart from her?

Bryn reached for him, and it was all the encouragement he needed. He fell on top of her, settling himself between her legs. She tensed, ready and willing, but he didn't take her.

Instead, he kissed her. No, he claimed and dominated her, but he wouldn't hurt her. She understood it like she understood the sun would rise every morning. He reached out to close the drapes around the bed, but she brushed the back of his hand with her fingertips.

"No. I want to see you."

His hand drew into a fist around the velvety fabric. She waited for him to decide. Darkness or light.

He grabbed her hand in his, pressed it into the bed, and buried his face in her neck. "My God, Brynmore, please." His voice was strangled, almost tortured. Nothing like the smooth, velvety brogue she'd grown used to.

She cupped his cheek and forced him to look at her. His eyes were sad and wet with tears. Forlorn and heartbroken.

"I love you. Maxwell, I love you. Don't you know that?" she whispered the words over and over. The moment they settled on him, his expression morphed into something primal.

Still holding her gaze, he entered her with a hiss, his lids settling low. This was what she'd been craving all night. His pace was slow and decadent, his hips rolling with each thrust. Her eyes closed, her pleasure dancing along the edge of a climax.

"No, look at me," he growled.

She popped her eyes open. His eyes reflected the firelight, and his magic carried her away. The voice calling his name and her love for him over and over was hers. She writhed under him as he released inside her.

He collapsed on top of her with his face buried in the pillow, still inside her and unmoving. She gloried in the press of his weight and traced his spine with her fingers.

He rolled to her side, pulled her close, and fluttered kisses along her jaw until he found her mouth in a gentle, sweet kiss. The storm that had consumed him had passed.

"How could you love me?" His voice was hesitant.

"How could I not?" Listing the many and varied reasons she loved him would only expose her vulnerabilities.

"We're going to marry in the morning." Although his voice retained a gentleness from their lovemaking, a familiar, implacable tone had invaded.

"We don't know if I'm with child or not."

"I don't give a damn about that. You're in danger. The only way to stop Armstrong is to take marriage off the table."

She didn't understand him. He was now willing to marry her just to protect her from a threat that may never materialize? Not a single word about love or even lust. Nothing about admiration or respect. She loved him, aye, but she wouldn't spend her life wondering if he secretly resented her.

Grabbing at the cover and pulling the edge over her body, she propped herself up on an elbow and put space between them. "You're willing to sacrifice your freedom to protect me?"

* * * * *

Was the woman daft? Sacrifice his *freedom*? Maxwell would give up everything to keep her safe. He would bloody well lay down his life for her. Did she not understand that?

The frisson that had passed through his body with her declaration of love had nearly undone him. He wouldn't have to capture her heart after all. She'd given it to him freely, and by God, he vowed to keep it safe.

Doubt crept in even with her words still singing through his blood. "Do you not want to marry me because I grew up a poor bastard?"

"This has nothing to do with your birth. You see judgment in everyone's eyes where there is none. The earl, Mr. Masterson, the men and women entrusting you with their money. None of them hold your birth over your head. Neither do I."

"Then marry me, dammit." Desperation turned him autocratic.

She turned her face away from him, neither refusing nor agreeing. There was one way he could declare himself. One place his heart and mind and body didn't war against one another.

He pushed her on her back and propped his head up on his hand. She had covered herself with a corner of the sheet, the curve of her hip and one long leg exposed. Like a little owl, she watched him with wide eyes, suspicious and missing nothing.

He quelled his impulse to tug the sheet away and instead brushed her hair back from her face, letting his fingers dance along her sharp cheekbones and soft mouth. "You're beautiful, lass."

She tried to pull away but didn't get far in the fluffy pillows. "No."

"Yes. Beautiful. Inside and out." He kissed her in an effort to convince her of the truth, but as her lips moved against his, he got lost in the sensation. Her hands circled his neck and tugged at his hair.

She gave herself freely and without artifice. Her love was almost tangible and knitted together years of fissures on his heart.

He whispered her name against her lips before moving over her. She opened for him without hesitation. His heart stuttered, and he took a bite of her soft neck to keep from speaking his heart aloud.

Moving lower, he lavished attention on her nipples until her hips bumped against him. He spread his hand over her belly, still taut and flat. It didn't matter anymore. Satisfaction rushed through him. She would be his wife on the morrow, but tonight she would be his in a more primal way.

Farther down he slid, pushing her legs apart and using his tongue to drive her as mad and wild as she made him feel. Their tastes mingled and drove the primitive beat of his heart against his ribs. *Mine.*

"Wait." She sat up and pulled his hair hard enough to sting. "My turn."

"What? No. I want to feel you come against my mouth."

She scrambled to her knees. "Lay back."

He obeyed as much out of surprise at the power in her voice as his curiosity. Lying back on the pillows, he waited, his body tensed in anticipation for her touch.

She ran a finger up his hard cock, swirling the fluid around the tip. "In the wardrobe, I would have given anything to have you bare in my hand as you touched me."

Her words made his cock jump, and he fought to keep his hips still. Her touch was the most erotic thing he'd ever experienced.

She leaned over him, her hair spilling forward to brush his belly and thigh. Her tongue rasped over the head of his cock. He was wrong. *This* was the most erotic thing he'd ever experienced.

She engulfed the tip in her hot mouth. He closed his eyes, and his hips rose instinctively toward the pleasure she offered. She moaned with her mouth full of his cock, and the vibration spiraled him into another world where nothing mattered but her.

She sucked him deep before releasing him with a pop. Her breathing was fast and shallow. He raised his head. She looked up at him while brushing kisses over his cock. Her eyes were glassy and unfocused, her lips puffy and reddened. Without breaking eye contact, the temptress opened her mouth and welcomed him deep inside once more. He fisted his hands in the bedclothes to keep from spending.

"Not like this," he muttered.

Scooping her up, he guided her to straddle him, a physical manifestation of the emotional power she held over him.

"What do I do?"

"Use me. Seek your pleasure."

She took a sharp breath and didn't move for a moment. Bracing her hands on his chest, she circled her hips and rubbed her wetness over his cock. He grasped her thighs and helped her establish a rhythm against him.

She tossed her head back and rose up. He fit himself at her opening, and she took him in a swift stroke, her nails digging into his chest as she climaxed around him. Grabbing her hips, he slammed her up and down until he followed.

She collapsed over him, her body boneless. He stroked her hair, kissed her temple, and settled her into his side. Tomorrow. Tomorrow he would get on his knees and declare his love before reality intruded.

CHAPTER TWENTY-FIVE

Maxwell slowly came to consciousness as light leaked into the room. His sated calmness faded. Bryn's warm, lithe body wasn't tucked into his. He sat up. She wasn't in the room. Worry rose even as logical reasons for her absence scrolled.

He rolled out of bed and pulled his breeches on.

A breathy exclamation came from the door. Maxwell grabbed his shirt and pulled it on before turning.

"I'm sorry, sir. I have Miss Bryn's water." Gertie stood in the doorway, her expression half-fearful, half-scandalized.

"Is Miss Bryn not already up and downstairs?"

"No, sir. No one has stirred." Her gaze darted from the rumpled bed to him and back again. "Where is she?"

Maxwell had neither the time nor ability to soothe the little maid as his own worry morphed into terror. After rousing Mrs. Soames and Henry to search the house from top to bottom, it was clear Bryn had disappeared like a wraith. The only explanation chilled his soul. Somehow Armstrong and Sutherland had managed to snatch her. He called for his horse. The ride to Sutherland's was swift along deserted streets.

Maxwell roused a stable boy and tossed him Primrose's reins. He pounded on the entry door. As he was contemplating ripping it off its hinges, a butler in a night wrapper opened it and peeked out of a narrow crack. It was ungodly early for a call, but social niceties didn't concern Maxwell.

"Where's Sutherland?"

"He's not to be disturbed, sir."

Maxwell pushed by him and strode toward the study. If he wasn't there, then Maxwell would rouse him from bed. The butler begged ineffectually for him to stop.

"Sutherland!" In the resulting silence, Maxwell tried the door. It was locked. "Open the door, man, or it's coming down."

Not even the rustle of movement came from the other side. The scenarios flashing through his head sent him into a berserk frenzy. Was Bryn helpless and hurting on the other side? Maxwell slammed his shoulder against the door a handful of times before it surrendered with a splintering sound.

Ready to do battle, he tore into the room with a yell. Bryn was nowhere in sight. Shock replaced his fury.

"'Tis the devil's work," the butler said with a mirroring shock.

"Fetch the magistrate. Immediately."

Maxwell stepped gingerly, careful not to touch the two bodies or the assortment of weapons on the floor. Having seen his share of bodies, Maxwell guessed the two men had been dead for hours.

A cord circled Sutherland's neck, his eyes bugged and his tongue so swollen his mouth couldn't close. The cord was wrapped around the handle to the wardrobe he and Bryn had hidden inside. He was sitting up with his legs sprawled in front of him, his breeches open. A gun hung loosely from his hand.

The other man in the grisly tableau was Dugan Armstrong. He was naked and on his back. His legs crossed Sutherland's, forming two X's, and indicated how close they must have been when the shot was fired. Dugan's stomach was a mass of tissue and darkened blood. Maxwell's stomach churned, the scene casting him back to battlefields.

This wasn't two enemies coming together but two lovers exploring forbidden practices. With the shock came relief. It was over. He and Bryn were free.

Except he didn't have the slightest inkling where Bryn was. Had she left on her own? But why? The magistrate would arrive soon with questions to be answered. Maxwell closed the study door behind him. The house stirred. Was news of their master's demise already spreading? He stopped a scullery maid. "Miss, I'm looking for a new footman named Pendleton. Do you know if he's about?"

"He's still abed, sir."

"Wake him. Tell him Mr. Drake is downstairs on urgent business." Maxwell pressed a coin into her hand, and she left with a curtsy. All these servants would soon be out of a job during the heart of winter.

Maxwell paced outside the corridor that led to the servants' stairs. The *clomp* of boots didn't take long. Penny ducked under the low doorframe, eyes red-rimmed and his clothes rumpled. "What the devil, Drake?"

Maxwell shushed him and motioned him to follow. Not saying a word, he pushed the study door open with his foot.

"Bloody hell," Penny muttered, treading closer. "I've heard of such practices, but something went terribly wrong."

"An understatement. The magistrate is on his way. As I found them, he'll require me to make a statement. And if I leave, suspicion will fall upon me." Asking for help was uncomfortable, but finding Bryn trumped everything. "I need your help."

"Anything," Penny said without hesitation.

"Miss McCann's gone, and I have to find her. Ensure her safety." It came out in a rush of words. "That's why I'm here. I thought…" He gestured toward the study.

"I understand. Since she's not here, any other idea where she may have gone and why?"

Maxwell shoved his hand through his hair. Pain seared at her defection. Last night had been perfect. The start of their life together. Why had she left him?

Rejection squat in the background of his thoughts. A familiar misery. Where would she go? Whom did she know? "Perhaps to Molly's or mayhap to her grandmother in Kinross."

"Molly's is a brothel, Mr. Drake."

"Bryn is old friends with Molly's man." Whether it was an earl, a whore, a street urchin, or even a vicar, Bryn managed to collect friends along the path of her life. Unlike Maxwell.

Penny patted Maxwell's shoulder and squeezed. "I'll send word as soon as I find her, sir."

A clatter of footsteps on the main staircase interrupted them. Penny inclined his head and disappeared back up the servants' stairs. Mary's shrill voice echoed above the lower tones of her husband. Maxwell closed the study up again as best as he could and blocked access to the hallway.

Mary wore a long-sleeved, winter dressing gown sashed round her waist. A vee exposed a long sliver of her bosom. "My maid was chattering about the magistrate and an accident. What have you done, Maxwell?"

"We should discuss this someplace private." Maxwell tried to usher them into the drawing room.

Mary pushed by him, and this time Maxwell let her go. She gave a little scream and covered her mouth. Craddock joined her at the study door, his already pasty face going gray.

Mary turned toward him. "I'll see you hanged, Maxwell. You and my sister." The threat lacked her usual vitriol. Whatever dreams and plans she had nurtured withered in the middle of Sutherland's hallway.

"The magistrate will be arriving soon." Maxwell gestured toward the drawing room, and this time they docilely preceded him.

"Sutherland was exposed and Dugan was…" She swallowed,

emotion squeaking her voice.

"Did you know about Sutherland and Armstrong?" Maxwell asked Craddock.

"I suspected," Craddock whispered.

Mary turned with a gasp. "What did you suspect?"

"Sutherland's proclivities are well known. Dugan enjoyed women on occasion, although boyish ones. It's why he pursued Brynmore. But I caught him with a stable boy once."

Mary fiddled with her sash. "Knowing Dugan preferred men, you pushed marriage to my sister?"

Craddock shrugged. "Their betrothal had nothing to do with sex or love."

"Was it all Bryn's inheritance and control of the vote?" Maxwell asked.

"How did you know about that?" Mary clutched her dressing gown together as if secrets were hiding in her cleavage.

"Bryn's grandmother is still alive, you know, and hired me to see to her estate. It didn't take a huge leap in intelligence to piece it together. Your schemes were confirmed by the marriage contract Sutherland kept in his study."

Maxwell relished the look of utter stupefaction on their faces. They'd been bested by the poor bastard of Cragian.

A grim-looking magistrate arrived. Sutherland was a powerful member of Edinburgh society. The shockwaves of his death would resonate through all areas and strata of the city—from his business partners to the apprentice gangs that roamed the night. New powers would rise and fill the vacuum, for better or worse.

Maxwell glanced at the door and prayed Penny was making some headway in finding Bryn.

* * * * *

Bryn stomped her feet and pounded on the door to Molly's.

The sun had long ago risen. She had been wandering the city for hours, her memory failing her. Only when the city woke did she find someone to point her in the right direction.

But as the city stirred, Molly's shut down. She slapped the door again. "Hello? Anyone?"

Finally a coarse middle-aged woman cracked the door open. "Whatcha want then? Molly's not in the market for new whores."

Bryn clutched the handle of her bag tighter. "I'm not looking for work, Mrs...."

"Easterly. Just Easterly."

Bryn tried to smile, but she was so cold her lips were stiff. "I'm friends with Thomas Kennedy, Molly's betrothed and—"

"They's married now."

"Oh how wonderful. Thomas and Molly told me if I ever needed help to call on them."

Easterly narrowed her eyes. Bryn was ready to drop to her knees to beg sanctuary when the old woman swung the door wide. "Well, in with you then. You look 'bout frozen through. There's a fire in the kitchen. I'll rouse the missus."

Easterly pointed her down a set of stairs, and Bryn followed her nose to where two girls rolled dough and gossiped. The scene reminded her of the hours she and Sarah had passed in the kitchens of the manor house growing up. How things had changed since then.

They stopped, but Bryn waved them back to their work with a stiff smile. "It's bitter cold outside."

"Would you like a bun, miss? They's still hot."

"That would be most appreciated. It smells lovely in here and feels even better." Bryn planted herself on a small stool by the fire and ate the bun in three bites. She pressed a hand to her throbbing belly.

The ache in her womb had woken her. It had always

287

happened to her like this. A few hours of belly pain before the blood flowed.

Still wrapped in Maxwell's arms with his scent marking her, a decision had loomed. Selfishly stay and let Maxwell bind himself to her out of some misguided need to protect her, or leave him free to find a woman he could truly love. She loved him enough to want happiness for him. Anyway, she wasn't alone anymore. She had a grandmother in Kinross.

She would survive the loss of him. Surviving is what she did.

The heat from the fire settled in her bones. Would Maxwell go in search of her? She'd ask Thomas to send a boy around with a note so Maxwell wouldn't worry. What a relief that would be for him.

Thomas strolled into the kitchen, and she popped off the stool. "Brynmore, what the devil? Tell me you didn't walk all the way from Drake's? What was he thinking letting you out on the streets in this cold? You could catch your death or worse."

Thomas towered over her, berating her just as Maxwell would have done, worry in his eyes and a frown on his face. She tried to swallow, but a sob tore from her throat. Her strength of will had been weakened by the warm fire and the kindness of her welcome at Molly's. Tears trickled down her cheeks. She wiped them away with the heels of her hands.

Thomas looked as disconcerted as any man would be in such a situation. Molly rounded the corner, looking younger without her rouge and with her hair in a plait.

"What did you say to her, Thomas Kennedy, you brute?" Molly wrapped an arm around Bryn's shoulders and led her to the table. A thin gold band winked on Molly's finger. "How about fixing us a cuppa, girls?"

Bryn was crying all over the newlyweds. She took a deep, shuddery breath and regained a semblance of control. "Con-congratulations. On your marriage. I'm so happy for you."

"Yes, you're obviously thrilled," Molly said dryly but with twinkling eyes.

"I really am. I'm not normally a watering pot, it's just… Maxwell."

Thomas propped a foot onto the bench behind Molly and loomed over them like a bear. "What's the blighter done? Do I need to kill him?"

"No, he hasn't done anything. Not really." He had turned Bryn's childhood infatuation into love, but he didn't love her back. If he had, he would have admitted it last night. It was hardly his fault though. No woman would have been immune to him. "I love him, but… but…"

Molly took Bryn's hand. "My dear girl, do you find yourself with child?"

Thomas slammed a fist on the table, rattling the teacups the kitchen maid had set in front of Bryn and Molly. "Bloody hell, I'll have him here within the hour by his bollocks to marry you, Brynmore. I promise you that."

"I'm not with child, but Maxwell planned to marry me anyway. That's why I left."

"I'll—what?" Thomas deflated. "I don't understand. Drake wants to marry you, but you determined you're not with child, so you ran away? You said you loved him."

"I do. I love him so much." Bryn pressed a hand over her chest where her heart should be. She was empty inside. "He doesn't love me."

"I understand," Molly whispered. In Molly's eyes, the same pain Bryn faced was reflected. The fact Molly had found happiness with Thomas slivered a needlelike feeling of hope into Bryn.

"I'm glad one of us does," Thomas said darkly. "You sure I don't need to go smash some heads?"

"Miss Bryn would be quite distressed if you smashed poor Mr. Drake's head." Molly poured the tea and dropped a lump of sugar in each cup. "You're welcome to stay here as long as you want. Thomas and I will make sure no one bothers you."

"Thank you for the offer, but I discovered I have a grandmother in Kinross. Do you have a horse I could borrow or know of a supply cart headed in that direction? My grandmother will be able to pay on my arrival." Bryn hoped she spoke the truth. She'd posted her letter with the vague promise to visit only a day before.

Thomas squatted down on his haunches so he could look her in the eye. "Brynmore McCann, after what you did for my family, it would be a small favor to ask and one gladly given on my part."

Tears welled behind her smile. "Thank you."

"Have your tea, then go lie down for a bit while I get everything fixed for your journey," he said roughly.

After sharing tea, Molly led her to a dark little room in the back. "No one will bother you here. Rest for a bit if you can. It will be a long trip to Kinross."

Molly tucked her under a quilt and smoothed her hair back like a big sister. The late night and early morning caught up with her quickly, and she drifted into a dreamless sleep.

CHAPTER TWENTY-SIX

As Penny stomped to the door of Molly's brothel, he told himself this was it. He would insist on heading south as soon as this debacle was cleared up. He missed Wintermarsh and the way his boring days taking care of his flowers flowed into weeks and months without a single wall to scale or document to steal or murderer to avoid. By God, if that little garden whelp Lily had hired in his stead had let his roses die, there would be hell to pay.

He'd found enough dead bodies for a dozen lifetimes. He wanted to relax, read some poetry, tend to the garden. He didn't want to be chasing runaway women to a bloody brothel in the middle of a blustery Scottish winter.

An old lady with a hairy mole answered his knock, and Penny prayed she wasn't one of the working women.

"Whatcha want?"

"I'm looking for a young lady—"

"Yer here too early fo' that, sir. They're all still abed." She waved him off and tried to shut the door, but he toed his boot in the crack.

Penny looked heavenward, seeking a measure of patience from the almighty. "Let me state that another way. Did a young lady with reddish hair find her way to you this morning?"

A deep voice from inside rumbled. "Let him in, Easterly."

Easterly opened the door and gestured him inside with an ironic flourish. A man stood at the bar—a worthy adversary by the looks of him. Penny had learned to recognize the loose-limbed stance of an experienced fighter. Hands held to the side to grab a weapon from under a coat or from a boot. Not to mention the man was as big and hairy as a bear.

"What can we do for you this early morn, sir?" the bear asked.

"I'm looking for a young lass with red-gold hair that may have made her way to your door this morning."

"Who's lookin' exactly?"

"I'm here on behalf of Mr. Maxwell Drake."

"Why didn't he come himself?" A woman carrying a stack of tinkling glasses appeared from around the corner and walked behind the bar. She was pretty and carried herself with confidence. She met his eyes with a boldness that spoke of a rare intelligence in these parts.

How much should he divulge? He wasn't dealing with French spies—true—but the desperation in Drake's eyes that morning had been of the life-or-death variety. "Mr. Drake has been detained on business."

"More important business than Miss Bryn?" The bear raised his bushy black brows and set his feet a little farther apart, a protectiveness obvious in the man's voice. The man was ready to champion Brynmore McCann if necessary.

"He's occupied with the magistrate." Curiosity flashed over both their faces. They'd hear soon enough. The news would fly from house to house through the servants' quarters. "Sutherland and Dugan Armstrong are dead."

The big man plopped down on a barstool. "Dead? Bloody hell. Did Drake…" He waved his hand around suggestively.

"Ah, no. It appears they did each other in. After he discovered Miss Bryn missing this morning, Drake suspected the worst and went to Sutherland's looking for her but instead discovered a rather grisly scene."

The silence lengthened until the woman broke it in a cheerful voice. "This news deserves a celebratory drink." She pulled a bottle of brandy and three cups from behind the bar. "Nothing quite so warming as some coffee and brandy. Would you care to join us, Mr.... I didn't catch your name, sir."

"Pendleton. But everyone calls me Penny. And I would love some."

"I'm Molly, and this is Thomas, my husband."

After she poured brandy-laced coffee for the three of them, Molly raised her cup. "A toast. To the death of the most depraved bugger in all Edinburgh. May he rot in hell."

"Here, here," Thomas seconded as he took Molly's hand.

Penny took a sip of the bracing coffee, secrets swirling around them. He wasn't here to discover Molly's past but to determine Mr. Drake's future. "Drake sent me to make sure Miss Bryn is well and safe."

"She's quite safe," Thomas said, a protective frown back.

Molly's half smile was more circumspect. "I realize you may not be at liberty to discuss such matters about your employer—"

"I don't work for Drake. I'm doing this out of the goodness of my heart," Penny said drolly.

"In that case, your friend should know that Miss Bryn is under the impression he doesn't hold tender feelings for her. Based on his willingness to take on Sutherland, I'm wondering if Mr. Drake might indeed care for Miss Bryn very much." Molly leaned over the bar on her elbows and waited.

"Mr. Drake keeps his feelings close to the chest." He met Molly's eyes. "But I would venture to say he cares for her very much indeed."

Molly looked over at Thomas. "What should we do, love? Mr.

Drake will come here for her eventually. Should we send her on or keep her?"

"Where is she going?" Penny asked.

Thomas ran a meaty finger over his lips. "To her grandmother in Kinross."

"Perhaps we should send her on. Mr. Drake needs a good kick in the pants. Will he go after her?" Molly asked.

"If he does, he'll have to admit the depth of his feelings," Penny said. "And if he doesn't, then he doesn't deserve her, and she'll be better off with family than waiting around here for him to swallow his pride."

The three of them nodded and clinked their cups together once more to bind their pact. He thanked Molly and Thomas and took his leave, curious to see Maxwell Drake's reaction at his news. Penny hoped the man was smart enough to follow his heart.

* * * * *

It was early afternoon before the magistrate released Maxwell. Penny was in the entry, leaning against a side table and flirting with a maid who was absently dusting and giggling.

"Did you find her?" Maxwell wasn't up to any polite preliminaries.

"Yes."

"Where in bloody hell is she?"

"At Molly's, as you suspected. Tuckered out and upset by the sound of it. Thomas wouldn't let me see her, said she was sleeping, but he and Molly assured me they would take care of her."

Anger climbed the mountain of his distress. "You left her? In a brothel? I meant for you to bring her back to me."

Maxwell wanted to punch the placid expression off Penny's face. "Those weren't your instructions. Miss Bryn is a grown woman with an uncommon amount of pluck. I'm not getting paid enough—or at all, for that matter—to kidnap her and deposit her on your doorstep. *Sir.*"

His last word was imbued with such withering sarcasm, shame flooded Maxwell. Was he any better than Armstrong or Mary or Sutherland?

"Bloody, bloody hell!" Maxwell's voice echoed through the entry. He ran his hands through his hair and laced them at the nape as he paced. "She doesn't want to come back to me?"

"As I said, I wasn't allowed to speak with her, but by now she's well on her way to Kinross."

"Perhaps that's for the best." Maxwell would retreat to his town house and rebuild something resembling a life without her. He'd offered her everything and still she'd rejected him. Through his own pain, something Penny had said niggled. "Wait. She was upset? What about?"

"You, of course," Penny said mildly.

Maxwell pivoted to face Penny. "Me? What did I do? We left things quite satisfactorily last evening, and then I woke to find her up and gone. Christ, I don't understand women."

"What man does? But I believe it's perhaps what you didn't do rather than what you did do that was so upsetting to Miss Bryn."

A feeling of foreboding washed over Maxwell. "What didn't I do?"

Penny cleared his throat and looked heavenward a moment before meeting his eyes again. "The lass is under the impression you don't hold tender feelings for her."

Maxwell rocked back on his heels. Bryn believed he didn't love her. After whispering her sweet confession over and over, he hadn't had the courage to tell her what was in his heart. But he'd planned to. He had. Yet he didn't. And now it was too late.

Or was it? He'd been desperate for her love but hadn't understood she might feel the same for his. Maxwell strode toward the door.

"What are your plans, Drake?" Penny asked idly.

"I'm going back to the town house to pack. Then I'll go after the bloody infuriating woman." Maxwell only caught a glimpse of the smile that crested Penny's face before he was gone.

* * * * *

Complications arose when Maxwell arrived back at his town house. All he wanted was to ride like hell for Kinross and beg Bryn to come back to where she belonged—in his arms and by his side—but waiting in his study was his brother. Under the exhaustion writ large on Albert's face was pride.

Maxwell pasted a smile on his face. Their burgeoning friendship was a fragile thing. "This is a surprise. I expected you'd be on the road back to Cragian this morn."

"I realized who Lord MacShane is this morning. *Me*, not my mother. I roused Pickett and demanded to see my father's will. I have it right here." Albert patted his breast pocket.

Maxwell sank down behind his desk. "What's it say then?"

Albert's smile faltered. "I attempted to plow through it, but it was full of legal folderol. Couldn't make out what everything meant. Give me a tome on plants, and I'll devour it, but this"—he pulled out a sheaf of papers and dropped them in front of Maxwell with a flourish—"was Greek to me. No, actually, I understand Greek quite well… It was Arabic to me," he finished with a chuckle.

Given time, Maxwell decided he could come to enjoy Albert. Maxwell smoothed the papers out on the desk and scanned them for the pertinent information.

"Old MacShane did indeed leave you with the money and estate." Maxwell flipped through several more pages before a name caught his attention.

Eden Drake. He read through the paragraph twice, unable to speak. His heart and stomach initiated a fistfight.

"What is it? Is it bad? My father could be an arse. Lord knows, there were times—"

"No, it's... Here. You read it."

Albert cleared his throat and read aloud. "I acknowledge I begat a son onto an innocent maid at Riverwalk. I wished to set the girl up as a mistress and take care of the child, but my lady wife forbade such actions, instead forcing me to cast her out. It is my greatest shame. I sent money through the vicar to buy the boy a commission, with the understanding he was never to know it was from me. As death stalks close, I confess my sins and bequeath to Maxwell Drake, my natural son, a parcel of land that includes the cottage in which he was raised and a yearly stipend from my estate. I hope this token of penitence will gain his forgiveness."

Maxwell contemplated their father's words from the grave. Forgiveness? Not yet but perhaps one day.

"I wish I had done more," Albert said haltingly.

"You were a child. Please don't carry a guilt that is not yours. And the commission our father bought me changed my life. Got me out of Cragian and into the world where anything was possible."

"That's some prime land he left you, Drake. Good for sheep, if you're so inclined. Or you can croft it out. The cottage is quite nice," Albert said.

Maxwell barked a laugh. "That cottage was falling down around my ears even as an adolescent. The thatch had more holes than a sieve."

"Not anymore. Miss McCann had it repaired for your mother. Didn't you know?"

Maxwell stared at Albert. "Where did she get the money?"

Albert looked down at his father's will. "The vicar would know for certain, but my guess is it was from our father."

Maxwell could foresee a trip back to Cragian sooner than he'd planned—which had been never.

After seeing Albert out the door, he ordered hot water and climbed the stairs, the memory of Bryn drawing him into her room. He averted his gaze from her bed and opened her wardrobe. The beautiful blue gown she'd worn the night before had been hung back up. He fingered the delicate fabric and brought it to his face, searching for her scent and warmth but finding little solace.

"She's gone then?"

Maxwell dropped the dress as if it was on fire. Mrs. Winslow meandered into the room. Maxwell had dismissed her as a distracted, ineffectual chaperone, but her gaze was dagger-sharp and threatened a slow, painful evisceration.

"Aye, she's gone," he said solemnly.

"Well?"

"Well, what?"

"You must go after her. You're bloody well in love with her." She propped her hands on her hips.

Why was it everyone else could see so clearly while he was stuck looking through frosted glass? He sputtered a few choice words before saying, "It's none of your business—"

"She's my charge, isn't she? I've come to care for her and admire her spirit. Come now, Drake. She loves you so. You mustn't let her escape."

Maxwell cleared the lump from his throat. "She's left for Kinross and her grandmother."

"See that you don't tarry too long before you claim her." She ran her fingers over all the dresses Maxwell had commissioned for Bryn. "Since you no longer require a chaperone, I'm going back to the earl and Lionel. Should I direct Gertie to pack up Miss Bryn's dresses and send them on?"

"No," Maxwell said forcefully. He was being selfish. She

deserved fine things even if she chose never to see him again. "Yes. That would be kind of you, Mrs. Winslow. Thank you for everything you've done."

Mrs. Winslow cocked her head and gave a slight nod. "Of course, my dear boy. We've all become very fond of you and Miss Bryn. Will you write and let us know how you got on?"

Her offer felt almost like... friendship. How the last months had changed his life.

Maxwell ran his hands over his face. His love for Bryn surpassed his fears. The hot water arrived, and he bathed and dressed in riding clothes, self-consciously tugging at his waistcoat and examining himself in the looking glass. A shot of optimism quickened his movements. His first stop would be Molly's. Transportation to Kinross would be hard to come by in the winter. Could she still be there? Was there time to right his foolishness?

He was too serious and dour for a sprite like Bryn, but babe or no babe, he loved her and meant to make her his. Forever, if she'd have him.

* * * * *

He rapped sharply on the door to Molly's. An old crone with thin gray hair and a bitter, downturned mouth cracked the door open.

"Whatcha want?"

"I'm looking for a young lady—"

"It's a bit early, ain't it?" She looked him up and down but waved him inside. "What color hair are you interested in?"

Maxwell nearly choked on his tongue. "I believe you misunderstand me. I'm looking for a *particular* young lady who made her way here this morning with red-gold hair."

"She's gone. Can I not find another girl that might satisfy you?"

Maxwell's stomach dropped to hang at his knees. "Is Thomas or Molly available?"

"Wait here." The lady shuffled off, which left Maxwell pacing the floor like a trapped wolf.

Both Molly and Thomas followed the old woman back into the room, and Maxwell approached them warily, not sure if they were friend or foe in his quest.

"Mr. Drake, how lovely to see you again." Molly's voice was friendly and welcoming, but behind her, Thomas's bared teeth counteracted any hope they would help.

"Where is she?" Maxwell's desperation colored his voice.

Thomas stepped forward crossing his arms across his chest. "Gone to Kinross. I put her in the coach meself."

Maxwell ripped his hat off and beat it on his leg. "You knew I was looking for her. Penny must have made that clear. Why didn't you keep her here until I came for her?"

"Mr. Drake, no one knew when or if you would come." Her tone sympathetic, Molly cocked her head to the side, a master at soothing men. "Her intention is to set you free to find someone you can love."

"But I love *her*. How could she think I don't? Why would she leave me after… I don't understand." Maxwell dropped in a chair.

"Her courses started," Molly said so matter-of-factly it took Maxwell a moment to process the implications.

When he did, he leaned back in the chair and ran a hand over his jaw. "She's not with child and means to release me from our agreement. How long has she been gone, and what did she take? Is there any hope I can catch her?"

"A mail coach," Thomas said. "You don't want to be on the road at night. You'll freeze to death or get accosted. Anyway, she's about to meet her grandmother, Drake. You don't want to stop that reunion, do you? It was hard for Miss Bryn without a family who cared for her growing up. She needs this."

Maxwell stared into Thomas's understanding eyes. "Dammit, I know you're right, but I hate to think Bryn is out there thinking I don't..." He swallowed. Expressing his deepest feelings wasn't easy considering he'd spent the past dozen years attempting to deny he had any feelings whatsoever. "I love her. Very much."

Molly's smile was kinder than he deserved. "Tell her that, and I have the feeling all will be right with the world."

Jamming his hat back on his head, he rose and crossed to the door but stopped short of leaving. These two unlikely people had been true and kind to Bryn. And him, in their way. "Thank you for taking care of her."

Thomas said gruffly, "O'course. I would do anything for Miss Bryn after what she did for my family. Kept us from starving, she did. Don't know where we'd have ended up without those baskets."

Maxwell swallowed past the sudden lump in his throat and turned to face Thomas. "What did you say?"

"Baskets. Miss Bryn would leave us baskets full of food, even some clothes and shoes for the little 'uns. Saved our lives after Papa died. There were too many mouths to feed on the meager coin I earned. It was a while before I caught her at it. Stayed up for three nights in a row until I spied her creeping up the lane. At first I truly thought she was a fairy, but we both nearly screamed the house up when I grabbed her arm. We kept it a secret from Ma. Didn't want to hurt her pride."

His world spun and clicked into place. It had been Bryn. It had always been Bryn.

In Thomas's eyes was a shared experience. He must have felt something very similar to Maxwell when he'd opened his door to find that first basket.

"I got baskets too," Maxwell said.

"Aye. I know. I asked her once what made her start helping people like she did. Most people would want the recognition. But she said the first boy she helped had too much pride. That he wouldn't have accepted help if she'd tried to give it freely, so she snuck him baskets. Said he was special, and she didn't want him to die."

"She was so young... How could she..."

"Loads of people have helped her with her little project through the years. Cadell, Mrs. Kidd, old Busby, Vicar Mitchell, me—once we were back on our feet. She has people on the lookout for shoes for the children, clothes, books, whatever their need." Thomas raised his bushy black brows. "Surely you've noticed the way she has with people."

"Of course. She charms them."

Thomas laughed. "That she does. And she chose you. Of course, my Molly would call it destiny." He held a hand out to her, and she strolled over to lay a buss on his cheek.

"That's right, Drake." Molly smiled. "She saved you, and then you come back and save her in a different kind of way. She's your destiny. Just the way Thomas is my destiny." Turning serious, she laid a hand on Maxwell's arm. "Go after her."

Maxwell took Molly's hand and squeezed it. "You should count yourself a lucky man, Thomas, to have such a lady as Molly by your side."

Thomas put his arms around Molly's waist and pulled her close. "Don't you worry. I know how very lucky I am."

At that, Maxwell took his leave of the brothel, unsure of his destination. Selfishly he wanted to ride for Kinross and bring Bryn home, but Thomas was right. Bryn needed to reconnect with her grandmother after a lifetime apart.

The business about his father's bequest weighed him like an anchor. Before he could claim Bryn, he needed to break the chains of his past. Then with nothing but possibilities ahead of them, he would win her back.

CHAPTER TWENTY-SEVEN

The mail coach rumbled to a stop. Bryn peeked out the window, seeing nothing but a wide lane off the main road. Winter had stripped the landscape barren. The misty fog only added to the feeling of foreboding. She clutched the door handle, her brain directing her to open it but her body not complying.

This was it. Her grandmother was in reach, yet fear of her welcome—fear of the future—ground her to a halt.

The carriage rocked as the coachman dismounted. He opened the door, letting in a blast of bracing air. "This is it, miss. If you're still wanting to be left here."

The uncertainty in his voice added to her trepidation. She had no choice. Once Molly had informed her of Dugan and Sutherland's deaths, the last tie binding her to Maxwell had been snipped. No babe and no need for protection. He was free, and so was she.

From the outset, her goal had been freedom. She'd achieved it. She just hadn't expected freedom to be so lonely. Or sad.

"Yes. I'm ready. Thank you." She accepted his hand out of the carriage. Thankfully, she'd only shared it with one other woman, and she'd been dropped in town. The man gave her a tip of his hat and climbed to the driver's bench. With a slap of the reins, the mail coach lumbered away, quickly swallowed by the mist.

She trudged down the lane, peering through the fog. A stately manor house materialized through the swirling white. Withered ivy clung to the dark bricked façade. What did she really know about her grandmother, except her mother had married the baron and never looked back? She almost turned around, cold feet and nose be damned.

No. She wasn't the scared mouse she'd once been. At one time the situation may have triggered a panicked episode, but she'd made it through worse with her wits intact. She'd dodged bullets, delivered a babe, dueled barbs with her sister while wearing a fine ball gown, and got dealt a broken heart. She'd survived it all.

She squared her shoulders and picked up the knocker, rapping three times. Good or bad, this place was her birthright and her only family.

The door creaked open. "It's a mighty cold day to come calling, I'd say. Who's there?"

Framed in the crack was a woman with graying red hair and features so familiar Bryn blew out a breath like bellows emptying. Her voice came out thin and reedy. "I'm Brynmore McCann, ma'am. And you're my grandmother."

The woman swung the door fully open to stare at Bryn, her expression still a mystery. Suddenly she clapped her hands and smiled. Her eyes crinkled like laughing was a favorite pastime. All Bryn's worries and trepidation melted away under the warmth.

Her grandmother took both her hands and pulled her inside, kicking the door shut behind them. She chafed Bryn's cold hands in her own. "Alasdair, of course, sent word he'd run across you most unexpectedly. It took an enormous amount of self-restraint to stay here and wait, but it's a good thing I did, or you might have found an empty house."

"I'm sorry to appear on your doorstep. I sent a letter, but it's not arrived. There were unforeseen circumstances, and I wasn't sure where else... to go." To her utter horror, a tear leaked out. She dashed it away but not quick enough to escape her grandmother's notice.

"Oh dear. Alasdair mentioned a gentleman. In my experience, these kinds of tears are the direct result of dealing with a stubborn arse of a man." Her grandmother led her into a cozy sitting room with a warm fire.

A small laugh at her grandmother's quip helped quell her emotions. Her grandmother went to a sideboard and poured two large tots of amber liquid, handing one over and keeping one for herself. Bryn took a sip and grimaced.

"All of it, dear. You'll feel better for it. Warmer too." She waited for Bryn to finish the glass. "You traveled on the mail coach? Alone?"

Bryn nodded.

"Alasdair thought perhaps your man would accompany you."

"He's not my man. Not anymore." Bryn's voice cracked. "He never was. Not really. Circumstances brought us together for a time, but everything has been satisfactorily settled. We're both free to move forward with our lives. It's good. The way it should be." Bryn wasn't sure which one of them she was trying to convince.

"Whatever brings you to my door, I'm thankful. My darling girl, if I'd had the slightest inkling of your existence, I would have swept into Cragian and brought you back here, the baron be damned. I never approved of the marriage, but Katherine was nearly as hardheaded as I was and determined to leave Kinross. She wanted to experience the world."

"But Cragian is a poor, out-of-the-way village."

"Aye, but she was lady of the manor there. She begged me for a season in Edinburgh, but I've never been one for the social whirl and refused her. I expected she'd settle down and find a lad in Kinross, but being a farmer's wife wasn't her fate. If I hadn't been so stubborn..." Her grandmother trailed off, regret dampening the twinkle in her eyes.

"She seemed happy enough. Papa wasn't a cruel man."

"I'm glad to hear it." Her grandmother's smile didn't reach her eyes. "Tell me everything about yourself and your childhood and what you've been up to in Edinburgh."

As Bryn talked about her years in Cragian, she found there were more good times than bad to share. Telling her grandmother about Cadell and Maxwell and the baskets filled her with a kind of peace. The most recent events elicited gasps, although Bryn glossed over the intimacies she'd shared with Maxwell.

In return, her grandmother shared stories about her mother, Katherine. She even gave Bryn a small miniature she had commissioned when Katherine was eighteen. In it, her mother looked happy and beautiful and full of hope. Much like she remembered her looking her last days in Cragian.

A comfortable silence fell as Bryn stared into her grandmother's eyes.

"It's uncanny," her grandmother said.

"I look just like you." Bryn smiled. A feeling of homecoming washed over her and smoothed the rough, raw edges of her hurt, not gone but honed to something that wouldn't cut her to ribbons.

The next two days were filled with discoveries interspersed with a desolation that stole her breath. Alasdair Lowry, her step-grandfather, returned from Edinburgh with equal delight to find her in residence. The day her trunk arrived was the day she gave up on Maxwell.

The pain was almost unbearable. The only thing missing was the midnight-blue ball gown. She'd wanted the dress if for nothing but the memories it held.

Her grandmother patted Bryn's hand. "The grief gets easier after a time. I've lost many people over the years, but if you keep your heart open, you'll learn to love again. There's many a handsome lad in Kinross when you're ready."

She'd never love another man, but she gave her grandmother a smile in an attempt to placate her obvious worry.

The winter winds calmed and the sun emerged, burning off the mist. Winnie, as her grandmother had insisted Bryn call her, took her to see the house she had inherited. Winnie prattled on about their ancestors, and Bryn drank in the most trivial details.

Filled with heavy old furniture that harkened back to a different era, the house was old and drafty yet beautiful in its simplicity. Bryn's mother had grown up in the house, and laughter seemed to echo through the great entry. Aye, there might be ghosts here, but they were happy ones.

Bryn could picture it in the summer with wildflowers and children running and playing. It was meant to be filled with life. The dream would remain unfulfilled.

"Come the spring, perhaps we'll hold a country dance to introduce you around Kinross?" Winnie asked with an expectation Bryn couldn't bear to disappoint. Perhaps her heart wouldn't be as broken then.

"Perhaps," she replied noncommittally.

Her half-hearted acquiescence made her grandmother clap her hands and launch into plans. Mary had wanted to keep Bryn closeted away, but Winnie wanted to show her off. After one last glance around the house, Bryn joined Winnie in the carriage.

"We're already halfway to Kinross, and it's such a pretty day. The inn lays out a handsome tea," Winnie said.

Bryn didn't relish meeting new people and making small talk, but she nodded anyway. She couldn't hide forever. "Sounds lovely."

Winnie rapped on the door, and the carriage jumped forward. Kinross reminded her of a more prosperous Cragian. The homes were well kept and the businesses more numerous. Winnie seemed a popular figure in the village. She poured her considerable love and energy into her home and its people.

Many of those people stopped to stare at Bryn, especially the older residents who had known Winnie in her youth, to comment on their striking similarity. It made her feel self-conscious and proud at the same time. The strain of maintaining a happy façade throughout tea wore her flat and dry like a piece of parchment.

"You're tired," Winnie murmured.

"A bit." An understatement if she'd ever uttered one.

"Go on and wait in the carriage while I make our excuses."

Her head down, Bryn threaded her way through the tables toward the door. The crisp air would be a balm to her lungs after the smoky common room, and the silence of the carriage would be a balm to her soul.

She bumped into a man who entered as she exited the inn. She jerked back, her body igniting with recognition. From the tips of his boots, up his legs, hips, chest, her gaze finally came to rest on the face of Maxwell Drake.

Had her subconscious summoned him as a spirit? No. The dark circles ringing his eyes and the strain at the set of his mouth were new. He was grim, like someone had died.

"Maxwell." Inanely she asked, "Do you have business in Kinross?"

A half smile lightened his face considerably. "Business of a sort. But that's a rather pragmatic, unsentimental way of approaching such matters."

Her heart took a flying leap off the nearest cliff.

"And who might you be, young man?" Winnie took Bryn's arm protectively.

"I can see now why Mr. Lowry was so shocked." Maxwell blinked, his gaze flitting between them. Turning his hat in his hands in a rare show of nerves, he said, "I'm Maxwell Drake, a friend of your granddaughter's."

"A friend, eh? A *friend* wouldn't break my granddaughter's

heart," Winnie replied hotly.

* * * * *

Maxwell caught Bryn's horrified expression and her whispered plea. "Winnie, no."

She was wan—a bit thinner, pale, dark eye circles, and freckles standing out prominently. Christ, she looked nearly as bad as he had in his shaving mirror that morning.

Bryn's grandmother—Winnie?—steered her out the door. "We are taking our leave, Mr. Drake. My granddaughter is tired. You may call on us tomorrow if she so desires."

Not bloody likely. He'd waited too long already. He'd not be put off another hour. Even if he had to do battle with her dragon of a grandmother.

"I've ridden two days straight from Cragian, and I'll see Brynmore today."

Bryn cast glances between them. "Follow us, Maxwell. It's time we finished things once and for all."

Her words pierced him, and he took her arm as she was turning to leave, whispering, "Things will never be finished between us, Brynmore McCann. You need to understand that once and for all."

She stiffened but leaned into him infinitesimally. The small betrayal gave him hope.

The weather was cold, and his welcome at the house even colder. Bryn's grandmother spent a fair amount of time energetically rearranging the ancient battle swords hanging on the wall of the drawing room.

Bryn dropped a whispered word in her grandmother's ear. The woman harrumphed, and with one last scathing glance in Maxwell's direction, she retreated but left the door cracked. Maxwell wouldn't be at all surprised to find her ear pressed against the seam. Bryn's meddlesome, protective grandmother aside, he would have his say.

After they settled themselves on the settee as if they were old, amiable acquaintances, Bryn fired the opening salvo. "My trunk arrived. I have money now and can pay you back. The blue gown wasn't included though. I'd like it back."

Maxwell had vowed to reveal the truth of his feelings no matter how difficult. "The blue gown reminds me of you, so I kept it."

A portion of her distant coldness evaporated. "That's... sweet."

"Is it? I wasn't feeling sweet the morning you left me without a word or note. Do you have any idea of how terrified I was when I found you gone in the morning like a wisp of smoke? I thought one of Sutherland's men—" He was unable to put the dark, twisty paths of his imagination into words.

"I wasn't sure you would care."

"I did—I do—care. I went to Sutherland's straight away and found... Well, I assume you've heard."

"I have."

"After the magistrate arrived, Mary and Craddock made insinuations that I might be responsible for their deaths. Eventually though, the truth emerged."

"I know Vicar Mitchell would be mightily disappointed in me, but all I felt was relief it was over. And then unbearable sadness that *we* were over."

"But we aren't over. Why do you keep saying such?" He tucked a piece of her hair behind her ear and let his fingertips brush her cheek. Her skin was soft and sweet, and he had to hold himself back from taking her in his arms.

"My courses started that morning. Then after I heard about Dugan and Sutherland, I didn't require your protection anymore either. I was free."

"I almost chased you down the road. Maybe I should have." He rose and paced, too agitated now the moment was on him to pretend this was a normal social call. This was life and death. "But I had urgent business in Cragian."

"What sort of business?"

"I needed to see to *my* inheritance," he said drily.

Bryn's eyes widened. "MacShane left you something after all."

"A small stipend, the cottage I grew up in, and some prime land around it." Maxwell stopped and faced her. "Bryn, the cottage. You had it repaired and expanded for Mother. It's lovely."

"It was falling down around Eden's ears." She squirmed and dropped her gaze to his knees. "After you left, there was no one to plug the holes that grew bigger by the week. I gathered up some of the local lads who owed me favors and appealed to Lord MacShane."

So many owed so much to one woman.

"The baskets. Why didn't you tell me it was you all along?" he asked. Her words from weeks before haunted him. *Of course I care. I always have.* He had been blind. She had never failed him from the time she was twelve. Twelve years old and she had recognized and eased his pain. She had been the one he prayed for daily.

"I didn't want you to feel ashamed or, even worse, *obligated* to me. Not like that."

"Most children either called me names or ignored me. How did you notice?" He'd left his shame in Cragian. What he felt now was more akin to awe.

"You don't remember, but you were kind to me once after I took a tumble off my horse. You acted a gentleman and treated me like a lady. I took to spying on you when you came to work in the gardens. Sometimes I would climb a tree, sometimes I would hide behind a hedge. I was drawn to you even then." Her tentative smile made his heart ache. He had to clench his hands from pulling her to him.

* * * * *

Maxwell's hands were balled in fists at his side and his body taut. If she didn't know him better, she would label it anger. But it wasn't. Or at least not just anger. It was a passion and fear and need he kept well hidden.

"Do you think me too stoic? Too unfeeling, Brynmore?"

She popped up to face him. This was her final stand. She'd not live her life filled with regrets like Winnie. She was stubborn, too, but in a different way—too stubborn to give up on Maxwell Drake.

"I can't read your mind, Drake. You must tell me."

"Christ! It's a lark really, the fact you can't see what feels etched on my heart." Maxwell's face was pained, and he ran his hands through his hair.

The man who'd scaled a wall to ransack an office and chase a would-be killer into the dark night was scared. Of her. The truth hit her like a bolt from the sky.

"Tell me." She gentled her voice and cupped his cheek. He let out a long breath, his body curling into hers enough to signal his surrender.

"I feel too damn much. The pain of my father not acknowledging my existence, powerlessness to help my mother, the humiliation I endured as a boy. It was like a knife to my heart, bleeding it little by little until your sister finally tore it into a thousand pieces. I buried the scraps deep. I protected myself from the good and bad of life, and I was perfectly content."

His voice crackled with emotion now; his eyes danced with it. He'd never looked as handsome.

"Is that what you want? To go back to being content?"

"I can't go back, damn you." His jaw worked. "You made me feel again. Live again. I bless the day I found you waiting in my bed. You're the first thing on my mind in the morning, and you haunt my dreams at night. I would give my life to protect you and want nothing more than for you to be happy. Even if that means you destroy me and marry another, probably more deserving, man. I love you, woman, don't you know that?"

His words melted the ice that had formed around her heart and made it leap into a rhythm that breathed life back into her soul.

"I do now." She wrapped her arms around his neck and feathered kisses over his face.

Her lips slid to his. The kiss was one of rediscovery and exploration. He roamed his hands over her back, her hips, her bottom. It felt like they'd been apart for months instead of days, and the passion between them grew at a rate she couldn't control. If he lay her down on the rug in front of the cracking fire, she wouldn't peep a protest.

"I've missed this." The rawness in his voice had only been partially smoothed.

"What? My arse?" she asked.

Maxwell laughed and nuzzled behind her ear. Erotic shivers coursed through her. "All of you but most especially your arse. I love you."

His kiss seemed imbued with all the love and passion he'd kept dammed up for too long. It stole her breath and tried to steal her reason.

She turned her head away and pushed lightly against his chest. She had something to say. "You know I love you and want to marry you more than anything in the world, don't you?"

Maxwell's smile was sweet and knowing but most of all full of love. "I do now."

EPILOGUE

At their small wedding in Kinross, the earl, Mr. Masterson, Mrs. Winslow, and Penny proclaimed their intention to depart Scotland, perhaps back to Wintermarsh, the earl's home. When Mr. Masterson idly mentioned a set of druid ruins in Northumberland he wanted to investigate, good-natured groaning rose all around. Bryn would be sorry to see them go.

"I can't express my thanks to all of you. We wouldn't have survived without your help, of that I'm sure. But for all the danger, it brought Bryn back in my life, and for that I'll be eternally grateful." Maxwell took her hand and bussed the back.

"It was great fun, Drake. A story to tell for certain. I'm glad it had a happy ending, and I couldn't be more thrilled the two of you finally made it official," the earl said with twinkling eyes. "In fact, I have my own glad tidings to share. Mrs. Winslow has most kindly consented to become *my* wife."

Mrs. Winslow blushed as David Drummond, the earl of Windor, brushed a kiss on her lips. Back thumping, hand shaking, and hugging occupied them in the aftermath of the announcement.

"Drake, you and Miss Bryn—ahem, excuse me, Mrs. Drake—must come to Wintermarsh for a visit. I'm sure Rafe and Minerva would be thrilled—as would we all." The earl's sincerity wasn't in doubt.

"We'll do that. I'd like to show Bryn London. It is one of the great cities of the world."

"Excellent, excellent. Just send a note ahead—or don't. I love a good surprise." The earl laughed.

After two nights in Kinross and with promises they would return soon, Bryn and Maxwell traveled back to the Barrow Street town house in Edinburgh. She stepped inside, and contentment filled her. It was home. Actually, Maxwell was her home.

Maxwell scaled back on the number of appointments he kept over the next days, but he was working hard to establish himself. Plus he had work to do in Cragian. When he shared with her his plans for his inheritance, she was torn between thankfulness and amazement.

His old cottage would be turned into a school where everyone was welcome. Vicar Mitchell would oversee it but hire a tutor to see to the actual teaching. If a family was poor and they needed their son or daughter to work instead of attend, Maxwell would provide jobs on his land, tending sheep or small plot farming to allow the children to make coin while they received a decent education.

Maxwell would manage his brother Albert's properties. The commission would be paid back into the school to buy books, clothes, shoes, or even food if needed. He'd also met with Craddock and Mary and convinced them—blackmailed might be closer to the truth—to donate money as well. It seemed a fitting use for the cottage where Maxwell spent his youth. And Bryn would see Sarah, Mrs. Kidd, and all the others on their trips back. The meld of past and present was perfect.

On their fifth morning as man and wife, Bryn settled herself in the bed of the master suite in their home on Barrow Street. The sheen of sweat from their rather energetic lovemaking against the door of his study had chilled her, and she burrowed under the covers, waiting for Maxwell to join her. She'd left him recovering on the study floor, his breeches around his knees and his shirt ripped from collar to hem.

Served him right for working her into such a fervor at ten in the morning. The things the man whispered in her ear at the breakfast table were positively indecent. Now that he'd stopped suppressing his feelings, the man was downright scandalous expressing his love and desires. She loved every debauched minute.

His heavy tread sounded on the stairs, and she flipped the covers down, exposing her nakedness in the sunlight. The door crashed open, and he stood there looking like a pirate with his mussed hair and torn shirt. He hadn't even managed to get his breeches properly fastened.

"You left me," he said accusingly and kicked the door closed with his heel.

"What was I to do? You couldn't do more than lie there and grunt at me. I got cold."

"I'll have you know Elspeth walked in to clean the grate. I'm surprised her scream didn't bring the entire house running. My breeches nearly at my ankles, my shirt torn—she probably thinks she's out of the pan and into the fire coming from Sutherland's to here."

A fit of giggles overtook her at the picture he painted. As soon as they'd returned from Kinross, she'd insisted they find and hire the young girl. She was skittish and quiet but settling in well, according to Mrs. Soames. Maybe Bryn hadn't been able to save them all, but she could make sure Elspeth and Gertie had a safe, decent place to work, minus some midday mischief from her and Maxwell.

He shed his clothing and joined her in bed, pulling her into his body. The best part of every day had been waking to stare into Maxwell's sleepy, love-filled eyes as the dawning sun cast its light into their room, knowing neither of them wanted to escape the other's embrace. Knowing that every morning for the rest of their lives, she would wake in his arms and could stay there forever if she wished. And as she closed her eyes, exhausted and sated, she wished for just that.

An Indecent Invitation
Spies and Lovers, Book One

Keeping her safe is difficult, keeping a proper distance from her is downright impossible.

Lady Lily Drummond understands only too well the danger of spy work. Her father, a preeminent master spy, has been missing for months, and her brother barely survived his final mission for the Crown. Lily is still determined to help find her father, no matter how hard her brother and his best friend try to keep her in the dark.

Busy trying to untangle the web of deceit surrounding the Earl of Windor's disappearance, Crown spy Gray Masterson also has to ensure Lily Drummond, the gangly, awkward child who was his constant shadow growing up, doesn't get herself ruined at her London debut. But the girl with scraped knees and elbows has evolved into a lush, sensual beauty surrounded by a bevy of suitors.

Realizing Lily is going to investigate on her own if he doesn't let her join the hunt for her missing father, Gray assumes he can give Lily a few minor tasks to pacify her, but he quickly learns she is a valuable asset. Moreover, she fairly crackles with life and warmth—things he craves after his dark years in service.

Warning : This book contains spies, scandals, naughty liaisons in houses of ill repute, men who think they know everything and women who know they do not.

A Brazen Bargain
Spies and Lovers, Book Two

Love soothes the deepest of scars.

Minerva Bellingham is at her wits' end. Her younger brother, Simon, will have them penniless and on the streets if his extravagant gambling habit isn't curtailed. An enormous debt to Lord Rafe Drummond is the final indignity. Signing over her dowry is their only choice. Until Lord Drummond suggests something much more scandalous. She can keep her dowry—in exchange for the Bellinghams working three months as a housemaid and stable boy.

Scarred from his service to the Crown, Rafe recognizes the young Simon Bellingham has the makings of a good duke. Minerva is a different story. Her pure, delicate beauty only underscores Rafe's tarnished, bleak soul. Yet he delights in cracking Minerva's icy reserve to reveal a fiery, stubborn woman. And Minerva discovers the gruff master of Wintermarsh has the heart of a poet. But before they can find a future safe in each other's arms, a menace from Simon's licentious past slithers back into their lives, forcing Rafe to plan the most important rescue mission of his life.

Warning : Contains a paragon of the beau monde who gets the hang of polishing silver, and a master of the house who'd like her to make his bed— preferably with him in it. Also passion unleashed with the mere touch of a finger. Readers are encouraged to swoon.

AUTHOR NOTE

I want to mention a couple of historical footnotes to *A Reckless Redemption*. The former occupation of Maxwell Drake, the hero, is an exploring officer for Wellington during the Napoleonic Wars. Before this time period, spying was thought to be quite ungentlemanly and to be avoided. But it wasn't long before Wellington and his officers discovered they knew very little about Portugal or their enemy's movements and created the Depot of Military Intelligence. It was the precursor to modern spy agencies such as MI-6 or the CIA. Exploring officers began by mapping the countryside, then would move behind enemy lines and send back reports. It was solitary and very dangerous work. The most famous of the exploring officers was Colquhoun Grant, the youngest of eight brothers from the Scots aristocracy.

Another historically significant piece of *A Reckless Redemption* involves roving gangs of apprentices in Edinburgh. The early nineteenth century was a time of great social upheaval and poverty for many. Work was difficult to find. The young out-of-work apprentices banded together in Edinburgh and took to the streets at night, robbing and beating well-off gentleman they would catch alone. They carried bludgeons and would cry, "Mar him!" before falling onto the unfortunate victims. Their activities culminated in the Tron riot and led to laws giving more power to the police in Edinburgh.

ABOUT THE AUTHOR

I hope you enjoyed *A Reckless Redemption*! If you have a chance please leave a quick review! Although, many readers know me from my Southern-set contemporary romances, the first books I wrote were the Spies and Lovers series! I grew up reading the historical "bodice rippers" of the late eighties and early nineties along with wonderful gothic romances. Now that I have the opportunity to publish all of the Spies and Lovers series, I'm so excited! There will be (at least) five full length books, but I have ideas for more...

I was born and raised in a small town in Northwest Tennessee. Although, I loved English and reading in high school, I was convinced an English degree equated to starvation! So, I chose the next most logical major - Chemical Engineering- and worked in a hard hat and steel toed boots for several years. Now I live in South Carolina with my husband and two children. In between school and homework and soccer practices, I love to get lost in another world, whether it's Regency England or small town Alabama.

My first two Falcon Football books received TOP PICKS from RT Book Reviews and a STARRED review from Library Journal. KISS ME THAT WAY, Cottonbloom Book 1, won the Stiletto Contest for Best Long Contemporary and finaled in the National Readers Choice Award. THEN HE KISSED ME, Cottonbloom Book 2, was named an Amazon Best Romance of 2016 and was a finalist for the National Excellence for Romance Fiction. TILL I KISSED YOU, Cottonbloom Book 3, is a finalist in the Maggie contest. LEAVE THE NIGHT ON, the latest Cottonbloom book, was named an iBooks Best Book of the Month and a Recommended Read from NPR. AN INDECENT INVITATION and A BRAZEN BARGAIN were both finalist for the 2014 Golden Heart® Award.

Printed in Great Britain
by Amazon

40682073R00182